ORIENTAL VALIANT

Richard Regan

ISBN: 978 0 6483542 4 6

 A catalogue record for this
book is available from the
National Library of Australia

This is a work of fiction. Names, characters, places and incidents either are products of the author's imagination or are used fictitiously. Any resemblance to actual persons living or dead, businesses, companies, events or locales are entirely coincidental.

CHAPTER ONE

Forenoon, Monday 1 December 1941

'**H**ow's the prickly heat?'

'Och, shite! Was I scratching again, Skipper?'

Second Mate Ian Lamont glared accusingly at the fingers scrabbling at his chest.

'I've got a tin of Meritt's powder in my cabin,' I said. 'You're welcome to borrow it.'

'I've tried that, and Johnson's. Best thing I've found was the bottle of calamine lotion from the Medical Hall in Singapore. I've nearly run out.'

'There's bound to be a chemist in Bangkok that can fix you up.'

I raised my binoculars to study the white-painted hulk moored off the mouth of the Chao Phraya River. The pilots were stationed there. We were waiting for one to navigate us across the bar and upriver to the city. I had wired our estimated time of arrival before leaving Hong Kong, and the flag whipping on the signal halyard in the brisk nor-easter confirmed our request. As yet, there was no sign of the pilot cutter and high water was less than an hour away.

'I wish they'd get a bloody move on. If we miss high water, we'll be stuck here until tomorrow morning.' I reached into my pocket for the tin of Senior Service, and swore. I had given up smoking.

I strode to the end of the bridge wing and gazed down at the muddy water of the anchorage. Its brown surface was chopped into sharp wavelets by the stiff breeze. Thick clumps of vegetation swirled around the ship in the eddies, where the last of the flood tide met the outflowing river current. It was the dry season when the flow of the normally swollen river slackened. It was also supposed to be the cool season but, even at the start of the forenoon watch, the temperature was already over 70 degrees and the humidity approaching 80 percent. Sweat trickled down my chest but, unlike

Lamont who had joined me out on the bridge wing, at least I had not erupted with miliaria.

'Take your shirt off. The breeze will cool you.'

'Och, that would never do, Skipper. Can't go letting the side down by appearing semi-naked. What would Mr Khoo think?'

'I'm sure the chairman's seen a man's chest before. Anyway, Second, what are you doing up here? It's your watch below.'

'Couldn't sleep.' His hand lifted involuntarily towards his chest. Grimacing, he forced it down again. 'Too bloody hot.' The grimace turned into a grin. 'I told the clerk at the Reserve Pool that I was looking for a nice quiet berth in a Clyde Puffer, running out to the Western Isles on nice days only. Rothesay, Oronsay, Taransay. How was I to know that Cathay was on the far side of the world?'

'Didn't they teach you geography in Inverness?'

'Aye, they did. But I must'na been paying attention that day.'

The previous second mate had contracted influenza which turned into pneumonia. Lamont had been sent down by the Merchant Navy Reserve Pool to replace him. The Pool had been established in May, to ensure the supply of officers and ratings for merchant ships. More importantly, it guaranteed their pay if their ships were lost or they were taken prisoner.

I was surprised the Pool had sent Lamont. He bore the clear hallmarks of a future captain and probably deserved something better than a berth in an ageing, coal-burning tramp steamer. Their loss was my gain. He was short and stocky, almost as wide as he was tall, with a face that looked as if it had been hewn from granite with a blunt chisel. Brimming with confidence, he was a born seaman with the briny blood of the Norse Gaels flowing in his veins. His father was a minister in the Scottish church and he had a younger brother in the Royal Navy, but I could not hold those against him. Apart from ebullient cheerfulness and the pipe he smoked, there was little to fault. He was also DEMS trained and happy to assist Petty Officer Bullen and his gunnery team.

'I still find it hard to believe you've been at sea all these years and never been to Asia,' I said.

'Aye, never left the Atlantic. It was all trips to the Med for iron ore and sugar from Cuba. The owners, Maclay and McIntyre, were men of little imagination.'

He had also never crossed the equator. We rectified that on the passage to Singapore. King Neptune appeared at noon as we crossed the line off the Gulf of Guinea. A trident wielding Brian Cramp, the shipwright, had been accompanied by an elderly Nefertiti played by Chief Engineer Fraser with the head of a mop plastered over his sparse grey hair. They dragged a weakly protesting Lamont onto the main deck. After the traditional punishment of a slathering with galley scraps and waste oil, they turned a fire hose on him. He took it in good grace, and I stood his afternoon watch while he shared a couple of bottles of rum with his shipmates to celebrate his new shellback status.

As a temporary distraction from the war, it had been good for morale. The Nazis had invaded Russia in May and Britain was no longer fighting alone, but the Red Army had crumbled and the panzers were on the outskirts of Moscow. The Royal Navy was doing its best but, at sea, the only thing that could be said of the war was that we had not yet lost it. Ships were still being sunk and merchant seamen lost at a terrifying rate.

We had been fitted with the long-awaited 4-inch naval gun soon after arriving back in Liverpool in February, and our anti-aircraft capability boosted by a 12-pounder on a high-angle mount. They provided some comfort that we could hit back, and Bullen claimed a share in a Condor shot down on a subsequent voyage. Despite that, I was glad when the Ministry of War Transport ordered me to take the ship back to the Far East. These were waters I knew, in which U-boats and surface raiders were few and far between.

They were warmer waters too, although Lamont was finding it hard to acclimatise. His thicker Scottish blood was better suited to the wintry reaches of the North Atlantic.

'Pilot cutter's on the way, Skipper.'

Third Mate Lakshman pointed towards the anchored hulk. A steam launch was puffing its way towards us.

'Nip below and tell Cramp to go forward to raise the anchor.'

Lakshman bounded down the stairs. Lamont continued to shadow me on the bridge wing. That was another of his faults. He had an insatiable curiosity about any place he was visiting for the first time.

'I can't promise you an interesting river passage. The country's as flat as a chart table and the river twists and turns until you imagine you're heading back on yourself.'

'I have my guidebook.' Lamont pulled a slim volume out of his pocket. 'Conrad took up his first command in Bangkok, the barque *Otago*. He describes steaming up the Chao Phraya on his way to join her.'

'*The Shadow Line* ... don't look so surprised. You and Lakshman are not the only ones who read. I've even seen the chief mate absorbed in a copy of *Fu Manchu*.'

Lamont reached into the other pocket for his pipe.

'You can put that away,' I snapped, before he managed to strike a match. 'No smoking on the bridge while I'm here.'

From the foredeck below, Cramp climbed onto the forecastle head. The pilot cutter had rapidly closed the distance. I raised an arm and circled my hand. Cramp's answering hail was followed by the clank and hiss of the windlass as he engaged the gypsy to haul the anchor in.

Twenty minutes later, the anchor was stowed, the pilot safely embarked and the ship steaming towards the Outer Bar lightship.

'What your draught please, Captain?' asked the pilot, an immaculately uniformed Siamese.

'Ten feet aft.'

He nodded. 'Fourteen feet over the bar today. Should be plenty clearance, but maintain good head steam and close boiler feed valves as far possible. Also, plenty weed. Keep eye on sea chests.'

I blew into the engine room voice pipe and relayed the instructions to Fraser.

'Tell him he's teaching his granny to riddle the fire grate.' The gruff Scottish brogue boomed up the brass pipe. 'It's the same every time we cross a bar, whether it's here, the Hooghly or the Rangoon.'

'Thanks Angus. No need to be so touchy.' I quickly replaced the cover, hoping the pilot had not heard.

Ahead of us, the broad expanse of muddy water stretched away to the low-lying coast, a brown smudge along the horizon. Beyond the Pilot Hulk, the Outer Bar lightship marked the start of the passage across the bar. It was hardly a channel; the chart showed a narrow gutter, between six and nine feet deep at low water.

As we passed the red-painted lightship at little more than half a cable to port, the pilot called a small course alteration. The helmsman spun the wheel spokes.

'Steady as she goes.' The pilot raised an arm and pointed right ahead. 'Five miles to Inner Bar Lightship. Steer straight to it. Then leave to port.'

I raised my binoculars and rotated the adjustment ring until the green painted lightship swam into focus. There was nothing else to mark our way, other than the gap between the fishing stakes thickly populating the shallows on either side.

Lakshman was standing beside the engine room telegraph, jotting down entries in a small notebook.

'Good work, Third, you'll need that to write up the log at the end of the watch.'

'It is also for my own education, sir,' he replied, his brow knotted with concentration. 'I make notes of all the pilotages I observe.' He finished the entry and looked up. 'If I might ask, sir. Why did the pilot suggest the boiler feed valves be partly closed?'

'That's a good question, Third. But this is not the right time. I suggest you ask Mr Fraser after we're safely moored.'

'I can answer that,' called Lamont, from the bridge wing.

'The third mate's got a job to do,' I growled. 'I don't want you distracting him. A moment's inattention and we'll be on the putty.'

Footsteps clattered up the bridge wing ladder and Chief Mate McGrath appeared in the wheelhouse. 'Both anchors ready for letting go, Skipper. Cramp's standing by on the brakes.'

I nodded in acknowledgement.

'What are you doing up here, Ian?' McGrath asked, seeing Lamont on the bridge wing. 'It's your watch below.'

'Making a bloody nuisance of himself,' I said, before Lamont had chance to reply. 'Distracting the third mate. And I had to stop him lighting that foul pipe of his.'

McGrath failed to suppress the smile that split his lips.

'And you can wipe that silly grin off your face.' I had suffered bouts of irritation ever since giving up smoking. There was an unopened tin of Senior Service in my day cabin in case of emergency. I took a deep breath and resisted the temptation to fetch it. It would be twenty minutes before we drew abeam of the lightship, and the pilot appeared to know what he was doing.

'It's in case we go aground, Third,' I said. 'The boiler feed valves are closed just enough to keep a full head of steam up, while restricting the amount of water in the boiler drums. It's not recommended by the boiler manufacturer, it's dangerous to starve them. But if we get stuck in the mud with them full of water, the steam demand by the engine will immediately drop. That'll send the boiler pressures soaring, blow the safety valves, possibly damage the drums and risk the loss of the feed water.' I paused, glancing across at Lamont. 'Anything to add, Second?'

Lamont looked down at his feet. 'No, sir.'

'Good. Well enjoy your sightseeing, but let the rest of us get the ship safely to Bangkok.' He still had the irrepressible grin on his face. 'And if you want to light that bloody pipe, keep well out on the bridge wing.' I grinned. There was a better alternative. 'On second thoughts, since you're up anyway, you can take charge on the forecastle. Keep Cramp company. He can point out the sights. That'll keep you occupied until we reach Bangkok.'

'Aye aye, sir.' Clamping the curved stem briar pipe between his jaws, Lamont climbed down the stairs.

Moments later, he reappeared on the foredeck, thick clouds of smoke billowing from his pipe. My nostrils twitched at the aroma of tobacco wafting aft on the breeze and I felt a desperate longing for a cigarette. Fortunately, Da Silva chose that moment to appear with a pot of coffee. I waited until he served the pilot, then savoured the strong, steaming brew.

The bright green Inner Lightship slid past close by to port.

'Port ten.' The pilot watched the bow swing onto a northerly heading. 'Midships the wheel. Steady as she goes.'

The helmsman had hardly settled onto the new course when the pilot again ordered the wheel to port. This time, he let the bow swing four points to the west, until Sunken Junk Lightship was fine on the port bow.

'Midships. Steady as she goes.'

The estuary narrowed as we cleared the bar and entered the deepwater channel leading upstream. Sunken Junk Lightship marked the gap in a line of stone laden junks sunk across the river mouth early the previous century. They, together with a heavy chain strung from shore to shore, were intended to prevent Europeans penetrating upriver to Bangkok. They failed, although Siam, or Thailand as it had been named since 1939, was the only country in South-East Asia not to succumb to western domination.

Beyond the lightship was the fortress at the end of West Point. Its white-painted fortifications concealed 6-inch Armstrong naval guns. Mangroves grew thickly along the tide line either side of the channel. Behind them, a tree-dotted network of paddy fields stretched away on either side. Bamboo houses thatched with palm fronds huddled amongst the trees. The occasional gilt spire of a temple gleamed in the sunlight.

After West Point, there were few marks to indicate the channel and the brown, vegetation strewn water provided no indication of its depth. The pilot stalked from one bridge wing to the other, watching the banks and issuing course corrections. McGrath and I took station in the wheelhouse, with all the windows lowered to catch the breeze. I had made the passage several times before, but never worked out what the pilots used to guide them.

Footsteps on the bridge wing ladder announced another arrival. Mr Khoo climbed up to join us.

'Good morning, Captain Rowden, gentlemen.' He nodded to each of us in turn, including the helmsman. 'Might I request your permission to join you on the bridge, Captain?'

'It's as much your bridge as mine. You don't need my permission.'

Despite the heat and humidity, Mr Khoo, the line's chairman, looked as cool and crisp in linen suit, white buckskin shoes and Panama hat, as if he had stepped out of the Peninsula Hotel in Hong Kong. He raised his hat as the pilot strode past. Pausing only to flick two fingers to the peak of his cap, the pilot continued out onto the other bridge wing. A junk scraped by, drifting down on the start of the ebb, its fan-shaped, battened sails spread wide to catch the breeze.

'Nevertheless, you are the captain. I am merely a passenger.' The smile creasing Mr Khoo's lips suggested he believed it less than I did. 'I have never been to Bangkok. Have I told you that before, Captain?'

He hadn't, nor explained why he joined us in Hong Kong. Our orders were to load a full cargo of rice and deliver it to Singapore. We were too big to cross the bar fully laden. Instead, we would part load in Bangkok and top up from barges at the anchorage outside the river mouth.

'No, sir, you never mentioned it.'

'It was Hong Kong merchants who developed the Siamese rice trade,' said Mr Khoo. 'Such as the Wang Lee family. Their junks arrived in Bangkok with ceramics, tea and silk, and returned to Hong Kong full of rice. They migrated here in the eighteen fifties. I am distantly related. It would honour me to meet the descendants of such forward-thinking people.'

Mr Khoo had a remarkably wide network of clan relations, including among my crew. Some of them had been pirates in the junks sailing from Bias Bay, north of Hong Kong. His nod to the helmsman was possibly more than mere courtesy.

'I didn't know that. So, it's something of a busman's holiday.'

Mr Khoo's soft chuckle brightened his steely eyes. 'Not at all. Merely sightseeing. We could have loaded the full cargo at the anchorage. But that would have meant hiring a steam launch to convey me to the city. What better way to arrive than on the bridge of my own ship?'

Following several ox-bow bends, the surrounding countryside became increasingly populated and industrial. Wood and bamboo dwellings clustered along either bank. Interspersed among them were godowns, factories and rice mills with chimneys belching smoke. Above them rose the gilt stupas of temples with glittering spires. Ships were ranged alongside rickety wharves loading bags of rice. Others were anchored mid-stream. I kept a wary eye on the pilot as he conned the ship past them.

Beyond the final bend at Bangkolem point, the industry thickened to include sawmills, slipways and oil tanks. Ahead, the city sprawled out on either side. The east bank was dominated by the grand buildings of the trading houses, hotels, diplomatic legations, the Dock Company and the Customs House, with the spires of the Royal Palace rising in the background. The west bank was densely populated with low housing, rice mills and temples. Many wooden houses fronted right over the water, supported on stilts. Women washed their clothes in basins dipped straight from the river. Children tumbled into its brown depths, splashing to the bank, uncaring of the current or the multitude of craft plying back and forth. A line of ships was anchored towards the western side of the stream, all with their bows pointing towards the city. Even at the height of the flood, there was usually enough fresh water flowing downstream, floating on the denser salt water beneath, to keep them from swinging around.

The pilot bustled in from the bridge wing, mopping the sweat off his face with a checkered handkerchief. He pointed to a space at the head of the line of anchored ships, opposite a large temple on the western bank.

'You anchor there, Captain. Six fathoms even at low water springs. Good holding ground.'

'Thank you, pilot. Slow ahead.'

I allowed the ship to slow until we were just stemming the tide and nosed her into position. My hail was followed by the splash of the anchor and the clatter and rumble of the chain tumbling over the gypsy. A cloud of rust enveloped the forecastle. The ship dropped slowly astern with the ebb, dragging the chain out of its locker, until I raised crossed wrists and Cramp furiously screwed on the windlass brake. Lamont peered over the bow as the ship snubbed up, watched until he was satisfied, and hailed to confirm the anchor was holding.

Lakshman recorded the time in his notebook. 'You can ring Finished with Engine, Third. We'll maintain sea watches. I've never dragged an anchor here, but you never know. Even in the dry season, the current can get up to four knots. So, establish some transits and keep a sharp eye on them. Call me if you have the slightest doubt. Let Mr Lamont know when he relieves you.'

'Aye aye, sir.' Lakshman rang the engine telegraph and made another note.

The journey upriver had occupied most of the forenoon watch. My stomach twitched at the welcome smell of curry wafting up from the galley. Free of the dreary restrictions of Britain's rationing, since Singapore our diet had returned to something approaching pre-war normality.

There was a polite cough and the pilot held out a chit for me to sign.

'Would you care for a drink and some lunch?'

'No thank you, Captain. The launch is coming alongside.'

I watched over the bridge wing until he was safely aboard the cutter, and went below to join Mr Khoo and the others in the saloon.

CHAPTER TWO

Afternoon, Monday 1 December 1941

'I expect you find it's hard to believe there's a war on out here,' said Mr Khoo.

He had accepted the offer of coffee in my day cabin after lunch and we were enjoying the strong brew. Da Silva had taken the opportunity of our return to Singapore to stock up on the dark-roast, fine-ground Java beans I preferred.

'Compared to Britain? It seems a million miles away,' I said.

'You must have been heartened when the navy sank the *Bismarck.* The Eighth Army seems to be coping with Rommel and the Blitz has eased.'

'We're still taking a terrible pounding at sea.'

Mr Khoo shook his head, sadly. 'I know, Captain. The newsreels show only the better news. The trouble is, people out here believe them. Your people that is. You have seen what it's like in Hong Kong and Singapore?'

I nodded. It was indeed hard to believe that Britain was in such dire straits, while in her eastern possessions life continued more or less as normal. There were Royal Navy ships in the harbours. The great and good flocked to their wardroom parties, while their sailors cruised the bars and brothels. Encouraging reports of the successes of Australian and Indian troops in North Africa, reassured the colonials the Empire was doing its bit. There was no blackout, no rationing, the shops were full, the garden parties at Government House were well attended, and the theatres, golf courses and tennis courts were packed.

'Life's still good, for the colonials,' I said. 'And the newsreels show we're doing what we've always done. Muddling through, but winning in the end, just like we did against the Kaiser.'

'You don't sound convinced.'

'Are you?'

'I might be, if there was just Hitler to worry about.' Mr Khoo reached into his pocket for a packet of small cigars. He offered me one, before changing his mind. 'Sorry, I forgot, you have given up smoking.'

'That's okay. I'll enjoy the smell.'

He rasped the flint of an expensive gold lighter. Aromatic smoke spiralled towards the deckhead where it was dispersed by the bulkhead mounted fan. It was warm in the cabin. Mr Khoo shed his jacket and loosened his tie.

'What was I saying,' he continued. 'Ah yes. If Britain only had Hitler to contend with. Hitler, of course, has something bigger on his mind. He thinks you're finished. The panzers are in the suburbs of Moscow. It's only a matter of time, days rather than weeks, before he seizes the capital and the communists collapse. Once Stalin's defeated, Churchill will have no choice but to sue for peace. I'm sure that's the view in Berlin.'

He took another puff on the cigar. 'How about a drop of that expensive cognac you save for sweet talking Poh into upping your percentage.'

Poh Ling Sing was the shipping line's agent in Singapore. I did my best to look shocked.

Mr Khoo's eyes crinkled and the corners of his mouth turned up. 'Don't worry Captain, your secrets are safe with me.' The smile in his eyes was replaced by a glint of diamond hardness. 'As are mine with you.'

I reached for the bottle of Renault hidden behind the Tanduay rum and poured two generous measures.

Mr Khoo raised his glass. 'To what shall we drink?' He pointed to the rose-pink ribbon edged with pearl grey, pinned to the breast of my khaki shirt. 'To the Order of the British Empire, so well deserved.'

'You flatter me. I did nothing anyone else couldn't have done.'

'Finding the tiny speck of one lifeboat in the middle of the Atlantic, and taking on a U-boat. I think you're being overly modest.'

'I lost two good men in the process.' I raised my glass. 'To absent shipmates.'

'I was very sorry to hear of the loss of that dashing young man, Griffith, but Commodore Lowther survived the sinking of his ship. He is leading convoys again?'

I nodded. 'Last time I saw him was on the Pier Head in Liverpool, in February. On his way to report back to Naval Control of Shipping.'

'I believe you suffered more casualties.'

It was not a question. How much did he know? I stuck to the tale recorded in the log.

'The third mate, Jeffreys, suffered a mental breakdown. He lost both his father and elder brother several years before, and was disturbed by the convoy losses. A ship exploded right before our eyes. He became obsessed with one of the women we saved from the lifeboat, and shot her. In the struggle to disarm him, the gun went off and killed him.'

'So your report says, but I have heard there was a connection between you and this woman, dating back some years.'

His dark eyes narrowed and reflections of light danced in them like fire agate. His clansmen amongst the crew had probably told him the whole story. It was better to confirm what he already knew.

'She was a prostitute I met in South Wales. I killed her pimp in a fight after he drew a knife on me. Jeffreys was his younger brother. I didn't know that when I signed him on. He discovered the truth after we rescued her from the lifeboat.'

'Payback. You injure my family, I injure yours. A dish best served cold, like Shanghai style Lun Mien noodles.'

'I don't know about that. He was ranting and quoting the Bible when he blew the back of her head off. I wasn't sorry when I wrestled the gun from his hand and … it went off.'

'You had feelings for her?'

'If things had been different … maybe.'

He reached across and patted my forearm. 'All men suffer in love. That pimp … he had no other relatives?'

'Not that I know of, apart from his mother.'

'Good. Can the police prove you killed him?'

'Apart from me, the only witnesses are dead.'

'Well then, you are in the clear. I should hate to lose a good captain over such a minor affair.' The hardness in his eyes melted into a smile.

'Anyway, that is all many miles astern. I am glad you are here.' He paused to take another drag at his cigar. 'Were you pleased to be ordered back to the east?'

'There's a war on, I go where I'm told.' I returned his smile. 'And at least we got away from the miserable weather.' I pulled the shirt away from my skin as drops of sweat rolled down my chest. 'Although there are days when I wish it was a little cooler.'

Mr Khoo stubbed the butt of his cigar into the ashtray and drained the last of his cognac. He shook his head when I offered him a refill. 'And what are your orders now?'

I tried not to let the surprise show in my face. 'To part load milled rice in Bangkok, top off at the outer anchorage at Koh Sichang and proceed to Singapore.'

Through the open porthole, the clank and hiss of steam winches confirmed loading was underway. Barges had come alongside almost as soon as the anchor splashed into the river. Slings of bagged rice were already filling our holds. It was all quite normal, but a hint of suspicion crossed my mind. The last time Mr Khoo had sat in my cabin and talked about a cargo; it had been tea in which he had a particular interest.

'There's nothing I need to know about this rice?'

'No. It's just milled Thai fragrant rice. Jasmine rice your English ladies call it.'

'The same English ladies who prefer Darjeeling tea.'

'Very possibly. Ha, ha.' He wiped away tears of laughter with a starched white handkerchief. 'Really, Captain, it is just rice. To stock the emporiums in Singapore. Nevertheless, I have not been entirely honest with you.'

I had tried to master the oriental art of inscrutability. My old friend Grim Jim Coffin likened it to having a poker face. I had never been any good at poker and, despite his claims, neither had Grim Jim. Mr Khoo, on the other hand, would have made a fine living gambling on the Mississippi paddle wheelers.

'I told you I had never been to Bangkok. That is true. It is also true that I intend to pay my respects to the Wang Lee family. But there is another reason I am travelling with you.'

'You're not answerable to me, Mr Khoo. It's your ship, you're welcome to sail in her whenever you choose.'

'I'm sure you prefer not having to entertain guests.' There was a malicious twinkle in his eye. 'Although not all the ones we have imposed on you have been as old and unattractive as I am.'

I was about to interject, for form's sake, but he held up a hand to silence me.

'I have decided to leave Hong Kong,' he continued, the twinkle fading. 'This is a matter of much regret, it has been my home for over thirty years. I have already sent my family on ahead to Singapore. We have closed up the house. All items of value have been placed into secure storage. Everything portable I have with me. I have made arrangements for the staff, many of whom feel like family.'

His shoulders slumped and I glimpsed the ageing man behind the steely facade of the Tai-pan. The war had shaken Britain to its core, but Hong Kong and Singapore seemed like solid refuges, bastions around which the tide of violence swirled but did not break. It was an illusion, but Mr Khoo's leaving smacked of more than just prudence, it sounded like self-preservation.

'And the shipping line? Your life's work was in Hong Kong,' I said.

'We will manage it from Singapore. Poh will be busier, but he will cope. I have rented a very nice bungalow in Tanglin. You will have to join Mrs Khoo and me for dinner once we are established.' He paused and ran a bony hand over his neatly oiled but sparse grey hair. 'You remember that cargo of Darjeeling tea … and what it was for?'

I could smile about it now. The tea had been opium that Mr Khoo hoodwinked me into smuggling into Shanghai. It almost got me killed.

'It was used to bribe Chinese warlords to protect Shanghai from the Japanese.'

'Not entirely true. It was mainly to protect British interests. The Japanese seized most of Shanghai, but left the International Settlement alone. As they have to this day, but for how much longer? You asked if I was convinced Britain would muddle through and I said it might if all there was to worry about was Hitler. Well, there may soon be something else to worry about, sooner even than Mr Churchill thinks.'

'You're much better informed than me. I thought the Japanese were fully occupied fighting the Nationalists in China.'

'So they are, but they are not doing as well as they hoped. The Nationalists continue to hang on, supplied by America under its Lend Lease program and the Burma Road. The Japanese are short of tin, rubber and oil which are denied them by Roosevelt's embargo. From where can they acquire them?'

'The Dutch East Indies, Malaya, Burma,' I said. I'd had a similar conversation with Major Spencer some years before, his official role as military attaché just a cover for his real work with British Military intelligence.

'Please forgive me, Captain, if I offer a history lesson. The Chinese are very resilient. We have survived the Mongols, the Manchus, the Europeans and we will survive the Japanese. There are Chinese throughout Asia, ruled over by colonial masters. Because they think they are strong, the masters don't listen to the voices of those they rule. But we Chinese know how to listen, our survival depends upon it.' He paused to light another cigar, took a deep drag and exhaled with a soft sigh.

'What do you think those Chinese would tell you? Care to hazard a guess, Captain?'

The fire burned in his agate eyes, but his face stiffened into its mask of inscrutability. I had seen and listened to enough of life in the Far East to know the answer.

'If Russia is defeated, we're on our own. If the Japanese attack us, then we're finished out here. Not just the British, but all Europeans. The Malays, the Indians, the Chinese, they'll resist the Japanese, but they won't lift a finger to help us. Why should they?'

Mr Khoo nodded and the corners of his mouth twisted with sadness. 'Some will. The way the Japanese behave in China, and will behave elsewhere, will unite peoples against them. We will survive them, but you won't. One way or another, the British Empire will become just another footnote to history.'

Mr Khoo took another drag of his cigar and we both sat in silence as the stream of blue smoke spiralled to the deckhead.

When he spoke again, his face brightened and the twinkle returned to his eyes.

'But we are not there yet. The Japanese are poised but who knows when they will spring. As a wise man once said, no matter the difficulties or how painful the experience, if we lose hope, that is our real disaster.'

'Confucius?'

'Possibly, but if he really uttered all the sayings attributed to him, he would have talked non-stop. No, the source is a Tibetan monk.' He stubbed out the cigar and reached for his jacket. 'I've taken enough of your time, Captain. I shall proceed ashore at five. The agent will send a boat to take me to the Oriental Hotel where I shall reside until you are ready to sail. I should be honoured if you would join me there for dinner. Shall we say, eight o'clock?'

'Thank you. I'd be delighted.' I knew better than to refuse an invitation from the chairman. In any case, the Oriental Hotel was the swankiest in Bangkok. There would be exotic cocktails, fine food, a jazz band and good-looking women. Some of the latter might even be persuaded to put up with my two left feet.

'Excellent. I will meet you there. Not in uniform. If you still have a white dinner jacket that would be preferable. There may be some interesting company.'

He pushed himself out of the chair and allowed me to accompany him one deck down to the passenger suite. After he closed the door, I stepped across the alley into my own quarters. It was only midway through the afternoon watch, but I was feeling drowsy with the heat, the effects of the curry lunch and the cognac. Da Silva, who seemed increasingly blessed with second sight, was already turning down the bed. I asked him to rouse out my dinner jacket and press it for the evening. Kicking off my shoes, I stretched out.

Mr Khoo's predictions would be laughed at or denounced as treasonable in the fashionable bars and nightclubs along Orchard Road. I had listened to the overconfident chatter of planters and their wives, secure in what they referred to as Fortress Singapore. As far as they were concerned, the Japanese were a weak-witted, short-sighted, rabble and no match for proper soldiers. As my mind wandered, I imagined countless millions of Asians listening to their colonial rulers while eagerly anticipating their downfall. They understood the increasingly precarious foothold of Europeans in Asia far better than we did. Lulled by the familiar clatter and clank of the steam winches my eyes started to close. My last thoughts were of a good dinner and the nature of Mr Khoo's promised interesting company.

CHAPTER THREE

Evening, Monday 1 December 1941

'**A**re you sure you wouldn't rather a run ashore to see the exotic dancers at the Siam Hotel, or pay a visit to the ladies in Wind Mill Road?'

'Normally, aye,' said Lamont. 'But it's the first time I've been here and I've always wanted to visit the Oriental Hotel. Conrad went there while making the *Otago* ready for sea. If you don't mind me stringing along, I'll buy you a drink at the bar while you wait for Mr Khoo. Then I'll go for a wee wander and soak up the atmosphere, find somewhere to enjoy a quiet beer and some local food.'

We were leaning against the main deck bulwark, gazing over the dark, swirling river at the bright lights of the city. Launches bustled up and down the broad reach, ferrying passengers between its banks and to and from the ships anchored mid-stream. Close to the bank, fishermen drifted on the current. Families clustered on the verandas of their riverside homes. The smell of cooking fires wafted over the water, together with the enticing aromas of charcoal grilled meats and exotic stir fries.

I checked my watch. The hands had just ticked past the hour. 'The agent was supposed to arrange the launch for seven.' I tapped my fingers against the steel rail.

'Think that's him now.' Lamont pointed towards a slim launch speeding from the bank. Its skipper put the wheel hard over and throttled back. The launch inscribed a white flecked arc on the inky water, and slid alongside the gangway with the merest touch. The bowman hooked on and Lamont and I scrambled down the swaying steps.

'Mind those lovely white sleeves, Skipper. You would'na want to arrive with oil stains on them,' said Lamont.

Da Silva had sponged and pressed the dinner jacket during the afternoon, almost restoring it to the glory of its first wearing in 1937 when, in addition to opium masquerading as tea, we carried Lady Helen Ashworth to Shanghai. I had lost weight as a result of the war-time diet, and it fitted perfectly.

As soon as we were aboard, the bowman let go and the launch accelerated away in the throaty roar of a powerful diesel engine. The river's surface was choppy from the wakes of numerous craft bustling up and down, and we ducked inside its tiny cabin to shelter from the spray. It was a mile upriver to the Oriental Hotel. Passing close to the eastern bank we sped past a rice mill, several temples, grand waterfront homes and the Bangkok Dock Company's slipways. Easing back on the throttle, the skipper angled towards a jetty beside a neat lawn dotted with palm trees. Beyond them rose the hotel's imposing, white, floodlight edifice.

I pressed a five-dollar bill into the skipper's hand as he saw us safely ashore. 'Return at midnight.'

He nodded. 'Okay, boss. Midnight.'

I paused on the lawn while Lamont gazed at the famous facade. Light spilt out of the ground floor ball and dining room windows. Above them stretched a row of tall, wooden shuttered windows behind which were the bedrooms. Crowning the centre was the ornate pediment with its rising sun motif.

'Come on Second, what does your guidebook say?'

'Conrad didn't write much about it then. He couldn't afford to stay here when he commanded the *Otago*, he just hung around the Billiard Room. When he finally slipped anchor, he said guests waved to him from the lawn, but that's probably just his imagination. I do know that in its heyday it was one of the most famous hotels in the world. The future Tsar of Russia, Crown Prince Nicholas, visited in eighteen ninety-one and Nijinsky danced in the ballroom in nineteen sixteen. Conrad stayed in later years, as did Somerset Maugham and Noel Coward.'

'Impressive. If you're ever short of a berth at sea, you can get a job as a tour guide,' I said, chuckling.

I led the way across the lawn and through to the lobby. The bar was off to the side. I spotted an empty table and signalled to a waiter. Settling back into the cane chair with an iced rum sling in my fist, I gestured to the throng of dinner suited and uniformed men accompanied by women in glittering cocktail gowns. 'Hard to believe there's a war on.'

'Well there isn't, here,' said Lamont, taking a swig of his drink.

'But you're right, Skipper, this is unreal. Only a few weeks ago we were in Liverpool, the city blasted almost beyond recognition. Then we ran the gauntlet of bombs and torpedoes, before slinking off alone to Singapore. And now this.' A door opened and the notes of *Bugle Call Rag* burst out of the ballroom. 'Back then, I thought I was passing through the outer reaches of hell on my way to an early, watery grave. Now, it's like we're at the gates of paradise.'

'A fools' paradise,' I said. 'Look carefully at those uniforms. They're mostly Japanese, with a few Nazis and a smattering of Vichy French. The Japanese already look as if they're holding a mortgage on the place.'

Raucous groups of Japanese officers were gathered around the largest tables, their surfaces forested with bottles of champagne and aged whisky. Gorgeously clad Siamese women, bright red smiles painted onto their doll-like faces, simpered and giggled at the jokes and roaming hands of their hosts.

'Shameless brutes,' said Lamont.

'They're behaving no differently to whichever race claims mastery over parts of the Far East. You'll see the British doing the same in bars and nightclubs from Suez to Shanghai.'

'Aye, you're right, we're a beastly race … men that is.' Lamont's face was a mask of disapproval. 'Ever since that woman led Adam astray in the Garden of Eden.' He paused, his lips cracking into a wide grin. 'Dinna fash, Skipper, I'm not going all Kirk on you. If I'm not mistaken, that's Mr Khoo making his way over.' He pushed back his chair. 'I'm away for some quiet contemplation over a few beers and a curry.'

'Last call for the Skylark's at midnight. After that you'll have to negotiate with a bum boat.'

Lamont waved a hand in reply, wished Mr Khoo a good evening and disappeared through the lobby.

'Was that your second mate, Lamont?' asked Mr Khoo, dropping into the chair opposite.

I nodded. 'He wanted to have a look at the hotel. Joseph Conrad, the author, stayed here. Lamont enjoys his books.'

'I tried to read Lord Jim once. I never understood the chapter about Stein's butterflies and beetles.' He caught the eye of a passing waiter. 'A refill for the captain and the same for me.'

'I think it has something to do with man's dual nature, a creature of both earth and air. Lamont can probably explain it better, he comes from a literary family. His father published several books on the local history of Inverness, and he has a younger brother called Alistair, currently in the navy, who wants to be an author.'

Loud angry voices interrupted us. A tall French Army commandant confronted a Japanese captain. A head shorter, the captain blocked the commandant's path and shouted at him in Japanese. The Frenchman looked down his Gallic nose, pursed his lips and forcefully emitted a contemptuous, 'Phuh.'

They glared at each other, refusing to give way, until the head waiter intervened. He stepped between them like a referee separating two prize fighters. After several whispered exchanges, during which they both remained rigidly at attention, the commandant raised his fingers to the peak of his kepi. The captain snapped a salute in return. After a short pause, both bobbed their heads in the slightest of bows. Honour apparently served, the commandant strode off towards the bar and the captain returned to his table. Back slapping comrades poured him a large scotch.

'Hostilities narrowly averted there, thank goodness.'

A trim, sandy haired man with a clipped military moustache approached the table. The white dinner jacket made a change from the uniform he usually wore.

He reached out a hand and I rose to grasp it.

Captain Rowden, you old pirate.' His blue eyes twinkled and his lips curled with pleasure.

'Major Spencer!'

He was the last person I expected to see but, from the smiles on his and Mr Khoo's faces, I had the sudden feeling I was the butt of a joke that felt decidedly unfunny. Spencer's presence invariably foreshadowed trouble. After seeing him safely ashore in Davao, after our adventures in Shanghai and the Pelews in 1937, we caught up for a drink or a meal on the rare occasions I called at Port Moresby. He disappeared as soon as war was declared.

'Colonel now, please. Well, Lieutenant-Colonel actually, but that's a bit of a mouthful.'

'Colonel Spencer will be joining us for dinner.' Mr Khoo spoke as if to dispel any doubt on the matter. 'I suggest we move.' He nodded in the direction of the Japanese officers. 'Before any more attempts are made to satisfy honour.'

We followed him through the door to the airy calm of the dining room. Fans circled overhead and the open windows overlooked the floodlight lawn and the darker backdrop of the river. Potted plants added splashes of tropical green.

Having been taken by surprise, I was in no hurry to ask why Spencer had been invited to dinner. I was saved from having to say anything by the arrival of the head waiter.

'I apologise for the altercation.' He led us to a discreet corner table screened by a large potted palm. 'It is a game the younger officers play, trying to force anyone in uniform to bow to the emperor. We have requested they desist, but the Japanese have much influence with the king. It makes them overly bold.' A wry smile creased his lips. 'There has been no bloodshed yet, thank God.'

'You diffused the tension without too much trouble,' said Spencer.

'I am Swiss,' said the head waiter, with a proud toss of his head. 'Living at the heart of Europe, surrounded by nations whose politics and interests frequently conflict, we have become masters of the art of avoiding trouble.' He pointed to the wine list. 'Would you care to select a wine, Monsieur Khoo?'

'Does either of you gentlemen know anything about wine? I rarely drink it, red with meat and white with fish is my limit.'

'My father swore by a simple rule.' Spencer accepted the wine list and snapped it shut. 'Find a wine you like, know why you like it and order it on all occasions.' He turned to the head waiter. 'I don't suppose your cellar runs to Australian vintages?'

The head waiter's nostrils briefly wrinkled. 'Non monsieur.'

'Pity, in that case have you a bottle of the twenty-nine Vieux Télégraph?'

'Oui, monsieur. A good year for the Rhone.'

Spencer's lips curled into a playful smile that persisted as the head waiter returned with a bottle cradled in a silver basket. After deftly extracting the cork and closely examining it, he poured a small amount into a glass. Spencer held it up to the light, swirled it around and sniffed like a bloodhound. Apparently satisfied, he took a mouthful and swished it around his mouth, before swallowing.

'Excellent,' he pronounced.

'What was all that for?' I asked, after our glasses had been filled. The wine tasted fine, better for the fact that my tongue was not furred by cigarette smoke, but I knew no more about it than Mr Khoo.

'Makes one look as if one knows what one's doing. Justifies the price if nothing else,' said Spencer, still grinning.

Mr Khoo took a mouthful and savoured it. 'Very pleasant. Tell us why you picked it.'

Spencer grinned so broadly that even the corners of his moustache turned up. 'Simple. In nineteen twenty-nine, I was a young subaltern on secondment to the British Army. The opportunity arose for a field trip to the south of France, Provence to be exact. It was late summer, vintage time. In between training exercises and route marches, we found time to fraternise. Funny how a French word meaning to treat men as brothers, means something entirely different in connection with the opposite sex. Anyway, there was a young lady. Her father kept a cellar and introduced me to the old telegraph. I've no idea if it's any good. The experts say it's rich in tannins and the scent of the wild herbs that flourish in the garrigue, the rocky limestone hillsides on which the grapes grow. To me, it just brings back pleasant memories of a better time.'

Mr Khoo raised his glass. 'To better times, and to knowing one's wine. Now, let us order.'

The Oriental Hotel prided itself on serving the best European food in Bangkok. To the head waiter's barely concealed displeasure, Mr Khoo ignored his recommendations and ordered a selection of Siamese dishes. There were curries, stir fried noodles and vegetables, steamed rice fragrant with pandanus and coconut, and a sour, fiery soup. The wine quickly gave way to cooling bottles of locally brewed Singha beer for Spencer and me, while Mr Khoo sipped on expensive cognac drowned in Canada Dry ginger ale.

Hunger satisfied, we relaxed back in our chairs while the waiters cleared the table.

'Well, Captain Rowden.' Mr Khoo reached into his pocket for a cigar. 'Are you not curious as to why I invited Colonel Spencer to join us this evening?'

Spencer eyed me watchfully, just the hint of a smile playing across his lips. He accepted the offer of a cigar and raised an eyebrow when I declined.

'He's given up smoking,' chuckled Mr Khoo. 'Makes him irritable at times. Pity the poor officer who feels the scourge of his tongue.'

'He was always a bit tetchy, as I recall,' said Spencer. 'I remember the small matter of a cargo of tea. Certain gentlemen felt more than the power of his tongue.'

I clenched my jaw and forced a smile. 'All right. I'll play the game. What are you doing here … Colonel?'

'I thought you'd never ask. I've missed our little chats since I was posted from Moresby. What dragged me away was an order to join the Australian Sixth Division when it went to North Africa to see off the Italians. Had a bit of trouble dislodging them from a place called

Tobruk, but we eventually sent them packing. Then it was off for a few weeks' sightseeing in Greece. Wandered all over the country being bombed and shot at by the Hun, before the navy finally pulled us off the beaches in the Peloponnese. Picked up the Bath Star to go with the Crown there. Spot of mountaineering in Lebanon after that, taking a crack at the Vichy French.'

'Sounds like you've been busy,' I said.

'I hear you've been busy too, bagging yourself another U-boat and picking up an OBE.' His smile faded. 'I was really sorry to hear about David Griffith and Tom Sayce. We can't afford to lose good men like that.' He shook his head. 'Terrible business, too, about the third mate and the ENSA woman, Mrs D'Angelo. And that after you'd found her and the others in a lifeboat in the middle of the ocean. Sounds like it was a rough trip. You deserve that gong.'

'Are you still keeping tabs on me?' None of it was secret, but it was annoying to know he was still tracking my movements. I had fouled up one of his intelligence operations in New Guinea. I thought I had repaid the debt, not least by saving one of his double agents from the NKVD. 'Have you nothing better to do, or is Hitler not high on your list of priorities. Why don't I make it easy and send you a daily cable of my movements?'

'Keep your shirt on, Bill. I ran into an old friend of yours in Suez, told me the whole story. Tall chap, wearing a commodore's broad stripe. Name of Lowther.'

'You bastard, you could have said that in the beginning.'

'And spoil the fun. Anyway, a good intelligence officer shouldn't disclose his sources.'

'Sorry, I'm afraid my sense of humour's been tested these past couple of years. Stopping smoking hasn't helped.'

'Not that we've noticed,' said Spencer, his eyes twinkling.

'Okay, now you're making me sound like a fool.' My cheeks blushed. 'You haven't answered my question, though. What are you doing here?'

Spencer took a long drag at his cigar and blew a plume of blue smoke towards the ceiling.

'Someone finally had enough sense to see that the eastern outposts of King George's empire are like an unchaperoned debutante. Ripe for the … well you can fill in the rest yourself. The Japanese have had their eyes on them for years, and the French and Dutch colonies. Not to possess them mind, nothing so vulgar as that. They want to help the locals kick out the white man, and set up what they call the

Greater East Asia Co-Prosperity Sphere. All under the wise guidance of the Chrysanthemum Throne, for which the gratefully liberated citizens will exchange their rubber, oil and tin.'

'You told me something similar once before,' I said. 'Of which Mr Khoo reminded me this afternoon.'

'The soundings are on the chart, as you sailors would say,' continued Spencer. 'It's only a matter of time before the Japanese army tears itself away from its pleasures in China and grabs at one or another of the white man's jewels. Hong Kong, Singapore, Batavia, Manila, Hanoi, Rangoon. I don't count Shanghai, they've already got the keys to the gate.'

'Any idea when?'

'Next week, next month, next year.' He shrugged his shoulders. 'Your guess is as good as mine. What I can tell you is that the Japanese have over one and a half million men, fifty squadrons of frontline aircraft and a first-rate navy. What have we got? What's left of the British Army is defending the Suez Canal. The RAF's got it hands full bombing Germany and the Navy's barely hanging on in the Atlantic. What does that leave? Two men and a dog. No, I'm not being quite fair. There are six battalions in Hong Kong and three divisions in Malaya and Singapore. But they're better on paper than in reality. They're a cobbled together mix of British, Australian, Indian, Malay and New Zealand troops. Mostly poorly trained, ill-equipped and hardly speaking the same language.'

'Forgive me interrupting,' said Mr Koo. 'But I thought Singapore was an impregnable fortress.'

'To attack from the sea, maybe. But what if the Japanese attack down the Malay peninsula? Common wisdom says armies can't fight through the jungle. I'm not sure about that.'

'But to do that, they'd have to go through Indochina and Thailand,' said Mr Khoo.

'Or mount a seaborne invasion,' said Spencer. 'The Japanese have already set up bases in Indochina, with the cooperation of the Vichy French, and they're on very good terms with the Thais. It's no surprise there are so many of them in Bangkok, and you've seen for yourselves how they behave.'

Finally, the penny dropped. 'Which is why you're here, to find out which way the Japanese will jump, and when.'

'My dear Captain Rowden. You make me sound like a spy. I'm just the Military Attaché at His Britannic Majesty's Diplomatic Legation to the government of His Majesty King Rama the Eighth.'

'So, what's this got to do with me? Call me suspicious, but the last time you lectured me on the military situation in the Far East, I ended up taking on Chinese Warlords, the NKVD and a Nazi U-boat.'

Spencer's laugh was almost convincing. 'Nothing at all, Bill. Mr Khoo heard I was in Bangkok and thought it would be nice to renew old acquaintances. And I must say it's been a most pleasant evening.' He turned to Mr Khoo. 'Thank you for dinner, sir. You've been a marvellous host.'

'Not at all, Colonel, the pleasure's been all mine.' Mr Khoo's mouth curled into a mischievous grin and the fire gleamed in his eyes. 'And you can put Captain Rowden's mind at rest? We can complete loading our cargo of rice and go about our lawful business in peace?'

'As far as the Japanese are concerned? I think you've nothing to fear. The drums may be beating, but they're faint. As for the Nazis, there could be U-boat wolf packs assembling in the Gulf of Siam for all I know.'

'I think we should have heard, were that the case,' said Mr Khoo. He raised a hand to summon the waiter. 'Now, if you'll excuse me gentlemen, I'll settle the bill and retire. If you'd like another drink just charge it to my room.'

We rose to bid him good night, and watched him pick his way through the bar to the lobby.

'No rest for the wicked.' Spencer refused my offer of one for the road. 'I've a meeting with the minister, sorry.'

'At this time of night?'

'His Majesty's government is ever vigilant.' He stuck out a hand. 'I expect you'll be in Singapore for a couple of weeks discharging that rice. I might find an excuse to pop down and you can buy me that drink at the Singapore Club.'

'I'm not a member.'

'Neither am I. Didn't stop us getting into the Shanghai Club.'

After he had gone, I ordered myself another large rum, topped it off with soda water and took it out onto the terrace. The night was cool, the air rich with the scent of frangipani and hibiscus. A jagged fork of lightning flashed in the distance, followed by the faint rumble of thunder. I took a large pull on the rum, mulling over what Spencer had said. The thunder sounded like the distant beating of drums, but if the threat was as far away as he implied, why had Mr Khoo suddenly packed up his family and moved to Singapore?

'Ah trust ya had a braw evening?' A hand clapped me on the shoulder and the sour reek of whisky assailed my nostrils.

A swaying, wild eyed Lamont grinned at me. His hair draped askew, his tie hung under his ear, the tail of his shirt flapped loose, several suspicious stains sullied his linen suit and he sported the beginnings of a black eye.

'So much for a quiet beer. What the hell happened to you?'

'Hell had'na any part of it. I've drunk fro' the well o' happiness. Supped on the sweetmeats of a thousand delights. Loved to the limit of ma loins and fought for the honour of a lady.'

'Did you win?'

'Ya ken the damage. But you hav'na seen the other fella.'

'Who was he?'

'Nae idea. He took a dislike to ma face.' He ran a hand over his jaw as if to reassure himself it was still there.

'And the lady?'

'The prettiest wee lassie this side of Pitlochry. Ungrateful hussy robbed me while I was otherwise occupied. Nae matter, I was down to ma last few coppers anyway.' He swayed as he gazed around the darkened lawn. 'Sure, it's a braw city, so it is, and I'm reet glad to ha' made its acquaintance.'

A hail from the riverbank indicated the return of the launch. Lamont weaved his way to the jetty, waved away the helping hand, stepped aboard with all the dignity he could muster, tripped on the sill at the entrance to the cabin and collapsed giggling onto the deck.

The ten-minute ride downriver was not long enough to sober him. I should have called for a rope and lashed it around his waist. Instead, I climbed the gangway behind him, praying he would not slip and send both of us tumbling into the river.

He was late for his watch, but in no state to stand it. I sent him to bed and told Lakshman to split it with McGrath. They would make him pay a well-deserved price for it.

I took a last stroll around the deck to make sure all was well, before turning in. My last waking thoughts were of Colonel Spencer. Whatever he chose to call himself, Spencer was a spy and Bangkok the centre of his attention. My ship was anchored in the heart of the city. It could have been coincidence, but I had long ago learnt not to believe in it. I rubbed my hands together to relieve the tingling in my fingertips and fell into a troubled sleep.

CHAPTER FOUR

Forenoon, Thursday 4 December 1941

The final slings of bagged rice had been swung aboard and the crew were lifting the hatch boards and canvas covers into place. There was no need to batten them down, we were only heading as far the anchorage.

From the bridge wing, I watched the last Siamese dockers climb out of the holds and scramble down rope ladders onto the empty barges lashed alongside. The crew cast their lines off, a tug took the strain and towed them upstream, back to the rice mill. Working from dawn to dusk, it had taken almost three days to load 3,000 tons, the maximum to cross the bar with sufficient clearance under the keel. Before proceeding to Singapore, we still had to load another 6,000 tons at the outer anchorage off Koh Sichang.

McGrath joined me on the bridge wing. 'Hatch covers are on. I'll leave the derricks topped but secure them. Any news of the pilot?'

'Last message from the agent said Mr Khoo was staying ashore until this morning. There's been nothing since about him, or the pilot.'

'They're cutting it fine. If we're not underway by nine, will miss high water at the bar.'

'I'm well aware of that, Mister Mate. Tell me something I don't know.'

'Sorry, Skipper. I didn't mean to—'

'Forget it.' I shook my head, annoyed at my outburst. 'If I'd known it would make me this irritable, I wouldn't have given up smoking.'

'Why did you?'

'I'm asking myself that question. I thought I was doing well, with neither you nor young Lakshman being smokers. And then Lamont comes along with his bloody pipe. By the way, what retribution did you extract for having to split his watch on Tuesday morning?'

'Nothing serious. He took my watch yesterday afternoon. Gave me a chance to take Lakshman ashore. Show him the sights and buy him some stir fry noodles and a green curry.'

'Was that all you bought him?'

'No chance of anything else. It was the temples he wanted to see. Apparently, there's a strong Hindu tradition in the Siamese version of Buddhism. He pointed out some of their shrines ... Vishnu, Ganesh and Brahma. Don't ask me who they are.'

'Whatever is the world coming to, when young sailors would rather gaze at painted idols than drink beer and go for a haircut. You did show him Wind Mill Road?'

McGrath nodded, grinning. 'Only in passing. He said it compared favourably with Grant Road, but not up to the standard of safe gully, where Bombay's white girls work.'

'I've never been to either, so I'll take his word for it.'

I glanced at my watch; it was approaching 9am. High water was at noon. In the absence of instructions from the agent, it looked as if we would spend another night anchored in the city. There was a second high water at midnight, but I was reluctant to attempt the river passage in the dark, with no buoys to mark the channel and countless fishermen and other small craft plying its waters. It was none of my business if Mr Khoo wished to spend longer ashore. He was paying the bills, and one more day hardly mattered. Still, I found it strange. He did not part with money needlessly and I had expected him to want us to sail as soon as we were ready. Whatever was detaining him—clan social obligations probably—was unlikely to be serious. Bad news, on the other hand, usually travelled fast in my experience. I put my irritation down to the frustration of not knowing one way or the other, and the absence of nicotine. Fortunately, there was still the pleasure of strong Javanese coffee. My nostrils told me Da Silva was busy in his pantry.

The chink of crockery was like a starting gun, and I darted back to my day cabin to find the coffee pot and a freshly poured cup awaiting me. I carried it onto the bridge wing and nodded to McGrath. 'Help yourself. Thank God there's no shortage of coffee out here.'

'Looks like we might be in for an afternoon rainstorm.' McGrath re-joined me with a cup grasped in his fist.

The usual dry season nor-easter had not picked up with the dawn. It was caused by cool winter air flowing down from the mountains in central China. Instead, the air seemed thick and towering banks of cumulonimbus filled the northern horizon. I could almost smell the rain.

'Have you written and told your parents you're back out east? If Colonel Spencer's right and things stay quiet, there's a reasonable chance of a call into Sydney.'

In Singapore, McGrath had received a letter from his mother. His father had fallen off a horse while mustering sheep and broken a leg. It had not mended well and he would limp for the rest of his life. McGrath had not been home in four years. He was worried, but trying not to show it.

'I dropped them a line from Hong Kong, but I didn't want to get their hopes up. They seem to be coping okay. My eldest brother's still at home. The other one volunteered for the army.' He took a mouthful of coffee and smacked his lips in appreciation. 'I'd almost forgotten what good coffee tastes like.'

'You've come a long way from the Royal George. Brand new master's ticket in your pocket. You could try for a mate's berth with Burns Philp or one of the other Australian lines. You'd get home more often.'

The Royal George Hotel in Sydney was where I first met him, as a young, hot-tempered, hard-fisted third mate out of a job. He had matured since then and earned his promotions to second and chief mate. I had sent him on leave in Liverpool to cram for the master's examination. He passed first time.

'Thanks, Skipper. I'm happy where I am.' He took another mouthful of coffee and changed the subject. 'Bit of a coincidence, don't you think, Colonel Spencer turning up here in Bangkok?'

'Like a bad penny? Actually, Mr Khoo knew he was here, so it wasn't that much of a coincidence. I suppose, with the war on, we were bound to run into him again sooner or later.'

McGrath raised an eyebrow. I was not sure I believed it either.

Thunderclouds were still piling up, but the city and the river remained peaceful. Several ships had weighed anchor and were heading downstream. The usual bustle of small craft criss-crossed between the river banks. On the foredeck, Lakshman was supervising the securing of the derrick booms. Down below, Fraser had a full head of pressure in the boilers. The excess steam whistled softly through the relief valves.

'Better let the engine room know we're still waiting for word from ashore.'

McGrath strode into the wheelhouse and blew into the voice pipe. He returned just in time to watch a launch pull alongside and the agent scramble up the accommodation ladder. I went below to my cabin to meet him.

The news went some way to easing my irritation. Mr Khoo's short, handwritten message, scrawled on notepaper bearing the logo of the Oriental Hotel, stated that he was unavoidably detained and our departure delayed by 24 hours.

'Looks like we've a quiet afternoon and evening ahead of us,' I said, re-joining McGrath on the bridge wing. 'I've sent word down to the chief that he can relax. If anyone wants a few more hours ashore they may as well take them now.'

Footsteps clattered on the ladder and Lakshman climbed up from the boat deck.

'All the derricks are secure, sir. May I know if we are still departing this morning.'

'Why? Do you need to be somewhere else, Third?' It was meant as a joke, but was met by an uncomfortable silence. McGrath cast a sly wink in Lakshman's direction.

'As you're so keen to know, Third,' I said, ignoring his widening smile. 'There are customers in the markets and grocery stores of Singapore anxiously awaiting the arrival of *Oriental Venture* and her cargo of the finest grade fragrant rice. But, out of the goodness of his heart, the owner has decided to grant you a further twenty-four hours to enjoy the fleshpots of Bangkok.' I glared at him until the smile vanished. 'Well, Mr Lakshman, what do you say?'

He bit his lower lip. 'Thank you very much, sir. I have, however, exceeded my budget for sightseeing and purchases. The tailor has run me up some excellent uniform shirts and shorts, and I have purchased rolls of mudmee pattern silk and cotton for my mother and my sisters. If Mr McGrath or Mr Lamont wanted some time off—'

'Stow it, Third. Or I'll think you're trying to take the mickey. There are plenty of things to keep you busy, and if you can't think of any, I'm sure the chief mate can. Now, I'm going below to catch up on some paperwork.'

I ignored the chuckles that followed me down the stairs. On my way to my cabin, I paused to examine the repairs to the bulwark where the 88-mm shell had torn through on its way to exploding in the radio room. The Freetown dockyard boilermakers had riveted roughly fashioned plates across the missing section and over the jagged hole in the radio room bulkhead. A new radio station had been installed in Liverpool. It, and its new operator Gilmore, now occupied the newly outfitted space next to my cabin.

It was no cooler there, even with the portholes wide open to catch the breeze. I angled the electric fan and sat at the desk. Reaching into the drawer, I pulled out the master's official log in which I made all the entries required by the Board of Trade to record the progress of each voyage. There was little to add since our arrival on Monday evening, and I entered a short note to explain the 24-hour delay. Flicking through the pages was like turning the clock back. The tersely worded descriptions of events, and the accompanying coordinates of the positions in which they occurred, brought flashbacks of the past. There was the sighting of the *City of Richmond*'s lifeboat, and the rescue of Lakshman and the survivors plucked from the burning ship. There, too, the bare facts of the fight with the U-boat and the loss of David Griffith and Tom Sayce. Several entries later was the stark, but untruthful account of the deaths of Olwyn D'Angelo and Third Mate Jeffreys. The log was quite clear, he was out of his mind when he shot her, and his death an accident as I wrestled the gun from his grasp. In truth, he had murdered her and I had killed him—executed was the word others might have used—but, apart from me, no one could attest to it.

Jeffreys had been no loss, other than to his mother, but Lakshman was a welcome gain. I signed him on for the voyage back to Liverpool, expecting he would be recalled by City Line as soon as they received word of his return. Instead, there had been a curt letter stating that his services were no longer required. I sensed his anger and disappointment, even as he tried to hide them. Perhaps they really didn't have a berth for him, or maybe they were ditching an inconveniently coloured officer as soon as they had the chance. In any case, it was City Line's loss. Wartime sinkings meant there were plenty of other ships clamouring for officers, including mine.

He looked at me with confusion written all over his young face. It had evidently never occurred to him that City Line would not want him back.

'I guess I'm stuck with you then,' I said.

His Adam's apple bobbed. 'If you are not happy with my services, Captain ...'

'I never said that.' I kept my voice gruff. 'But if you're going to stay, we need to get a few things straight. You can have an advance on your pay to buy yourself a replacement sextant. I'm saving mine for the next third mate I pluck out of the ocean. And you can drop all the City Line bullshit. We're not officers and gentlemen here and we don't dress for dinner. You call me and the chief engineer sir, everyone else is mister, unless they give you permission otherwise. And the rules are simple. You do your job right, you do as I say and no fighting on board. Think you can live with all that?'

'Yes, sir.' His mouth was compressed into a straight line, but there was the beginning of a twinkle in his eyes.

I stuck out a hand. 'Welcome aboard Mr Lakshman.' He grasped it and winced at my grip. 'That bit about the sextant. If you'd rather save your money that's okay. Buy one when you can. And write to your mother and give her the good news. We might not be as genteel, but you'll learn far more of your profession in a rough tramp steamer than you ever will poncing about the bridge of a passenger liner in starched white number tens.'

Since then, he had given me no cause to regret my decision, and if ever I came across the City Line manager who signed the dismissal letter, I would gladly shake his mistaken hand. The only weevil in the biscuit was the love of reading he shared with Lamont. The two of them spent hours comparing the literary merits of their favourite authors. If I had to sit through another meal listening to them debate the difference between metonymy and synonymy, I would banish them both from the saloon.

I closed the logbook and placed it back in the drawer. The mouth-watering smell of the lunchtime curry was wafting up from the galley. With the ship secured and ready to proceed downriver, it promised to be a peaceful afternoon. One in which I might even enjoy banking a few precious hours of sleep against the inevitable long nights to come. I pulled the rum bottle off the rack and poured myself a stiff tot. The low rumble of thunder sounded like distant gunfire, and I shivered as a gust of cooler air blew through the porthole. The rum warmed on the way down, but did nothing to ease the tingling in my fingertips.

CHAPTER FIVE

Middle Watch, Friday 5 December 1941

Another bomb exploded, deafeningly close this time. I yelled at the helmsman to spin the wheel hard over. Zig-zagging was the only way to put the bombers off their aim. The man stared straight ahead; the wheel spokes frozen in his grip. He couldn't hear me. I struggled to reach him, my feet sticking to the deck, and woke with my legs thrashing against the sweat-damp sheet.

I shook my head to clear the last of the sleep and reached for my watch. An eyeball searing flash of lightning revealed it was 2am, before the violent clap of thunder battered my eardrums. As they recovered from the shock, I heard the roar of torrential rain. Water puddled on the linoleum and I dragged the portholes closed. Pulling on shirt and shorts, and slipping my feet into sandals, I darted up the stairs to the wheelhouse.

Lamont was sheltering inside, puffing on his pipe and gazing at the faint lights of the city, barely visible through the tropical rain-storm.

'It's been building for the last couple of hours.' He shivered as a strong wind gust drove rain through the open bridge wing doorway. 'Tide's just turned. There's more water flowing down with the ebb, but the anchor's holding.'

Another searing, jagged fork of lightning sizzled into the ground on the west bank less than five cables away. The simultaneous thunderclap rattled the bridge windows.

'Hope no one was underneath that.' I dragged the sliding door closed. The rain turned ferocious, blotting out the city and the river. The forecastle was barely visible and the water beating onto the decks sounded like a giant waterfall.

'If this is the dry season, I'd hate to be here when it really rains,' said Lamont, surrounded by a cloud of blue smoke.

'That just means it rains less often than in the wet season.' I would not have admitted it, but the smell of his pipe tobacco was pleasant. I was tempted to retrieve the Senior Service from my cabin. 'It's unusual though. Must be some very unstable air blowing out of China.'

Another crackle of lightning, farther away this time, was followed several seconds later by the boom of thunder. As the rain eased, the city lights emerged as if from behind a muslin curtain. 'Did you get the duty man to check the hatch access lids are closed and the covers aren't leaking. Be a disaster if the rice gets wet.'

'Aye, Skipper. Sent him down over half an hour ago, before it started.' He checked his watch. 'Blighter should be back by now. Probably sheltering in the poop enjoying a cheroot. I'll have words when—'

He was interrupted by frantic knocking on the bridge wing door. I yanked it open. A Chinese seaman, his hair plastered over his scalp, streamed water.

'Boat come, Captain. Ask lower gangway.'

I darted to the edge of the bridge wing and peered over the side. The deck lamps cast just enough light to see a motor launch, its bow angled alongside the hull, holding station against the current with the thrust of its engine. The skipper poked his head out from under the awning and waved furiously. If anyone else was aboard, they had the good sense to be sheltering in the cabin.

I ran back into the wheelhouse. 'Go and find out what he wants. It's probably some of the crew coming back late. Get their names and send them aft. I'll deal with them in the morning.'

Lamont disappeared down the stairs and I went in search of a towel in my day cabin. Rubbing my hair dry, I felt wide awake. Was it too early to call Da Silva?

Returning footsteps thudded on the stairs and Lamont called, 'Skipper?'

'In here.'

He poked his head around the door.

'Well?'

'It's Mr Khoo. He's come back aboard.'

'At this time of night! Why the hell couldn't he wait until morning?'

'He's not alone. There are three passengers with him. I've put them in the saloon while we get their baggage on board. Da Silva's fixing them up with coffee.'

'Tell me this is just a joke.' I shook my head in frustration. Mr Khoo had made some unusual requests over the years, but had never arrived in the middle of a tropical downpour, in the small hours of the morning, requiring me to carry passengers. 'We're not ready for more guests. Most of the cabins have Bullen and his DEMS party bunked down in them.'

'Sorry, Skipper, it's no joke. If it's any consolation, one of them's a woman. She looks a bit bedraggled, the rain and all that, but she's a stunner. Auburn hair and the most amazing green eyes. One of the men looks a bit of a brute. The other's—'

I held up a hand to stop the flow. 'Okay, I get the picture. Never any rest for the wicked.' I swung open the porthole. The rain had almost stopped, the lights of the city burned bright in the clearing night air, and the rumble of thunder was fading as the storm moved away. 'The rain's swollen the river. Keep an eye on the anchor and watch for anything large and heavy floating downstream. I'll go and sort out Mr Khoo and his passengers.'

I left him to it and returned to my cabin to change my sodden shirt. Running a comb through my hair, I considered shaving. Lamont had said the woman was a looker but, if she chose to arrive unannounced in the middle of the night, she would have to put up with the stubble.

It was one flight down from my cabin to the main deck, the stairs ending beside the ante-room to the saloon. The chatter of voices was loud as I descended. One of them belonged to Mr Khoo and another almost certainly to Colonel Spencer. The other two ...? Recognition hit me like a body blow.

The voices ceased as I stepped into the saloon. Three expectant faces turned to me. The fourth combined the stony gaze of the Sphinx with the warmth of Al Capone.

In a wet, crumpled dinner jacket, Mr Khoo looked as if he had not been to bed since the previous evening. His ashen tinged face and dishevelled hair gave him an air of desperation. Spencer, on the other hand, looked ready for parade ground inspection. There was barely a crease in his uniform and his shoes shone with the patina of black pearl.

As Lamont had said, the third man, the one with the stony gaze, was a brute, with short cropped hair over the dome of a block shaped head. The arm muscles strained the seams of his ill-fitting suit, and a vile smelling Belmorkanal cigarette was clamped between the nicotine-stained fingers of his giant fist. A smile of recognition creased his thick lips.

'Ah! Captain Rowden, you seem to lead a charmed life.'

I ignored him and turned my attention to the woman. Her face was still achingly beautiful. The almond shaped, green eyes burnt fiercely. Thick tresses of auburn hair tumbled to her shoulders. An ivory holder containing a pink Sobranie cocktail cigarette was poised between her fingers, the smoke curling upwards to the deckhead. Theoretically she was dead, or at least two of the women she had been were. I had buried them at sea off Formosa. The one before me was Elena Markova, the rising film star whose name was already touted as a future Oscar winner. The ones I had buried were Helena Kovtoun, an émigré Russian, and Lady Helen Ashworth the woman she became upon marrying a minor member of the British aristocracy. As Lady Helen, she gained a title, if not wealth and respectability. She was also a double agent working for British Intelligence. Spencer and I had once rescued her from the clutches of the Belmorkanal smoking thug; Soviet NKVD General Ivan Maslennikov.

I dragged back a chair and dropped into it.

'I beg your pardon Mr Khoo, I wasn't expecting you until tomorrow. Well, later today anyway. And I wasn't expecting any … guests.' I levelled my gaze at Spencer. 'Judging by past events, I'm guessing you'll be the one best equipped to explain your unexpected and … untimely arrival.'

My words disappeared into an empty silence. Spencer had the irritating habit of lighting a cheroot whenever someone asked him a question he was reluctant to answer. I contained my frustration, as he fiddled about with cigarette case and lighter. What were they doing here and why? With a lit cheroot grasped between his lips, he blew a stream of smoke to the deckhead.

Mr Khoo broke the lull. 'When can we be ready to sail, Captain?'

'We're ready now. We were ready yesterday morning. Why the hurry all of a sudden?'

He stiffened at my tone and his eyes hardened. 'My words were ill chosen. When can we sail?'

I pointed to the brass clock mounted on the bulkhead. 'High water was at one o'clock. The tide's ebbing. If we leave now, we'll arrive at the bar at five, two hours before low water. We're drawing fourteen feet, too deep to cross, except within an hour either side of high water. The earliest will be noon today, in which case there's no point weighing anchor before ten.'

Mr Khoo ran a hand over his dishevelled hair. 'But if we went now,

36

and anchored at the river mouth to wait for high tide?'

'Apart from the fact the channel's unmarked, we've no pilot and the river's full of fishermen showing no lights? Yes, I could manage that, but we wouldn't gain anything. We still couldn't cross the bar until noon at the earliest.' I paused as realisation dawned. 'Is there some reason you need to be clear of the city before dawn?'

'Bravo, Bill Rowden.' Spencer clapped his hands in mock salute. 'I've learnt never to underestimate you. A group of sodden, disreputable characters rouse you from your beauty sleep in the middle of the night asking how soon they can leave. It's a fair bet they're in a hurry.'

'Sorry to disappoint you, I was already awake. And you can be in as much of a hurry as you like but, like King Canute, I can't command the tide. Anyway, we're only going as far as the anchorage at Koh Si-chang. I've got a cargo of rice to load.'

Mr Khoo cleared his throat. 'A change of plan, Captain. We'll be heading straight for Singapore.'

'Fine! I go where you tell me.' I struggled to keep the frustration out of my voice. 'But I'd still like an answer to my question.'

I didn't get one. Ignoring me, Spencer turned to Mr Khoo. 'If we weren't seen and the launch skipper keeps his mouth shut, then no one knows we're here.'

Maslennikov mashed the butt of his cigarette into the ashtray. 'No one followed us from the embassy. I can have the launch skipper taken care of … if that's a problem.'

Mr Khoo raised a hand. 'That won't be necessary, General. He's one of Wang Lee's men. I trust them with my life.'

'I would not trust anyone that far.' Maslennikov's grin revealed a row of stained, crooked teeth. 'Possibly not even myself. You have anything to drink in this ship, Captain?'

I called for Da Silva and asked him to fetch scotch and rum from my cabin.

'We're about to embark on another journey … and you have no vodka?' The woman spoke for the first time. Overlaid with a newly acquired American accent, her voice gave little clue to her origins, but it brought back memories, some of them painful, of the previous occasions she had travelled in the ship.

'I wasn't expecting to be entertaining any Russians. What do I call you, by the way? Lady Helen? Miss Markova. You were Helena the last time you sailed in my ship.'

'Helena's as good a name as any I've had.'

Da Silva returned with the bottles and five glasses on a tray. Spencer, Helena and Mr Khoo chose scotch. Maslennikov and I took rum.

'*Za vstrechu*, to our meeting.' He raised the glass, downed it and poured himself a refill.

Spencer took a sip of his scotch. 'If no one, apart from present company, knows we're here, then it's better we depart in the morning, as Captain Rowden suggests. If he leaves now, without a pilot and without clearance, it'll only arouse suspicion. The Japanese have good connections here. They're quite capable of putting two and two together.'

'I concur, Colonel.' Maslennikov swallowed another mouthful of rum and pulled out the pack of Belmorkanal. Grinning, he offered me one.

I shook my head. 'I've given up smoking.'

His laugh sounded more like a deep throated growl. 'Crazy Englishman.' He held up his glass and the cigarette. 'Two of life's pleasures. If they provide a little comfort amongst all the suffering, who cares if they might kill us. We can't cheat death. Especially now there's a war on.' He raised his glass to Spencer. 'You are right my friend. We are safe here.' He gestured toward Helena with his cigarette. 'She is safe here. For tonight anyway. Tomorrow, who knows. It is out of my hands.' He levelled his gaze at me. He was smiling, but his eyes had the stare of a dead fish. 'In your hands now.' He chuckled softly. 'So, no problem, eh?'

'Well, maybe just a little problem,' said Spencer. 'Assuming we do cross the bar at noon tomorrow, when will we arrive in Singapore?'

'It's eight hundred and thirty miles to Keppel harbour.' I ran the calculation in my head. 'That's just under three and a half days. We'll be alongside shortly after midnight on Tuesday morning.'

Spencer sucked his teeth. 'Any chance of bringing that forward?'

'For God's sake! If you're in that much of a hurry, why don't you fly? There must be an air service between Bangkok and Singapore.'

'There is. It leaves at noon. But it's less … private.'

'So, what the hell are you hiding from?' I turned to Helena. 'What does Maslennikov mean when he says you're safe here? Last time it was him we had to save you from.'

'Safe here? Is that what he thinks?' Her eyes flashed with anger. 'What is it the psalm says? *God deliver me from the workers of iniquity, and save me from bloody men.*' She drained the last of her glass and pushed her chair back. 'I'm surrounded by iniquitous bloody men and I'm sick to death of them. I'm going to bed.'

Da Silva had been hovering in the pantry. Hearing her chair scrape the linoleum, he poked his head into the saloon and beckoned Helena to follow him. His sole eye sparkled and his aged face beamed with pleasure. 'Come. Come, Lady Helen. One deck upstairs.' His head wobbled from side to side. 'No suite this time. Mr Khoo occupy. But single berth cabin, same for maid last time. Own bathroom. Bed is made. What time shall you be wanting tea?'

His voice faded as they climbed the stairs.

I rapped my knuckles on the table. 'Come on Colonel, spit it out. The last time you did a pierhead jump in Shanghai, you'd just pulled Lady Ashworth from the clutches of your sudden friend Maslennikov there. Her back was a mass of cuts and bruises from the beating he gave her. I saw the mess he made myself. The last thing she told me was that she was off to Hollywood to make a new life for herself. She's got a new name, and I've watched her at the cinema. But as far as I can see, she's back where she started. Dragged aboard between the NKVD general who beat the daylights out of her and the Australian spymaster happy to pimp her to him, as long as it suited his purpose.'

Spencer gazed down at his hands. 'The bit about pimping was below the belt, old boy.'

'*Da*, but it was my belt,' said Maslennikov, his mouth a crack in a mask of chiselled granite. 'Listen to me, Captain Rowden. It is true, I beat her. It was not personal, you understand, strictly business. Just like it was business for her when she shared my bed and went through my papers. Bah, it is a rotten world, but maybe it takes rotten people to protect the good ones, *da*?' He reached for the rum bottle and topped up our glasses. 'You know the expression, the enemy of my enemy ...?'

'Is my friend. Yes.' I picked up the glass.

'We Russians are the only friends you have right now.'

'But for how much longer? I hear that German tanks are already at the gates of Moscow.'

'Don't believe all you hear on the BBC. A new general has just taken the field. He doesn't have an army, but he'll fight the Nazis to a standstill.'

'Is that so. He must be some general.'

'He's the best we have. Defeated Napoleon, and now he'll do the same to Hitler.' He raised his glass. 'To General Winter.' He downed the rum, grimaced and banged the glass onto the table. 'That is a drink fit only for sailors. As you have no vodka I shall retire also.' He nodded in the direction of Spencer. 'If you seek answers, maybe the colonel will provide them.'

I pointed towards the alleyway leading to the passenger cabins. 'Take the outboard one on the right. You might have to share with a soldier.'

'I have shared with worse. Lice, pigs, fleas.' He reached for the rum bottle. 'To help me sleep.' He disappeared down the passage. There was a rattle and click of a door handle.

Mr Khoo remained silent, sipping his scotch. His face was grey and lined with fatigue, the half-closed eyes red rimmed and dull. 'I know I owe you an explanation, Captain. I am afraid that at the moment I cannot offer you more than you have already heard. We must cross the bar as soon as depth permits and make for Singapore with all possible speed. Please let Colonel Spencer know as soon as we are in international waters.'

He pushed back his chair, made to rise, but sank down into it. I jumped to his aid. His hand was bony and fragile as he grasped mine, and I gently helped him to his feet. Spencer also rose and between us we assisted Mr Khoo up the stairs to the door of his suite.

'Thank you, both of you. It has been a long, tiring day. And for me also a very disturbing one. I fear sleep will be hard to come by. But please, wake me when the pilot is aboard.'

After Mr Khoo had closed the door, I nodded in the direction of my office. The curtains were drawn back and the first rays of dawn filtered through the porthole.

'And then there were two,' said Spencer, accepting my offer of a chair.

I dropped into the one opposite him. 'So, are you going to tell me, or do I have to beat it out of you?'

'Do you still have that Webley?'

I nodded. 'Do you want me to shoot you?'

One corner of his mouth curled into a rueful smile. 'I don't trust Maslennikov. Keep it handy.'

'For Christ's sake, Spencer. I don't trust any of you. If you don't tell me what's going on, how will I know when to shoot him?'

He tapped his nose. 'Need to know basis, old boy. That's not information I can share with you at the moment.' His head drooped and he ran a hand over his sandy hair. 'I can tell you this. Those drums I mentioned, they're beating louder.'

'The Japanese?'

He nodded 'I'll have a radio message to send to Far East Command as soon as we reach international waters.'

'What about radio silence?'

'I'll write you an order to override that. Now, I've got to get coding, so I'll leave you to enjoy what little peace you have left before we get underway. Once we're out in the gulf, your job's to get us to Singapore as fast as you can.' He heaved himself out of his chair. 'I'm sorry we were sprung on you like this. Events moved faster than I anticipated.'

He let himself out and crossed the alleyway. I pointed to the remaining empty passenger cabin and then trudged wearily up the stairs to the wheelhouse. McGrath and Lamont were leaning against the bridge wing rail deep in conversation. They fell silent when I joined them and listened, mouths agog, as I told them the little I knew. After sending Lamont below to get some rest I sent for Cramp. Spencer and Maslennikov might have reached a truce as a result of Hitler's attack on Russia, but it was unlikely to be permanent. If I needed someone to watch my back there was no one better than the former tier ranger, who's ability with his fists was more than matched by his stealth. Finally, I climbed back down to the main deck. Fraser would not welcome the news but, if Spencer was to be believed, it was vital he squeeze every last tenth of a knot out of the ship's ageing machinery.

CHAPTER SIX

Forenoon, Friday 5 December 1941

'**P**ilot launch approaching, Captain,' called Lakshman from the bride wing.

'Thank you, Third. Nip down to the gangway to meet him and on your way call in on our passengers. Tell them not to leave their cabins until we've dropped the pilot outside the bar. With the exception of Mr Khoo. Let him know we're about to get underway and he's welcome to join me.'

Lakshman bounded down the stairs. I rang the engine telegraph to Stand-by Below, crossed to the front of the bridge and cupped my hands around my mouth.

'Heave up short.'

McGrath's answering hail was followed by the slow clank of the windlass as the cable was hauled in.

The overnight rainstorm had swollen the river and the current was racing past at three to four knots. With a line of ships anchored astern, and the river less than a quarter of a mile wide, there was not much room to turn. Footsteps on the boat deck ladder announced the pilot's arrival. I shook his outstretched hand.

'Good morning, Pilot. We're heaving the cable short. I'll turn the ship around for you and you can take her down river.'

'Thank you, Captain. The current may be up to four knots. You have deep water to within one hundred feet of the west bank, upstream of the temple.'

I beckoned to Lakshman. 'How wide is the river at this point?'

'About one and a half cables, sir. Nine hundred feet.'

'So, allowing one hundred feet either side, we've got two ship lengths to turn in, a four-knot current and no tugs. Have you thought about how we're going to do that? You're almost certain to be asked in the oral exam for your mate's certificate.'

His customary smile faded and his eyes widened with surprise. 'I'm … I'm very sorry, sir. I have not anticipated that question.'

'Get your note book ready, you're going to see it done now.'

As he reached into his pocket, there was a hail from the forecastle and McGrath waved his arm straight up and down. I replied with a circling hand and the windlass continued to clank.

'Well, Lakshman, the anchor's about to break free, we need to get some way on and stem the current. Listen carefully and make a note of the orders. Half ahead.'

'Half ahead, aye aye.' He rang the telegraph.

The furious ringing of the forecastle bell confirmed the anchor was aweigh.

There was a woosh of air as the engineers opened the fire dampers and the deck trembled as the engine beat to life.

'Now we need to angle the ship towards the bank … Port ten.'

'Port ten,' repeated the helmsman.

The ship moved ahead, the combined thrust of the rudder and the current swinging the bow towards the bank. I clenched my fists as the distance narrowed. The gleaming stupas and spires of the temple looked only a heaving line's throw away.

'Midships … Starboard ten … Steady.'

The ship steadied to run parallel with the shore. I could clearly see the faces of the children splashing around the bamboo supports of their river front homes. They waved as we passed.

'Okay, now we're going to turn into the stream … Hard a starboard.' The helmsman confirmed the order. 'Watch, Lakshman, the current flows faster in the centre of the river than at the edge, it'll swing the bow downstream.' I glanced astern to judge the distance from the bank. 'The ship pivots roughly in the middle, so you have to leave sufficient room not to drive the rudder and the propeller into the mud.'

My heart rate quickened as the ship continued to swing. The distance between the bow and the east bank was narrowing, and the current starting to slide us downstream.

'Stop engine … hard a port … full astern.'

Lakshman repeated the orders and scribbled them into his notebook.

I pointed to the line of anchored ships. 'Not much room for error. Full astern, with the rudder hard over, will hold us against the current and continue canting the stern to port.'

I held my breath. The ship continued to pivot until the bow was pointing downstream. All that remained was to steady her, check the stern way and go ahead on the engine to gain steerage.

'Stop engine … Midships the wheel … Half ahead … Steady as she goes.'

The orders followed smoothly. I let out a deep breath and clenched my jaw to stop smiling with relief.

'Well, Lakshman. Think you'll be able to manage it next time?'

The sideways wobble of his head conveyed his doubts.

I nodded to the grinning pilot. 'She's all yours now, sir.'

The line of anchored ships slid rapidly past as we forged ahead. Rounding Bangkolem point, the pilot took her wide to avoid the sandbanks. The city disappeared, the rice and timber mills thinned until we were again sailing past checker-board paddy fields interspersed with clusters of bamboo and thatch dwellings, and the spires of temples.

I had not slept since being woken by the night's thunderstorm. There were dark circles under my eyes, but a close shave, a hot bath, a breakfast of nasi goreng with a fresh fried egg flipped on top and several cups of Da Silva's best coffee, had restored my body, if not entirely my temper. I hoped Spencer, Maslennikov and Helena heeded my warning to stay out of sight. There were no passengers on our departure manifest, so any sighting of them on deck would raise questions to which I didn't have answers. There was also the matter of topping up the cargo. We were only cleared to sail as far as Koh Sichang. What would the authorities make of it when we failed to appear?

I pondered these questions, while keeping a weather eye on the pilot. He was concentrating on conning the ship around the twists and turns as the river meandered its way to the sea. We were not the only ship heading down river, the one ahead disappeared and reappeared as we followed it around each bend. Numerous small craft were also heading seawards. Thickets of junks and sampans opened out as we approached and slid down our sides within spitting distance.

'Good morning, Captain. I hope you managed some rest after the excitement of last night.'

I had not heard Mr Khoo approach. He was casually but immaculately dressed in linen slacks, loose cotton shirt and soft-soled loafers. Restored by several hours' sleep, he looked refreshed and fully in command of himself.

'I haven't slept a wink, but nothing that a hearty breakfast and strong coffee can't fix.'

'I am sorry to hear that.' He glanced around. The pilot was out on the starboard bridge wing. He nodded his head towards the other side and I followed him out the door. 'I also apologise for our unexpected arrival in the middle of the night.' He dropped his voice. 'Has Colonel Spencer explained the reason to you?'

'He said only that the prospects of a Japanese attack were closer than he suggested over dinner on Monday evening.'

Mr Khoo nodded and his mouth tightened. 'So he has told me also.'

He held a finger to his lips. The pilot crossed to the port bridge wing, checked whatever landmarks he used to keep inside the deep-water channel and returned to the wheelhouse.

'Are they planning to attack Singapore?' I asked. Mr Khoo was on his way to join his family there. If the Japanese assaulted the city, the consequences would be devastating for him and for all of us.

'Not directly. Colonel Spencer has all the details. That is why he needs to send a cable as soon as we reach international waters.'

'How did he find out?'

And what roles were Helena and Maslennikov playing in what was obviously another of Spencer's intelligence operations? The stakes were clearly enormous. Sufficient to resurrect the double agent we had buried at sea four years before.

Mr Khoo shook his head. 'I am not able to tell you that.'

'Look, I know there's a war on.' Frustration tinged my voice. 'But I'm master of this ship. I'm responsible for the lives of everyone in her. I think I've a right to know the risks I'm asking them to run.'

Mr Khoo stiffened and his eyes narrowed and hardened. 'There's nothing special about you or your crew, Captain. We're all just following orders ... and running the same risks. Colonel Spencer will decide how much you need to know and when. Right now, your job ... this ship's job ... is to get him into international waters and then to Singapore as quickly as possible.'

I had a sudden, desperate longing for a cigarette and the calming effects of nicotine. Instead, I took a deep breath and counted to five while exhaling slowly. 'I had a word with Chief Engineer Fraser this morning. He's confident he can coax an extra quarter of a knot out of the engine.'

'Please thank him for me. Every little will help. And please thank the stokers and firemen. I know it will mean harder work for them for the next three days. You may have Mr Fraser assure them their efforts will not go unrewarded.' He caught the smile that crossed my lips. 'What? You don't think I value my own safety as much as help-ing Colonel Spencer satisfy whatever deadlines he is working to?'

'On another, practical note.' I pointed towards the foredeck and the thicket of raised derrick booms. 'If we're putting to sea, I need to have those lowered and secured. Doing it now might arouse the pilot's suspicion … if we're only supposed to be going as far as Koh Sichang. I can leave them until we've dropped him outside the bar, but won't the authorities ask questions if we don't turn up to top off the cargo?'

The hardness in Mr Khoo's eyes softened. 'I do not expect any trouble from the authorities. The house of Wang Lee has much influ-ence.'

McGrath appeared beside me. 'Both anchors ready for letting go, Skipper. Cramp's standing by on the forecastle.'

'Thanks, James. You can lower and stow the derricks as soon as we've disembarked the pilot.'

'Aye aye. But what about Koh Sichang?'

'Mr Khoo's assured me the paperwork will be in order.'

'I'll get onto it.' He turned and headed towards the stairs, before glancing back. 'Anything else I can do for you, Skipper?'

'Just ask Da Silva for another pot of coffee. It's a beautiful morning for a river cruise. Might as well enjoy it.'

Watching the fertile, flat landscape slide by, sipping strong Java coffee and feeling the breeze cool the heat of the late morning sun, it felt good to be alive. All trace of the previous night's rainstorm had blown away with the nor-easter and the air bore the fresh, clean tang of the mountains. If the Japanese were poised to strike, it hardly seemed possible on such a benevolent morning.

'You must tell me where Da Silva buys these coffee beans.' Mr Khoo held up his cup, his face beaming with pleasure.

'In Singapore, somewhere. It's a closely guarded secret. Won't tell me or even the chief steward.'

'Have you tried ripping his fingernails off?' His smile widened. 'Is it true he lost the eye in a fight over a woman in Chittagong?'

It was my turn to smile. 'Apparently. You know he never leaves the ship, apart from the occasional run up the road when we're in Singapore.'

Mr Khoo nodded. 'So the bosun tells me.'

I raised an eyebrow.

'Ha! Don't look like that. I'm not spying on you. The bosun is a cousin, a distant one. But I'm sure you knew that. Maybe I shall ask him to have a discreet word with Da Silva about the source of those beans.' He glanced down at his watch. 'Eleven thirty. Will we be able to cross the bar at noon?'

We were just entering the sharp bend on the apex of which was the small town of Paknam. A large pagoda dominated the opposite bank. In front of it was a small fortified island.

'I checked with the pilot. With the rain there'll be well over fourteen feet over the bar at high water. We're drawing thirteen feet nine inches. We're a little early, but the pilot's happy to push on. The mud's very soft, we should be able to plough through any shallow patches.'

'And how long before we reach the three-mile limit?'

'By the time we drop the pilot, we'll already be five miles offshore. That'll be just before two o'clock.'

'Thank you, Captain. I'll leave you to your duties and inform Colonel Spencer on my way below. You won't be joining us for lunch I assume?'

The mouth-watering smell of cooking had been wafting up from the galley for the past half hour. I didn't need Mr Khoo's question to remind me I was hungry.

'Da Silva will bring trays up for the pilot and myself.'

Mr Khoo climbed down the stairs to the boat deck and disappeared through the door to his suite. Paknam dropped astern. Ahead was the final bend at East Point. Beyond, the river widened into Sunken Junk Reach and the ten-mile passage down the narrow gutter between the fishing stakes. Gilmore, the radio operator, had been warned to have his radio set warmed through and ready to transmit by 2pm. After that, I hoped Spencer would share the information sent to Singapore, and explain the sudden reappearance of Helena and General Maslennikov. Having taken so much trouble to get her away from him, why had Spencer felt it necessary to reunite them? And why had she agreed to it?

CHAPTER SEVEN

Afternoon, Friday 5 December 1941

I raised my binoculars to study the Outer Bar Lightship, the bright red hull swimming into clarity as I twisted the focus ring. Above the hull, the bulwarks were painted white. In the centre rose a tall, red lattice tower topped by a light. At night it shone red, visible for six miles. The lightship keepers also manned a short-range radio station.

I lowered the binoculars and rubbed my fingertips together to ease the tingling. Beyond the lightship, the broad expanse of the Gulf of Siam lay open before us. Astern, to the north, the low-lying countryside bisected by the Chao Phraya River stretched away to east and west, before curving abruptly south like two arms enclosing the waters between them. The long, narrow western arm stretched south to the Malay border and continued all the way to Singapore. The eastern arm merged with the landmass of Indo-China. The gulf between them broadened until it merged with the South China Sea.

The light vessel slipped astern no more than a cable to port. The pilot ordered a small course correction, and presented his chit for my signature.

'Thank you, Captain. The cutter will be alongside shortly. Continue this heading until you cross the four-fathom line. Bon voyage.'

I shook his hand and gestured to the bridge seaman to escort him down to the pilot ladder. Watching over the side until he was safely aboard the cutter, I waved a hand in farewell and strode back to the wheelhouse. Spencer was waiting for me.

'Is that necessary?' I pointed at the holster clipped to his Sam Browne belt.

He ignored the question. 'Are we outside the three-mile limit?'

'Theoretically, yes. Although it depends where you measure it from. The original limit was the longest range a muzzle loading cannon could fire a ball. That's irrelevant now, but the limit remains and it could be defined as three miles from the closest piece of territory. The Thais might take that to be the sandbanks of East and West Flat, which are dry at low water. They're submerged now, though.'

'Jeez, you pommy bastards can be so bloody pedantic,' said Spencer.

'I'll take that as a compliment. Anyway, you're the migrant with the ginger hair and freckles.' I turned to Lamont, whose watch it was. 'You have the deck, Second. Course is south by west until we sight Koh Samui. You can stand down the leadsman. The chief's giving her all the revs she can stand, so we should make ten and a quarter knots. Let me know the log reading every hour and tell the mate I'll be up at stars to check on progress.'

'Aye aye, Skipper.'

I nodded in the direction of the stairs and Spencer followed me down to the boat deck.

'You got your signal coded and ready?'

Spencer patted the breast pocket of his uniform and pulled out a folded sheet of paper.

'Care to tell me what's in it?'

'You're as persistent as a swarm of blowflies.' His face was grim. 'There's no time to waste. Is the radio operator ready to send it?'

'He's warmed the set and his fingers are poised over the Morse key. Lakshman checked earlier.' I pointed to a varnished wooden door, the external entrance to the radio shack. Come on, let's—'

A gunshot was followed by the sounds of smashing and splintering, as if someone was chopping up orange crates. I darted for the door with Spencer at my heels.

I yanked it open. Maslennikov clutched a Nagant revolver in one hand and a fire axe in the other. The revolver was pointed at Gilmore's head. The fire axe dangled at his side. Behind them, the radio installation was a shambles of twisted metal and broken valves.

Seeing us, Maslennikov dropped the axe, grabbed Gilmore and pressed the Nagant to his temple. A shoulder barged me aside. The Colt pistol in Spencer's hand was levelled at Maslennikov.

For a moment there was silence; Spencer's normally amiable expression replaced by a grim, steely hardness.

'You double-crossing, bastard,' he shouted. 'After all the trouble we went to to get this information'—he crumpled the message in his fist—'and now you've smashed the fucking radio so we can't warn anyone.' He advanced a step, white knuckles gripping the pistol butt, the muzzle unwavering. 'You won't get away with this.'

'My dear Colonel, it looks like we have a Mexican stand-off.' Maslennikov's lips compressed into a thin smile, but his eyes bore the icy coldness of a Siberian winter. 'But I assure you, I'll blow his head off before you can pull that trigger.' He wrapped an arm around Gilmore's throat.

The blood drained from the radio operator's face and his eyes were the size of saucers. The image of Jeffreys pointing my own Webley at Olwyn flashed into my head, and anger flooded my gorge.

'You touch so much as a hair on his head and I'll break every bone in your body,' I snarled.

'Brave words, Captain Rowden. I'm not afraid to die. But do you really want to sacrifice one of your crew?'

'Keep out of this, Bill,' said Spencer. The smile returned to his lips, but his eyes narrowed, the pupils glinting between half-closed eyelids like a cobra poised to strike. 'I don't give a damn whether you kill him or not,' he hissed at Maslennikov. 'Not when the fate of the British Empire's at stake. What's one more life matter.' He held out his other hand. 'Come on, General, game's up. You can't escape. Hand over the gun. Let him go and I'll let you live.'

'For what? So your people can go to work on me. Try and beat out of me every secret I've carried for the last thirty years.'

'That's up to you, General. You can make it easy on yourself. Or we can do it the hard way. Sure, you'd kill the radio operator and maybe even one or two others. But you don't know Captain Rowden and his crew. This ship's armed to the teeth.' Spencer pointed to the ribbon over my shirt pocket. 'He didn't earn that for helping little old ladies across the street.'

'Maybe you're right, Colonel. Or maybe a Siberian snow leopard's too old to change its spots. I'm a dead man, whatever happens. If you let me go, Stalin will wonder what deal I did to save my skin. I can assure you the NKVD has more ways of extracting the truth out of a man than you ever dreamt of.' He tightened the arm around Gilmore's throat, the muscles straining at the fabric of his sleeve. 'What is your name, son?'

'Gil … Gilmore … sir.' The reply was stammered through chattering teeth.

'Well, Mr Gilmore,' continued Maslennikov. 'Give me the benefit of your professional opinion. Is there any way you can repair that pile of scrap?'

There was desperation and appeal in Gilmore's eyes as he shook his head. The mess of smashed glass tubes, severed wires from which sparks still jumped and twisted, torn metal seemed eloquent enough.

The Nagant pressed harder into Gilmore's temple until he winced with pain. 'I can smell lies, boy,' growled Maslennikov.

'I'm not lying. I swear it.'

'I believe you.' Maslennikov shook his head and his eyes softened into a look of sadness. 'But I can't take that chance. It's not personal Mr Gilmore, it's just business. I can't take the risk.'

His fingers whitened around the trigger.

A brawny arm reached around the internal doorway and a fid thudded down on Maslennikov's head. He collapsed as if poleaxed.

'He'll 'ave a sore crust for a week.' A grinning Cramp stepped in from the alleyway. He bent down and placed his fingers on the side of Maslennikov's neck. 'Sleepin' like a baby, but the pulse is strong. His skull's not broken.'

'You cut that fine.' I wiped away the cold sweat that had broken out on my brow. 'Tie him up in my office.'

Cramp dragged the unconscious Maslennikov into the alleyway. I turned to Gilmore. He was still shaking, but the colour was returning to his face. 'Can you fix it?'

'No, Captain. He's smashed the vacuum tubes in the main and reserve transmitters. I don't have enough spares even to jury rig something.'

'I'll fucking kill him.' Spencer's face flushed puce and the veins in his neck looked like purple knotted tree trunks.

'Might first be worth trying to find out why he did it.'

'It doesn't matter why he did it.' The Colt wavered erratically. 'It was all for nothing, if we can't send the warning.'

'Put that away before you accidentally kill someone.' I gingerly reached for the barrel and pushed the pistol down.

'If I kill someone it won't be an accident.' He holstered the Colt, ran a hand over his sandy hair and smoothed down his moustache. 'When did you say we would be in Singapore?'

'Early Tuesday morning. If the boilers hold together and the stokers don't die of exhaustion.'

'Maybe we can salvage something.' He jerked a thumb in the direction of my office. 'You want to know what's in that message?'

Leaving Gilmore to clean up the mess, I lead the way. Maslennikov was slumped in a chair, his hands and feet tied and his chest bound to the chair back. Cramp was admiring his handiwork.

'Trussed up like a Christmas turkey.' He grasped Maslennikov's jaw in his massive fist and raised his head. With the other hand he served several stinging slaps to the ashen cheeks, eliciting a faint groan.

'Thanks Brian, with that fancy ropework we'll make a sailor of you yet. Find Mr Khoo and Helena and tell them what's happened. Give Lamont my compliments and tell him we've no radio, but no one's dead. After that, stand guard at the door. Keep any nosey parkers away.'

Cramp disappeared up the stairway and I pointed Spencer towards the arm chair. 'Make yourself comfortable, I suspect this is going to be a long story.' I reached into the drinks' cabinet for the scotch and poured three glasses.

Spencer reached for one and took a long swallow. Pulling a cigarette case out his pocket, he flipped it open and offered me a cheroot. 'I think you might need a gasper. To steady the nerves if nothing else.'

My hand was halfway towards the gold case before I managed to haul it back. Spencer laughed softly as I reached for the scotch instead.

'Okay, Arnold. It's about time you levelled with me. What was in that cable that so nearly cost my radio operator his life?'

Maslennikov groaned and struggled against the ropes.

'Should he hear any of this?' I asked.

'It makes no difference. Even if I let him live, he won't be going back to Russia in a hurry.' Spencer paused to take another pull of scotch and a long drag of his cheroot. His face was drawn and the customary sparkle had faded from his eyes. 'It'll be quicker if I start at the end rather than the beginning. What was in that cable? Only the dates, times and places of the Japanese entry into the war ... on the side of Hitler and Mussolini.' He pulled the crumpled ball out of his pocket and tossed it onto the table. 'Midnight on Sunday. That's when the axe falls, on Hong Kong and Malaya.'

'At the Oriental, on Monday, you said the Japanese were no immediate threat. What changed in a week?' I asked.

'We knew they were coming. We knew it was soon. Quite how soon will be a shock to some, but not to me. The runes were all there, we only had to read them correctly.'

'So, you lied.' I should have felt anger, or at least resentment that he hadn't trusted me. Instead, I shook my head. 'I'd laugh ... if it wasn't so funny.'

'Sorry Bill, you should know me well enough by now to know I'm economical with the truth. Anyway, it's water under the bridge. A Japanese fleet sails from Hainan tonight. It'll enter the Gulf on Saturday. They'll land troops in southern Thailand, and at Kota Bharu in northern Malaya, around midnight Sunday.'

'That puts us right in its path.'

'My bloody oath it does.' Spencer dropped his clipped tones for a broad Australian accent. 'How ironic! Even if we sail slap bang into the middle of the Imperial Fleet, no one can hear us cry for help.'

'No wonder Maslennikov seemed so calm about it. He probably thinks we're doomed anyway.' I took a mouthful of scotch. 'We're making as much speed as we can. We should be into Malayan waters by noon on Sunday. If we hug the coast there's a chance we'll pass ahead of them, and blacked out we'll be harder to spot against the coastline.'

Spencer shook his head. 'But we still won't be in Singapore until Tuesday. It'll be too late then for Operation Matador.'

'Operation Matador!' I parroted.

'In the event of an attack aimed at Malaya, Far East Command's plan is to launch a pre-emptive advance into Thailand. The idea is to grab and hold the peninsula at its narrowest point, to prevent the Japanese using Thai airfields and landing at Singora, the best port on the east coast. Meanwhile, the RAF and the navy will deal with the invasion fleet. The battleships, *Repulse* and *Prince of Wales* arrived on Tuesday.

'And if we're too late with the news?'

'The Japanese will be ashore and the road down the peninsula from Thailand will be open.'

'To Singapore?'

'Yes. Their General Yamashita's promised the emperor he'll capture the city by New Year's Day.'

'How the hell do you know all this?' I asked.

Spencer gestured to the slumped Maslennikov. His head rested on his chest, but he had stopped struggling and was breathing normally. 'He's a bloody good spymaster is our general. It'll be a shame if I have to kill him.'

'I shall take that compliment to my grave,' said Maslennikov, raising his head. He glanced at the table where a full glass of scotch remained. 'Is one of those for me?'

'With the headache you've got, I thought you might need it.' I picked up the glass, held it to Maslennikov's lips, slowly tilted it back and emptied it down his throat.

'*Za vstrechu.*' He licked his lips. 'I won't drink to your health. It might bring you bad luck. Any chance of another?'

I refilled the glass. 'Don't push your luck, General. I'll take the colonel's word that you're a good spy. But you still look like a thug to me. I haven't forgotten that you flogged Helena's back to a pulp.'

'You are too sentimental, you English. You still believe in fair play. We are building a new man in the Soviet Union, without fear, without pity. He will bury you.'

'Wars might not be exactly won on the playing fields of Eton, old boy,' said Spencer. 'But the British didn't win an Empire by playing fair.'

'That's all very well, but something's not right here,' I said. 'If the Japanese are invading Hong Kong and Malaya, what's it got to do with the Russians.'

'The answer to that's simple,' said Spencer. 'There's been bad blood between them since nineteen oh four, when the Imperial Navy attacked the Russian fleet at Port Arthur. The Japanese have had their eyes on the mineral wealth of Siberia for years. But if they have their hands full fighting us, they can hardly take on the Russians at the same time. Am I right, General?'

'*Da.* Even as I sit here enjoying your pleasant company, the Red Army is withdrawing the bulk of its divisions in the east back to Moscow. The little corporal is about to find more than General Winter waiting for him. You should be grateful.'

'For what, throwing us to the wolves.' Spencer's face again flushed with anger. 'You got what you wanted, so why destroy the radio and prevent us preparing a reception committee for General Yamashita?'

'Don't worry, comrade. The Americans will save you.'

Spencer was silent for a moment. Finally, he raised a hand and slapped his palm against his forehead. 'My God! You really are double crossing bastards.'

'Comrade Colonel, this is what Mr Churchill has dreamt of. Your entire British war strategy is based on the Americans … what you say … pulling your testicles out of the fire.'

'Chestnuts.'

'Whatever. The Red Army is going to kick the Wehrmacht in the chestnuts and the Americans are going to boot Tojo's arse all the way back to Tokyo. All you have to do is hang on in Singapore until the cavalry arrives.'

'I don't understand,' I said. 'Apart from sounding like a bad impersonation of a Hollywood gangster, what does he mean about the

Americans? Why would they want to defend Singapore?'

'Because it's not just Malaya,' snapped Spencer. 'It's the Dutch East Indies. And Pearl Harbour, the Philippines and all the American possessions in the Pacific.'

'Pearl Harbour, the naval base in Hawaii?' I could hardly believe my ears. 'That's nearly three and a half thousand miles from Tokyo.' The implications hit me like a bouncer's boot in a Manila nightclub. 'That means they're already there.'

'The Japanese fleet sailed at the end of November. Six aircraft carriers with over four hundred aircraft. The strike's timed for 8 o'clock Sunday morning, zero one hundred Monday in Singapore. The whole American Pacific Fleet will be in harbour, looking forward to church parade and a day at the beach.' His voice rose in anger. 'And because he's smashed the radio, they're sitting ducks.' His hand strayed towards the holster. 'I could shoot the bastard right now.'

'Don't you at least want to know why … before you kill him?' I asked.

'What does it fucking matter why? God, I'm going to enjoy them ripping his fingernails off.'

Maslennikov's laugh was disturbingly casual. 'They can't do that if you kill me. And like I said, I'm a dead man whatever happens. Ask yourself this simple question, Colonel. What would happen if you had sent that message?'

'The Americans have the chance to save their fleet, get all the ships out to sea.'

'And then?'

'They can bloody well fight back.'

'You will never make a chess player, my friend. You need to see all the ways the game might end before you commit your pieces. Do you think we are the only ones with spies on the board? If the Pacific Fleet sails now, the Japanese will know they have been warned. They will recall their fleet, claim they were just conducting an exercise, make a humble apology and bide their time. There will be no war with America, for a while at least. In the meantime, they still have a free hand to grab as much of Indochina, Malaya and the East Indies as they want. Maybe even Australia and India. How long can you fight on after that?'

'But all those ships. All those men,' I said.

Maslennikov's laugh bore the chill of an exhumed coffin. 'Nothing like dead bodies to spur the Americans to seek revenge. You need them in the war right now. I'll let you into a secret, we need them in the war now too. If the price is a few sunken ships and some dead sailors?' He shrugged his shoulders.

'There's a flaw in your argument, General,' said Spencer. 'The Americans won't be much help to us ... or to you ... if their entire fleet's at the bottom of Pearl Harbour.'

'America is a sleeping giant. Maybe it won't waken quickly enough to save Singapore, but when it does ...'

Spencer opened his mouth to reply, but was silenced by angry voices in the alleyway. Cramp was protesting that we were not to be disturbed. Helena's reply, in her plummiest version of Lady Ashworth, insisted he let her past. She burst through the doorway. Maslennikov's smile froze when he saw the hatred in her eyes.

Helena strode over to him and reached into her handbag as calmly as if feeling for a powder compact. The hand emerged clutching a tiny pistol.

She pulled the trigger. A neat round hole appeared in Maslennikov's chest and his head slumped forward.

CHAPTER EIGHT

Afternoon, Friday 5 December 1941

'W hat the hell did you do that for?' Spencer jumped to his feet. He checked Maslennikov's breathing and pulse. 'He's dead! For God's sake, Helena, there was no need to kill him.'

'Wasn't there?' Helena's face was deathly pale, save for the red spots burning on her cheeks. He eyes blazed, the pupils like black diamonds surrounded by glittering emerald. 'After what he's done to me ... that was strictly personal.' She raised the pistol again and levelled it at Spencer. 'Tell me why I shouldn't shoot you too?'

Spencer glanced down at the pistol muzzle, inches from his chest, and smiled. 'Because, my dear Helena, no one's going to ask too many questions in Singapore about the whereabouts of General Maslennikov. But a missing colonel in His Majesty's Australian Army, that'll take some explaining.' He held out his hand. 'What is that?'

Helena handed him the tiny pistol.

'Baby Browning, twenty-five calibre.' He whistled softly. 'Always thought it was a toy.' He turned it over in his hands, ejected the miniature magazine, and handed both back.'

'I could hardly miss at that range, and they told me it was good for killing vermin.' Helena's mouth twisted into a smile, but her eyes retained their hardness. 'If I had shot you, Captain Rowden's an expert in making people disappear. But maybe you're right.' She dropped the gun into her handbag. 'Is no one going to offer a lady a seat?' She gestured toward the slumped form of Maslennikov. 'And for God's sake, get that thing out of here.'

Cramp was hovering in the doorway with a look of apology on his face.

I nodded. 'Parcel him up and dump him over the side, well weighted.'

He produced a knife and sliced the bonds holding Maslennikov to the chair. Gathering up the ropes, he hoisted the bulky corpse over his shoulder as if it weighed no more than a child, and headed towards the stairs.

I pointed to the arm chair. 'Please Helena, sit down.'

She sank back with a sigh and crossed her long legs. One hand rested on the handbag in her lap. The other settled lightly onto the chair arm. The colour returned to her face, and only the fire smouldering in her eyes betrayed the passionate rage that had driven her to murder.

'I'm surprised how easy that was, and how little shocked you appear to be,' she said.

'I've seen too many good men killed over the past couple of years, to shed tears for a Soviet thug,' I said. 'But I don't know how you can sit there so calmly. I've never seen a woman kill a man before, and certainly not with such cold-blooded efficiency.'

'Cold blooded! The man was a monster. I still have the scars to prove it.'

'I know you had every reason to hate him,' said Spencer. 'But he'd have been more use to us alive.'

'He'd have told you nothing. *'Twas the women, not the warriors, turned those stark enthusiasts pale.'*

'For the female of the species is more deadly than the male.' Spencer completed Kipling's rhyme. 'Shocked? Yes. Christ, that was an execution! But am I surprised? No. Not after all the trouble we went to.'

'We! It was easy for you … and Maslennikov.' She turned to me. 'He's told you the what and the why. I bet he hasn't told you how.'

Spencer held up a hand. 'Just a moment, Helena. By rights, I should remind you of the Official Secrets Act.'

'Pah. Do you think you can frighten me into silence? You've taken over his ship. I think that demands an explanation. If you don't tell him, I will.'

'I think I can guess part of it,' I said. 'You knew we were going to be in Bangkok.'

Spencer nodded. 'Sorry, Bill. We couldn't tell you. We've been trying to break into the Japanese legation for weeks. Then Maslennikov came up with a plan. It worked, but we couldn't be sure the Japanese or the Thais weren't monitoring the British Embassy's communications. So we had to have a way out, and a secure way to deliver the message. Your ship was ideal. What better cover than a tramp steamer loading rice in Bangkok.'

'Did Mr Khoo know?'

'We needed him to smooth things over on the ground. Amazing network of connections the expatriate Chinese have built for themselves in South-East Asia.'

I shook my head. We had been jerked around on invisible strings. 'But Maslennikov? Why was he mixed up in it?'

'Like he told you last night, the enemy of my enemy makes a strange bedfellow. The Russians needed the information as badly as we did, and we're allies now. Or so I thought. It was all going according to plan, until he smashed up the bloody radio.'

I eyed him warily. 'And if you hadn't got what you wanted, until tonight, say?'

'Plan was the same. Get into international waters as fast as possible. Send the message and take our chances.'

'Of trying to thread our way through the Japanese fleet?' The implication was like a punch in the guts. 'So, we were expendable.'

'It was our necks too, and Mr Khoo's.'

It was still touch and go whether we could outrun the invasion fleet. And even if we got to Singapore, it would not be in time to make any difference. But ... did we have to reach Singapore? I kicked myself for not thinking of it earlier. 'There's something Maslennikov overlooked.'

'What do mean?' asked Spencer.

'We'll be off Kota Bharu by noon on Sunday. There's no port there, the Kelantan River's unnavigable. But I could land you by boat.'

Spencer's eyes lit up. 'Of course! There's an army base and an airfield there. I can telephone Singapore. Twelve hours' warning might not be enough for Operation Matador, but it could save the American fleet.' He turned to Helena. 'Turns out our efforts might not have been entirely in vain after all.'

'My efforts you mean.' Helena's reply was icy enough to freeze vodka. 'And right now, I'm not sure it was worth being dragged away from a glittering career in Hollywood, to take the lead role in your sordid scheme.'

Spencer's lips curled into a smile. 'My dear Helena, as far as your adoring fans and the Hollywood studio are concerned, you're on a whirlwind tour to promote your most recent film, or movie as you Americans say. Honolulu, Manila ... where you met General MacArthur among other admirers.'

'What happened in Bangkok wasn't on the itinerary agreed with my agent,' snapped Helena. 'And I'm not your *dear* anything.'

'Nevertheless, as soon as we reach Singapore, I guarantee you a seat on a flying boat to Sydney and a berth on the next Matson liner to San Francisco. You'll be back in front of the cameras before you know it.'

'And apart from the sightseeing and the travel tickets, what else were my ... services worth?'

Spencer's lips widened to reveal his teeth, but the veins throbbed at his temples. 'The honour of serving your country during wartime, and a continuing and lucrative career in Hollywood. Friends in high places.'

Helena reached into her handbag for a Sobranie and lit it herself with a gold lighter. Uncrossing her legs, she stood and walked to the porthole. For a moment she gazed at the sea which, clear of the sediment of the river, was a deep blue. Turning back towards us, she took a deep drag on the cigarette and folded her arms.

'Whose honour ... and for which country? What was it Wilfred Owen wrote? *The old lie: Dulce et decorum est pro patria mori.*'

'For goodness' sake Helena. Don't be melodramatic. You haven't died for your country.'

'But what I did was hardly sweet and fitting.' She tossed her head and sorrow clouded her face. 'You don't know how much of me died back there.'

'You'll get over it. It's hardly the first time you've done something similar.'

'You utter bastard.' Her eyes blazed fire again. 'With Maslennikov? That was the first and, up until now, the only time. And it was my choice. I did it for *my* country. The one the Bolsheviks hijacked and turned into a death camp. Do you know how many people those monsters Lenin and Stalin have killed between them? Eight million! Eight million Russians, murdered or starved to death during the collectivisations. I'd gladly do it again, if it might bring the end of the Soviet Union one step closer.'

'And if what you did was to help end Hitler's regime?'

'You British! You change the colour of your coat to suit whatever cause you're fighting for. After the last war, Churchill sent British troops to fight the Red Army. He said he wanted to strangle the Bolshevik state at birth. Now he's sucking up to Stalin'.

'It's called survival. Anyway, I don't recall you raising too much objection.'

'What choice did I have?' she shouted. She turned to me, her chest heaving. 'They told me to do what they wanted or be exposed as a

Nazi sympathiser, and an illegal immigrant with false papers.' She jabbed a finger at Spencer. 'The papers he gave me.' As her voice rose, the aristocratic layers peeled away to reveal the tones of her origins. 'My new career in ruins. Deported ... to where? I can't go back to Russia.'

'It's over, Helena,' said Spencer, gently. 'You did what we asked of you and we'll fulfil our end of the bargain.'

'Until the next time. And what do you mean we? You can't speak for the NKVD, now Maslennikov's dead.'

'It was you that killed him.'

Her laughter was bitter and laced with contempt. 'He deserved to die. You were just too weak to do it yourself. And then listening to you both calmly discussing the outcome, as if it was all a game. Thousands of young men are going to die. Men whose lives I thought I was trying to save. Well, it wasn't a game to me.' She jabbed the butt of the Sobranie into the ashtray, reached for Maslennikov's unfinished scotch, downed it and hurled the glass into the corner. It shattered against the bulkhead.

'You pimped me to the Japanese military attaché. I had to lie there and pretend to enjoy it, while he pawed and sweated and grunted his gratification. And all for nothing.'

'It wasn't exactly for nothing. We know a damn sight more about the Japanese plans than we did a few days ago.'

'You make me sick, all of you. And the smug, self-satisfied male world you've created for yourselves. We'll, I'll tell you this. I'm glad I killed him and I'd happily do it again. And you can count yourself bloody lucky, Colonel Spencer, that I didn't put a bullet in your miserable backside at the same time.' She sprang out of the armchair. 'I'm going outside to blow the stench of you out of my nostrils. You can tell Da Silva to bring dinner to my cabin along with a full bottle of that scotch.'

The door slammed behind her.

For once, Spencer was not smiling. 'It's a dirty business.' His fingers trembled as he fumbled to light a cheroot. 'You know, I think she meant it.'

I reached for the scotch bottle and refilled our glasses. 'About killing you? You might want to keep out of her way until we reach Singapore. I don't want to fabricate any more log entries.'

The raised eyebrow was reply enough.

'On the other hand. Maybe then you'd leave me alone.'

The chuckle and the returning smile were reassuring. 'Just as long as I know who my friends really are.' He took a drag on the cheroot. 'How were you thinking of explaining Maslennikov?'

'Easy. He smashed up the radio and took Gilmore hostage. You had to kill him to save my radio operator.'

Spencer shook his head. 'Actually, old boy, none of us was ever here. You'll have to find another excuse for the radio.'

I nodded. 'Someone sneaked aboard in Bangkok. A saboteur maybe.' I glanced up at the bulkhead clock. It was after 4pm. McGrath had the watch. 'I'm going up to the bridge to check on progress. I'll let you know if there's any change.' I pointed to the scotch bottle. 'You're welcome to stay and finish that. I'll send Da Silva in with coffee, and to clean up the broken glass.'

CHAPTER NINE

Forenoon, Saturday 6 December 1941

L akshman finished plotting cross bearings on the chart, noted down the time and used the dividers to step off the distance steamed over the previous hour. 'We're still making ten and a quarter knots, Captain.'

I followed him back onto the bridge wing and rested my arms on the dodger, allowing my binoculars to dangle from my neck on their strap. The breeze generated by our passage was cool on my skin. To the west, the low hills of Koh Pha and Koh Samui were smoky-blue in the late morning sunlight. To the east, the ruffled blue surface of the gulf stretched unbroken to the horizon. Isolated thunderclouds suggested the afternoon would be punctuated by rain showers.

'Alter course to south-east by south at noon,' I said.

'Aye aye, sir.'

I raised the binoculars and scanned the horizon. Blue painted fishing boats dotted the waters around the islands, and there were smudges of smoke from the coastal steamers that connected them to the mainland. Apart from that, the gulf appeared empty of shipping. If there were other ships heading to Singapore, they would be closer to its centre, following the shortest route.

'You know why we're over to this side of the gulf, Third?'

'Yes, sir. Mr McGrath explained about the Japanese fleet.'

'The first warning we get is likely to be from planes scouting ahead. So, keep the lookouts on their toes. Don't assume that any aircraft is friendly. Sound action stations immediately.'

'Aye aye, sir. If it is Japanese, do you think they'll attack us?'

'Hostilities aren't supposed to start until midnight Sunday. But if they think we'll report them and give away their location, then yes, probably. At least we've got something to hit back with.'

The high angle 12-pounder had been placed atop a specially constructed turret on the forecastle. Two more Lewis guns were supplied before we left Liverpool, and machine gun mounts fitted at all four corners of the Monkey Island. With those and the 4-inch gun on the stern, we packed a reasonable punch. Bullen's DEMS party had grown accordingly.

I turned to look aft. The wake stretched away astern, reassuringly straight. The hot boiler exhaust streaming from the funnel contained only wisps of grey smoke.

A movement on the boat deck caught my eye. Helena emerged from her cabin in a pale blue sun dress. She walked to the rail and shook her shoulder length hair. Both it and the loose skirt billowed up in the breeze. I enjoyed the sight of her long, slender legs. She raised a hand in greeting.

'You can manage here, Third. Alter course at noon and let me know if there's any change in speed.'

'Aye aye, Captain.' His soft chuckle followed me down the stairs.

I joined Helena at the rail. 'Good morning. I trust you slept well?'

'It would've been a miracle if I hadn't, after half a bottle of scotch.'

'You look remarkably well on it.' It wasn't true. Her make up barely concealed the pallor of her face and the dark smudges below her eyes.

'Well, that's one way to wish a lady good morning.' Her lips parted in the semblance of a smile. 'Actually, I feel like shit. There's nothing like alcohol induced remorse.'

'For shooting Maslennikov?'

'Not for that. I'm glad I sent him to the devil. No, I regret some of the things I said. It wasn't Arnold's fault that Maslennikov smashed the radio. And it certainly wasn't yours.' She reached into her handbag for her enamelled cigarette case, then slipped it back. 'Sorry, forgot you'd given up. Anyway, were you enjoying the view?'

I pointed to the islands slipping slowly astern to starboard. 'The big one's Koh Samui. The pilot book says it's almost entirely unspoiled, with beautiful beaches and safe anchorages.'

Her husky laugh put some colour back into her face. 'Not that view. I saw you ogling my legs. A gentleman would have averted his gaze.'

'A gentleman is something I'll never be. But you're right, sorry, I shouldn't have been looking.'

'Apology accepted.' She offered her delicate hand. 'Friends?'

'Friends.' I gently shook it, then glanced down at my watch. 'Half an hour to noon. Sun's over the yardarm. Do you fancy a drink before lunch?'

'Yuk! I don't think the hair of the borzoi that bit me will do any good at all. But if Da Silva can rustle up some of that lemon squash he makes.'

I turned towards the door leading to my cabin, and had second thoughts.

'Let's go upstairs. I don't fancy being haunted by Maslennikov's dead face.'

Up in my day cabin, Helena lounged back on the couch while I took the armchair. Da Silva appeared with a jug of iced lemon squash and filled two tall glasses.

Helena reached for the drink. 'Don't let me stop you, if you want to add something stronger.'

I shook my head and raised the lemon squash. 'What shall we drink to?'

Helena was silent for a moment, before her lips curled into a smile. 'There's a Russian toast that goes something like this. Pain makes you stronger, tears make you braver, heartbreak makes you wiser ... but vodka makes you forget all that crap.'

I raised my glass and we chinked. 'Shame I don't have any vodka.'

'I really couldn't face it right now. But don't worry, we'll make up for it in Singapore.' She raised a finger to her lips. 'And don't tell me we just have to get there, first.' She took another sip and reached into her handbag. 'I'm sorry, but I do need a gasper.'

She screwed a pink cigarette into the ivory holder, handed me her lighter and rested a hand on my wrist to guide the flame. Her fingers were dry and cool and the hairs on the back of my hand bristled.

'Do you still get the tingling in your fingertips?'

'Yes, occasionally.' Had I mentioned it to her the last time she sailed in the ship?

'Are you feeling it now?'

'No, but it's not always reliable. Maybe that means I'm safe ... for the moment.'

'Mmmm. I wasn't thinking of shooting you.' She took a delicate drag of the Sobranie. 'Do you think I was too hard on Spencer?'

The unexpected question caught me off guard. I thought for a moment before replying. 'No, I think he deserved every word of it. Anyway, you weren't half as hard on him as you were on Maslennikov.'

'Maslennikov!' she snorted softly. 'He beat me. He pimped me. But do you know why I really shot him? He threatened my family. My mother still lives in Paris. God knows how she's coping with the occupation. Sewing buttons onto Nazi uniforms, maybe. My brother, Tomas, was in the French army. After France surrendered, he managed to get to Britain and join that colonel with the big nose, De Gaulle. Maslennikov said it didn't matter where they were, the NKVD would kill them eventually if I didn't cooperate. Can you imagine what it's like, being forced to have sex in order to save the lives of your family? Of course you can't.'

'Did Spencer know he'd threatened them?'

'I don't know. But if I even thought it was his idea, I'd kill him too.'

Spencer was quite capable of selling his own grandmother, if it aided whatever cause he thought he was fighting for. I kept that thought to myself, but Helena read my face.

'You too, huh? But the worst you face if he betrays you ... is death. For a woman there are fates worse than that.' She mashed the butt of her cigarette into the ashtray. 'Or at least that's what the romance writers would have you believe.' Slapping the back of a hand to her forehead, she slumped down on the couch. 'Oh no, Sir William! I would rather die a thousand deaths than you should rob me of my honour.' Her flashing eyes narrowed and fixed me in their gaze. 'Tell me, as a man, have you ever made love to a woman you didn't find attractive? Don't answer that ... of course you have. Answer me this, then. Did you walk away from her feeling you'd lost some of your honour ... whatever that is ... or despising yourself and vowing never to do it again?'

I had deflected awkward questions from nosey officials on many occasions, but the look in Helena's eyes seemed more intimidating than any of them.

'No.'

'And if she was a prostitute, did you rush back to your room and scrub yourself down to remove the taint of her?'

I flushed with embarrassment. 'No. Well, only ... selectively ... if I thought there was a risk of catching something.'

'Or that you might fall pregnant?' Her husky laugh filled the day cabin. 'Of course not. That's not your problem.' She sat up straight and took a long drink of squash. 'I respect your honesty, Rowden. So, I'm going to tell you the truth. Yes, I slept with that Japanese diplomat. More than once. He wasn't especially attractive. I didn't like him, but I'm a very good actress. And as any actress will tell you, the casting couch is a damned sight more comfortable than the cold, hard floor of poverty.

'I didn't need to act all of it, though. He was a very competent lover, he knew how to pleasure a woman far better than Maslennikov. After we had sex, he slept so soundly that it was easy to photograph the documents on his desk. The silly man thought it was safe to leave them lying about because he thought I couldn't read Japanese. Spencer gave me a Minox camera and taught me enough Japanese characters to know what to look for. The night of the rainstorm, I found a copy of the invasion orders in his briefcase and photographed them. He was still asleep when I slipped away. After that, we needed somewhere safe to hide in case they realised the briefcase had been tampered with. If so, I hate to think what they've done to him. Of the two of us, I think he'll suffer far the worse fate.'

She paused to light another Sobranie. 'And you know the silliest part? There was no need for Maslennikov to threaten my family. Spencer's threats were quite enough. But he couldn't help himself. He liked to see the fear in my eyes, just as he had when he beat me. Even sillier, it was an empty threat. His was a one-way mission. His job wasn't to make sure Spencer found what he was looking for, it was to stop him sending the warning. Once he was aboard, he knew there was no way out, he knew too much. He could destroy the radio, he could kill Spencer and me, but he couldn't kill you all. You'd have handed him over to the authorities in Singapore. After that he was a dead man if he ever went back to Moscow. My family were never in any danger.'

'How did you find out?'

'I only pieced it together the other night. It's the only explanation that makes sense.'

'And you killed him in spite of it?'

'No, I killed him because of it. Not very sporting, was it?'

'Not very sporting of Stalin either. Why did Maslennikov do it, if it was a one-way ticket?'

Helena shook her head. 'Who knows. Maybe they threatened his family the way he threatened mine. Perhaps it was for letting me escape in Shanghai and the failed attempt to get me back. God knows, I'm hardly a master spy. I just got mixed up with the wrong people. I hoped I'd heard the last of Colonel Spencer when I went to Hollywood. Shows how wrong a girl can be.' She paused to take a long drag of the cigarette. The smoke streaming between her pursed lips and the rich smell of Balkan tobacco awoke my craving for a Senior Service. I reached for the desk drawer.

'I think I will have that drink after all,' said Helena. 'Mother's ruin will do, if you really have no vodka.'

It was a welcome distraction and I pulled a bottle of export strength Tanqueray out of the cabinet. 'Water, bitters? I don't have any ice.'

Helena wrinkled her nose. 'As it comes.'

I found two lowball glasses and poured stiff tots.

Helena raised her glass. '*Za nashu druzjbu,* to our friendship.'

We drained the glasses. Helena spluttered and coughed. 'God save me from such unholy drinks.' She reached for her lemon squash and emptied it. 'Maybe the second one won't be so bad.'

Smiling, I refilled her glass. 'Absent friends.'

'Absent friends,' she chinked her glass against mine. 'I heard about the death of David Griffith. Such a lovely young man and so good looking. He'd have made a fortune in Hollywood.'

Olwyn D'Angelo had said something similar the previous year, as we looked at his blood-drained corpse.

'He was cut down by a steel splinter when a U-boat's gun punched a hole in us. It killed Tom Sayce, the radio operator, too. We gave the U-boat a headache, though.'

Helena nodded. 'Spencer told me. He said you were awarded an OBE, for that and finding a lifeboat that had been adrift for three days.'

'For a spy, Spencer's very free with information about other people's lives.' I felt a flush of annoyance.

'Please don't be cross, Rowden. Despite what I said about him, I think you're the only real friend he's got. Or at least you're one of the few men he trusts. He arranged with the Ministry of Shipping to have you sent to Bangkok.'

'I'd already joined those dots. I like him too, but I still wouldn't trust him on the other end of a stage.'

'That's a theatrical reference I'm not familiar with.'

My hoarse laugh was hardly likely to melt a woman's heart, but it was the best I had. 'A stage is a length of wood on which two men sit suspended when working aloft or over the side. The supporting ropes are at either end. Your life depends on the other man securing his rope correctly. I doubt Spencer could tie a granny knot.'

'I think you'd be surprised what that man can do. He managed to turn me into a convincing corpse, remember?'

I laughed again. Spencer and I had saved Helena from being seized by the crew of the Soviet freighter that intercepted us off Shanghai. She shot herself with a theatrical pistol, and Spencer completed the deception by administering just enough neurotoxin to fool the Soviet captain into thinking she was dead. 'Your resurrection, after we got you back, frightened the life out of Peter Lowther. What else did Spencer tell you?'

'He told me Peter was back in the navy and promoted to commodore. I'm very happy for him. He's reconciled with his brother and got his career back.'

'The navy's gain was my loss. After he left, I promoted Griffith and McGrath. When Griffith was killed McGrath stepped up. I've two new junior mates now. Fraser's still here, though. And Cramp and Da Silva you've already met.'

There was knock on the door and Da Silva's head appeared, his sole eye glinting. 'Lunch is being served in the saloon. Will you be wanting to eat there, or shall I bring trays?'

Helena shook her head. 'I'm afraid I'm not very hungry. Is there a soup?'

The glint in Da Silva's eye faded.

'We don't run to three courses at lunch,' I said. 'A curry followed by jelly and custard is the best the cook normally manages.'

Da Silva's head wobbled and his lips parted to reveal his stained, crooked teeth. 'The crew are having chicken soup with noodles. Perhaps they are being persuaded to spare you a bowl.'

'I swear sometimes the crew eats better than we do,' I said. 'Now we're back out east, the victualling rate goes much further, and the crew use some of their war bonus to add a few luxuries.'

'Chicken soup would be lovely. Can I please take it in my cabin?'

'Atcha Memsahib.' Da Silva bustled away, grinning fiercely.

Helena rose. I joined her and she laid a hand on my arm.

'I know there's a war on and we're running for our lives, but I'd like to join you and the others for dinner, for old time's sake if nothing else. I'll put on a nice frock, but don't you go to any trouble. Oh, and please invite Mr Cramp. I've never really thanked him for helping me disappear by sewing what was meant to be my corpse into a canvas shroud.'

'It's a deal. If Spencer's right we shouldn't be in any danger until tomorrow night.'

She leaned forward and kissed me on the cheek. 'Until tonight then.'

CHAPTER TEN

Evening, Saturday 6 December 1941

W e were a motley bunch gathered in the saloon, waiting for Mr Khoo to escort Helena to dinner. Colonel Spencer was in khaki; Lamont, Lakshman and Gilmore were sweating in their reefer jackets; and Cramp had managed to find a clean pair of dungarees and a blue shirt. Only Fraser and I donned the white dinner jackets we wore the last time Helena sailed with us, four years before.

On the stroke of seven, in a pale, green gown of flowing silk, Helena swept into the room with all the combined grace, elegance and allure of the Russian aristocrat and Hollywood movie star she was. On the previous occasion, she had bewitched like a remote and mysterious female deity, with the ability to reduce men to blushing silence or chattering imbecility. This time, she warmly shook hands and exchanged greetings with those she already knew. Fraser was blessed with a kiss on his shining pink cheek, while Cramp was teased about his earing and the sewing skills he had learnt in Wandsworth gaol. Finally, I presented the new crew members to her.

'Ian Lamont our second mate,' I said, as she reached for his hand. 'He's from Inverness in Scotland. This is the third mate, Vijay Lakshman, from Bombay. He was in charge of the lifeboat we rescued last year. And David Gilmore, our radio operator, who's currently enjoying a pleasure cruise after someone smashed his radio station.'

There was no point spoiling the evening by even mentioning Maslennikov's name. In any case, his body had been dumped over the side before dawn without ceremony. There was no mention of him in the log and, as far as the rest of the world was concerned, he had disappeared without trace. There were no bloodstains in my cabin, and I could almost imagine he had never set foot there.

'I'm very pleased to meet all of you,' said Helena, shaking each of their hands in turn. 'Now, take off those jackets before you melt. And please call me Helena, there's to be no formality this evening.'

We gathered around the table. Helena sat at one end, flanked by Fraser and Lakshman, while I took my customary place at the head underneath the portrait of King George. Mr Khoo and Spencer took the seats on either side. The rest filled up the chairs in the middle.

The Goanese cook had done his very best to prepare as good a meal as any found in a top restaurant in Hong Kong or Singapore—ones, that is, suffering under similar wartime restrictions. It would hardly have mattered what he served. With a beautiful woman at the table, whose familiarity had lowered the drawbridge protecting her approachability, and with tongues loosened by alcohol, the food was consumed unnoticed. Helena flirted outrageously, drank toasts with the flair and capacity for which Russians were justifiably feared, and revelled in being the centre of attention. If anything, she seemed to be trying just a little too hard, as if desperate to use the uncritical adoration of the men around her to recover her sense of self-worth, diminished by what she had done in Bangkok.

'Stop staring.' Spencer nudged my elbow. 'You look like a school-boy with a crush.'

'Is it that obvious? You can't blame me. Helena looks particularly attractive this evening.'

'I'll drink to that,' said Mr Khoo, raising his glass. 'In China we have a saying. The tree may be old ... but the wood is just as hard.'

Spencer almost choked on his whisky. 'You'll have watch out, Bill. Looks like you've a rival there.'

'No, no,' said Mr Khoo, patting my arm. 'Take no notice. It was just a vulgar joke. And Mrs Khoo ...' He chopped the edge of his palm against the table top.

Laughter and conversation swirled around the other end of the table, where Helena presided like a queen. At my end, Mr Khoo's eyes hardened and his face creased with concern. 'Tell me, Colonel Spencer, if the Japanese do make it ashore, will the British be able to stop them reaching Singapore?'

'From what I can tell of their plans, we outnumber them two to one,' said Spencer. 'Although our forces are spread out across the peninsula, so they'll enjoy local superiority at first. But if Operation Matador successfully seizes southern Thailand, we can cut them off from reinforcements. If we don't deliver the warning in time, Matador has no chance of success. Even so, our weight of numbers should tell eventually.'

'And can the Japanese fight their way through the jungle?' asked Mr Khoo.

'I'm afraid it's not as impenetrable as it seems. It's crisscrossed with roads linking the rubber plantations with the towns. But we have the numbers to defend them.'

'And if the Japanese should reach Johore?'

'We'll withdraw across the causeway and turn the island into a fortress. As soon as Far East Command knows what's happening, they'll call for reinforcements. With *Prince of Wales* and *Repulse*, and whatever else the navy can spare, we should be able to control the sea lanes.'

'I hope so,' said Mr Khoo. 'But what of Hong Kong?'

'Ah! The garrison there numbers only fourteen thousand. They'll fight hard.' Spencer shook his head. 'But there's no chance, I'm sorry.'

'Thank you for being honest, Colonel. Let's hope fate shines more favourably on Singapore.'

The chatter from the far end was interrupted as Lamont pushed back his chair.

'If you'll excuse me Helena, Captain, I'll relieve Mr McGrath for dinner.'

McGrath arrived moments later and took the vacated seat. Da Silva placed a plate in front of him and he joined in the conversation between mouthfuls.

'Good evening, James,' called Helena. 'Last time we met you regaled me with tales of sailing ships, battling storms around Cape Horn while eating meals with one foot on the table. What will you tell us about this time?'

'Good evening to you too, Lady ... Helena. I'm afraid the foot was only on the table when we were not battling storms. Did I mention having to tap the ship's biscuits before eating them ... to dislodge the weevils, and soaking the oak-hard joints of salt horse in seawater for twenty-four hours.'

'Salt horse? It sounds revolting.'

'That's the sailor's name for any meat that's been salted for long periods. Even when boiled in fresh water for hours, it's still salty and as tough as leather. It keeps you alive, though. Anyway, I think you should ask Mr Lakshman about his experiences, he's our youngest member now.'

All eyes turned on the third mate, whose own widened with apprehension.

'And have you sailed before the mast too? Is that the correct expression?' asked Helena.

'Oh no, Madam,' said Lakshman. 'My apprenticeship was conducted in the Indian training ship *Dufferin*, and then aboard ships of the esteemed City Line. In no way can I emulate the sailing ship feats of our captain and chief officer.'

'A madam is a woman who runs a bordello,' said Helena, frowning. 'If you want to address a lady correctly it's Ma'am as in harm, unless you're talking to the Queen, when it's M'am as in jam.'

Lakshman's eyes sparkled with mischief. 'I am so sorry, Ma'am as in harm. But perhaps Helena would be simpler.'

The saloon echoed with laughter and Helena wiped the tears from her eyes with a small handkerchief.

'I'm sure you're being too modest,' she said, struggling to regain control of herself. 'I'm told you sailed a lifeboat with a crew of only soldiers and entertainers, and almost made it to the Canary Islands.'

Lakshman's head wobbled. 'That is so. But we would have been interned. Fortunately, Captain Rowden found us first.'

I crossed my fingers under the table. I avoided questioning where Lakshman's loyalties lay. The King had declared war on behalf of India, but I doubted the average Indian was as committed to saving the British Raj as he was to seeing the back of it. Indian troops were fighting well in North Africa against the Nazis and the Italians. No doubt they would fight well against the Japanese, and probably better than we deserved. Lakshman had proved a competent and cheerful third mate, loyal to his ship and shipmates. How far it extended beyond that, I preferred not to ask.

'Your family must be very proud of you,' said Helena.

I breathed a quiet sigh of relief.

'I am sincerely hoping I can live up to their expectations of me.' Lakshman glanced at the bulkhead clock which was approaching 8pm. He pushed back his chair. 'Please excuse me, Helena. With your permission, Captain, it is time for the change of watch.'

I nodded, 'I'll be up shortly, Third.'

'Do you have to go too?' asked Helena.

'I'm afraid so. These days I spend most of my nights on the bridge. If I'm lucky, I might doze in the pilot chair. Every second counts if we spot a periscope or a torpedo. I'm no use to the mate on watch if I'm sound asleep in my cabin.'

'Are there U-boats operating in the China Sea?' asked Helena.

'I've heard no reports of any. What about you, Colonel?'

'As far as we know there are none east of the Cape.'

'It'll be a quiet night then. Probably the last one for a very long time, if you're right about the invasion fleet.' I pushed back my chair. 'But don't let me spoil your evening. Just remember to keep the blackout curtains drawn and don't smoke on deck. Da Silva will probably kick you out when he judges you've had enough to drink.'

Mr Khoo rose. 'I think I shall retire, gentlemen. It has been very pleasant to spend such an evening aboard one of my favourite ships, in attractive and stimulating company. These last few days have been tiring and I am not getting any younger.'

'In that case.' Helena reached for her handbag. 'Mr Khoo, would you be so kind as to escort me to my cabin.'

Fraser jumped to his feet and held Helena's chair as she rose.

I followed them up the stairs. Mr Khoo bid Helena good night and pushed open the door to his suite.

Helena turned to me. 'Have you time for a stroll about the boat deck?' Without waiting for an answer, she took my arm.

Stepping through the accommodation door was like walking onto a darkened, spotlight stage. The wind had dropped and the sky cleared to reveal a breathtakingly full moon, twenty degrees above the horizon and almost directly abeam to port. The buff-coloured accommodation glowed in the cool silvery light, and our shadows stretched across the deck keeping pace as we walked.

Helena gripped my arm tight. 'I've never seen the moon so beautiful.' She held a hand up to the light and shivered. 'I can almost feel it bathing my skin.'

'The old-time seamen used to say that sleeping on deck in the moonlight sent you blind.'

'Is that true?'

'No. Night blindness is caused by vitamin deficiency, like scurvy. It was their diet that was lacking in fresh meat and vegetables. The treatment was cod liver oil.'

'Yuk! My mother used to give that to my brother and me when we were young.'

'That was to prevent rickets. Fresh food was in short supply then. Your mother—'

Helena sealed my lips with a finger. 'I don't need a walking encyclopaedia. Can you dance?'

I slipped an arm around her waist and extended the other one. She swivelled to face me, reached for my outstretched hand and placed the other on my shoulder.

'Music, maestro,' she said.

I stepped off into a foxtrot. It was the one dance in which I could be reasonably sure of keeping time and not crushing the toes of a partner. Helena proved a far better dancer than the taxi girls of Singapore and Hong Kong. She was a head taller for a start, which made it easier to hold and keep pace with her. We skipped and gyrated our way around the boat deck, its teak sheathing—scrubbed white by frequent holy stoning—an ivory dance floor gleaming in the moonlight.

'What tune are we dancing to?' whispered Helena into my ear.

'*Let's Face the Music and Dance.*'

'Ginger Rogers and Fred Astaire in *Follow the Fleet*, that's perfect.' She pulled me closer and sang. '*There may be trouble ahead. But while there's moonlight and music and love and romance. Let's face the music and dance.*'

'I'm no Fred Astaire, I'm afraid,' I said, skipping to catch a missed beat.

'Thank goodness, he's balding with big ears. You're more like Randolph Scott, dark and brooding ... and clumsy, ouch that was my foot.'

'Sorry.'

She reached up and ruffled my hair. 'Don't worry, I've got another one.'

I raised my arm and Helena pirouetted beneath it, swung in and pulled me close.

'That was lovely, just hold me for a while.' She rested her head on my shoulder; her arms circled my waist.

Underneath the flowing silk gown, her body was firm and I felt her chest rise and fall with each breath. My hands gently gripped her shoulders, my fingertips tingling as they brushed her skin.

'I'm short on practise. I'm out of breath and ... flushed.'

'I'm sweating myself,' I said. It was sultry, there was little breeze and trickles were running down inside my shirt.

'Horses sweat, men perspire but ladies simply glow,' chuckled Helena. She untangled herself from my arms. 'Your palms are making wet patches on my gown.'

I was tempted to suggest she take it off. Diligent Lakshman may have been, but I doubted even he could concentrate on keeping a lookout with a semi-naked woman bathing in moonlight on the boat deck.

'A shower would cool you down.'

'If that's the best on offer.'

A loud hissing interrupted us. Billows of thick smoke streamed from the funnel and black specks rained onto the deck. I grabbed Helena's hand and dragged her to the doorway.

'Slow down, sailor. I didn't know you were in that much of a hurry.'

I closed the door behind us. 'The engineer is blowing steam into the boilers. He does it every night to clear the build-up of soot from the boiler tubes.' I pointed to my dinner jacket which was sprinkled with black spots. 'I'll need to give this to Da Silva to soak. And then I really must check how Lakshman's getting on.'

Helena glanced down at her dress and grimaced. 'He'll have to do my gown as well.' She held out a hand. 'Take off that jacket and I'll give them both to him.'

'Thank you for the dance. I won't be down until dawn. Don't wait up.' I handed the jacket to her and bowed my head, intending to kiss her cheek.

'Don't worry, I won't.' She twisted away and disappeared into her cabin.

CHAPTER ELEVEN

Saturday night and Sunday morning, 6-7 December 1941

I f Lakshman had watched Helena and me foxtrotting around the boat deck, he was too discrete to say anything. After ducking into my day cabin to ditch the bow tie and roll my sleeves up, I found him on the port bridge wing, scanning the horizon through binoculars. With the moonlight gilding the ship's silhouette she was, to anyone close enough to target her, invitingly illuminated against the black backdrop of sea and sky. Bright moonlit nights in the North Atlantic always brought an unwelcome chill to the pit of the stomach. Now, without the threat of U-boats, it was possible to enjoy the untroubled beauty of the moon. It seemed so large and so close I could almost reach out and touch it.

'See anything, Third?' The question was hardly necessary. Since Koh Samui dropped astern, we had sailed at the centre of an empty disk, its edge continually receding into the distance ahead us.

'Nothing, sir.'

'If Colonel Spencer's correct, the Japanese invasion fleet will be inside the Gulf, off the coast of Indochina. Strange to think they're looking up at the same moon as us.'

Lakshman nodded. 'Yes, sir. According to the Vedas, the moon is home to the ancestors where our spirits go to be reborn. It is also sacred to the Japanese.'

'The Vedas?'

'They are ancient Sanskrit texts, the oldest scriptures of Hinduism. Like the earliest books of the Old Testament.'

'Sacred or not, there's more than a few will have gone to meet their ancestors by this time next week. Let's hope we're not among them.'

'Do you think we'll make it to Singapore, sir?'

'The Japanese will have aircraft scouting, but they won't risk coming close enough to the coast of Malaya to be spotted from ashore. If we stay close to it ourselves, we should be safe. It's what happens after we get to Singapore we should worry about. If the Japanese Navy can bottle up the Straits while its army advances down the peninsula, we could be trapped like rats in a barrel.'

Lakshman's frown was clear in the moonlight. 'My elder brother is in Singapore, sir. He is a captain in the Mahratta Light Infantry.'

'You never mentioned him before. You could have had some time off to see him, last time we were there. You can go next week.'

'I don't know how to find him, sir. His letters don't say where he is based.'

'Colonel Spencer, he'll be able to find out for you. I'll mention it to him.'

'I would not like to cause him any bother, sir.'

'Nonsense, Mr Lakshman. He's a colonel in the Intelligence Corps. He'll know how to find your brother.'

The frown melted. 'I shall be most grateful, sir. Now, if you will excuse me, I shall check on the lookouts.'

It was pleasant to have the bridge wing to myself. I paced up and down the short length of teak decking, enjoying the cool breeze in my hair and the shimmering silver light turning my battered old tramp into an elegant, romantic steamer. Or perhaps it was the thought of Helena sleeping peacefully in her bed stirring my overactive imagination. The only thing missing was the added comfort of a cigarette. I tried tricking myself, holding out the promise of one if I completed ten lengths of the deck, then upping it to twenty and thirty.

Da Silva arrived at four bells, just in time to save me, bearing a pot of strong coffee. The caffeine temporarily quelled the nicotine cravings and I continued my pacing, reviewing the chart of the Gulf of Siam projected inside my head. We were heading southeast by south with the coast of Thailand 60 miles away to the west. The Japanese fleet was to the east, heading into the Gulf. At some point, the ships designated to attack Kota Bharu would detach and steam southwest, putting us on converging courses. Provided we maintained steam pressure and the propeller kept turning, we would pass ahead of them. If anything went wrong, we could end up right in their path.

Fraser had managed to squeeze an extra quarter knot out of the ship since leaving Bangkok. Before dinner, he warned me that continually operating the boilers above their normal limits could damage the furnace walls and crack water tubes. There were also the stokers to consider. The higher the steam pressure the more coal the boilers consumed, coal that had to be shovelled by hand from the bunkers and into the fire boxes. Each stoker was shovelling over one ton of coal per watch; continuous, back-breaking work in temperatures well in excess of 100 degrees. How much longer before they started to flag? With twelve hours steaming before we reached Kota Bharu, and our last chance to warn High Command, there was no alternative but to push on and risk the consequences.

The change of watch at midnight brought welcome distraction in the form of Lamont. He waxed lyrical about the moon, which reached its zenith just after 1am, its light so bright that he fetched a copy of an old *Daily Mirror*, determined to see if he could read it. He managed the headline—'Avenged. Last hours of the *Bismarck*'—but the longer he stared at the smaller print the more it seemed to fade away. There was nothing wrong with his eyesight. He spotted the faint light of a lone fisherman, several miles off the starboard bow, before the lookouts reported it. The boat slid astern less than a mile off the beam. Through the night glasses it looked deserted, the crew apparently resting in between hauling their net.

By the end of the watch, without the constant nagging dread of being hit by a torpedo to keep me alert, boredom set in and I struggled to keep my eyes open. Lamont seemed as sharp as ever and, with McGrath about to relieve him, I decided to take the risk.

'I'll be in my day cabin. Call me if anything at all happens.'

'Nae worries, Skipper,' said Lamont. 'You'll be the first to know if we sight so much as a flea on a tick's testicles.'

I kicked off my shoes and stretched out on the couch.

The furious ringing of the wheelhouse bell, followed by McGrath bellowing, 'aircraft sighted,' dragged me awake.

It was daylight. I sprinted for the bridge in my bare feet, grabbed my binoculars and darted onto the starboard bridge wing. McGrath and Bullen had beaten me to it.

'Where away?' I snapped.

'Fine off the port bow, thirty degrees above the horizon,' said McGrath.

I followed his outstretched arm. It took several seconds of searching the blank sky before my eyes picked out a tiny dot. I watched it grow in size.

'Seems to be headed north,' I said.

'Japanese?' asked McGrath.

'Unlikely, sir,' said Bullen. 'Coming from the wrong direction. But he's in for a surprise if he is.'

I glanced up at the Monkey Island. The Lewis guns were on their mounts, with determined looking, tin hatted gunners squinting through their sights.

'Might give us a chance to blow the cobwebs out of the 12-pounder, too.' Bullen studied the approaching aircraft through his binoculars.

Lamont joined the gunnery team grouped around the 12-pounder gun mounted on its turret on the forecastle. It was already training towards the aircraft, its barrel elevating as the layer spun his hand wheel.

I studied the aircraft again. It appeared to be a flying boat with a hull shaped fuselage slung under a single wing. The wing dipped as it altered course to look us over.

'It's a friendly. Catalina,' said Bullen.

'Royal Air Force, operating out of Singapore.' Spencer's eyes were glued to a pair of binoculars. 'Any chance of contacting him. Warn him there's a Japanese fleet to the north?'

The Catalina flew straight towards us. I reached for the signal lamp, flicked it on, and cursed. What the hell was the signal to attract an aircraft's attention? Was there one? I aimed the lamp, grasped the shutter handle and flashed a stream of AA … AA … AA.

'What's that?' asked Spencer.

'International Morse for, I want to communicate with you. Works for ships. Don't know about aircraft.' The shutters clacked again as I fired off another series of AAs. 'Someone get the sparky up here, quick.'

There was a change in engine note and the Catalina's nose tilted into a dive. I flashed more AAs, followed by L … L … L. At sea it meant: Stop I have something important to communicate. Did it mean the same to aircraft? How could it stop, anyway?

Levelling out at 500 feet, the Catalina flew over the ship, the noise of its engines roaring to a crescendo.

'Hoist the ensign, anywhere will do,' I shouted, continuing to flash AAs interspersed with Ls.

Tilting its wing, the plane started to circle around us. The pilot's pale, flying helmeted face peered through the cockpit window. A hand touched my shoulder and I moved aside to let Gilmore take over. McGrath was hoisting the Red Duster on the signal halyard.

'Tell him we're a British ship, send our signal letters and warn him there's a Japanese fleet bearing north-east about one hundred and fifty miles.' The shutter clacked rapidly. 'Slow down, I doubt they can read Morse as fast as you.'

The Catalina continued to circle, droning around and around us. Gilmore slowly spelt out the message, but there was no response.

'For Christ's sake! Why don't they answer?' shouted Spencer. 'Surely they can read plain English.'

I watched with mounting frustration. Gilmore repeated the message, even slower this time, but the Catalina continued to mutely circle. Finally, it dropped to masthead height for a last, roaring pass and, with a waggle of its wing tips, streaked off to the north-east. Within moments it was a small dot climbing in altitude, the noise of its engines fading into the distance.

'Shit!' I banged my fist against the rail. 'Why did he ignore us?'

'Probably thought we were just being friendly,' said Spencer, who had recovered his composure. 'Once he'd checked us out to determine we weren't hostile ...' He shrugged his shoulders. 'Or perhaps he read the message but couldn't reply. If he keeps going on that heading, there's a good chance he'll spot the invasion fleet.' His lips split into a wide grin as he noticed my bare feet. 'You seem to have dressed in a hurry. Forget a couple of items, did you?'

Spencer was not the only one grinning at me. Only Bullen and the helmsman had straight faces. Bullen probably because he had years of experience ignoring the eccentricities of naval officers, while the helmsman's eyes were fixed firmly on the horizon.

'You can stand the men down from action stations, Bullen.'

'Stand down from action stations.' His bellow was deafening, easily carrying to the forecastle where Lamont raised an arm in acknowledgement.

'All right, fun's over,' I snapped. Da Silva waved an arm from the wheelhouse. 'I'm going below for a moment, James. You can brief me on progress when I get back.'

I didn't wait for a reply and stalked off. Da Silva had laid out fresh uniform shorts and shirt in my cabin. I shaved while he fetched a fresh pot of coffee. Refreshed and fortified, I returned to the bridge. McGrath showed me his position for morning stars. We were still well inside Thai waters, 40 miles east of Pattani. Our speed had dropped to a shade over ten knots.

Spencer joined me at the chart table. He stabbed a finger towards the centre of the gulf. 'If my rough translation of the documents

Helena photographed is correct, the Japanese fleet should be about there. Flying north-east, that Catalina can hardly miss it.'

'In which case he'll report it to Singapore,' I said. 'That'll give High Command about seventeen hours' notice. Is that sufficient time to launch Operation Matador?'

'Barely, but it's better than nothing. Trouble is, it does nothing to warn the Americans. And the Japs are bound to have air cover. If that Catalina gets shot down ...'

'So, we press on. We've dropped speed a little, a weak current runs north-west in this part of the gulf, but we're only forty miles from the mouth of the Kelantan River. I'll have you ashore by mid-afternoon.'

'The airfield's about five miles south of the river. If you can put me ashore near there, somewhere close to a road, it shouldn't be too hard to find HQ.'

'Want me to wait and take you off again?'

'Too risky, for you. Get out of the area as fast as you can. I'll take my chances.' He turned for the chartroom door. 'I'll go and get my things packed.'

I headed back out to the bridge wing. The sea was a shimmering blue, the ship shouldering her way through the low swell with the familiar tumble and rush. To the west, brightly coloured fishing boats were setting drift nets. Behind them, the hills of southern Thailand were a blue-grey, jagged ridge along the horizon. The smell of breakfast wafted up from the galley. In the face of such normality, it was hard to imagine that, somewhere over the horizon, a Japanese fleet was poised to rain fire and destruction into such a peaceful setting.

CHAPTER TWELVE

Afternoon, Sunday 7 December 1941

T he north-east monsoon strengthened during the morning and, by 1pm, as we approached the mouth of the Kelantan River, the sea had risen. Waves crashed against the sandbanks and islets of the estuary. The river mouth was half a mile wide, with a small native settlement on the eastern bank nestling among tall palms. Fishing boats were pulled up on the shore. The chart showed water depths of five fathoms to within a mile of the coast, but the water was brown with sediment washed down by the river and I had the boatswain standing by to take soundings.

From the river mouth, the low-lying coastline stretched away to the south-east, fringed by a sandy beach. Beside me on the bridge wing, Spencer examined it through binoculars.

'There's quite a surf running. Not ideal conditions to land a boat,' I said.

'Never mind the surf, the beach appears to be mined and there are three layers of barbed wire.'

'There's a creek four miles east. If you can get ashore there, it's about a mile hike to the perimeter of the airfield.'

'Sounds good to me. I'll be able to hitch a lift to Brigade headquarters in the town.'

I watched the shoreline slide by. The wind was warm, but I shivered at the thought that, in just over 12 hours, men would be fighting and dying on that shore. Even though it was Sunday, I expected the airfield to show signs of activity, but not a single plane had landed or taken off. If anyone noticed the arrival of a lone tramp steamer, it certainly wasn't the air force. Perhaps the army had us in its sights. I hoped they could see the Red Ensigns fluttering at our stern and signal halyard.

I raised my binoculars, searching for the mouth of the creek. A break in the palms and the surf line looked promising.

'Hard a starboard, dead slow ahead.' I waited for McGrath's acknowledgement, and the ringing of the engine telegraph, before leaning over the bridge wing. 'Start the soundings.'

The boatswain waved a hand in reply. The lead swung in widening arcs, before sailing into the air and splashing into the sea forward of the bow. He let the line run though his palm, nipped it when it went slack, read the mark and hauled it in for the next swing.

'By the deep, eight.'

The ship slowed as she curved in towards the shore. The entrance to the creek opened into view.

'Midships the wheel.'

'And a quarter plus seven.'

'Steady as goes.' I turned to Spencer. 'You'd better get into the boat. I'll run in as far as I can.'

'And a quarter less seven.'

The water was shallowing slowly and the shore was over a mile away. With 25 feet still under the keel I could afford to close the distance a little more. I leaned over the rail and called down to Lakshman on the boat deck.

'Swing the boat out and standby to lower away.'

'And a quarter plus six.'

The boat swung out on its davit until it was level with the deck. Lakshman, Spencer and the boat crew clambered in. Cramp tossed in Spencer's holdall and moved to the boat falls.

'By the mark, five.'

I waited as the shoreline slowly neared.

'And a quarter less five.'

Close enough, on a falling tide.

'Hard a starboard, slow ahead.'

The ship turned into the wind, until we were almost parallel to the shore.

'Midships the wheel. Steady as she goes. Stop engine.'

We were just under a mile offshore. With the north-east wind blowing against the starboard beam, the port side workboat had a reasonable lee in which to launch.

'Lower away,' I yelled.

Cramp and a seamen unhitched the falls and lowered the boat, stopping when it was just clear of the water. Lakshman waited until it was poised above a trough and yelled for them to continue lowering. The boat dropped onto the back of the rising wave. The crew unhooked the falls, shipped their oars and rowed off towards the creek, the rise and fall of the blades resembling the stride of an ungainly water beetle.

Once the boat was clear of the ship's side, I ordered the engine ahead and the wheel hard over, completed the turn until we were heading into the wind and dropped anchor in six fathoms to await its return.

With the assistance of the breeze, the boat reached the shore in 20 minutes. As I promised Spencer, it disappeared into the creek just before four bells in the afternoon watch. Having taken cross bearings to fix our position, Lamont climbed down from the Monkey Island.

'Let the engine room know I expect to be here for about an hour, until the boat gets back. But keep sufficient steam pressure up in case the anchor drags and we need to move in a hurry.'

Lamont strode into the wheelhouse to relay the message, while I continued to study the shore. The land behind the beach was table-top flat, stretching away towards a distant line of rugged hills, with only the occasional clump of palms or the minaret of a mosque as landmarks. Towering banks of cloud were building up over the hills, and the wind was freshening, driving foaming waves towards the shore.

'Looks like they'll have a long, wet pull back,' said Lamont, re-joining me on the bridge wing.

'I wish they'd get a bloody move on.' I searched the creek mouth for any sign of the returning boat.

'Why would the Japs want to land here, anyway?' he asked. 'It doesn't look as if there's anything worth fighting for. It's miles from Singapore and jungle all the way.'

'It's the airfields,' I said. 'Apart from the one just beyond that creek, Colonel Spencer says there are two others farther south. If the Japanese seize them, they can easily mount air raids on Singapore.'

'And I wouldn't be too sure about the jungle, Mr Lamont.' We turned as Mr Khoo stepped out of the wheelhouse. 'It might look impenetrable but, as Colonel Spencer also said last night, you British have built some of the best roads in Asia to serve the rubber planta-tions and tin mines.'

Mr Khoo was in shirtsleeves, his linen trousers suspended from braces. The lines and creases in his face had deepened and there were dark smudges under his eyes.

'I don't wish to interfere, Captain,' he said. 'But now that Colonel Spencer has gone ashore to deliver his message, when can we get underway.'

'As soon as Lakshman returns.' I glanced at the Rolex on my wrist. It was already half an hour since the boat disappeared into the creek. 'He was ordered to drop Colonel Spencer at the first convenient place and return as soon as possible.'

'Let me know the moment you have any news. I am taking lunch in my cabin with Miss ... Lady Ashworth.'

'Lucky blighter,' said Lamont, as soon as Mr Khoo was out of ear-shot. 'I wish I was having lunch with Lady Ashworth, or Helena, or Elena, or whatever she calls herself.'

'You had dinner with her last night.'

'Yes, but I had to share her with the rest of you. And I didn't get to dance with her in the moonlight afterwards.'

Was there jealousy or admiration in Lamont's voice? His grin faded when he saw the look on my face. I maintained the glare as long as I dared, without appearing melodramatic. In the past, I would not have tolerated a junior mate speaking to me with such familiarity. To my surprise, I seemed to be mellowing with age.

'Now then ... Ian. That's not the sort of thing you can say to your captain. It's no business of yours who I dance with. I'm Master under God, remember. I can have you flogged, logged and cut off your tobacco ration.' I squashed the grin that creased my face. 'But seriously, you can have your little jokes, but don't mess me around. My bite can be worse than my bark.'

'Sorry, Captain. Poor attempt at humour.'

'Okay, water under the stern. Now go and find that rogue Da Silva and tell him to fetch a pot of coffee.'

It was hot and strong, but the caffeine did little to soothe my agitation and it was not long before the tingling in my fingertips had me pacing the bridge wing. At the end of each turn, I cast increasingly frustrated glares at the creek mouth.

With an hour to the change of watch, Mr Khoo climbed up from the boat deck, a look of deep concern on his face. 'We are running out of time, Captain. It will be dark in four hours and in nine this will be a war zone.'

I nodded. 'I can't imagine what's happened to keep Lakshman ashore. I don't want to leave him and the others behind, but ...'

'Neither do I, but I fear we must. We will all be dead if we are trapped by the Japanese. What did Bentham say ... the greatest good for the greatest number.'

Lakshman was a resourceful young man. He had already demonstrated that by taking charge of a lifeboat with a crew of landsmen, after the sinking of the *City of Richmond*. Was he resourceful enough to keep himself and six Chinese seamen out of the clutches of the Japanese? It was just as likely we would never hear from them again.

I glanced at my watch. I knew the time; I had been checking it constantly for the past hour. 'I don't want to have to write to another mother to explain the loss of her son. I'll make a decision at five o'clock. If we left at six, we would still be sixty miles away by midnight. That should be enough to keep us safe.'

Anger flared in Mr Khoo's eyes, before his poker face clamped down. 'It's your decision, Captain.'

He didn't need to say anymore. Of course it was my neck on the line. That went with the four gold stripes.

Mr Khoo turned away, but not before I caught the desolate, haunted look in his eyes that even the poker face could not conceal. What was it? Fear? Fear for his life? The ship? Everything he had worked for? He did not display emotion easily and, although I had seen him happy and angry, I had never seen him afraid. If Mr Khoo was afraid, was Spencer's confidence misplaced? Would high command take his warning seriously, even if he delivered it in time?

'What about lowering another boat to go look for them?' Lamont climbed down from the Monkey Island after checking the cross bearings.

'I've thought of that, Second. But I don't want to risk another boat and its crew. There must be a good reason he hasn't returned.' I checked my watch for the thousandth time. Whatever was holding up the boat's return was unlikely to be good.

By 4.30pm the sky had clouded over and the wind stiffened, whipping the sea into a confused mess of white-crested, steep-faced waves. Mr Khoo took shelter in the wheelhouse. He had not spoken to me for almost an hour, and I took his silence for disapproval. McGrath relieved Lamont at the change of watch, and joined me on the bridge wing. The chilly breeze whipped our shirts and hair.

My eyes were aching from being jammed into the eyepieces of my binoculars, and the desperate longing for a cigarette finally overwhelmed me. I darted into my day cabin and grabbed the tin of Senior Service. Back on the bridge wing, I cupped a matchbox in my fist and struck a light.

'Skipper, something's moving in the creek mouth.'

I dropped the match, spat out the unlit cigarette and snatched up the binoculars. A boat swam into focus. It looked awfully frail against the breaking white water.

'That's them. Shit! It's going to be a bloody hard pull against that sea.'

The workboat was a 25-foot double ended whaler with oars for five men. It was a good sea-boat and, with buoyancy tanks, almost unsinkable. Still, a mile-long pull against the wind and seas was a daunting prospect for even the best trained oarsmen. The crew's stroke was already ragged, and Lakshman was bailing furiously with one hand while steering with the other.

Clear of the confused cross seas at the creek mouth, Lakshman was able to restore some order. The strokes were less ragged and the boat made more headway. It was already 100 yards offshore and the crew were pulling strongly. Perhaps too strongly, they would need to pace themselves or the conditions would overwhelm them.

By the time they were 500 yards from the shore, it was clear they were flagging. The strokes were again ragged and progress slowed to a crawl. Several waves broke over the boat, four men continued to row while the others bailed. An audience gathered to watch the drama. Mr Khoo joined me on the bridge wing, while Helena watched from the boat deck. Down aft, the Chinese crew crowded the taff rail, probably taking bets on their shipmates' return.

'If they're not going to make it, signal them to return ashore,' said Mr Khoo. 'I'd hate to see them drown. There's a railway station close to Kota Bharu. They can take a train from there to Singapore. Tell them to contact Poh Ling Sing. He'll look after them when they arrive.'

It was a sensible suggestion, one I should have thought of myself, but there was another way. While we had been talking the boat gained another 50 yards.

'Lamont, find Cramp, tell him to stand by to veer the anchor cable, one shackle at a time. Then get back up here. James, get someone to fetch an anchor buoy and as much line as he can quickly muster. Stream the buoy downwind. I'll tell Lakshman to pick it up. Once he's got it secured, haul the boat in. And get the bosun to take soundings as we drop astern. Sing out if we reach twenty feet.'

As they both darted below, I grabbed the signal lamp. Slowly, I flashed the message to Lakshman to make for the buoy and secure the line attached to it. The response was a raised fist, which I hoped meant he understood.

I rang the engine telegraph to Stand-by Below and watched the buoy drift towards the shore, dragging the line with it.

Raising the speaking trumpet, I bellowed into the wind.

'Veer the cable, one shackle.'

Cramp raised a fist in reply. He eased off the break and the cable clanked over the gypsy, link by link, as the ship dropped astern propelled by the force of the wind. One shackle of cable measured 30 yards. Not much, but every yard would help Lakshman's exhausted crew.

Cramp screwed on the brake and crossed his fists.

The buoy had drifted almost 200 yards. The boat gained another fifty. Encouraged by the reduction in distance, the crew seemed to gain a second wind.

'Veer one more shackle,' I bellowed at the forecastle.

The chain clanked out and the crew veered more line. In a matter of minutes, the distance to row had closed to 100 yards. I could almost hear Lakshman yelling to the men to put their backs into it for one final effort. The five oars rose and fell in unison, the stroke as precise as any crack naval crew in a whaler race. The boat surged ahead, the bow thrusting the breakers aside. The bowman snared the buoy with the boat hook. It was heavy and others leaped to help him. Between them they dragged it in and secured the line to the towing post.

Lakshman raised his arms and crossed his wrists.

The seamen at the poop clapped onto the line. With the boatswain calling time, they heaved together, the last man taking in the slack around a mooring bitt. With the combined effort of oars and rhythmically grunted heaves, the distance rapidly closed.

With a final heave, the boat ran under the stern and was hauled along the ship's side until it lay under the falls.

'Dead slow ahead, hard a port.'

There was a woosh of smoke from the funnel and the ship began to turn.

Holding the stern into the wind with short bursts of the propeller, and with the bow held by the anchor, the ship lay across the wind, providing a lee while the lifeboat was recovered. Even so, retrieving it was as dangerous as launching. With the boat heaving up and down, it took careful timing to ensure it was hooked on at both ends and hoisted at just the right moment. Any mistake could result in crushed limbs, or the boat dangling from one end of the falls with the crew spilt into the water.

If Lakshman was conscious of the audience of seamen, all of whom were choking back the urge to shout advice, he did not show it. He waited until the boat rose on a wave, shouted to the crew to hook on and yelled to McGrath to heave away. There was a sharp twang as the falls took the strain and the boat rose safely up the ship's side.

'Dead slow ahead.'

Lamont rang the telegraph and I waved at Cramp, circling my arm in the air. He raised a fist and clutched in the windlass.

With the clank of the gypsy hauling in the anchor, and the re-assuring beat of the engine throbbing through the deck plating, the ship steamed slowly away from the coast.

The sun had set by the time the boat was secured. I checked my watch. It was 6.30pm. We had just over five hours to get clear before the gates of hell swung open.

CHAPTER THIRTEEN

Evening, Sunday 7 December 1941

With the boat safely hoisted and secured, Lakshman climbed up to the bridge. I motioned him to wait, while McGrath plotted his latest cross bearings on the chart. From the position he drew a course line to take us clear of the Perhentian Islands.

'West-sou-west will do it, Skipper. There are reefs and islets inshore, we don't want to blunder about there in the dark.'

'Make it so then. Lay courses to clear them and get us back on track to Singapore as soon as it's safe to do so.'

I left him to it and signalled Lakshman to join me on the bridge wing.

'You cut that fine, Third. We were on the point of leaving you behind. What happened?'

'We were being arrested, sir. Once inside the creek, I looked for a place to land Colonel Spencer. About two cables from the entrance there was a pillbox close to the shore. When we got there, soldiers surrounded the boat.'

'They saw the British flag?'

'Yes, sir, but their lieutenant pulled out his revolver and told them to seize us. Colonel Spencer explained who he was and demanded to be taken to the nearest command post. There was an argument. I have heard that Australians have a wide vocabulary of swear words, now I am knowing the truth of it. The lieutenant was not intimidated, though. He told his men to guard us while he took Colonel Sahib to Brigade headquarters in Kota Bharu.'

'Christ, that was six miles away.'

Lakshman's head wobbled from side to side. 'I am sorry, Captain. The men were armed. I tried talking to their havildar, a very fierce Bengali from the Dogra Regiment. He thought the boat crew were

Japanese.'

'But they let you go?'

'Yes, sir. After three hours the lieutenant is returning. He was most apologetic. We are all back in the boat double quick.'

'Did the lieutenant say whether Colonel Spencer delivered his message?'

Lakshman shook his head. 'No, sir. He did not tell me that. He was a very nice chap after all. From Calcutta. His father was a subedar-major in the same Dogra regiment. In his family it is—'

'That'll do for now, Third. You did well bringing the boat back through those seas.'

'Thank you, Captain. I shall go below and check on the boat crew. Their hands suffered most cruelly from the oars.'

'I'm not surprised. Take them to the sick bay and ask Mr Lamont to have a look at them. He can show you what to do about blistered palms.'

With the sky totally overcast, twilight was short. The coast and the cluster of inshore islands disappeared into an inky darkness broken only by the flicker of lightning away to the north-west. I checked McGrath's latest position on the chart. We would be clear of Pulau Redang, the last of the islands, by midnight. It was unlikely the Japanese fleet would approach Kota Bharu from the south, but there was always the possibility of a warship, or even a submarine, scouting the flanks. If so, we would just have to hope that no eagled-eyed lookout spotted our profile. Moonrise was just before 9pm but, blacked out, with the cloud cover promising rain showers and six-foot seas running, we would be hard to see. I found McGrath in the darkness of the wheelhouse.

'I'll take over for a bit. Have a walk around the external decks. Make sure there's not a chink of light visible anywhere.'

He disappeared below, leaving me alone with the helmsman. Only his ghostly face and disembodied hands were visible in the faint glow of the binnacle lamp.

By the time McGrath returned, we were in the midst of a tropical downpour, the rain hissing and splattering onto the decks and sluicing down the scuppers in torrents. The wind had a keen edge and I sent Da Silva below to fetch me a lightweight jumper.

'Almost feels as if we're back in the North Atlantic on a dirty night, thankful the U-boats might not spot us,' said McGrath.

'Something like that. Come midnight, if not before, we'll be fair game for any Japanese that happens to sight us. You got your abandon ship kit packed?'

'Never unpacked it.'

'Are you happy if I go below for a bit? I need to have a word with Helena and Mr Khoo. Make sure they're prepared if we have to take to the boats. I'll be back up at the change of watch.'

'No worries, Skipper. I'll holler if anything happens.'

I found Helena and Mr Khoo in the saloon. Dressed for dinner and enjoying a cocktail, they were in jarring contrast to the reality that our lives could be snatched away at any moment by shell or torpedo. The unvarying routine, and the familiar shipboard surroundings seamen called home, made it somehow possible, even in the direst of situations, to maintain an illusion of normality. It was that illusion which allowed men and women to go about their duties when common sense should have told them it was hopeless. Even if we made it to Singapore, there would soon be no patch of ocean in which to hide. The waters of the Far East had been an oasis of calm, compared to the horrors of the North Atlantic. No longer. As of midnight, every scrap of sea and ocean was part of the battlefield.

Helena and Mr Khoo were deep in conversation when I joined them, but accepted my offer of a refill. I poured myself a rum, topped it up with iced water and dropped into a chair beside Helena.

'I'm sorry to interrupt your conversation.'

'That's quite all right,' said Mr Khoo. 'We were just talking about what might happen when the Japanese attack.'

'I doubt we'll see any trouble during the night,' I said. 'There are rain showers about and the visibility's poor, but we shouldn't take any chances. You ought to pack a small bag in case we do have to abandon ship in a hurry. It's also a good idea to sleep fully clothed with your lifejacket beside you. If we take a direct hit the ship could go down in minutes. So, every second counts.'

Mr Khoo nodded, his careworn face grave, the fear in his eyes replaced by concern. He need not have worried about Helena. In contrast, she was a picture of equanimity. Her face broke into a broad grin.

'I can't possibly go to my death without at least an hour's warning. A girl needs to look her best. Full war paint, hair and nails done. I'll also need to contact my agent so I get at least half a column in the *Los Angeles Times*. "Future Oscar Winner slaughtered in vile Japanese surprise attack." That should improve my chances with the Academy.'

The image of Olwyn D'Angelo scrambling up the side netting, in slacks, overcoat and headscarf, flashed into my head. I blinked, and saw her hanging out her underwear on the boat deck, casually smoking a cigarette as we lured the U-boat closer.

'Are you all right, Rowden?' asked Helena, the grin fading. 'I was only joking. You look as if you've seen a ghost.'

'I see too many ghosts. I don't want you and Mr Khoo among them.'

'In China, we believe that a man who dies a violent death becomes a hungry ghost. One whose desires can never be satisfied. I have no wish to torment my descendants as a hungry ghost.'

'Neither do I, Mr Khoo. But I'd be tempting fate if I said I could guarantee our safe arrival in Singapore.'

'We also say of a man, first destiny, second luck. I knew you were a lucky man the day you brought *Oriental Venture* safely to Hong Kong. How many times since then has it proved so? But what is your destiny? To do what you came to do in this lifetime. But can we ever truly know the destination before we arrive there? Perhaps not, but of one thing I am sure. It is not your destiny to perish at the hands of your enemies.'

He spoke with such conviction that, for a moment, I was tempted to believe him. Sure, I'd had my share of luck, good as well as bad. Too much to discount its potential to wreak havoc as easily as bestow good fortune. A wiser man than me had once said that good luck was mostly a matter of preparation. If that was true, it should be plain sailing all the way to Singapore and beyond. A large part of me wanted to believe that too.

Helena broke my train of thought. 'And what about women, Mr Khoo. Do the same rules apply to us?'

Mr Khoo's face brightened and the twinkle returned to his eyes. 'I am afraid that Master Confucius did not have a very high opinion of women. But our ancient tradition says it was Nu Gua, the Divine Empress, who created all of humanity. Sadly, she grew tired of the process and invented marriage and procreation, which have placed an unequal burden upon your sex. Still, as Mrs Khoo frequently reminds me, if you want something done in a hurry, ask a busy woman.'

It was pleasant to hear Helena laugh.

'I've been declared dead once, so perhaps I'm already a hungry ghost. There are certainly plenty of men I could haunt.' Her smile faded and uncertainty clouded her face. 'But seriously, what are our chances of reaching Singapore?'

I rubbed my fingertips together to ease the tingling. I had come to accept it as a sixth sense. It had saved my skin more than once, but it didn't always signify danger, at least not the physical kind.

'I'd say there's every chance you'll be shopping in Robinsons or John Little at Raffles Place before the end of the week. The Japanese have more important targets than one ageing tramp steamer.'

'But how safe will we be there?' persisted Helena. 'Mr Khoo has very kindly invited me to stay at his bungalow while I arrange my passage home. But with the war lapping the shores of Hawaii, I wonder how easy it will be to cross the Pacific.'

'I'm sure things will work out favourably,' said Mr Khoo. 'The British will fight hard to defend Singapore. It is the lynchpin in the defence of their eastern dominions.'

'Colonel Spencer says the same.' Helena shrugged her shoulders. 'Still, as President Roosevelt once said, the only thing we have to fear is fear itself. We're none of us dead yet, and there's plenty of living to do.' She raised her glass. 'Live easy, play hard, die hard.' She drained the contents. 'I don't suppose you'll be joining us for dinner, Rowden?'

I shook my head. 'I'll be on the bridge. No dancing in the moonlight tonight but, hopefully, I'll see you at breakfast.'

I left them to it and climbed back to the bridge. Da Silva had laid a dinner tray and a pot of coffee in my day cabin. The stir-fried chicken with chilli and noodles was mouth tingling. I washed it down with two cups of coffee. The urge to smoke was strong. I was annoyed with myself for almost succumbing earlier, and locked the tin of Senior Service into my desk to minimise temptation.

By the time I finished, the watch had changed and Lakshman was on the bridge wing. The showers had eased, but the wind was still stiff. Seas breaking against the hull sent spray whipping across the deck. Shafts of moonlight penetrated the ragged clouds.

'Everything under control, Third?'

'Yes, sir. The cloud cover is breaking up. Mr McGrath should be able to take stars in the morning.'

I went back into the wheelhouse to study the chart. With the invasion fleet approaching from the north and the Malayan coast to the south, it felt as if we were about to be crushed between the jaws of a giant nutcracker. I could ask Fraser to force one more effort from the boilers, but the extra mile or two it would deliver was not worth the risk to men and machinery. We would be 60 miles away from the invasion beaches before midnight. It would have to be enough.

It was, although it took a few moments to realise that the distant rumble to the north, that erupted just after the change of watch, was not thunder but heavy gunfire softening up the defences.

'Pity those poor Indian chaps on the beaches. They'll be copping an awful battering,' said Lamont, who had relieved Lakshman.

I recalled the minefields, barbed wire and pillboxes that Spencer had pointed out. 'Let's hope they give as good as they get. Those Jap soldiers will be pretty green by the time their boats struggle through this lot.' If anything, the wind had strengthened during the evening whipping up a cauldron of short, breaking seas.

'Aye, well I wish them luck. The Indians that is. I hope they hurl the bastards back into the sea.'

I hoped so too. If Kota Bharu and its airfields were in Japanese hands by the morning, it would make every mile to Singapore feel like an eternity.

By four bells, the rumbling gunfire had faded into the whistle of the wind and the slap and rush of the sea. I spared a thought for those Indians who survived the shelling. They would now be slugging it out on the beaches.

As Lakshman predicted, the cloud cover continued to break up as the night wore on. In the clear patches, the moonlight lit up the undersides of the clouds and silvered the white-capped waves.

McGrath arrived at the change of watch, bringing a welcome pot of coffee with him. We enjoyed it out on the bridge wing as the darkness paled. With the moon and a good sprinkling of stars to choose from, McGrath took his twilight observations. I waited until he plotted the position on the chart, adjusted course to correct for set and leeway, and headed below.

I pushed open my cabin door and switched on the light, looking forward to a precious few hours in my bunk.

Helena was asleep on it. She was wrapped in a long silk nightgown knotted with a cord at the waist. I watched the swell of her breasts rise and fall beneath the gown.

She stirred and opened her dazzling green eyes. 'Have you brought breakfast?'

'I thought I told you to sleep fully clothed. And where's your abandon ship kit and lifejacket.'

'I'm sorry, Captain. I changed my mind and decided if I had to leave to meet my maker, I'd do so in the same state she sent me here.' She reached for the cord at her waist. 'You can check that I'm telling the truth. Unless, of course, you're too tired.'

'Who said anything about being tired.' I perched on the edge of the bed, all thoughts of sleep instantly banished, and watched, mesmerised, as she untied the knot and let the gown fall open. The silk slid apart to reveal her body.

Unblushing, she submitted to my scrutiny.

'I do declare that some men seem to take more pleasure at just looking at a naked woman. I don't mind, I just hope your eyes aren't bigger than your ...'

I stripped off my shirt and leaned down to kiss her, feeling her nipples brush against my chest.

Her fingertips traced over the tattoos on my forearms. 'What do these mean?'

'Drunken stupidity, mostly. I got the anchor after my first trip across the Atlantic. The rooster ... well there's an old saying, cock on the right never lost a fight.'

'Is it true?'

'I like to think it is.'

She squeezed the muscles in my arm. 'I hope the rest of you is as hard as that. Why don't you ditch the clothes so we can find out.'

I kicked off my shoes and socks, stood up and turned around to undo my belt.

'Why so modest ... oh my! Your back, what a lovely picture of a ship.'

'It's a schooner, fore and aft rigged. She was my first.'

There was a swish of silk and I looked over my shoulder to see her standing behind me, the gown discarded. Her hands reached out and her fingers played across my back.

'Does it hurt much? When they do it?'

'It helps if you're drunk. Why, do you want to get one?'

She pressed herself into my back. Her arms wrapped around me, her nipples raked my skin and her lips nuzzled my ear.

'What should I get?'

'A dragon perhaps ... that means you've served in the China trade. Or a swallow, so you can find your way home.'

'I'm not sure where home is anymore. A dragon might be nice. It's my Chinese birth sign.' Her hands dropped to my waist, finished unbuckling my belt and reached for my fly buttons.

I dropped my trousers and turned to face her.

She whistled, softly. 'I think I might know just the right treatment for that condition.'

'I can't lock the door.'

'Don't worry, I promise I won't try and escape.'

I reached for the light switch.

'Leave it on. I'm not shy.' She giggled. 'Anyway, I like to watch the mantelpiece while the fire's being stoked.'

'Someone might call me if they need me.'

'I need you.' The light danced in her eyes, and I shivered feeling them sweep over my body.

I reached out for her, but she wriggled away, pushed me onto the bed and jumped astride my thighs.

'Slow down, sailor. There's an old Russian saying. A woman in need wants a swain who can last.'

'I'll sign you on as my coxswain then.'

Her soft laugh had a devilish edge. 'Actually, I made that up. But they'll have to drag me off you if they want you back on the bridge.'

She lowered her head until her auburn hair tumbled over my chest.

I wrapped my arms around her and pulled her close. The musky, jasmine smell of her perfume filled my nostrils like a bewitching drug. I could feel her heart beating squeezed next to mine, and the rise and fall of her bosom as she breathed.

'This feels so good. I don't know why I didn't do it four years ago.' She raised her head and gazed into my eyes until I felt I was swimming in a sea of emerald. Then our lips fused, her body engulfed me, and all thoughts of the ship, the war and the Japanese invasion fleet were drowned out by our passion.

CHAPTER FOURTEEN

Forenoon, Monday 8 December 1941

A determined rap on the door jerked me awake. It was followed by Da Silva's harsh voice. 'Coffee Sahib.'

I checked my watch. It was almost 9am. We had slept for nearly two hours, but I felt as rested as ever I had since taking command. I glanced down at Helena. She was still asleep, breathing peacefully. I covered her naked body with the sheet.

The knocking resumed. 'Sahib, coffee.'

'Okay, put it on the table.'

The door opened and Da Silva's grizzled head appeared, followed by the rest of him bearing a tray with a coffee pot and two cups. He placed the tray on the table and whisked open the curtains. Bright sunlight burst in through the porthole. The second cup and the mischievous glint in his sole eye were the only acknowledgement of Helena's presence.

'Shall I be fetching breakfast, Sahib?'

'Yes please,' chirped a cheery voice beside me.

'Atcha, Memsahib'. He closed the door behind him.

'He might only have one eye, but I'd swear that man has second sight.' I padded naked to the table and returned with two brimming cups. 'How did he know you were here?'

Helena sat up, her long legs coiled under her, and accepted one. 'Perhaps he checked my cabin first and found the bed not slept in.'

'But why assume ...?'

'Well obviously, if I'm going to sleep my way around a ship I'll start at the top.'

She sipped the strong brew and a satisfied sigh escaped her lips. 'Well, that puts life back into a girl. If only you still smoked, I could enjoy a cigarette and the morning would be complete.'

'Don't let me stop you. Where are they?'

Helena pointed to the small, embroidered clutch bag on my desk. I reached for it and flicked the catch.

'A gentleman does **not** look inside a lady's handbag, even if he has kept her up half the night making love to her. Give it here.'

Duly chastised, I passed her the bag. She extracted the cigarette case, flipped out a Sobranie and handed me her lighter. I rasped the flint. She inhaled deeply and blew a long stream of smoke towards the deckhead.

'Look at you. A nude woman drinking coffee and smoking in your bed. There's your reputation ruined.'

I sat beside her and sipped my own coffee. It was a long time since I had woken up next to a woman, and even longer since doing so in my own bed. It was already over an hour into the forenoon. Lakshman would be on the bridge. I should have checked the ship's speed and position at the change of watch.

I felt Helena's eyes burning my cheek and turned to see her smiling at me.

'Do you need to go?'

'They've managed without me for three hours and the sky hasn't fallen in.' I put my cup on the floor and rolled over to face her. 'And if my reputation's already ruined.'

Helena gazed down at me. Her blazing green eyes turned my insides to jelly, but not the part that mattered.

'Ah, I see you're ready for an encore.' She dropped her cigarette into the coffee cup, reached for her bag and headed towards the bathroom. 'Don't go away.'

She saw my raised eyebrow.

'I'm not going to powder my nose. A girl has to take precautions. Something you men seem to always conveniently forget.'

She pulled the bathroom door closed.

The furious ringing of the wheelhouse bell was accompanied by Lakshman's bellow. 'AIRCRAFT SIGHTED.'

I scrambled into my underpants and sprinted for the wheelhouse.

McGrath and Bullen were already on the bridge wing, their binoculars trained on what looked like a distant flock of birds, low in the sky to the north-east.

'What are they?'

'Twin-engined bombers by the look of them,' said Bullen. He lowered the binoculars, saw the little I was wearing, coughed behind his hand to conceal his grin and looked away.

McGrath made no attempt to hide his amusement. 'Sorry, Skipper, but you appear to have forgotten … your shoes again.'

'Wipe those silly grins off your faces,' I barked. 'What the captain choses to wear on his own bridge…'

I felt a discrete nudge of my elbow. Da Silva clutched the rest of my kit. I scrambled into shorts and shirt, jammed my feet into shoes and pulled my cap on. Dignity restored; I studied the growing dots. Visible in between banks of heavy cumulus, there were over a dozen aircraft flying in loose formation.

'They look a bit like Hudsons, but they're Japanese alright,' said Bullen. 'Twin-engined, twin tail planes, long snout. High … probably ten thousand feet. No sign they're interested in us. Looks like Singapore's going to cop it, though.'

On the Monkey Island, shoulders pressed against the stocks of the Lewis guns, the gunners tracked the bombers through their gunsights.

'Keep your eyes peeled lads,' called Bullen. 'There might be a fighter escort.'

The drone of aero engines rose to a throbbing roar as the bombers crossed high and ahead of us. If Spencer's warning had got through, what reception awaited them from Singapore's defences?

'Aircraft! Six o'clock.'

All heads on the bridge swivelled at the startled yell from the Monkey Island.

Approaching rapidly from astern, half a dozen fighter planes had peeled off from a larger formation flying high cover for the bombers. Gull winged, with an enormous engine cowling, they looked like stubby, blunt-ended Stukas.

'OPEN FIRE.' Bullen's shout was almost drowned by the screaming engine as the first one bored towards us.

An ear-splitting crack from the forecastle was followed by the crump of a 12-pounder shell exploding behind the fighter.

The Lewis guns chattered in unison, sending a stream of lead into its path. It held steady. Lights flickered at its nose, and a double line of bullets hosed along the decks, gouging furrows into the hatch covers and striking sparks off steel.

As it roared away to the south, climbing to re-join formation, the next fighter streaked towards us.

The 12-pounder crew worked furiously. Shells exploded close to the gaggle of fighters, but a single anti-aircraft gun was hardly likely to deter them.

'Hard a starboard.'

It was too late to throw the pilot off his aim and more bullets ploughed and sparked along the exposed decks. Those on the bridge threw themselves down as it roared overhead.

I scrambled back my feet, ashamed that my instinct for self-preservation might be taken for cowardice. Apart from their tin hats, the gunners on the Monkey Island had no protection whatsoever. Undeterred by the flying bullets, they continued to fire into the path of the oncoming fighters, until it seemed neither could miss.

Yelling to the helmsman, to be heard above the roaring engines and the crack and crash of gun fire, I ordered rapid changes of heading. The ship responded slowly, but it was better than nothing and made it slightly harder for the pilots to sight their guns.

One by one, the fighters took their turn to rake us from stern to stem. The firing was continuous. Shells exploded overhead. Expended machine gun cartridges rained onto the deck. The 12-pounder swivelled to fire at the fighters as they swooped away at the end of their run. A gunner slumped back from his Lewis gun, his mouth gaping wide in surprise.

It was over almost as suddenly as it began. The fighters jinked away to re-join the slower flying bombers, the noise of their engines fading rapidly into the distance.

Bullen watched, stony faced, while the dead gunner was carried below. 'I'll check round the rest of the lads, sir. That's one nil to the Japs, but the fight ain't over yet.'

I ordered the helmsman to resume course, and sent McGrath below to check whether there were any more casualties. Ten minutes later, he re-joined me on the bridge wing, a look of relief on his freckled face.

'Apart from the dead gunner and a few bullet holes in the life-boats, we got off lightly. Cramp's plugging the holes. Why didn't they all attack us?'

'Saving their ammunition,' I said. 'Their job's to protect those bombers, not shoot up ships. Think of it as just a warning.'

'Standing up there, on the bridge wing in the open, while being used for target practice, felt like I was standing naked in George Street. Bloody uncomfortable experience.'

'Worse than being in a convoy under attack by a wolf pack?'

'Reckon so, Skipper. Surrounded by several dozen ships, at least there's a feeling of safety in numbers. A bit like being one small fish in a bait-ball attacked by a shark. But six enemy aircraft lining up to take turns? Jeez, that's like the poms bowling bodyline ... it's just not bloody cricket.'

'Maybe not. But it's hard-nosed bastards like Douglas Jardine who win wars.' I nodded in the direction of the wheelhouse. 'Can you keep an eye on things up here for a bit. If the Japs are launching air raids on Singapore there'll be more to come. I'll be in my cabin if you need me. Catching up on some breakfast.' I caught the slight raise of his eyebrow and the curl of his lips. 'Not one word. I was asleep when the alarm rang.' I clamped my jaw shut. There was no need to explain.

Pulling open my cabin door revealed Helena clutching a valise. Despite the worry etched on her face, in linen slacks and blouse, she looked as fresh as a newly plucked daisy.

'I've never had a man run out on me so fast. Do we have to abandon ship?'

'No. Some Japanese fighters took pot shots at us. But the bombers they were escorting left us alone.'

'Was anybody hurt?'

'One of the gunners was killed. Took a bullet straight through the chest. At least he never knew what hit him.'

'I'm so sorry. Did he have a family?'

I was ashamed to realise I knew very little about the man. Bullen kept a close watch on his gunners and they didn't mix much with the rest of the crew. 'I believe he did. Petty Officer Bullen will let me have the details so I can write to them. He died bravely, but I doubt it'll be much comfort to them.'

Helena dropped onto the couch and placed the valise on the deck. 'It's so sad, all those mothers receiving telegrams and letters confirming the loss of their sons.'

'And daughters. There are women fighting this war, too. I've seen more than enough of them dead already. I don't want to have to write to your mother. So, I suggest you stay inside, at least until sunset. There could be more attacks. We might not be so lucky again.'

'And after we reach Singapore?'

'You'll be someone else's problem.'

A frown wrinkled her eyes. 'I don't like the idea of being anyone's problem. And you said that as if you'd be happy to get rid of me.'

'Sorry Helena, that was a poor attempt at humour. I don't want to be rid of you and not just because of what happened last night. Which was wonderful. You were ... you are, wonderful.' I was beginning to sound like an infatuated teenager, but I couldn't stop talking. 'I don't know what you see in me, though. Just a fisherman's son from the wrong side of the river.'

The smile returned to her eyes. 'I seem to have a soft spot for boys from the wrong side. They've been my downfall more times than I care to admit. Even Bobby Ashworth, despite his title, could be as bad as any of them. He was just like the nursery rhyme. When he was good, he was very, very good. But when he was bad, he was better.' A soft chuckle escaped her lips. 'I've heard men say the same about me.'

'Well, if that was you being better, I'd happily settle for good.'

Her eyes narrowed like a cat sizing up her prey. 'Ooohh, I can be better than that. I'll show you, if you let me hang around.' Her laughter filled the cabin. 'My God. I'm asking a man if he wants to go to bed with me again. I've become an alley cat … with no morals.'

I had a soft spot for alley cats … with or without morals. 'Of course, I want you to stay. But why me?'

I submitted to her long, cool scrutiny.

'You know, bad boys never ask that question. And good men? Well, I don't usually explain myself to any man. They can accept as little or as much of me as I'm prepared to offer … or they can go hang.' Her expression softened. 'But I'll make an exception … because I like you. Because I thought you needed some loving. Because I wanted my self-respect back. Because … underneath that tattooed, rough exterior, I think there's a good man trying to get out.'

'For God's sake, don't tell the crew. I've spent a lifetime perfecting my impression of Captain Bligh.'

Her peals of laughter joined my guffaws.

'And on the subject of bad men,' she continued. 'I'm not sure how many thanks I owe you for consigning me to the tender care of Captain Coffin and his gang of pirates. I spent the whole voyage feeling like a hunted deer surrounded by lions. Fortunately, they were so busy snapping and snarling at each other, we made it to San Francisco before I got eaten.'

A knock on the door interrupted the conversation and Da Silva appeared with a breakfast tray. Apart from coffee, there were fried eggs, a small mound of toast and a jar of marmalade from my private stock. His sole eye glinted as he placed the tray on the desk. He flashed Helena a grin and pulled the door closed as he left.

'That man is a real treasure,' said Helena. 'I'm starving.'

'Don't wait for me, I need a shave.'

By the time I emerged from the bathroom, Helena had worked her way through most of the eggs. She paused to pour me a coffee.

'Good job I didn't take long.' I attacked the remaining egg with a fork.

'I told you I was hungry.' She reached for a slice of toast. 'If you're not going to eat all that, can you pass the marmalade?'

I gulped down the coffee. 'Would you mind …?'

'Go … go,' she said, between mouthfuls. 'Go to your precious bridge. But don't expect me to wait for you.'

She jumped up and grabbed me as I headed for the door. Her hands reached for my head and her kiss tasted of oranges. 'I'll wait, lover.' Her laugh contained a note of sadness. 'After all, there's a war on. I've got nowhere else to go.'

CHAPTER FIFTEEN

Monday afternoon to Tuesday morning, 8-9 December 1941

Mid-afternoon found us threading our way between Tioman and the chain of islets off Mersing in southern Malaya. Twelve hours from Singapore, Japanese aircraft were still a threat, but the day remained quiet. The north-east monsoon winds eased, the rain showers drifted away and, with the ship steadily forging through a shimmering blue sea, the earlier attack by fighter planes might never have happened.

I spent the day on the bridge, snatching a quick lunch off a tray in my day cabin. It wasn't just the threat of attack that kept me there, but the knowledge that, if I went below, I would go to Helena. Would it be so bad if I spent the afternoon in her arms, instead of pacing the bridge wing searching an empty horizon already scoured by the lookouts' anxious eyes. Even being caught in bed with her, while the ship exploded under a hail of bombs, didn't sound so bad. Who was it had said: *If it were now to die, 'twere now to be most happy?* 'Ah yes, Othello? Great general he may have been, but he was also a fool.'

'Sorry, Skipper. What was that you said?' As I turned to stride the few paces back to the end of the bridge wing, Lamont stood just inside the wheelhouse door.

'Are you eavesdropping on my private conversations?'

'No, Skipper.' He lowered his head to hide the grin. 'I just thought I heard you say something.'

'I was remarking to myself what a fool Othello was.'

'For killing the woman he loved?'

'For trusting his lieutenant, that snake Iago.'

'Great use of dramatic irony by Shakespeare.' Lamont's eyes lit up with enthusiasm. 'The audience knows exactly what's going on, but poor old Othello canna see what's right under his nose.'

I maintained the scowl long enough to stop the flow.

'Sorry, sir ... you're no' suggesting ...?'

'No, Lamont, I'm not suggesting that any of my lieutenants are not to be trusted. You'll be the first to hear if I have the slightest doubt about your abilities. One of which is not to comment, when the old man let's slip part of the inner workings of the great and mysterious mechanism of his mind.'

'No, sir.'

'Good, now turn your attention back to your watch and let me mutter to myself in peace.'

I resumed pacing, enjoying the breeze ruffling my hair and the rush and tumble of the water as the ship shouldered aside the low swell. Apart from passing islands and the smudge of mainland Malaya to starboard, the horizon remained peacefully empty.

McGrath arrived at the change of watch and joined me on the bridge wing.

'We should be at the pilot station just after midnight,' he said. 'Japanese air force permitting, we could be alongside and tucked up in our bunks by two o'clock.'

'Ever the optimist. You ready with your stores' request? Might as well stock up as much as we can. Who knows when there'll be another opportunity?'

'Has Mr Khoo said where we're going next?' asked McGrath.

'No, but it's not up to him. It's up to the Ministry of War Transport.' Even as I said it, I remembered Mr Khoo's remark that we had gone up river to Bangkok because it suited him. That had never been true. Was Spencer finished with us? My fingertips were not tingling, but I had the familiar feeling we had not heard the last of the colonel.

'We'd better make the most of it then,' said McGrath. 'I'm looking forward to a run up to the Great World and wheeling a few taxi girls around the dance floor.'

The Great World, on Kim Seng Road in Singapore, was a pale imitation of the one in Shanghai. Behind the tall spire of the entrance was a barn like dance hall. After paying the fifty-cent entrance fee, a dance with a taxi-girl cost twenty-five cents. If you didn't want to dance you could eat from the food stalls and drink your fill of Tiger Beer. There were also Happy World and New World with their circus stunts and cabarets. Personally, I preferred the nightlife around Bugis Street. The war in Europe had done very little to dampen people's enthusiasm to enjoy themselves in Singapore. What would happen when air raids rained destruction on the city, and Japanese troops marched down the roads from the Causeway?

'You sure you wouldn't like to join me and Cramp for a run up to Bugis Street to ogle the Kai Tais?'

'Jellied eels and porter, that's what Cramp promised the first time he took me,' said McGrath, laughing. 'Yeah, I'd be happy to come with you, Skipper.' The cheery smile on his face faded. 'It's just a shame David Griffith can't join us.'

'Life's for the living, James. As I'm sure he'd remind us. Make the most of it while we can. It's going to be a long, bloody war.'

McGrath and Griffith had once almost come to blows in Bugis Street, over Griffith's flaunting an especially beautiful Kai Tai. They'd been good friends and shipmates after that, until Griffith was killed.

Leaving me to continue my pacing, McGrath climbed up to the Monkey Island to take cross-bearings. We were converging with the coast of Southern Malaya, with about thirty miles to run to Pedra Branca, where the Horsburgh Light marked the entrance to the Singapore Strait. As the afternoon wore on, the wind strengthened, a few thunderclouds dotted the horizon but visibility remained clear.

The sun was low in the west, when the lookout reported smoke fine on the port bow. I jerked up my binoculars. At first it looked like wispy cloud. I slowly traversed either side of the smudge. The black speck of a topmast nicked the horizon.

'Get Bullen up here on the double. He's going to want to see this.'

By the time Bullen arrived, panting from the brisk climb from the main deck, a second topmast had appeared. His hand was halfway to his cap before he remembered my instruction that saluting on a tramp steamer was unnecessary.

I handed him my binoculars. 'Tell me what you make of that.'

He studied the growing masts, before emitting a low whistle. 'Two battleships. *Prince of Wales* and *Repulse* by the look of those fightingtops.'

'Colonel Spencer said they only arrived last week. Barely time to refuel and top up the gin.'

Travelling fast, they were soon hull up. With their upperworks and massive gun turrets highlighted by the setting sun, they looked menacing.

'That's a sight not to be missed,' said Bullen, continuing to study them. 'I served in *Repulse*, sir, as a young gunner.'

'At Jutland?'

'No sir, she wasn't in service then. Heligoland Bight, the following year. Hit the German cruise *Konigsberg*. Accepted the surrender of the High Seas Fleet at the end of the war. Happy days they was.' He swept the horizon either side of the battleships. 'There's four destroyers with 'em. Two look like E-class, one's an S and the other a V. Pretty weak escort if they're off looking for trouble.'

Travelling north-east, the six ships were soon approaching the beam. The westernmost destroyer flashed a challenge. McGrath replied with our name, nationality and call sign.

'By rights, we should dip our ensign,' said Bullen. 'They're a bit far away, but there'll be some eagled eyed Jimmy the One with a Snotty standing by just in case.'

McGrath darted into the wheelhouse and returned with a Red Ensign.

'I'll do the honours, sir,' said Bullen, handing back my binoculars.

He unrolled the flag and expertly re-folded it. Wrapping two turns tight around the bundle, he tucked a loop of the lanyard under them and bent the clips onto the signal halyard. He hoisted the bundled flag to the top and yanked. The flag broke out in a single red flash, streaming bar straight in the breeze. Bullen waited half a minute, before lowering the flag to half height.

McGrath and I studied the warships.

'My God ... they've all dipped their white ensigns,' said McGrath.

Bullen hoisted the Red Ensign back to the top of the halyard. 'Permission to signal, Good Hunting, sir?'

I nodded. He reached for the lamp and grasped the handle. The rapidly clacking shutter flashed out the message. There was a brief acknowledging blink from the nearest destroyer.

'Wish you were going with them, Bullen?' I asked.

'Oh, I don't know, sir. Reckon there's going to be enough trouble for all of us.'

With the six ships drawing rapidly away, we watched until their camouflage painted hulls disappeared into the twilight.

'On the subject of trouble, sir.' Bullen turned away from the empty horizon. 'I had words with the 12-pounder crew. They'll have to work a damn sight quicker if they're going to have a chance of hittin' anything.'

'How's Mr Lamont shaping up?'

'He's keen enough, and got a good eye for distance and elevation. Practice makes perfect.'

'There'll be plenty for all of us before this lot's over.' I paused, remembering that one of his gunners was dead. 'Tell me about the man who was killed.'

'Tom Watkins. Hostilities only rating. Flat feet, so he failed the army medical. Good with a machine gun, though.' Bullen shook his head, eyes downcast. 'The flat feet didn't save him. Saw enough men killed in the last show. Never gets any easier.'

'Let me have the address of his family and I'll write to them. They deserve more than just a telegram.'

'That's good of you, sir. With your permission, I'll check with HQ in Singapore. Might be able to rustle up a replacement.'

I nodded and Bullen disappeared below, leaving McGrath and me in the falling darkness.

By the change of watch we had cleared the Romania Shoals and, if our dead reckoning was correct, Horsburgh Light was only five miles ahead. Fortunately, the late afternoon thunderstorms had not materialised and, with a third quarter moon peering between the clouds, visibility was good. Nevertheless, the Singapore Strait was a tricky patch of water to navigate in the dark, made more difficult, now that Singapore had been bombed, by switching off the navigation lights.

Lakshman checked the chart and re-joined me in the wheelhouse.

'Fifteen minutes to the alter course, sir.'

'Aye aye, Third.' I checked my wristwatch, the luminous hands glowing green in the darkness.

Surprisingly, the lights of several ships were visible in the Middle Channel. We were still steaming without lights. Blacked out in the busy roadstead, suddenly seemed less than a good idea.

'Switch on the nav lights, Third. And tell the lookouts to keep their eyes peeled. There might be ships in the channel not showing any.'

After we altered course into the Strait, the next couple of hours were a tense exercise in searching for clues that we were not being set down onto the shoals on either side. Fortunately, the peaks along the coast of Johore were silhouetted against the clear horizon, and some of the city lights were still visible. If blackout restrictions had been announced, they were yet to be enforced.

Approaching Singapore roads, the peaks of Mount Faber and Fort Canning made good landmarks, and I adjusted course to head towards the anchorage. There were ships already moored there, most with at least one faint lamp hoisted to the forestay. Among them I noticed the steaming lights of a launch. A white light over red denoted it was carrying a pilot. On a hunch, I reached for the signal lamp and flashed a series of As to attract its attention.

The reply was instantaneous. Having confirmed our call sign, the launch altered course and raced towards us.

I called to Lakshman. 'Take one of the lookouts and get the pilot ladder over the starboard side. Hang a cargo lamp to show them where it is. Turn it off as soon as the pilot's aboard.'

I slowed the ship until we just maintained steerage way, and a big, powerful launch pulled alongside. On its deck, beside the pilot, was the familiar figure of Poh Ling Sing, dressed in a white linen suit. In the pool of light cast by the lamp, the pilot clambered up the ladder, followed, more hesitantly, by Poh. With the ship only part loaded, they had further to climb than usual. By the time they reached the wheelhouse, Poh was mopping his face with a handkerchief.

I greeted the pilot. He ordered the engine to half ahead and turned the ship towards the North Channel leading into Keppel Harbour. 'The navy's been mining the approaches,' he said. 'You need to obtain a chart from the Harbour Master marking where the minefields will be.'

I thanked him and turned to Poh. Apart from being the company's Singapore agent, he was one of the Straits Settlements' Lobang Kings, who knew all the right people and most of the wrong ones. Having recovered his breath, he was beaming at me, his moon-shaped facing seeming to glow in the darkness.

'Captain Rowden, welcome.' He reached for my hand and pumped it vigorously.

'Good morning, Mr Poh. How did you know to meet us?'

'We were expecting you. Colonel Spencer sent word of your departure from Kota Bharu. It was simple matter to calculate arrival time.' He clapped his hands. 'Everything is arranged. You go straight alongside West Wharf. Tug already standing by. First you unload rice, then top up bunkers. After that, we see what we have for you.'

'You've heard the news?'

'Yes, yes, dreadful business. But the Americans already declared war on the Japanese. Now they will get what coming to them.'

I turned to Lakshman. 'Nip down below and give Mr Khoo my compliments. Tell him Mr Poh is aboard. Then call the chief mate and the crew for mooring stations.'

An hour later, we were safely alongside West Wharf. Mr Khoo retired to his cabin taking Poh with him. Da Silva supplied them with a large pot of coffee and Mr Khoo invited me to join them. Normally I would have, but after only a couple of hours' sleep in the last two days, I was ready for the blissful oblivion of my bunk.

I told McGrath to take care of any officials that dared to venture aboard before breakfast, or to hand them over to Poh to deal with. He grinned—rather more cheerfully than the situation demanded—and wished me pleasant dreams.

All thoughts of sleep vanished when I opened my cabin door and smelled Helena's perfume. I quietly shut the door, left the light off and pulled open the blackout curtains. Sufficient moonlight filtered in through the porthole for me to see the outline of her naked body under the bed sheet. I stripped off my clothes and stepped into the shower in my tiny bathroom. A quick cold splash washed off the day's sweat and grime, and when I emerged, towelling myself dry, Helena was sitting up in bed, clasping the sheet under her chin.

'I wouldn't have minded the caveman, but that was thoughtful of you.' Her eyes sparkled in the dim light.

'It's been a long couple of days, I'm whacked.'

She dropped the sheet and held out her arms. 'You poor boy. I won't keep you up longer than necessary.'

She made room on the bed. I slid myself alongside her and the pale moonlight bathed our entwined bodies.

CHAPTER SIXTEEN

Forenoon, Saturday 13 December 1941

F our days later, I was leaning against the bridge wing rail, enjoying a late morning coffee and watching thunderclouds build up in the Strait.

The Inner Roads' anchorage had its usual bustle of lightering ships, and it was hard to believe there was a war on. There had been no further air raids and, reading the news in *The Straits Times*, one could be forgiven for thinking the Nazis were a greater threat than the Japanese, less than four hundred miles to the north. Even the sinking of *Repulse* and *Prince of Wales* was outranked by reports of Nazi attacks around Sevastopol, and an 18-month-old account of the British Army's successful evacuation of Dunkirk. It was not until page six, after the shipping notices and advertisements for the cinema—Ronald Reagan was starring in *International Squadron* at the *Alhambra*—that the headline read: *Testing Times*. Stunning as the news was, Duff Cooper, the British Resident Minister, reassured readers that, despite the sinkings and the Japanese landings, the defensive spring of the armed forces would hold until the pressure on it weakened, then snap back to give the Japanese a bloody nose.

To Singaporeans looking forward to the Japanese recoiling from a whack on the nose, the first air raids had come as a shock. I had seen the blown-out shop-front windows in Raffles Place and the partly demolished offices of Guthrie and Company, the oldest British Trading house in South-East Asia. Sixty people had been killed in Chinatown, but the Europeans seemed more concerned about the damage to the hallowed turf of the Padang.

Since then, the blackout was better enforced, although that brought the additional risk of being run over by cars driving with masked headlights. None of this had, as yet, affected work at the docks and our cargo of rice had been unloaded promptly. According to Poh it was badly needed. Rice was not grown in Malaya, and the Japanese had done their best to interfere with normal shipments from Thailand and Indochina. Once our holds were empty, we moved under the coal chute to re-fill our bunkers. It was a dirty process as ever, with coal dust hanging about the ship and penetrating every opening. I was glad when it was over and we moved out to the anchorage to await orders.

What they might be I tried not to speculate. Poh said large quantities of rubber were accumulating in the godowns, stockpiled by the trading houses hoping to cash in on a surge in demand. The wartime government had imposed an excess profits tax to discourage racketeering, but the glint in Poh's eyes suggested there were ways to circumvent it. If so, it would not be the first time we had carried illicit cargoes.

As for Helena, Mr Khoo had taken her to his newly rented bungalow in Tanglin. Amongst the bustle of officialdom and paperwork, there had been time for only a handshake and a brief kiss on the cheek. The following day, she sent an intimate note on scented paper inviting me to visit whenever my duties permitted. With the ship empty, safely anchored and all the paperwork in order, I decided to accept her offer. I broke the news to McGrath that I was leaving him in charge for a couple of days and moving ashore to Raffles Hotel. I asked Poh to reserve a room and handed him a note for Helena inviting her to meet me in the lobby for afternoon tea. I did not mention the room. I would surprise her with it if ... well, I was probably a bit long in the tooth to be crossing fingers. Poh, the old rogue, was enough of a romantic to keep a straight face when he told me the bridal suite was the only room available. He also delivered a note from Colonel Spencer inviting me to lunch at the Singapore Club and suggesting I come in uniform. It was less than a week since I had dropped him ashore at Kota Bharu. How had he evaded the Japanese and made it to Singapore so quickly?

I drained the last of the coffee and went in search of Da Silva. I found him in my cabin, neatly stowing enough clothes into a valise to last a week. Laid out on the bed were my best white uniform trousers and shirt, freshly pressed with the buttons polished.

'Where's Mr Poh?' I pulled off my khakis and changed into the crisply starched whites.

'He with Chief Engineer. Tasting whisky.' The fierce glint in his sole eye spoke of more than just tasting.

Miraculously, Poh had scoured Singapore's bonded warehouses

and managed to locate a case of Laphroaig, Fraser's favourite single malt. I was not surprised they were sampling its contents.

I pulled on my best cap and checked my appearance in the mirror. I had shaved that morning, but my jaw was already fringed in dark shadow. There were flecks of grey in the unruly hair escaping from under the cap, and even several nights of uninterrupted sleep had not totally erased the dark circles under my eyes. The deep wrinkles surrounding them were there to stay. I smiled, to reassure myself I was not about to frighten horses or small children, and headed for the door.

'Take that sea bag down to the launch. I'll go and fetch Mr Poh.'

I pushed aside the privacy curtain to the chief engineer's cabin and found them grinning like schoolboys. Judging by the level in the bottle, the sampling had been extensive.

'Sit ya'sel down an enjoy a wee dram, ya lucky bastard,' said Fraser.

'No thanks, Angus. I've been summoned by Colonel Spencer. Best bib and tucker.'

'Wondered why ya looked so smart. Thought ya might be wanting tae impress a certain person.'

There was no point narrowing my eyes or scowling, he knew me too well to react. In any case, he was right. I was a lucky bastard, and the smile on my face probably resembled that of a cat discovering a bowl of cream. There was a spring in my step and a sense of antici-pation I had not felt for a while; not since the previous November in Liverpool when I had met Teresa.

'If I didn't know you better, I'd say you were jealous.'

'Aye man, who would'na be. She's a fine lassie. Maybe if I was ten years younger, I'd give you a run for ya money.' He shook his head and took a large slug of whisky. 'Awa wi' ya William. Dinna keep the colonel or the lady waiting. It's not good manners.' He pushed him-self out of the chair and reached for my hand. 'You deserve a break, man. The auld ship'll still be here when ya get back. We'll tak good care of her.'

'Thanks Angus.' I shook his hand and nodded at Poh.

He followed me to the gangway and down into the waiting launch. It was some time since I had seen the ship from water level in daylight, so I told the launch skipper to take a turn around her. Close up, the evidence of her mounting years was clearly visible. Her black hull was in desperate need of scraping and painting. Rust streaked from the anchor pads, scuppers and overboard discharges. The hungry horse appearance of her bow plating, with its protruding ribs and stringers, spoke of years of battering into heavy seas. The draught marks were almost unreadable and I made a mental note to remind McGrath to have them repainted.

Above the hull, the superstructure, masts and derricks were a patchwork of white, cream, buff and brown, interspersed with eruptions of rust and splotches of red lead where the crew were battling the corroding salt. But, despite her worn, battered appearance, she still bore the eye-pleasing sheer and camber of a thoroughbred. She would never set any speed records. Even newly built, on sea trials, she had only managed ten and a half knots, but she was as sea-kindly a design as ever slipped down the ways of Thompsons in Sunderland.

The grey painted muzzles of the naval guns on the forecastle and poop struck an ugly, discordant note. She had been built to trade, not fight. Some sailors swore that ships had souls. Could she feel those guns, like two unsightly blemishes on the face of an otherwise beautiful woman? Even I would never have called *Oriental Venture* beautiful, but she was my first and, so far, only command and I looked upon her with all the affection of first love.

Poh watched me silently. I was not the only one with a soft spot for the old lady. She had served the owners well, and helped him secure his fortune. I was not jealous; I had also accrued a sizeable nest egg.

'Good ship. Make owners very happy,' he said, echoing my thoughts.

Once clear of the ship, the skipper opened the throttles and we bounced across the short chop of the anchorage towards the Master Attendant's Pier. It was a warm, humid morning and, even in the breeze of our passage, I could feel the sweat trickle down my back. Threatening clouds filled the sky and it looked like being a race between the arrival of a downpour and my own at the Fullerton Building.

Approaching the pier, the skipper throttled back.

I handed Poh an envelope. 'Please see this is delivered to Miss Markova. And have my suitcase taken to Raffles.'

'Of course, Captain. Enjoy your lunch. If there is any news I know where to find you.'

The launch nosed alongside the pier allowing me to step off. I walked up the decking to the shelter of the trees lining Fullerton Road. Approaching noon, the traffic was heavy. To my right, the sturdy low arch of Anderson Bridge carried the road across the

Singapore River. Waiting for a break in the traffic, I crossed to the other side. The massive, pale grey stone edifice of the Fullerton Building loomed over me. The southern end housed the General Post Office and the northern end the Marine Office. I walked around the corner towards Cavendish Bridge and Boat Quay, where sampans and tongkangs were thickly jammed in ranks extending almost across the river. Hundreds of families lived their entire lives afloat in them, lightering ships anchored in the roads and carrying their cargoes to the coastal settlements of Johore, Malacca and further afield. As the first drops of rain fell, I turned towards the building and sprinted to the discrete side entrance to the Singapore Club. A uniformed Sikh doorman checked my name against the guest list and escorted me to the staircase leading to the first floor.

Colonel Spencer met me at the reception desk and signed the register. His uniform was clean and freshly pressed, but he looked tired and drawn.

'Welcome to the Singapore Club.' He stuck out a hand.

'How did you manage to wangle your way in here?' It was the most exclusive in Singapore. Only Tuan Besars, the most influential and wealthy European men, were invited to join.

He tapped his nose. 'Friends of friends. I've been granted temporary membership.' He cast an approving eye over my whites. 'You scrub up well. Between the two of us we look important enough to belong here.' He touched my arm. 'Come along, I'll show you how the top five percent live.'

He led me upstairs to the club's main rooms on the second floor. Our footsteps clacked on the marblette tiles and echoed off the granite faced walls and columns. Pushing open an ornate brass door, he ushered me into an enormous room with a long, polished wooden bar. Despite the rain, the tall windows were open to admit a cooling breeze and offer a grand view across Fullerton Road to the anchorage.

'I haven't paced it, but they say this bar is over two hundred feet long.' Spencer found an empty table and summoned a waiter. 'I've booked for lunch, but there's time for a snifter first. What'll you have?'

'Tanduay and soda.'

Spencer chose whisky. As we waited for our drinks, I cast my eye around the bar. It was full of linen suited men, the top strata of the Straits' establishment, puffing on cigars and knocking back Stengahs, the Malay name for fifty-fifty whisky and soda water.

With the war raging only a few hundred miles away, it was also surprising to see that Colonel Spencer was not the only man in uniform; there was enough gold braid to delight a bullion dealer. On the far side of the room, a group huddled around a wireless listening to a news broadcast.

'Impressive, eh? There's a library and card rooms through there.' Spencer pointed towards open doorways at the end. 'There's also a six-table billiard room with a vaulted ceiling and, on the other side, facing Battery Road, is the dining room. The bedrooms are on the third and fourth floors. I didn't have enough pull to get one with a sea view, but it's a darn sight better than the officers' quarters at Tanglin Barracks.'

The waiter returned with our drinks, the amber-coloured spirits glinting in cut glass. He left a Schweppes' syphon on the table.

Spencer splashed soda water into his drink and raised it. 'To the Royal Australian Air Force.' He saw my raised eyebrow. 'How do you think I got here so fast? Hitched a lift in one of their Hudsons.'

I topped up the rum and took a sip. 'Did it make any difference, your delivering the intelligence about the invasion fleets?'

'Hardly a damn.' The knuckles of the fist gripping the glass turned white and, for a moment, I feared he would crush it. 'They already knew about the fleet in the Gulf.'

'The Catalina we sighted?'

Spencer shook his head. 'I don't know if it was the same one, but a Catalina was reported missing that day. It was probably shot down before it could radio a report. No, a Hudson from Kota Bharu had already spotted the fleet three hundred miles out on Saturday afternoon, twenty-four hours before I got there. Instead of launching Operation Matador straight away, the damned fools just sent the information up the tree to the C-in-C in Singapore and waited to be told what to do. He sat on his arse and did nothing.'

'Did they warn the Americans?'

'If they did, it didn't make a blind bit of difference. Caught the US Navy at Pearl Harbour with its pants around its ankles.'

I nodded. The news bulletins had reported nine battleships sunk or seriously damaged. Fortunately, the aircraft carriers had been at sea and escaped unharmed. 'Maslennikov got what he wanted, then. They've stung the Americans into the war.'

Spencer drained his Stengah and waved to the waiter to fetch another. 'That bastard got what he deserved. I should have killed him myself.'

'Still, it means the Yanks are coming.'

'They might be too late to save us here.'

'The news reports say we're holding on up north.'

'Do they?'

The waiter arrived with the whisky. Spencer splashed in soda and took a large swallow. 'I'm sorry you had to wait off Kota Bharu for Lakshman. An Indian lieutenant thought we were Japanese spies. It took a visit to Brigade HQ to convince him otherwise. Good man Brigadier Key, commander of the Eighth Indian Brigade. He patched me a call through to Singapore. All too late by then of course. But his men were ready when the Japanese came ashore just after midnight.'

'We heard them. The beaches seemed to be taking a helluva pounding.'

'It wasn't all one sided. The Indians spotted the ships just after midnight and opened up with their 18-pounders. The Australians managed to get five Hudsons into the air. They smashed up a cruiser, sank one transport and damaged several others. It didn't stop the landings, though. The beach you were anchored off was hit first. Two companies of the Dogra Regiment, including that lieutenant, bore the brunt of it. They fought bloody hard, until the Japs found the creek mouth, motored their landing craft up it and outflanked them. They drove the Dogras back off the beach, but they dug in and kept the airfield operational for a few hours.'

He paused to take another mouthful of whisky.

'How did you get away?'

'The surviving Hudsons were ordered south and I grabbed a seat in one of them. The airfield was abandoned after we took off. The maintenance crews headed for the railway, but the stupid bastards left the runway intact, and a bloody great stock of bombs and petrol as a gift. So next time there's an air raid ...' He reached for his glass, gulped the rest of the whisky and waved to the waiter for a refill.

'Would you not like to put a base under that?'

'You worried I might get drunk and embarrass you?' He pointed at my half-full glass. 'Not going temperance, are you?'

His cheeks were flushed and his eyes burned with a feverish light. 'You know what really gives me the shits about all this?'

I shook my head and waited for him to continue.

'The normality of it.' He waved his glass in the direction of the room, filled with men enjoying their pre-tiffin drinks and conversation. 'We've had two battleships sunk. There are Japanese troops swarming all over northern Malaya. They've seized Hong Kong, invaded the Philippines and smashed the American Pacific fleet. Yet here, you'd think the Empire was as solid as rock.' He reached into his pocket and dragged out a page of newspaper. 'Have you read this from bloody Brooke-Popham? Instead of ordering Operation Matador, he waits until the Japanese are ashore and then issues an order of the day.' He shook the paper under my nose. 'Here it is, the Commander-in-Chief, as published in *The Straits Times* on Monday.'

I reached my hand out for it.

'Don't bother, I know it by heart. *Japan will find that she has made a grievous mistake,*' he recited, in plummy upper-class parody. '*We are confident. Our defences are strong and our weapons efficient. Whatever our race, and whether we are in our native land or have come thousands of miles, we have one aim and one only. It is to defend these shores.*' He swallowed more whisky. 'Grievous mistake my arse. That's the sort of tripe only an Englishman could write. The Malays and Indians will wait and see who's winning before deciding where their sentiments lie, and why shouldn't they? They've seen bugger all benefit from the white man's so-called civilisation. The Malays have had their land taken over for rubber plantations and thousands of Indians have taken the jobs they used to do. Only the Chinese might support us, not because they give a damn about the British Empire but because, with what's going on in China, they hate the Japanese more than us.'

He pointed at my glass. 'For God's sake, drink up and let me get you another one.' He waved for the waiter. 'I've lost my appetite, but if you're hungry they do a good club sandwich.'

The waiter took the order and bustled away. Spencer reached into his pocket, pulled out a pack of cheroots and offered me one. I shook my head.

'Sorry, can't get used to not seeing you with a Senior Service smouldering between your fingers. You don't mind …?' He lit up without waiting for an answer and dragged in a lungful of smoke.

'Today's *Straits Times* is just as bad,' he continued. 'Judging by the reports you'd be forgiven for thinking it was all quiet on the northern front. The editor, whoever the hell he is, says we're fighting for time … and winning. Winning! God save me from armchair fucking generals.'

He fell silent as the waiter returned with the drinks and a neat row of triangular toasted sandwiches, picketed together with toothpicks. I topped up the rum with soda water and reached for a triangle. Spencer watched me eat, smoking furiously and taking frequent sips at his Stengah. With narrowed eyes, flushed face and a bristling moustache, he looked like a wild boar about to charge.

Frustrated by my silence, he leaned across the table. 'Well, aren't you curious to know what's really going on up there?'

'Should you be telling me?'

'What are you gonna do, call the head-up-his arse Governor, Sir Thomas Bloody Shenton, and tell him it's time to evacuate.'

'Is it?'

'Just a matter of time. He got that bit right, the editor at *The Straits Times*. We're fighting for time, but there might not be much of it.' He reached for the plate, grabbed a triangle and stuffed it into his mouth. 'Might as well make the most of this'—he flung out an arm to encompass the bar—'while it lasts.' He beckoned me closer with a finger. 'You remember what I told you about Operation Matador?'

I nodded. 'The planned advance into southern Thailand to stop the Japanese getting hold of it.'

'Yes, the one that didn't happen. Army HQ had over twenty-four hours' notice that the invasion fleet was on its way but, instead of rushing them over the border, they ordered the troops to sit tight. So the main landings at Pattani and Singora were unopposed, the Thais were easily brushed aside. That put the Japanese astride the main roads across the peninsula, which connect with the west coast roads running all the way to Singapore. Instead of stopping them before they got there, we're now fighting to hold those roads. The main one crosses the border at Jitra in the north-west. We had the whole Eleventh Division there. The other road winds through the mountains to Kroh. About thirty-five miles over the border in Thailand it passes through a ravine. The narrowest point is called The Ledge, six miles of winding road cut into the side of a very steep hill. Blowing it up would send the entire road sliding into the valley and delay an attacker for weeks. On the other hand, if the Japs get down that road, they outflank Jitra.' He paused to draw breath and take a drag at the cheroot.

'A battalion of the Punjabi Regiment was sent forward on Monday to seize The Ledge. God only knows why the hell they didn't start as soon as they got word of the landings. Once they crossed the border, they were pinned down by a handful of Thai policemen taking pot shots from the jungle. Policemen! So they dug in for the night to wait for reinforcements. The next day the police felled logs in front of the trucks and the Punjabis manged to advance only five miles.' He slapped his hand against the table top. 'Five miles for Christ's sake! They eventually got to The Ledge on Wednesday evening having taken forty-eight hours to get there. And when they did ... they found the fucking Japs had beaten them too it. They'd twice as far to come from Pattani, and they still got there first. As we speak, the Punjabis are retreating across the border at Kroh with the enemy snapping at their heels.'

Spencer reached for the glass and took another swallow. His voice had risen and I glanced around. Over the hubbub of conversation no one appeared to have heard him. To be sure, I raised my finger to my lips. He nodded and continued in a calmer tone.

'As if that was not bad enough, the Japanese at Singora made quick time down the road to Jitra. Leading the way was a battalion and a half of infantry supported by a company of tanks. Last night that spearhead routed Eleventh Division, forcing it back over the Kedah River.' He shook his head as if in disbelief. 'Fifteen hundred men and a few tanks routed an entire division. And they're already outflanked. If the Japanese at Kroh can get down the road to the coast south of Butterworth, they'll have the whole Division in the bag. There are whispers we'll have to fall back to the Perak River.' He stabbed his finger onto the table top. 'That's one hundred miles further south.'

'Can they be stopped?' I asked.

'Of course they can. They have to be. They're not super human. The further south they come the longer their supply lines are stretched. They'll run out of steam eventually, then weight of numbers will tell. And there are more troops on the way from Australia and Britain.' He took another drag of the cheroot. His face was still flushed, but the familiar twinkle had returned to his eye. 'That's the plan anyway. Hold them as long as possible while we prepare defensive positions, wait for them to outrun their supply lines and ... seize the initiative.'

'What's your part in all this?'

'I'm to be attached to the Eighth Australian Division. At the moment they're in Johore training, ready to move north.' He stubbed the cheroot into the ashtray and drained the last of his whisky. 'I'm sorry. 'I've been a bore. I invited you to lunch, not to hear me prattle on.' A rueful smile spread across his lips. 'I probably shouldn't have told you all that. If I can't buy your silence, I'll have to kill you.'

'What are you offering?'

'What do you want?'

'Free passage to a deserted tropical island where I see out the war in peace.'

'Anyone in particular you'd like to share it with?'

'I'll send you a list.'

His laughter was hard edged. 'You drive a hard bargain, Rowden. Maybe I'll have to make you a counter offer.' He glanced at his wristwatch, raised his hand and waved for the waiter. 'Is there anything else I can get you? I've got to dash. Afternoon intelligence briefing at Command House.'

I shook my head.

Spencer signed the chit, pushed back his chair and reached out a hand. 'Give my regards to Helena.'

I shook his hand and watched him elbow his way through the crowd to the door. Draining the last of my drink, I consulted my own watch. It was almost 2.30pm. I had asked Helena to meet me at Raffles at three.

It had stopped raining when I stepped onto the pavement. I flagged down a taxi on Battery Road and settled back for the short ride across Anderson Bridge, past the Padang and over the Stamford Canal. Turning off Beach Road, the taxi pulled into the palm-lined driveway leading to the familiar white painted facade. I gave the driver a handsome tip, accepted the salute of the liveried doorman and stepped into the spacious lobby.

CHAPTER SEVENTEEN

Afternoon and evening, Saturday 13 December 1941

The lobby was crowded and abuzz with animated conversation. A camera flash bulb fired and I blinked to restore my vision. Elbowing my way through the commotion, I spotted Helena seated at a table opposite a young Eurasian woman clutching a notebook. Around them swirled a press of men and women with admiration—or was it longing—painted on their excited faces.

Helena glanced up as I squeezed out of the throng and beckoned me to join them.

'Sorry Scott, word seems to have spread that there's a Hollywood star visiting Raffles.' She waved me to a seat. 'This is Miss Chan. She writes the Social Spotlight column for *The Straits Times*. Miss Chan, meet Randolph Scott.'

Miss Chan scrutinised me through thick-lensed, tortoise shell spectacles. 'Excuse me, Captain Scott. I won't keep Miss Markova long.'

'I'm sorry to disappoint you Miss Chan,' I said, trying not to smile. 'I'm not Randolph Scott, nor a naval captain. Miss Markova is teasing me. William Rowden, master of a tramp steamer anchored in the roads.'

'Oh! How interesting. How do you come to know Miss Markova?'

I was about to reply, but Helena cut me off.

'Captain Rowden and I are old friends. I took passage in his ship back in nineteen thirty-seven. On my way home to Shanghai from Hong Kong.'

'I see.' Miss Chan jotted another entry in her notebook. 'And now you're on a whirlwind tour of the East, to promote your latest picture?'

'Movie, Miss Chan. That's what we call them in Hollywood, movies. But yes, I've visited Honolulu, Hong Kong, Manila and now

Singapore. I took tea with General MacArthur at the Manila Hotel. He's a great fan, and such a charming man.'

While Miss Chan took notes in shorthand, Helena expounded upon her trip in an accent blending California with her native Russian. Mixing colourful anecdotes with titbits of gossip about the co-stars with whom she had appeared, she wove lies into the truth with the ease of years of practise as spy and actress. I knew she had performed in racy cabarets in Paris and Berlin, and starred in plays by Oscar Wilde and Somerset Maugham on the London stage. She acquired a title by marrying a minor English aristocrat and was a double agent for British Intelligence. She had even faked her own death. This was just the latest role I had seen her play. Which one, if any, including the one she played in my bed, was the real woman? And did I care?

Miss Chan completed the latest entry in her notebook and opened her mouth to frame another question.

'I hope you'll forgive me, Miss Chan. But I do have another engagement.'

The notebook snapped shut. 'Of course. Thank you so much for your time. If I could ask just one more. Are you thinking of staying long, under the current ... circumstances?'

'I don't know. I've only just arrived. But everyone assures me that we are quite safe here in Singapore.' Helena leaned forward and offered her hand. 'So nice to meet you, Miss Chan.'

The journalist stuffed her pen and notebook back into her handbag, shook Helena's hand and disappeared through the lobby

'Tiresome woman,' said Helena, as soon as Miss Chan was out of earshot. 'So many questions.'

'You didn't seem to mind the attention.'

'Miss Markova didn't mind. She thrives on it. I, on the other hand...'

'But aren't you afraid of being recognised?'

'I can't hide for the rest of my life. And I'm not exactly inconspicuous. But it's years since I was in Singapore. And Lady Ashworth, despite her shady past, was hardly the stuff on which the society pages thrived. I'll just have to hide in plain sight. Now, would you mind summoning the head waiter. I've had enough of being gawped at. Find us somewhere more private.'

The dining room was less crowed, but we were still the focus of sly glances from those at adjacent tables.

'Now you know what it's like to be the centre of attention,' said

Helena. 'Ignore them, the novelty will wear off eventually.'

The waiter arrived pushing a trolley from which he unloaded an afternoon tea sufficient to sustain a small army. There were scones with jam and cream, profiteroles and thinly cut cucumber sandwiches. I reached for a sandwich while Helena poured tea. I disliked cucumber but, after missing lunch, I was ravenous. I had eaten half of the sandwiches before I noticed Helena eyeing me with curiosity.

'I know the best way to a man's heart is through his stomach. But have you not eaten today?'

'I was supposed to have lunch with Colonel Spencer at the Singapore Club. He said he wasn't hungry, ordered me a club sandwich … and then ate half of it.'

'Mr Poh told me Spencer had arrived from Kota Bharu.' She reached for a profiterole and bit off a chunk. Smears of chocolate clung to her lips. She rolled her tongue around them to lick it off. 'So! When were you planning to tell me you'd booked the bridal suite?' Her eyes narrowed, like those of a cat poised to spring onto its prey. 'And have you also organised a Russian Orthodox Priest?'

Humour seemed the best line of defence. 'If there's one in Singapore, old Poh will know where to find him. Do I need to get down on one knee first?'

Helena cocked her head to one side and frowned. 'Don't push your luck. And don't be presumptuous. I hate being taken for granted.'

'I wasn't. I decided the ship could spare me for a couple of nights, and that was the only room they could offer.'

'You'll have plenty of room for yourself, then. Unless you find someone to share it.'

'I was hoping—'

'Hoping! Is that the best you can do?' She shook her head in disapproval. 'Too busy hoping to get me into bed and stuffing your face to notice anything else.'

I had indeed been too busy satisfying my hunger to pay attention to how gorgeous Helena looked. She was wearing a slim-waisted, turquoise afternoon dress with a matching wide-brimmed hat. It was too late to attempt an apology.

'You look lovely.' I reached for a scone. 'Would you like half?'

'Pah! I might as well be wearing sackcloth.' She shook her head. 'Stop trying to ruin my figure, Rowden. A moment on the lips, forever on the hips. Anyway, I didn't dress up just for you. I have to look my best for my admirers.'

I finished the scone and washed it down with the last of the tea.

'Has Poh made any progress booking you a passage home to the States?'

Her eyes flashed, but I caught the twinkle in them. 'He hasn't seen me for three days. And already he wants rid of me.'

'That's the last thing I want. Actually, I'm just thinking of your safety. Things might get pretty hot around here.'

'Everyone assures me that Singapore will never fall to the Japanese.'

'Maybe not. But it doesn't mean it's safe to stay.' Having listened to Spencer earlier, keeping the Japanese out of Singapore seemed an even bet at best. No one would thank me for repeating it now.

'That's what Mr Poh says, too. But since last Sunday, there are no flights or passages across the Pacific. He's trying to book me a berth with P&O, at least as far as India. Now stop trying to scare me. If you've finished stuffing your face, call for the waiter and sign the chit.'

I could feel the eyes burning into my back as I escorted Helena through the lobby to the elevator.

'Scandalous, isn't it. Miss Markova and the mysterious captain heading off upstairs. And it's not even four o'clock.'

'We could always play snooker in the billiard room.'

'I've never understood the male obsession with sticks and balls. The only thing you're going to pot this afternoon … is me. And afterwards, if you don't wear me out, I expect to be taken to the Saturday evening dinner dance.'

The bridal suite was on the top floor and enjoyed a view across to the sea. I swung open the windows to let in the breeze and pulled the shutters closed for privacy. Dust danced in the thin shafts of afternoon sunlight streaming in between the wooden slats.

I pulled open the doors to the wardrobe to find my valise had been unpacked and my clothes hung on hangers. Helena's gowns hung alongside them. I turned to find her grinning at me.

'What? Did you think I was going naked for the rest of the day? I brought an overnight bag. Girl Guide's motto. Be prepared.'

'I thought that was the Scouts.'

'They're supposed to be clean in thought, word and deed.' Helena unpinned her hat and tossed it onto a chair. 'In which case they're no use to me.' She turned her back. 'I do hope you know what to do with a zip?'

I slid it down as slowly as my rising excitement would allow. With a wriggle of her hips, the dress puddled around Helena's ankles. She sashayed over to the bed in her underwear, lay down and beckoned me.

'I love a man in uniform ... but I love a man out of one even more. Ditch it. Then come and unwrap the rest of me.'

Free of the prospect of interruption by Da Silva's knock, or a yell from the watchkeeper, Helena made love with a passionate intensity that seemed to unravel the strands of my being and braid them back afresh. I felt as if I had awakened into a new world, in which everything looked the same but was utterly different. The feeling wouldn't last. It never did.

Afterwards, we dozed side by side and enjoyed the sea breeze cooling our sweat-burnished bodies. The sun was setting, the last of the light painting the undersides of the clouds in purple and scarlet. Above the low rumble of the evening traffic on Beach Road, the buzz of cicadas and the chuck, chuck of a gecko accompanied our breathing. Rolling onto my side, I watched the slow rise and fall of Helena's bosom. Her eyes were closed, but she was smiling.

'Are you asleep?'

'Yes. I'm dreaming.'

'What about?'

She rolled to face me and opened her eyes. Gazing into them, I again felt the sensation of floating in a sea of mesmerising emerald.

'I'm dreaming I spent the afternoon making love with a wonderful man. I'm afraid to wake up.'

'Why? In case he's gone?'

'No. In case he's still here.'

I glanced over my shoulder. 'Where?'

Her soft laugh set my pulse racing.

'Take a compliment when it's offered, Rowden.' She placed a fingertip over my lips. 'But don't spoil things by telling me I'm wonderful. Beautiful, perhaps. Do you know how many men have told me I'm beautiful? You don't want to know the answer to that ... more than enough to know it must be true. Good in bed? Well, I haven't heard many complaints. But there are plenty of fifty-cent taxi-girls that are beautiful and good in bed. Apart from that? I can't cook, I can't sew, I hate children and I refuse to clean house and wash dishes. I spend far too long in front of a mirror and I'm an accomplished liar. Oh, and I'm also a murderer. Honestly, how wonderful would a man have to be to put up with someone like that?'

'And here was I feeling grateful to find myself in bed with you.'

Her punch stung my chest.

'Grateful is what you are when a lady offers you a cup of tea. I ain't no lady, mister. I get too hungry for dinner at eight and I never go to Harlem in ermine and pearls'—she pronounced them Brooklyn fashion as oymin and poyles—'I'm just a tramp, or maybe a China Coaster, a woman getting by with whatever assets God gave her. You don't need to be grateful. I've given you a part of me, but it was a fair exchange. I've taken just as big a part of you.' She erupted in giggles and clapped a hand over her mouth. 'I didn't mean to sound so vulgar. But then you do know what bad girls say?'

I shook my head.

'It's hard to find a good man, but it's good to find a hard one.' She reached for me. Her jaw dropped and her eyes arched in feigned surprise. 'Oohh! Again? It looks like it's my lucky day.'

'And mine. And mine.'

To my surprise, Helena spent very little time in either the bath or in front of the mirror.

She chuckled when she saw me confirm by my watch that the entire transformation from lover to lady had taken just half an hour.

'I'm starving. I told you I couldn't wait until eight.'

It was just after seven, when she swept into the ballroom. Her ankle length, pale green, waist-tied gown accentuated her tumbling auburn hair, and heads swivelled in her direction. She was holding my arm but, even in the snug fitting dinner jacket, none of the eyes had time for me.

Poh's influence and her movie star status guaranteed us a central table close to the dance floor. I would have preferred something more intimate in a secluded corner, where we were not the centre of attention again. Transfixed in the gaze of dozens of pairs of admiring eyes, I felt pangs of jealousy until Helena nudged me and whispered, 'Most of the women in the room want to be me and the men want to be you.'

Having shown us to our seats, the head waiter snapped his fingers and the sommelier appeared with a bottle of Moët et Chandon Imperial.

'With the compliments of the house.' He deftly extracted the cork with a gentle hiss and poured two foaming glasses.

'We're lucky they still have any,' said Helena. 'The Nazis billeted troops at the winery and requisitioned most of its stock. What shall we drink to?'

I swirled the wine around in the glass, watching the bubbles form at its base and stream to the surface. 'May the best days of our past be the worst of our future, and may our stay in hell be as pleasant as the journey.'

'That was very eloquent, for an Englishman.' Helena chinked her glass against mine and drained it. 'Don't look at me like that. There's no law says you have to sip champagne.'

I refilled it while she studied the menu. It bore little resemblance to the rationing version offered by the Adelphi Hotel in Liverpool, the night I took Teresa to the dinner dance. There was clear turtle soup, a fillet of sole, medallions of beef and wild rose ice cream. We made our selections, sipped champagne and listed to the band playing swing and jazz hits. Under the table, Helena rubbed her leg against mine. The ballroom was full of women in elegant gowns and men in white or black dinner jackets, with only the occasional military uniform as an unwelcome reminder that the war was only a few hundred miles to the north.

Helena reached into her handbag for the enamelled cigarette case and screwed a pink Sobranie into her ivory cigarette holder. I reached for her gold lighter and rasped the flint. She took an elegant draw through pursed lips and my nostrils twitched at the smell of rich Balkan tobacco. The sudden urge to smoke was almost overwhelming. Had they not been pink I would probably have accepted one. Instead, I wrestled with temptation and was only saved by the sight of two uniformed officers and their companion, a young man in a cream linen suit, in animated conversation with the head waiter at the entrance to the ballroom.

'Is anything the matter?'

'That's my third mate, Lakshman.' I nodded in the direction of the entrance. 'I expect one of the army officers he's with is his brother.'

Helena turned towards the doorway. The head waiter was shaking his head. 'If there isn't a spare table invite them to join us.'

I pushed back my chair. 'Excuse me while I go and see what the trouble is.'

I could see what the trouble was well before I got there and heard the head waiter's emphatic, 'I'm sorry gentlemen, I cannot admit you.'

One of the officers was half a head taller than either of his companions. He wore the uniform of an Indian Army captain. He loomed over the head waiter, his dark eyes flashing outrage, but his voice was icy calm.

'What is the reason you are denying us entry?'

'I have already explained, gentlemen. This is a dinner dance. You are not correctly dressed.'

They paid no attention to my approach, until Lakshman's eyes lit up when he recognised me.

'Good evening, Mr Lakshman. Is there a problem?'

'Ah, Captain sir. The gentleman is telling us that we cannot enter the ballroom because we are improperly dressed.'

'Is that so.' I turned to the head waiter. If he was expecting support, he was about to be disappointed. I swept an arm in the direction of the ballroom where there was still a scattering of empty tables. 'I can see a number of uniforms, and even one or two lounge suits. These gentlemen are as well dressed as any of those.'

The head waiter's eyes flashed daggers. He was in a bind and he knew it. Unlike the exclusive Europeans only clubs, Raffles was open to anyone who could afford it, in theory. In practice, there were other ways of enforcing a colour bar. Imposing a dress code was one of them, even if there were Europeans dressed no differently. Most non-Europeans could not be bothered with the embarrassment of an argument.

'I am afraid all the tables are booked.' The head waiter was not going down without a fight. A braying shout made it unnecessary.

'I say! Move those wogs along. There are people here waiting to be seated.'

The young man who had spoken had a self-satisfied smirk on his ruddy cheeked face. Perhaps one too many Singapore Slings in the Long Bar had bolstered his courage. Or maybe he was trying to impress his male companion and their simpering girlfriends.

I strode towards him flashing my friendliest smile and offered my hand.

He shook it … and gasped with pain as I crushed his fingers and twisted his wrist.

'If that remark was aimed at these gentlemen, then I'd advise you to apologise. One is my third officer and the others are captains in the Indian Army, which, in case you haven't heard, is fighting for your miserable lives not three hundred miles away.' I squeezed harder, forcing another squeal of pain. 'If you don't, you and I are going outside where I'll teach you the benefit of good manners.'

'Let me go you thug. Jeremy, go and fetch a policeman.'

'Take one step Jeremy and this little shit will regret the day he was born.' I balled my left fist and cocked it in his face. 'What's it to be?'

'All right, all right. Let me go. I'm sorry.'

I released my grip and swung him around. 'Tell them.'

'I ... I apologise.' He flexed his fingers to check that none were broken.

'Now beat it before I change my mind.'

He hesitated, as if the effects of gin sling had reignited his courage, then grabbed his girl by the arm and stalked off back towards the bar. Jeremy muttered something which I chose to ignore, before he and the other girl followed them.

I straightened my sleeves and turned to find the taller Indian captain regarding me with thoughtful eyes. He drew himself to attention.

'Captain Lakshman. Seventh Battalion, Mahratta Light Infantry.' He gestured to his fellow officer, a turbaned Sikh with a thick black beard. 'Captain Mohan Singh, Punjab Regiment.'

'Captain Rowden, master of *Oriental Venture*. I have the honour of commanding your brother.' I stuck out a hand.

Captain Lakshman seized and pumped it. 'Thank you, sir, but that was unnecessary.'

'Maybe. But it made me feel better.' I turned to the scowling head waiter. 'Miss Markova has invited these gentlemen to join us.'

The scowl switched into a beaming smile as I pressed a tip into his hand. 'Welcome to the ballroom, gentlemen. Please accompany me.'

I turned, expecting them to follow, but Singh placed a restraining hand on Captain Lakshman's arm.

I could not understand the stream of fiercely whispered Hindi, but it's meaning was unmistakable. Lakshman's eyes dropped to the floor.

When the tirade stopped, Captain Lakshman turned to me. 'Thank you for your invitation, Captain. But we are not welcome here and do not wish to cause you or the lady any further embarrassment.' His voice was steady, but the veins in his temples bulged. 'Thank you again, but we shall leave you to your dinner.'

He took a step back, nodded and wheeled around as if on parade. Captain Singh said nothing, but the hatred in his eyes would have seared any of the diners who caught sight of it. He turned his back on me and stalked away.

Loyalties torn between his brother and his captain, young Lakshman hesitated.

'I am most sorry, Captain. I...'

I held up a hand. 'That's alright Mr Lakshman. The invitation still stands, but I understand if you wish to accompany your brother.'

'Thank you, sir.' His eyes filled with relief as he turned to follow the others.

'Is everything alright?' asked Helena, as I re-joined her at the table.

'I have a feeling those Indian Army officers were trying to make a point. I think they succeeded. The empire's subjects are good enough to die to protect the white man, but not to share his table.'

'You don't seem to like the idea of empire very much.'

'I've never been able to work out what the benefits are for those at the bottom of the ladder, of whatever race.'

Helena laid her hand on my arm. 'You can tilt at windmills another day.' Her smile would have melted the heart of a workhouse Beadle. 'But please don't let them spoil our evening.'

Bruno D'Angelo had also warned me about windmills, after learning that Olwyn had nicknamed me Sir Gawain for rescuing her from a pimp outside the Chain Locker in Barry. My chivalry had not saved her from Jeffreys' vengeance.

'Are you okay? You look as if you've seen a ghost.'

I forced a smile. 'Someone just walked over my grave.' The arrival of the waiter, with our bowls of turtle soup, saved me from further explanation.

Replete after the best meal either of us had eaten in weeks, our bodies glowing from foxtrotting around the dance floor, I escorted Helena back to our room. The faint strains of the band were still audible through the shuttered bedroom windows. Helena flung them open, the moonless clear night was incandescent with stars.

I switched off the light. 'There's supposed to be a blackout, in case of air raids.'

'I hope you can find your way by feel, then.'

I groped towards the bed, shedding clothes as I went. As my eyes adjusted to the dark, I saw Helena wriggle out of her gown and drop it to the floor. The underwear followed.

Gliding onto the bed she padded towards me like a large, pale cat. Her green eyes glinted in the darkness.

I tried to lie still as she slid her body over mine. Parts of me failed.

'Mmmm, that feels nice,' she whispered.

'I thought you liked to make love with the light on.'

'I like it in the dark too. I think I can remember where everything goes.'

'Here, let me help you.'

'Oohh! You wicked man. Stop it. I love it.'

CHAPTER EIGHTEEN

Forenoon, Sunday 14 December 1941

I awoke to hammering on the door of the suite. Helena jumped up in alarm and grabbed the sheet around her.

'Good Heavens! Who do I have to go to bed with to get some sleep around here?'

I reached for my watch. It was almost 7am; sunlight streamed in through the open windows.

There was more hammering on the door.

'If that's breakfast, tell them to come back at a reasonable hour.' Helena slumped back on the bed and wrapped the pillow around her ears.

I pulled on trousers and shirt and opened the door. A young soldier eyed me suspiciously.

'Captain Rowden?'

'Yes.'

He thrust an envelope at me. 'Corporal Mullens, Signal Corps. You're to report to Command House in Sime Road at zero nine hundred sharp. Orders is in there, sir.'

I shut the door and ripped open the envelope. The message simply confirmed Mullens' verbal instructions. Under the scrawled signature was the name: Lieutenant Colonel B.H. Ashmore GSO/I Malaya Command HQ.

'What is it?' I turned to find Helena wrapped in her silk nightgown. The loosely tied belt left little to the imagination.

'A summons from military headquarters. I'm to report there by nine. What the hell do they want with me?'

Helena reefed the belt tighter. 'You'd better get cracking then. I'll just have to be patient. But don't worry, I might even be here when you get back.'

She sat on the bed, smoking a Sobranie, while I showered and dressed. 'That really is a lovely tattoo of a … what did you call it … a schooner?'

'Yes. She was the *Sunshine*. Built in Whitstable in eighteen ninety. Owned by my uncle. She worked the coal trade when I was in her. Mostly Sunderland or Newcastle to the Channel Ports. Sometimes a trip over to France or Belgium. She went down off Zeebrugge in the twenties.'

I pulled on my white shirt with the four gold stripes on the shoulder straps. The short sleeves did nothing to hide the tattoos on my forearms.

'Sorry, I was never much good at history, you lost me around eighteen ninety.' Helena passed my gold braided cap. 'You didn't tell me about your lunch with Colonel Spencer yesterday. I take it my bedchamber exploits in Bangkok were largely for nothing.'

I nodded. 'By the time he delivered the warning it was too late. The Japanese still caught both us and the Americans with our sails furled. Things aren't going well. We're retreating in northern Malaya.'

'Another Dunkirk?'

'Maybe. Perhaps that's what this summons is about. Making ships ready for an evacuation.' I paused, recalling the conversation at the Singapore Club. 'After lunch, Spencer went to an intelligence briefing at Command House. That's where I'm going.'

Helena's brows knitted in thought. 'I like him, he can be quite charming, but he's as dangerous as a cornered rat. And believe me I've met a few of those, both the furry and the other kind. Be careful.'

She reached out her arms. I clasped her to me and we exchanged a long, passionate kiss that almost had me disobey orders. Finally, she disentangled herself.

'If you don't go now, I'll lock the door and throw away the key.'

I jammed the cap on my head. 'I'll be as quick as I can.'

'What would you like me to wear to welcome you back?'

'Nothing.'

Her laughter followed me down the corridor to the elevator.

The Sunday morning traffic was light, which was fortunate as the taxi driver was keen to prove that the next world racing car champion ought to be Chinese. We flashed past the low shop houses lining Rochor Road and were soon speeding northwest beside the canal along leafy Bukit Timah. Just past the Botanic Gardens, the driver wrenched the wheel. With a scream of tyres, we swerved in front of the oncoming traffic into Adams Road and sped north towards the

Sime Road Army Camp. I feared for the life of the checkpoint sentry who stepped into our path at the entrance; the taxi screeched to a halt just short of his polished boots. Stony faced, he checked my name against a list and waved us through.

I breathed a sigh of relief as we rolled to a halt outside Command Headquarters, handed the driver the fare plus a large tip for keeping me alive and declined his offer to wait.

Clearly mistaking my gold bars for the real thing, the guard jumped to attention and snapped the stiffest of salutes. I did my best to return it navy fashion.

'Follow me please, Captain Rowden. The colonels is expecting you, suh.' The barked invitation sounded more like an order. I followed him up the steps and into the long, two storey, flat-roofed building.

He showed me into what looked like an operations command centre. A huge map of Malaya lined one wall, with coloured pins marking the latest positions of Japanese and British troops. Spencer stood gazing at the map smoking a cheroot. He turned when he heard the door open.

'Morning Bill, trust you slept well.'

'No thanks to you, hauling me away from my dreams. What am I doing here?'

'All in good time, we're just waiting for Colonel Ashmore to join us. He's a Royal Scot. Oldest regiment in the British Army. They claim they even provided a body guard for Pontius Pilate. He's the GSO one.'

'What the hell does that mean?'

'General Staff Officer, Grade One. He's in charge of operational planning and intelligence.'

'So, he's the one responsible for the mess you were telling me about yesterday?'

The amused snort was hastily disguised by a fit of coughing. 'Actually, he's the one charged with sorting it out. General Percival's blue-eyed boy. Although you wouldn't think it to look at him.'

The door opened and the man who stepped through it was certainly no one's idea of a dashing officer. Burly, with heavy jowls, he stalked forward with an air of grim determination but, when he spoke, his deep voice dispensed calmness and authority.

'You must be Captain Rowden. I trust we haven't torn you away from anything more pressing?' There was a disconcerting twinkle in his eyes. 'Colonel Spencer has told me a lot about you.'

I shook the offered hand; the grip was dry and firm. 'Colonel Spencer can sometimes be expansive with the truth. I'm just a tramp ship master, so I'm wondering why I'm here.'

'All in good time, Captain,' he said, in almost the exact tones of Spencer's earlier rebuff. 'While we wait for Admiral Spooner to join us, I'll give you a quick rundown of the current situation. No need to remind you that everything you hear in this room is classified.'

I nodded. I was used to keeping secrets and not just because of the war. Keeping one's eyes open and one's mouth shut had been a prerequisite for success in the pre-war China coast trade.

'Right you are then.' He grabbed a long, white pointer. 'The Japs have entered Malaya here, at Jitra and Kroh.' He pointed to the two northern towns on the Malay-Thai border. 'They've forced us back from Jitra along this road south. We're currently taking up positions around here, at Gurun.' He tapped the pointer on the map. 'It's a strong position in a narrow valley with the coast to the west and mountain ridges to the east. The only approach is along the trunk road passing through swamp and paddy fields. Easily observed from high ground with good fields of fire. We should have a chance of stopping them, or at least slowing them down. With me so far?'

I nodded. Spencer had told me the same story at the Singapore Club. 'Yes, Colonel. But what about the Japanese at Kroh?'

'Ah, you've spotted that eh? Good eye for the situation. Rare in naval types. Well now, you see this road here?' He traced a line on the map snaking south from Kroh through the central mountains. 'Joins up with the trunk road here.' He tapped the map far to the south of Penang. 'Not much point hanging on at Gurun, if the enemy get behind us here, at Taiping. Classic encirclement. Not to be recommended. At the moment we're still holding them at Kroh, and Twelfth Indian Brigade's been ordered up as reinforcements. Best trained troops in Malaya. Should give the blighters something to think about.'

He paused, staring at the map as if seeking answers to a problem only he had foreseen.

'Up to the field commanders now. See what they can do to hand out bloody noses, what? Still, if it comes to the worst, best be prepared. Boy Scout's motto.' He tapped the pointer again, south of Taiping. 'This is Ipoh on the Perak River. Mountains to the east and the river flowing down to the sea. If we have to make a fighting withdrawal, it's a good place to hit them hard.' He turned away from the map and stared at me with piercing dark eyes. 'Now then, Captain. Assume they do get to Gurun.' He pointed over his shoulder. 'The Perak River is there. What do you see in between, eh?'

I stared at the map. I was more used to looking at a chart, on which the coastal features and the water depths were of greatest importance. What the topography of the hinterland was like was of no concern to a mariner. Spencer gazed at me expectantly, as if I was a child confused by a simple question. Finally, I saw it. Snaking along the narrow plain between the mountains and the sea, often following the coast, was a thin black line.

'One hundred miles of coast road.'

'In one, old boy. In one. The farther south he comes the longer his supply lines get.' Ashmore pointed to the map again. 'There are only two roads south from Taiping. One inland skirting the mountains and the other along the coast. Now, if we cut those roads, disrupt their supply lines, sow some doubt into their minds.' His grim countenance dissolved into a bear like grin. 'Guerrilla ops, gentlemen. Strike from the sea, strike from the mountains. Strike fast, strike hard. But strike.' He rapped the pointer against the map for emphasis.

'We're going to set up an operations' base at Port Swettenham. Everything the army needs for commando raids along the coast as far as Penang. The navy will ferry them there in small boats. Dead of night, blow up roads, bridges, cut telephone lines, set ambushes, cause havoc up and down the coast.' There was something in his eyes that reminded me of a mongoose eyeing off a cobra. 'We need your ship, Captain. It's going to be the floating depot in Port Swettenham. A treasure chest of everything that goes whizz and bang.'

Our heads turned as the door swung open to admit two high ranking naval officers.

'Ah the navy, come to join the party. Captain Rowden, let me introduce you to Rear Admiral Spooner, in charge of all naval operations in Malaya, and Captain Mulock head of coastal patrols. Admiral, I was just briefing Captain Rowden on our irregular scheme.'

With the double row of braid on his cap brim and the shoulder boards gleaming gold, Admiral Spooner looked a formidable man. The hook nose and narrow mouth reminded me of a hawk. His gaze swept over me like a searchlight. Was he expecting a salute? Instead, he stuck out a hand.

'Good morning, Captain Rowden.' He glanced down at the tattoo on my forearm. 'Cock on the right, never lost a fight.' His thin mouth split into a grin. 'I know a bit about you.'

I glanced at Spencer, wondering just how many more people he shared my secrets with. He shook his head.

'Not guilty this time, Bill. The admiral knows a good friend of yours.'

'Commodore Lowther,' said the admiral, smiling wider. 'We were shipmates in the last war and I caught up with him when I commanded the Northern Patrol.' He pointed to the medal ribbon on my shirt. 'Mulock, let me introduce you to the man who rammed a U-boat last year, and lived to tell the tale.'

'Damned good show,' said Captain Mulock, pumping my hand.

'Now then, Colonel Ashmore,' continued the admiral. 'I take it you've explained to Captain Rowden what we expect of him.'

'Yes sir, load his ship with everything to support several weeks of guerrilla and coastal patrol operations, take it to Port Swettenham and set up as a depot ship.'

'Anything to add, Spencer?'

'Only that Captain Rowden will be working with a handpicked force that'll do the actual patrolling and fighting. I'm going along to see what intelligence we can pick up from the raids, sir.'

'Right then. Mulock, hand the captain his orders.'

Captain Mulock thrust out a large, sealed buff envelope. I hesitated, wondering why a tramp ship with a crew of civilian merchant mariners had suddenly been caught up in the defence of Singapore. The ship was under charter to the Ministry of War Transport, had they or Mr Khoo been consulted?

Admiral Spooner read the reluctance in my face. 'Ah, I see you haven't been told the whole story. Your ship's been requisitioned as a naval auxiliary. The owners have been informed, of course. She'll fly the blue ensign of the reserve, and need a commissioned officer to command her.'

My stomach churned and I clenched my fists. 'I'll be damned if I'll hand over command to—'

Admiral Spooner raised a hand. 'No need for that, Captain. Included amongst your orders is a temporary commission into the Royal Navy Reserve. Lieutenant's the best I can do I'm afraid. There's no extra pay, more paperwork and a better chance of being shot at. You'll report to Captain Mulock. If I were you, I wouldn't even think of changing uniforms just yet, otherwise you'll have to salute anything that moves. Any questions?'

I had dozens, but I knew they were better aimed at Spencer. 'None, sir. Except, when do we start?' I had a sinking feeling I already knew the answer to that.

The admiral's eyes hardened. 'There's not a moment to lose, Captain. The dockyard's waiting for you. Proceed there as soon as possible … today. If that's all, carry on.'

He turned on his heel and strode to the door, Captain Mulock and Colonel Ashmore trailing in his wake. Left alone with Spencer, I glared at him with the most malicious expression I could muster.

'You do know who you've dragged me away from? Is there any chance the Japanese might kill you on one of these hare-brained commando raids?'

'Yes, on both counts.'

'Have I told you you're a dangerous son-of-a …' I shook my head in frustration. 'I should have left you on the bloody quayside in Shanghai.'

'Too late for that. Anyway, if you had, Helena wouldn't be here. Look, if it's any consolation I didn't dream this up. That's Ashmore. He said he needed a cargo ship with a reliable captain. You're the only one I know. I thought you'd prefer it to swinging around an anchor, and I wanted someone with a cool head. There'll be a bunch of young naval officers all thinking themselves the next Nelson. England expects and all that bullshit … never mind manoeuvres just go straight at 'em. You're a survivor. It'll be no picnic up there in Port Swettenham. The Japs are bound to bomb the docks.'

'The navy must have bloody little to do, if it takes an admiral to tell the master of a worn out, old tramp that his ship's suddenly vital to the defence of Singapore.'

'That's the navy for you. After they managed to throw away *Repulse* and *Prince of Wales,* it has rather struck them that they've left a huge gap in the notion of Fortress Singapore. With the air force being shot out of the sky, it falls to the poor bloody infantry to pull the chestnuts out of the fire, as usual. The admiral's suddenly very keen to support us as best he can. He's only got a handful of destroyers. Most of them are occupied escorting ships into Singapore, what's left are laying mines in the Singapore Strait. He's pressing all sorts of old and odd cargo craft into service, not just *Oriental Venture.*'

He glanced down at his watch. 'Sorry Bill, the admiral meant what he said. If you're going to have half a chance of a decent farewell with Helena, you need to get a wriggle on. If you write me a note for Poh, I'll see he gets it so everything's ready as soon as you're back aboard. I'll rustle up a car to take you to Raffles.'

The journey back was more sedate. I had to resist the urge to tell the Indian driver to hurry up. Every minute spent on the journey was one less in Helena's arms. Still, it gave me time to think, although my thoughts were not optimistic. If the navy was pressing old cargo ships into service, it probably meant they thought them expendable. Shaking the unfortunate master's hand and presenting him with a commission was perhaps just the admiral's way of saying thank you ... and goodbye. Not for the first time, I cursed the day I crossed paths with Spencer. Although, if I was being fair, I was just as much to blame, for sticking my nose into business that should not have concerned me. I still had Wolfgang Eberhardt's small arsenal on board. It had proved as much blessing as curse. The way things were heading, it looked as if it might be needed again.

CHAPTER NINETEEN

Forenoon, Wednesday 17 December 1941

T he hammering of rivet guns did nothing to ease my headache. Naval dockyard workers were supplementing our anti-
aircraft defences. Two 20-mm Oerlikon rapid-firing cannon
were being installed on the Monkey Island, and gangs of men were
riveting sheets of steel to provided simple but, hopefully, effective
armour protection to the bridge, radio room and other exposed areas
of the ship. Hinged, bullet proof shutters were being fitted outside
the wheelhouse windows. When lowered during an attack, they had
slits for the helmsman and watchkeeper to see through.

Apart from the guns and the armour plating, wireless techni-
cians had repaired our radio, and the passenger accommodation
was being converted to provide berths for naval officers and ratings.
The DEMS gunners had been relocated to the forecastle, where naval
carpenters added more bunks and lockers to those already built by
Cramp to house the soldiers previously rescued from the *City of
Richmond*.

The headache was entirely self-inflicted, the result of a long evening in the officers' mess at *HMS Sultan*, the barracks adjacent to
the Sembawang naval dockyard. It had all started quietly, with an
invitation from Captain Mulock to meet some of the officers who
would command the launches and the other small craft attached to
the commando raids. The overall impression was how young they all
were, lieutenants and sub-lieutenants no older than Lakshman. Survivors of the sinking of *Repulse* and *Prince of Wales,* they should have
had little to celebrate, but they drank with the intensity of young
men whose mortality had, for the first time, been so closely demonstrated to them. When the higher spirited cleared the furniture for
mess games, I took my queue to leave.

To add to the suffering, I had a mound of paperwork to attend to.

Admiral Spooner had been right, the navy apparently functioned for the primary benefit of pen pushers. Its ability to fight seemingly only a secondary consideration.

The privacy curtain whisked aside and Da Silva appeared with a pot of coffee and a bottle of aspirin tablets. I was tempted to add a shot of rum to the coffee, but the skin of the crocodile had never seemed a sensible remedy to me. A cigarette would probably have helped and the smell of pipe tobacco drifting in from the chartroom added to the temptation. I swallowed a couple of aspirin, washed them down with a mouthful of coffee and took the cup with me. Lamont was hunched over the table, his pipe clamped between his teeth. I took a deep, surreptitious breath of the soothing, nicotine rich smoke trailing from the bowl.

'Morning, Skipper. I'm just plotting the positions of the minefields the navy's been sowing.' He put down his pencil and reached for a stapled sheaf of instructions. 'These are the pilotage directions for the Johore Strait and the approaches to Dockyard Reach. I was hoping one of the pilots from the warships could talk me through them and add any tips.'

I nodded. 'Good work, Second. I'll have a word with Captain Mulock. I'm sure he can find someone to help you. And leave those directions where I can find them. I'd like to read them myself'

I walked out to the bridge wing, hoping a few lungfuls of fresh air would finally send the headache on its way. They didn't. The air was hot and oppressively humid. Threatening clouds to the north-east over Johore, promised the usual early afternoon thunderstorm.

Apart from *Oriental Venture*, the only ships at the dockyard were a destroyer undergoing the repair of damage incurred rescuing survivors from *Repulse* and *Prince of Wales*, and a couple of old coastal steamers being modified for minesweeping. The naval base had been constructed to support a squadron of capital ships sufficient to defend Britain's Far East possessions. With the two sent for that purpose now at the bottom of the Gulf of Siam, it might be argued that the only reason for defending Singapore was to stop the base falling into Japanese hands. From our berth alongside the west wall, there was a grandstand view of the King George V graving dock. It could accommodate the navy's largest battleships, but the lone destroyer resting on the keel blocks looked like a toy boat in an outsize bathtub.

A line of trucks was parked on the quayside, from which sling loads of stores were being hoisted in by a dockside crane. Fresh meat and vegetables were still readily available in Singapore's markets, but most of the foodstuffs being loaded were pickled, powdered, dried, bottled, canned or otherwise preserved. The bottled stores included sufficient cases of rum, gin and beer to float the destroyer off her blocks in the graving dock

In addition to the food, we still had to load dozens of drums of diesel oil to fuel the launches, and large stocks of weapons and ammunition. With naval officers and ratings berthed in the ship between operations, and a raiding party of 50 Australian soldiers to support, it looked as if we were loading enough to maintain commando operations for several months. Colonel Ashmore obviously had high expectations of the raids. I hoped they were not misplaced. The thought of being bombed while full of fuel and munitions was distinctly unpleasant, as was the prospect of being cut off in Port Swettenham if the Japanese advanced quicker than expected.

Sailing in convoy, there had at least been some comfort from safety in numbers, even if that was more wishful thinking than reality. And even if attacked, there was still the possibility of escape in the lifeboats. Being ordered to deliberately place the ship in harm's way, was an entirely new and unappealing experience.

I had been around the ship earlier and briefed Fraser, the chief steward and the boatswain on the dangers we were facing. There was little comfort to offer. Service in merchant ships was an alternative to conscription, any man refusing to sail would quickly find himself in uniform, at least as far as British crew were concerned. If our Chinese or Somalis refused to sail, they would most likely end up in gaol until they could be sent home. For the Chinese, with Hong Kong under the Japanese heel, that might be a very long sentence. Even so, the boatswain's reaction surprised me.

'You say go Port Swettenham … we go Port Swettenham,' he said, with a fatalistic shrug of the shoulders. 'Maybe Singapore fall, but Japan no can win. Plenty Chinese people in Asia. They cannot kill all. We drive Japanese out. Then you British.' His normally inscrutable face split into a wide grin. 'Not personal, Captain. You good man, but when war end, all change. Same India, same Africa, same Singapore … Hong Kong. British go. Maybe after … if you still captain … we sail with you again.'

It was the longest I had ever heard him speak in English. I watched his departing back, recalling Mr Khoo's own predictions of the demise of the British Empire. For a moment, I sensed just how precarious was the position of the handful of Europeans who claimed a God given right to rule countless human beings whose skin was darker than their own. I could count on the loyalty of the Chinese crew for only as long as I ran the ship to Mr Khoo's—and to their —satisfaction. One misstep and the whole pretence would crumble. My own little realm, of which I was master under God, being just a microcosmic metaphor for the fate of an empire, when the consent of the governed was finally and fatally withdrawn.

I shook my head, glad to feel the last of the headache receding. The fate of the British Empire was too big a subject to be tackled in one forenoon watch. In any case, I had more pleasurable things to consider. Reaching into my pocket, I pulled out the perfumed note Helena had sent, and returned to the privacy, if not the peace, of my day cabin to read it again.

Our parting at Raffles, after the conference at Command House, had been short but memorably energetic. Afterwards, there had been little time for reflection. I returned to the ship as fast as taxi and bumboat could carry me, and she returned to Mr Khoo's bungalow in Tanglin.

I was not used to receiving perfumed letters, in fact I had never received one. There were no endearments or passionate effusions. She simply wrote that Poh was still trying to secure her a passage to India, but that the governor's office was discouraging Europeans from leaving in case the local population sensed defeatism. It was the final sentence that stirred longing. She stated that, whatever the governor had to say in the matter, she was in no hurry to leave and was looking forward to another dinner dance at Raffles.

I reached for a sheet of paper, unscrewed the cap off my pen and stared down at the blank, white surface. What to write? Did her reference to another dinner dance encompass the complete range of the evening's activities? Staring down at the paper, lost for words, I had no idea how to reply. Would I end up sounding like a lovesick schoolboy, a smug lounge lizard or a cold-hearted cad? And would it matter anyway? My orders left no scope for dalliances, I was to be ready to sail at a moment's notice, and either or both of us could be dead before we had a chance to meet again.

'Writing love letters, old boy?'

My head jerked up in surprise to find Spencer grinning at me from the doorway.

'Told the gangway sentry you were expecting me. He sent me straight up.'

That was news to me. 'I'll leave clearer instructions next time. Can't have any odd riff-raff from the dockyard snooping about on board.' I pushed the still blank paper aside.

'I hear Helena's pining away for you at Mr Khoo's bungalow.' He gestured towards the paper. 'Go ahead and write. I can deliver it for you, if you want.'

'Surely you've not come all this way just to play postman?'

'Or cupid. No. I've news. Can I sit down?' He dropped onto the couch without waiting for an invitation. 'The dockyard foreman says it's all going well. They'll have you ready to sail by the weekend.' His eyes light up as he read the anticipation on my face. 'Sorry, shore leave's forbidden. Can't chance any loose lips wandering around the bars of Singapore. Admiral's orders … no exceptions.'

'There's no need to sound so pleased about it. You dragged me away from Raffles without a hint of warning. We hardly had time to say goodbye.'

'Don't worry, I'll put in a good word for you. Now, forget Helena for a minute and let's focus on more important matters. The navy's located two Harbour Defence Motor Launches. Built for the Straits Settlement naval reserve and almost brand new, ideal for what Ashmore has in mind. Seventy feet long, twin diesels, top speed of fourteen knots, over a thousand-mile range and armed to the teeth with a three-pounder on the foredeck, an Oerlikon aft and multiple Lewis guns. They even have eight depth charges.'

'They'll come in handy if we come across any U-boats.'

'Don't scoff, the Japs do have submarines patrolling off Malaya. You're lucky you didn't run into one after Kota Bharu.'

I pointed at the coffee pot. 'It's cold, but I can get Da Silva to fetch a fresh one.'

Spencer shook his head. 'I'd rather a scotch.'

I reached for the bottle and poured him a large tot.

'Thanks. Now, where was I? Ah yes, the launches. They're the mother hens. The navy's also requisitioned half a dozen civilian pleasure craft. They'll ferry the soldiers up the rivers and creeks, and land them as close as possible to the targets. The launches will tow them there and back, and ride shotgun.'

'That must have been popular at the yacht club.'

'It wasn't. The owners removed bits of the engines to disable them. I had to enlist the help of your Mr Poh. He persuaded enough rich Chinese to donate their boats in service of the greater cause.'

'Donated!' I said, smiling.

'The less said the better.' Spencer tapped his nose. 'So much for the boats. The army hasn't been idle either. An officer's been appointed to plan the raids. Major Thorne, Argyll and Sutherland Highlanders, specialist in jungle warfare. The expedition's been named Thorne Force.' His face broke into a broad grin. 'It's meant to be a thorn in the side for the Japanese. The Australians have been asked for fifty volunteers. They'll be divided into two platoons commanded by Captain Nettles from Thirtieth Battalion. Technically, Australian soldiers can't take direct orders from British Army officers, so I'm the liaison ... between Thorne and Nettles. And don't tell me the army doesn't have a sense of humour.'

The rivet guns ceased hammering, and the sudden quiet amplified our laughter. I glanced at the bulkhead clock; the hands were approaching noon.

'They must be knocking off for their lunch.' I reached for a glass. 'Think I'll join you. Refill?'

Spencer nodded and held out his glass. 'Now, what else do you need to know? I believe you met some of the navy chaps last night. They'll command the launches and the boats.'

I nodded. 'Most of them look as if they're straight out of school. They seem as keen as mustard, though.'

'The navy breeds them that way. Captain Mulock's provided them with a headmaster. Lieutenant-Commander Barker, another survivor from the *Repulse*.'

I took a sip of whisky, wishing I'd poured myself a rum. 'Someone seems to be going to an awful lot of trouble. But are you sure this isn't just a stunt? To make it look as if the army knows what it's doing?'

Spencer's grin widened. '*And England's far and Honour a name, but the voice of a schoolboy rallies the ranks ...*'

'Yeah, I know the rest. *Into the valley of death rode the six hundred.* When do we charge?'

'Australian army HQ is still choosing its volunteers. Hundreds of the mad buggers put their hands up. There'll be a few days' training before they transport them to Port Swettenham by truck. I expect you'll be on your way before Christmas.'

'Are you sure there's no chance ...?'

'None. She'll just have to wait.' He paused and the grin faded. 'Now, tell me about the incident at Raffles the other night, with those two Indian Army officers.'

I glared at him, speechless. Did he have eyes everywhere?

'Don't look at me like that. There were other officers there, in mufti. You weren't the only one offended.'

'I didn't see anyone else rush to their defence. One of these days we're going to get what we deserve.'

One side of Spencer's mouth curled upwards. 'I'm afraid to pour cold water on your idealism, but most of them were offended by the presence of the Indians, not the Johnnys you threw out. Look, I agree with you. Why should we expect Indian soldiers to defend an Empire that won't allow them into its best clubs and hotels? And why is that important? Because the bulk of the troops facing the Japanese are Indian Army.' He paused to pull a cheroot out of his pocket. 'Do you mind if I ...?'

I pushed the ashtray towards him.

'You're probably not following developments in India,' he took a drag of the cheroot and exhaled. 'The Indian National Congress didn't take kindly to the Viceroy declaring war on behalf of all Indians without their consent. One of its leaders, a chap called Subhas Chandra Bose, called for mass protests. He was arrested, but after a stint in jail he escaped from India. He's now living in Berlin and has set up what he calls the Free India Legion, which is already recruiting Indian soldiers captured in North Africa.'

'So? What's this got to do with my third officer and his brother.'

'What was the name of the captain accompanying them?'

I scratched my chin. 'Singh, he's a Sikh. Mohan Singh. I think that's what Captain Lakshman said.'

'And what happened?'

'After I'd dealt with the young Johnny, I invited them to join Helena and me. I thought they would, until Singh said something in Hindi. Whatever he said, I had the feeling it changed Captain Lakshman's mind. His brother looked pretty embarrassed too. I didn't make an issue of it.'

'That sounds right. Captain Singh's got form for this sort of thing. Suggests to his fellow officers that they should go for dinner or a drink, and then takes them to places he knows will cause a fuss. I'm not saying it's wrong of him, God knows we have enough problems in Australia with people who think the country should only be populated by white men—and blow the Aborigines, but Singh's a troublemaker, trying to sow discord among Indian soldiers, making them question their loyalties.'

'And is he succeeding?'

Spencer shrugged his shoulders. 'Hard to say. The army's been keeping an eye on him. I don't suppose ...?'

'Not on your life. Young Lakshman's a good officer. I don't give a shit what his politics are. If you want to know about his brother, go ask him yourself.'

Spencer shook his head. 'Too late for that. The Punjabis and the Mahrattas have been sent forward to join the Eleventh Indian Division at Gurun.

'Well then, let's hope they slow the Japanese down long enough for your hare-brained schemes to work.'

CHAPTER TWENTY

Evening, Sunday 21 December 1942

D espite the navy's supposed love of urgency, it was a week since I had rushed to Command House, been commissioned into the Naval Reserve and had my ship requisitioned. Meanwhile, the Japanese had forced their way farther down the peninsula. Penang had fallen on 19 December, but still the commando raid was not ready to proceed. How much longer before events rendered it pointless?

There was nothing to do but wait and read *The Straits Times*. Despite the optimistic tone of the news' reports, it was obvious the British Army was retreating before an enemy that had, until very recently, been ridiculed for its physical weakness, short-sightedness and lack of intelligence.

I saw nothing of Helena during the week. Poh sent word that she had left Mr Khoo's bungalow and taken a room at Raffles. The naval base was on the other side of the island. I could hardly invite her to visit me there and everyone connected with the raid was still confined to base. So, when one of Poh's clerks delivered another perfumed note, I felt a keen sense of frustration and retired to the privacy of my day cabin to rip open the envelope.

Rowden,

It's days since I heard from you. I'll be dining at Raffles tonight with some new and not so new friends. If you can drag yourself away from your mistress, then please do join us.

Yours, Helena.

It was brief and brusque and I felt guilty at not having replied to her earlier note. I had never been a letter writer, there was no one to write letters to … until now. Leaving the ship was another matter. I considered telephoning her at Raffles to make my apologies, before annoyance at my irresolution spurred me to action. I had never let petty restrictions stop me in the past, so why now? And if the worst happened? Well, Colonel Spencer owed me enough favours. Instead, I sent Lakshman ashore to telephone Poh and ask him to send a car to take me to Raffles.

Even though shore leave was banned, it was apparent that senior naval officers came and went without question. Helena had not specified evening dress. Would a bored sentry notice that the four stripes on my shoulders were Merchant, not Royal Navy?

During the afternoon, Da Silva pressed my best white uniform. He starched it so heavily that it crackled when I forced my limbs into the sleeves and legs. When the car arrived, he subjected me to a final inspection that would have wilted a Guardsman on Horse Guards Parade. The Sikh driver flashed a salute and held the car door open. I climbed into the back seat, feeling like a minor potentate. The sentry on the gate took only a perfunctory glance at my uniform, raised the bar and waved us through.

Despite the shaded headlights, from which only slivers of light escaped, the driver sped south along Bukit Timah Road as if blessed with the night vision of a cat. He only slowed when the traffic thickened nearing the city, but still squealed the tyres rounding Dhoby Ghuat into Stamford Road. It was strange to see the city bathed in darkness, and Raffles seemed very quiet as we pulled up the drive. The doorman opened the car door and ushered me into the foyer. Behind the blackout curtains, the hotel was ablaze with light and noisy with the babble of voices. Raffles was famous for its Saturday night dinner dances, which continued in defiance of the Japanese advance. Sunday was more sedate, with the Tuan Besars and planters enjoying evening cocktails and dinner with their wives and families.

The head waiter greeted me with polite indifference, until I told him who was expecting me. He then welcomed me as if I was the returning prodigal and guided me towards a corner table. Helena had her back to me. Seated to one side of her was an American Army officer. On the other side was an older couple whose faces I recognised from the society column of *The Straits Times*. The woman was eye catching, with an oval shaped face, a small mouth with bright red lips, and pronounced cheekbones framed by bangs of wavy hair. Her cocktail gown was a shimmering profusion of grey-silk.

Helena turned as the head waiter caught her attention.

'Ah, Rowden. Glad you could finally make it. Let me introduce you. Lady Diana Cooper, Alfred Cooper the British Resident Minister, and Colonel Miles Beckwith the Third, the American Military Attaché.'

She waved a hand towards me. 'Everyone, this is my friend and sa-viour, Captain William Rowden.'

The gentlemen rose to shake my hand. Cooper was thick set, with heavy jowls, dark, brilliantined hair slicked back over a high fore-head and a neatly trimmed moustache, flecked with grey. Unusual for the tropics, his suit was dark, pin-striped and double-breasted, but he seemed cool enough. The enigmatic smile playing around the corners of his lips reinforced the impression.

I reached for his hand.

'Pleased to meet you, Mr Cooper.'

'Duff, everyone calls me Duff ... and we're all friends here. Would you prefer William or Bill?'

'Either is fine ... Duff.'

I turned to the American. A blond crew cut bristled above a tanned, boyishly handsome face from which pale blue eyes twin-kled. The shoulder straps of his Army green jacket carried the silver eagle of a full colonel. He grabbed my hand with a firm grip.

'Call me Miles.'

Lady Diana extended her hand, palm down as if expecting me to kiss the back of it. *The Straits Times* had reported that she arrived in Singapore along with one hundred suitcases. It had also, some-what uncharitably, mentioned she was approaching fifty. She looked younger, and close up I understood why she had once been named the most beautiful young woman in England. She allowed me to take her fingers in mine and I gently waggled her limp hand, glancing between her and Cooper. He had a reputation for gambling, drinking and womanising. What bound them together? She released my hand and glanced up at me, catching the flicker of my eyes. Her mouth opened in amusement and her hazel eyes lit up her whole face.

'Stop wondering ... and sit here.' She patted the seat beside her. 'If you don't mind, I'm going to call you Captain. I like the sound of it. And you can call me Lady Diana, that's what I was born.'

I took the vacant seat between her and Colonel Beckwith. Sitting almost opposite Helena, I compared her with Lady Diana. Despite the difference in age, it was hard to say whether one outshone the other. Helena saw me staring and winked.

Cooper signalled to a passing waiter. 'The ladies are drinking champagne, Miles and I are drinking whisky. Name your poison, Bill.'

I ordered a rum and soda. The waiter bustled away to fetch it while we consulted the menu. A trio played soft chamber music. There was the steady burr of conversation. Men were fighting and dying less than three hundred miles from where we sat. It was hard to believe the two worlds existed side by side.

'So, Bill. Tell me. Is it true you saved Elena's life?' Beckwith was gazing at her with puppy-like devotion. He had called her Elena, her screen name in Hollywood. Did that mean he knew nothing of her past? If he was the new friend she referred to in her note, Duff and Lady Diana must be the old ones who, presumably, knew her as Lady Helen Ashworth.

'What has she told you?'

'That you gave me passage in your ship to Davao, to escape Shanghai when the Japanese seized most of it in thirty-seven.' The half-truth tripped off her tongue.

'I didn't know the Royal Navy accepted passengers,' said Beckwith.

'I'm not a naval captain. My ship's a tramp steamer.' Was there relief, or a touch of scorn in Beckwith's grin? 'Although the navy's requisitioned her. For what purpose, I'm not allowed to say.'

'Quite right, too,' said Cooper. 'Half the staff might be on Tojo's payroll for all we know. Miss Markova, excuse me, Elena, was telling us about the ship which took her from Davao to San Francisco. Something called the *Nimrod*, under the command of a friend of yours.' His subtle stressing of Helena's new names confirmed Beckwith was not privy to the deception.

'Grim Jim Coffin, yes. His ship's a sister to mine, both built on the Wear during the last war.'

'Grim Jim,' laughed Lady Diana. 'How did he get a name like that?'

'He went to sea in the last of the American whaling ships. It was a hard life. They say no one saw him smile from the start of a voyage until he paid off at the end. And then only if he was satisfied with his share. There's not many will call him it to his face.'

'Times have changed then,' said Helena. 'He smiled from the day I set foot on the *Nimrod* until we arrived at San Francisco four weeks later. I felt like I was being pursued by a hungry shark.'

Cooper rested a hand on Helena's arm. 'I'm sure you could handle him, my dear. What was it Mae West used to say? A dame that knows the ropes ain't likely to get tied up.'

The laughter was interrupted by the return of the waiter with the soup and my rum. I savoured a large mouthful of the latter and then tasted the soup. It was cream of chicken—with both cream and chicken. It was delicious and I was hungry. The waiter refilled the ladies' champagne glasses and fetched two more whiskies. For a moment there was silence as we plied our spoons, until Cooper and Beckwith interrupted each other in their enthusiasm to engage Helena in conversation.

'Like moths to a flame.' Lady Diana's voice was barely audible as she leaned towards me. 'If I was twenty years younger, I'd be jealous.' She sighed. 'They're old … friends, by the way.' Her voice dropped to a whisper. 'He'll chase anything in a skirt.'

Was she referring to Beckwith, or Cooper who looked old enough to be Helena's father?

'What's that about a skirt, Diana darling?' asked Cooper. 'Bill looks as if you've scandalized him.' His hearing must have been acute, either that or he could lip read.

'I was just telling Captain Rowden about the skirt I wore when you forced me to accompany you to Batavia for that ABDAB thingy.'

'ABDA, Diana. The American-British-Dutch-Australian command meeting. Yes, but I didn't force you. You demanded to come along.' He leaned forward across the table, beckoned us close and dropped his voice. 'She can be very persuasive. The poor old loadmaster told her women were not allowed to fly in bombers. She wouldn't take no for an answer. The fellow tried to put her off by telling her she'd have to wear a parachute for the entire flight. Made no difference. She strapped herself in the harness like a trooper, waddled aboard the Hudson and off we went to Batavia.'

Lady Diana waited for the laughter to subside. 'You have *no* idea how shameful a woman looks in a skirt with straps between her legs.' She fanned her face with her hand, provoking more laughter.

The waiter took advantage of the interlude to clear the soup plates and replace them with the next course. Both Helena and Lady Diana had chosen fish. Beckwith had ordered steak, Cooper and I the roast beef. There was another silence during the silver service of vegetables. Beckwith had chips and slathered them with tomato ketchup.

'Shall we have a claret to accompany this beef?' mused Cooper. Without waiting for a reply, he summoned the sommelier and ordered a bottle of Chateau Latour.

'Marvellous year, twenty-nine,' he said, sniffing the cork. 'Very hot, but with rain at just the right time. Not much of a market for it during the Depression. Good news for those of us looking for it now, though.'

I took a sip and swirled the liquid around my mouth, trying to identify the different flavours, and made appreciative noises until Cooper seemed satisfied. He took a mouthful and beamed with pleasure. 'Marvellous that. What do you think, Diana old girl?'

'Duffie, you know I can't tell a claret from a chianti. And a bit less of the old girl, if you don't mind.'

The beef was good, served with all the pre-war trimmings. Beckwith set about his steak with the efficiency of a mechanical digger. In between mouthfuls he engaged Helena in non-stop conversation, as if afraid to let her attention wander. I felt a gentle nudge on my arm and Lady Diana's soft voice filtered into my ear.

'I'm sorry if that was a surprise ... about Duffie knowing Helen. Actually, we've both known her for years, ever since she married Bobbie Ashworth ... well Duffie a bit before that. He was very cut up to hear she'd died, although I must say we never really believed the suicide bit. She seemed to have dealt with Bobby's loss rather well. It's hugely entertaining to see her resurrected as a Hollywood actress. But I expect you know all about that. And don't worry, we'll keep her little secret. Mind you, she always was good at playing a role. Duffie's got a pretty good idea now of what she's been doing out here. He's very close to Ducky, and all that cloak and dagger stuff.'

'Ducky! Sorry, you've lost me.'

'That's my pet name for Winston ... Churchill. Duffie's his personal representative here. Got a line straight to the old bulldog. Anyway, to cut a long story short, I know Helen's not all she seems. She says you helped fake her death, but I suppose the less I know about all that the better.' She paused to dispose of a delicate mouthful of fish. 'Beckwith has no idea by the way. Nice lad. Seems keen to get into her bloomers or whatever Helen wears, probably none knowing her. He seems to have made good progress.' She fluttered her eyelids. 'Oh dear, I'm afraid that sounds rather vulgar.' She laid down her knife and fork and turned her attention to Cooper, who was methodically clearing his plate, leaving the peas until last.

'Don't forget your greens, Duffie dear. Remember what your old nanny used to say.'

'I don't know about your nanny. Mine used to force me to eat spinach. Hated the stuff ever since.'

'What's the name of that sailor, the one who eats spinach?' asked Helena, laughing.

Beckwith launched into the opening verse of *Popeye the Sailor Man* and Helena joined in with a "toot-toot" at the end of every line. They were interrupted by the waiter returning with servings of apple pie and ice cream.

Cooper finally pushed his chair back and patted his stomach.

'Make the most of it, Diana. It's back to rationing shortly.'

I was almost sure I saw Beckwith's ears twitch.

'So, you're going home?' he asked.

'Just for a flying visit. Only be away a few days.' Cooper winked at Helena. 'We might be able to take Miss Markova with us. She should be able to get back to the States from London.'

'I'm not sure if I want to leave just yet. I'm having such a marvellous time.' Helena smiled as Beckwith reached for her hand and squeezed it.

'Made better progress than I thought,' whispered Lady Diana, raising her hand to conceal her lips. Was she deliberately teasing me, or had they …?

'If you don't mind my asking, sir,' said Beckwith. 'What will you be telling Mr Churchill?'

'My dear, Colonel,' said Cooper, raising one bushy eyebrow. 'You'll be asking me state secrets next.'

'Well, we are allies,' said Beckwith. 'Friends don't keep secrets from one another.'

'I don't know about that,' said Cooper, grinning broadly. 'There are some things I wouldn't tell even my closest friends.'

'I'm sure there are things you don't tell me, Duffie,' said Lady Diana, her face giving nothing away. 'And a good job too. But you've made no secret of your views here, and I don't think the colonel will be very surprised.'

'Hmmph. Very well then.' He fixed his eyes on Beckwith. 'But if I hear my name mentioned, I'll deny ever having said any of this.'

Beckwith nodded. Even so, I was surprised that Cooper thought any of us trustworthy, with the possible exception of his wife.

'First thing is, are we going to hang on here? Long enough for the cavalry to arrive, preferably ours but yours would be just as welcome. Although after Pearl Harbour there's little chance of that. Look, man for man, we might be able to beat the Japs, but we're outnumbered in the air and there's nothing left that can stand up to their fleet. Even so, there's a reasonable chance we could hang on. Trouble is, the army's fighting with one hand tied behind its back. The Governor just can't see the need to take the gloves off. The nobs raise hell whenever someone suggests digging up the golf courses and tennis courts for trenches and gun emplacements, and the governor won't release the labour. He's too busy worrying about civilian morale and keeping the economy going. So, there are no trenches, hardly any air raid shelters, no gas masks and not even any tin hats for the civilian authorities. It's madness. That's what I'll be telling Churchill.'

Cooper's round face flushed and his voice had risen.

'Keep your voice down, Duffie,' said Lady Diana. 'You don't want to frighten the horses.'

He paused and glanced around apologetically. 'Sorry. I'm being a bore.'

'Not at all, sir. Please carry on,' said Beckwith.

Lady Diana raised an eyebrow and Cooper responded with the barest nod. 'I've said too much already.' He glanced at his wrist-watch. 'And look at the time. Way past our bedtime, old girl, we really must run along. You young people can party on if you wish.'

He rose and Beckwith jumped up to help Lady Diana with her chair. After we had said our farewells, he escorted them to the door.

With Helena alone at last, I switched chairs to sit beside her. 'Thank God! I thought they'd never leave. Can we get rid of Beckwith too?'

'Hold your horses, that's hardly polite. I've known the Coopers for years and Beckwith's good company. I can't just send him packing.'

'I've missed you.' I cringed. It sounded so ... needy.

'I've missed you too, but that's not my fault. I've been here all the time, while you disappeared with hardly a word.'

'We're all confined to the naval base.'

'I know, and I'm glad you got away, but you weren't ordered not to write to me were you. You do know how to write?'

'Of course I do.'

'Well, I wasn't expecting sonnets, but a few words of appreciation would be nice. Anyway, you're here now. I hope you enjoyed the dinner.'

'The food was good. Duff seems alright, but Diana's a bit of a gossip.'

'You seemed to be getting along very well with her. What did she say about me?'

'She said they knew you ... from before. And that you and Duff were old friends.'

'Old friends!' Her sigh sounded more like a snort. 'We were lovers.'

'I guessed that's what she meant. She also thinks you and Beckwith are more than just friends.'

Her eyes flashed. 'You don't believe her, do you?'

'He was all over you.'

'I beg your pardon! We were just talking? Surely you're not jealous?'

'It looked like you're well past the talking stage. I'm beginning to wonder why I was invited.' The words were past my lips before my brain could stop them.

Helena went white. 'Do you think I invited you just to make you jealous? Or to make up the numbers for a stable of my lovers. You bastard, Rowden. If we weren't in public, I'd slap your face.'

She glared at me, her blazing eyes painfully searing my heart. How had it suddenly come to this? I was jealous, jealous of Duff who had been her lover, and of Beckwith showering her with attention in an attempt to become one.

'I'm sorry, Helena. I didn't mean that. The words slipped out without thinking.'

'But they did, and if that's how you really feel ...' Her face was set like granite, but the red spots burning on her cheeks showed she was battling to contain her anger. 'I really thought you better than that. You should go, before I say something I might regret.'

She glanced over my shoulder and stiffened. Beckwith had slipped back into his seat, a satisfied grin on his well-fed face.

'Can I buy you both a drink.'

Helena crumpled her napkin. 'I'm sorry Miles, but I've developed a shocking headache. If you don't mind, I'm heading off to bed. Captain Rowden's leaving too.'

I was not going to give up that easily.

'Look Miles, I need a quiet word with Elena. Line me up a rum in the bar and I'll see you in five minutes.'

For a moment, I thought he was going to refuse. Then he stood, wished her good night and stalked off.

'I meant what I said. I'm going to bed ... alone.'

'Helena, listen. I shouldn't have said that. I admit I was jealous, but that's no excuse.'

'You're damn right, it's no excuse. I've given you no cause to be jealous, but even if I had, I never promised you anything. The only man I ever promised anything to was Bobby Ashworth, and look where that got me.' Her jaw set with determination. 'I mean it, Rowden. Go. Go! Beckwith's waiting with the rum you ordered. Come back and apologise, when you're in a more amiable frame of mind.'

I pushed back my chair, feeling the blood pounding in my chest. 'We sail any day, I don't know when I'll be back. You should consider leaving with the Coopers. It's not going to end well here.'

'You're right, it's not ending well. Good night.'

She stood and walked away, while a voice in my head screamed at me to call her back.

Beckwith was in the bar with a gloomy look on his face. It turned into a sly grin as I took the seat next to him.

'I thought I ...'

'Well, we both thought wrong.' I shrugged my shoulders, reached for the rum and downed it.

'Women!' said Beckwith, draining his glass. 'Can't live with 'em, can't live without 'em.'

'Don't worry, Elena will be upstairs saying the same thing about men.'

I nodded when he signalled to the barman.

'Keep 'em coming. We've both got sorrows to drown.'

CHAPTER TWENTY-ONE

Tuesday 23 to Wednesday 24 December 1941

'For God's sake man. Have you forgotten how to salute?' shouted Lieutenant-Commander Barker.

'No, sir. Sorry, sir.' Bullen stiffened to attention and snapped his palm to the peak of his cap; in an identical repeat of the salute he had just delivered.

'Who are you anyway?'

'Petty Officer Bullen, sir. In charge of the guns and the DEMS party.'

'DEMS? What the devil is that?'

'Defensively Armed Merchant Ship, sir.'

'What flag are we flying, Bullen?'

'Blue ensign, sir.'

'Exactly! You're back in the navy now Bullen. I don't know what nonsense you've been allowed to get away with. But it all stops now. Do you hear me?'

'Is there a problem, Lieutenant Barker?' I kept my eyes fixed on the compass binnacle. We were making the final turn, rounding Changi Point, before entering the broader waters of the Singapore Strait.

'No, not now Rowden, and it's lieutenant-commander if you please. Or just commander for short.'

I counted to ten before turning to Lamont. He was calling out bearings and headings as I conned the ship down the narrow, twisting channel separating Singapore from Johore. 'Keep her on this heading until we're clear of the Johore shoal. Then set course for the Main Strait.' I glanced at my wristwatch, thankful I managed to keep the anger out of my voice. It was just after 7am, long past the end of Lamont's watch. 'Once she's steady on the new course, hand over to McGrath and get your head down.'

'Aye aye, Skipper.'

I stepped out onto the bridge wing. The early morning mist clouding Dockyard Reach had burned off as we slipped downstream. Already, the morning was hot and bright, a hint of breeze ruffling the sparkling waters of the strait. Astern on either side, like two large chicks following their mother duck, the launches carved effortlessly through the low swell. Behind each of them, two motor boats tugged at the end of their tow lines. Barker was, no doubt, pleased to command a fleet of his own, even if his flagship was only a tramp steamer, but he had made a nuisance of himself from the moment he stepped aboard the previous evening. He demanded to know why I had not met him in person, criticised the crew's dress standards, and insisted on being saluted. He even complained about his cabin, wiping a white-gloved finger over the surfaces and loudly dressing down Da Silva over its dustiness. It was all a petty act to assert authority in unfamiliar surroundings. He was treading dangerous ground; Da Silva was not a man to cross. There were plenty of ways he could make Barker's stay on board very uncomfortable.

From inside the wheelhouse, Lamont called the helm orders to bring the ship onto its new heading of west-south-west. Moments later, he joined me on the bridge wing.

'Mr McGrath has the watch, Skipper. I've marked all the minefields on the charts. The courses give them as wide a berth as possible. Permission to go below.'

'Yes please, Second. You did a good job of pilotage in the Johore Strait.'

'Thank you, sir.'

'Okay. Go and get your head down for a couple of hours.'

His feet clattered down the ladder to the boat deck. Astern, the white flecked arc of the wake marked the point of the course change. The ship slowed in the turn, allowing the launches to creep forward towards the beam.

'Signalman!' Barker's angry yell was almost right in my ear. 'Signal those launches. Keep better station.'

A naval rating, one of several that boarded with Barker, leapt for the signal lamp. The rapid clacking of its shutter was followed by a blinked acknowledgement from the launches.

Barker rapped his knuckles on the rail with annoyance, as if their station-keeping was our fault. 'What's the most you can get out of this ship, Rowden?'

'Ten knots. As I told Captain Mulock.'

'Pah! I suppose your chief clanky will tell me his precious boilers can't stand an increase in pressure. That's what they all say.'

'You don't need to ask him. I'll tell you the same. Ten knots, down-wind on a good day. Take it or leave it.' I pointed at the launches, now back in position on either quarter. 'Conditions are fine now. But if the nor-east monsoon picks up they'll be struggling to make even ten knots, towing those boats.'

'We'll see about that. This is the navy, Rowden, we don't make excuses. Who's the officer in charge of your guns?'

'The second mate, Lamont.' Anger flushed my face. Barker was barely out his twenties, little older than McGrath. I clenched my fists behind my back, fighting the urge to knock the sneer off his face.

'Well get him up here. I want all the gun crews exercised. If they're as sloppy as that Petty Officer Bullen, God help us when the shooting starts.'

'I've just sent him below. He's been on watch since four o'clock.'

'This is not a debate, Rowden.'

I raised a hand and jerked a thumb towards the far end of the bridge wing. 'Unless you want the bridge crew to hear me tell you your fortune, I suggest we move out of earshot.'

I stalked away, wondering if he would follow me. When I reached the end, I glanced over my shoulder. Barker was right behind me. I turned to face him. He was a couple of inches taller than me, but slender. His white uniform hung loosely on his bony frame. Under the brim of his cap, his eyes bulged and there was a pink flush to his face.

'I'm in command here, Rowden. You can't speak to me like that.'

I stepped towards him until our chests were almost touching and looked him straight in the eye. 'Who's in command of this ship?' I kept my voice level, not just to keep the conversation private, but also in the hope of appealing to his reason.

'You are, but—'

'No buts. I'm in command of the ship,' I pointed to the four gold bars on my shoulders. 'That's what these mean, and though, technically, I'm only a reserve lieutenant, when I'm aboard I'm entitled to be called captain, even by you. Are we clear so far?'

Barker's face darkened as his eyes flashed with anger. 'I could have you court-martialled for insubordination.'

'If I'm going to be court-martialled, then I might as well punch your fucking lights out and be done with you.' I maintained the most inoffensive smile I could muster. 'I don't know for whose benefit your little performances have been. They're not going to win you any respect here. You're just making enemies and earning yourself the possibility of a knife in the back, or an accidental shove overboard.'

'Are you ... threatening me?' He spluttered the words, as if unable to believe his ears.

'Threatening you? That was just my morbid sense of humour. You'll know when I'm threatening you.' I raised a clenched fist, giving him a good view of the cock tattooed on my forearm. 'I didn't get here by allowing myself to be pushed around by upstarts, in or out of uniform. But I tell you what. Maybe we got off on the wrong foot. I know you're the senior officer in charge of the naval operation, but this is still my ship, and all her crew, including Bullen's DEMS party, work for me. If you've anything to say about it, or them, you come to me first.'

Barker's mouth opened to reply but, before he had a chance to speak, I saw Bullen still in the wheelhouse. 'Petty Officer Bullen. Can you spare me a moment?' My command voice would easily have carried to the forecastle. Bullen marched out of the wheelhouse and drew himself to attention, warily eyeing Barker.

'Commander Barker has suggested we exercise the guns' crews. I should have thought of it myself, where we're going there are bound to be enemy planes looking for targets.'

Bullen nodded. 'Yes, sir.'

'Make my apologies to Mr Lamont and ask him to take his normal station aft. The general alarm will sound shortly.' I turned to Barker; a polite smile pasted to my face. 'Anything to add Commander?'

'I'll time them with a bloody ... I suggest you use a stopwatch.'

'Excellent idea. Make it so Mr Bullen.'

Barker waited until Bullen was out of earshot. 'You can call yourself captain, but of what, this old rust bucket? She's nothing but a floating ham and jam depot for those doing the real fighting. I won't forget this. You called me an upstart. Well, you can call me what you bloody well like. But make one mistake, and I'll personally make sure the only thing you ever command again will be a shit scow at the arse end of the world.' He glared down at me, the red spots glowing on his cheeks, his lips compressed into a tight line. The corners of his mouth twisted into a feral grin. 'No offence meant, of course.'

I returned the grin, not sure whether I had made a mortal enemy. 'None taken, Commander Barker.'

'Right then.' He raised his wrist to consult a gold watch. 'It's eight bells. We have two hundred miles to run. I expect to be alongside before zero eight hundred tomorrow. Now, sound the alarm and let's see how fast your DEMS people can bring their guns to readiness.'

I ordered Lakshman to ring the bell. Yelled orders were followed by the thud of boots as the gunners raced to their stations. Behind me, men scrambled up the ladder to the Monkey Island, pulling on steel helmets, grabbing the stocks of the Oerlikons and Lewis guns and swinging their barrels skywards. Barker impatiently rapped his fingers on the hand rail while we waited. It was a little over three minutes after the ringing of the bell when Bullen finally reported the gun teams closed up. It seemed reasonable to me, but the sardonic grin on Barker's lips suggested he was unimpressed.

'It's your ship but, if they want to stay alive, they need to do better than that. Try again later in the morning, but don't give them any warning.' He turned towards the ladder. 'I'm going below. Have the officer of the watch keep an eye on the launches. Call me if there's the slightest change.'

I was grateful to see him go. There was little to occupy him on the bridge, apart from looking over my shoulder. There was equally little to occupy him in his cabin, apart from the inevitable paperwork the navy seemed to thrive on.

The appearance of Lakshman reminded me the watch had changed. He climbed up to the Monkey Island to take cross bearings, dodging the gunners securing the weapons and packing the ammunition back into the ready use lockers. I waited until he plotted the position on the chart and checked our progress. The sharp ridges of Saint John's Island were visible fine on the starboard bow. The bulk of Singapore Island lay to the north, with the green clad slopes of Bukit Timah rising behind the city. There were ships anchored in the roads. It all looked so normal and peaceful.

I wondered if Helena was awake and enjoying an early breakfast at Raffles. In the twenty-four hours since she sent me packing, I had heard nothing from her. Nor had I expected to; my ears still burnt from her parting words, *It's not ending well.* I could have telephoned to apologise, but I didn't think all the fault was mine, and I didn't know what to say to bridge the chasm that had suddenly opened between us. There had been occasional romantic interludes in my life, usually as fleeting as tides and sailing schedules permitted. Some finished amicably, but mostly one or other of us had been glad to call an end. Teresa, whom I had met in Liverpool the previous year, had been an exception. Even though already married, she was the closest I had come to imagining a wife or a lover in whose arms I could forget the rough-edged existence of the merchant seaman. The war had only increased that longing. Helena was different. There was no prospect of her settling down to enjoy the companionship of another marriage, an institution that would never cage or tame her. Nor of tying herself to a man who might be gone for months or years at a time. She was a wanderer, a free-spirit, who lived and loved on the strength of her own wits and resources. We had that in common, and I might as well have dreamed of snaring the westerly winds that forever circled the southern oceans. But I had felt her fire, had held it for a time in my arms, and it had burned an indelible impression that left me wanting more, as if the only way to quench the fire was to feel its heat again.

I had always laughed at the feverish emotions of lovers depicted in romances. Now, the thoughts swirling in my head resembled one. I shook it to try and dislodge them. It was pointless daydreaming about the unattainable. We had a war to fight.

For the next couple of hours, we steamed steadily on, keeping within the channel between the minefields. Approaching Coney Islet, where Raffles Light marked the centre of the Main Strait, I sent Lakshman down to tell Barker we were about to alter course towards the Malacca Strait.

He emerged through the chartroom just as we steadied onto the new course. This time the launch skippers were more alert and maintained station astern. The wind had freshened, chopping up the waters of the strait, and the motor boats yawed at the end of their tow lines. Monsoon rain clouds were building up to the northeast and it looked like being an uncomfortable afternoon for those in the open bridged launches.

Barker glanced at his watch. I took the hint.

'ENEMY AIRCRAFT SIGHTED,' I roared, at the top of my lungs. Grabbing the whistle lanyard, I blew the emergency signal.

The unexpected blasts and the repeated yells of enemy aircraft resulted in a mad scramble. Men pulling on boots, clothes and helmets while climbing stairs, reminded me of the Keystone Cops. Even Barker suppressed a grin, especially when he saw the startled launch crews jump to the conclusion we were under attack and race to man their own guns.

When Bullen's call announced the guns' readiness, I realised I had forgotten to start the stopwatch. I glanced at Barker, who was glaring at his wristwatch.

'A few seconds faster, but I'm sure if PO Bullen puts his mind to it they can do better. Eh, Bullen?'

'Yes, sir.'

'Good. I'll leave you to it then.' He stalked away.

Bullen's face relaxed into a grin. 'You had us going there, sir. Blowing the whistle and yelling like that.'

'Have to keep Commander Barker happy.' I returned his grin.

'Old school he is, sir. Mostly all bark. If you'll pardon the pun.'

He went off chuckling, leaving me to wonder whether I had misread Barker.

The next few hours did little to enlighten me.

By noon we were passed Tanjong Bolus, the southernmost tip of Malaya, and steaming north-west by west through the Malacca Strait. With the monsoon wind settling in, thunderclouds ringed the horizon and torrential rain showers frequently blotted out visibility.

In a break between showers, Lamont took cross bearings to fix our position. I joined him in the wheelhouse. His unlit pipe was clamped between his teeth. I almost felt guilty that my presence stopped him lighting it.

'You have checked the pilot book?'

'Yes, Skipper. I'm following the recommended track for steamers.'

I nodded. The track followed the centre of the deep-water channel between the sandbars on either side of the strait. 'And the current?'

'It's two hours to high water, so I've allowed for the easterly set. The current will reverse towards evening. I'll make certain Mr McGrath knows when to make an adjustment.'

'You might want to bear in mind that anyone coming the other way might also be following the steamer track. It wouldn't hurt to be five cables to the east. Hopefully, we'll sight Mount Formosa before sunset and get a check on our position.'

The horizon disappeared behind another rain squall, the thick, heavy drops temporarily flattening the sea and raising a low cloud of spray that looked like smoke on the water's surface.

'Pity those bastards in the launches. You'd better keep an eye on them.'

'Aye, Skipper.' Lamont pulled an oilskin off a peg, slipped it over his shoulders and darted onto the bridge wing.

Predictably, the launches and their tows made heavy weather of the monsoon conditions, pitching and rolling in the steep, choppy seas. It was not long before the first tow line snapped, quickly followed by another. I sent word to Barker. He arrived moments later and stalked out to the bridge wing. Ignoring the rain, he yelled curses and ordered sharply worded signals that he must have known would do little to help the skippers battling to reconnect their tows. Reducing speed eased the strain on the lines but not enough to stop them breaking in the heavier squalls. It was a long, dreary afternoon, the one consolation being that the murk effectively concealed us from any patrolling Japanese aircraft.

Conditions had not improved by sunset and I resigned myself to another long night on the bridge. I knew the coast of Malaya well. Malacca, Port Swettenham and Penang had all been frequent ports of call before the war. There had been lighthouses to guide us then. Now, the coast was pitch black, except where the faint light of hurricane lamps and charcoal fires illuminated coastal settlements. Fortunately, once past the Formosa River the sandbars trailed away leaving the broad waters of the strait unimpeded, except for the occasional shoal on the western side.

The weather conditions eased towards midnight, and the tow lines stopped breaking with such frequency. By 1am, a faint glow in the eastern sky announced that we were abeam of the old Portuguese and Dutch city of Malacca, and that the blackout regulations were not being enforced. With the rain also easing, I was able to pace the bridge wing, dragging in lungfuls of cool air to keep me awake. Da Silva, who seemed to need less sleep than I did, fetched regular pots of hot, strong coffee to the wheelhouse, which also helped restore my overworked sense of humour.

Fortified, I carried a mug out to Barker who had also remained on the bridge since the afternoon. He was facing aft, staring in the direction of the launches. They were keeping station two cables off either quarter, but all that was visible of them in the darkness was the pale tumble of their bow waves.

'Why don't you get your head down for a couple of hours? I'll keep an eye on them.' I handed him the steaming mug.

'Thanks, but no thanks.' He accepted it and took a sip. 'You're not going to sweet talk me that easily. Those bloody launch skippers. Not a decent seaman between them. I told them to increase the length of the tow lines.'

'Conditions are improving, they're doing better now.'

'I can see that for myself. But you were right, damn you. We won't see Port Swettenham until this afternoon.' Barker waved a ghostly hand in the direction of the launches. 'Left on their own, I doubt they'd find it anyway.'

I grinned at the back handed compliment. 'It's not that hard.

North-west by west most of the way. Keep going until Parcelar Hill bears due east, and turn right.'

'Easy for you to say, you do it all the time. I didn't do very well on the navigator's course at Dryad. Gunnery was a whole lot easier.'

'Is that what you were, in *Repulse?*'

'Yes, and a fat lot of good my 15-inch guns were against torpedo bombers.'

'We saw you, you know. The afternoon you left Singapore. It was Bullen who thought to dip the ensign and wish you good hunting.'

'Break a leg might have been more appropriate. Oh well, that's something you can tell your grandchildren. That you saw *Prince of Wales* and *Repulse* sail off into the sunset for the last time.'

I was reflecting on the unlikelihood of ever having grandchildren, when a light flashed out of the darkness.

'Fuck! That's another line parted,' said Barker.

I stopped the engine and we drifted until another flurry of Morse confirmed the tow had been reconnected.

We steamed on, and by dawn were well past Port Dickson, with Parcelar Hill visible at ten miles on the starboard bow. It was another bright morning with a gentle land breeze and, in calmer waters, the launches and their tows made better progress. By 9am we were rounding the western edge of Carey Island and steering north towards the white columned lighthouse on the tip of Pinto Gedong. Abeam of Pulo Lumut, I ordered the helm to starboard and swung the ship into the southern entrance channel to Port Swettenham. The mangroves on either side gleamed bright green in the morning sunlight. A pair of roosting sea eagles took flight, soaring skywards, their white breasts bright against the blue sky.

Approaching the northern end of Pulo Lumut, I rang slow ahead and swung the ship into Port Swettenham roads. There were several ships anchored midstream and a couple alongside the southern wharves. Our orders were to berth at the deep-water jetty south of the town. I raised my glasses and studied the signal mast beside the Harbourmaster's office. The red ball suspended from the northern yardarm indicated the tide was on the flood, the current flowing south in the roads.

'I hope you weren't expecting a tug. The navy doesn't believe in such luxuries.' I turned to find Barker with what looked suspiciously like a malicious grin written across his face.

I nodded at McGrath, who was waiting with his mate's whistle to pipe the crew to mooring stations

'Clear away the port anchor. Starboard side alongside. Signal the launches to keep clear while we dock.'

Slipping past the ships anchored in the roads, I swung *Oriental Venture* into a tight curve, watching that the tide did not sweep us too close to the wharf. Completing the turn, I stemmed the tide and crabbed the ship across it until the bow was close enough for the first heaving line to be grabbed by the waiting dockers. A short burst from the engine with full port rudder kicked the stern in. The ship glided alongside with only a gentle creak from the fenders. The rest of the lines snaked ashore and were swiftly made fast.

'Ring finished with engines, Third.' I waited until Lakshman had rung the telegraph and pulled off my cap to mop my brow with a handkerchief. It was a warm, humid morning, but that was not why I was sweating. I had berthed the ship in trickier places, but never under the critical eye of a man happy to see me make a fool of myself. Barker disappeared below without a word of acknowledgement.

'Something else to add to your journal, Third?'

'Yes, sir. I shall make some fair notes and sketches. If you would not mind checking them?'

'Drop them on my desk later and I'll take a look. First things first, though. Once you're all secure up here, get the derricks hoisted, but leave the hatch covers on until the army turns up.' I headed for the chartroom door. 'Oh, and don't get your hopes up about a run ashore. There's nothing here worth seeing and the jungle's full of mosquitoes, snakes and crocodiles. The Mariners' Club does a good meal and there's a swimming pool.' I hesitated, knowing he would not like what I had to say next. Despite its name, the club did not welcome all mariners. 'If you want to go there, my advice is to tag along with one of the other mates or one of the engineers. I'm afraid what happened at Raffles was not an exception.'

His head wobbled and his mouth drooped. 'Thank you, Captain. I understand.'

'Look, I'm sorry about what happened. But we're not all like that young idiot.'

'I know, sir. Still, it was painful to be reminded that the colour of one's skin marks one out as ... second rate.' The words were tinged with bitterness and resentment. Justifiably, but I didn't need him dwelling on it.

'Not in my ship, Mr Lakshman. Now, you've got a job to do.'

I left him to it and went below to find a throng of port officials in my cabin already drinking my coffee. Unshaven, unwashed and dog tired after 24 hours on the bridge, they were the last thing I wanted to see, but the only way to get rid of them was to deal with their paperwork as swiftly as possible. I was about to sit down and join them when Barker poked his head around the door. Despite being on the bridge almost as long as I had, he was clean shaven, dressed in a neatly pressed uniform and looked as fresh as if he had slept for eight uninterrupted hours. He saw the surprise in my eyes and grinned.

'Years' of naval training. I'm off to report our arrival to the authorities. The launches are rafted up alongside and their crews are getting some shut eye. I suggest you keep the lookouts posted watching for Japanese aircraft. The port will be a target and you're a sitting duck in the middle of it.'

'Cheerful sod,' I muttered at his receding back.

Slumping into the chair, I glared at the pile of papers on my desk all waiting to be signed and chopped by the assembled officials. I twisted my lips into the best smile my tired facial muscles could muster, and reached for my pen. 'Right, who's first. The sooner I get rid of you all, the sooner I can get my head down.'

CHAPTER TWENTY-TWO

Thursday 25 December 1941

T he cook had performed a miracle. The saloon tables groaned under the weight of a Christmas dinner that would hardly have disgraced the Raffles Hotel, and was heartily approved of by the officers and engineers of *Oriental Venture* and their Royal Navy guests. Sitting at my anointed place under the portrait of King George, I watched the men fill their bellies. There were chicken, goat and vegetable curries from which tantalising aromas wafted; heaped plates of rice and noodles and, for those who still preferred their food plain, mounds of fried potatoes, fish, eggs and thick slices of Spam. The navy supplied a generous issue of rum, which I supplemented with bottles of scotch and several cases of Tiger beer. The naval ratings and the crew were equally well catered for. Neither the Chinese nor the Somalis had ever bothered celebrating Christmas on board before, but they were not going to turn down the chance of a feast. The only challenge had been ensuring the Chinese did not slaughter and cook their pig within sight of the Somalis.

The 24 hours since our arrival confirmed the old saying—if any such confirmation was necessary—there was no peace for the wicked and even less for the righteous. No sooner had the arrival paperwork been completed, than the lieutenants commanding the launches were badgering McGrath to unload sufficient fuel drums to top their tanks up. Several army trucks turned up and a moustachioed, red-faced sergeant presented a list of stores and equipment to be unloaded. The crew worked the winches and derricks and a squad of sweating Tommies heaved the loads onto waiting trucks.

With the prospect of a prolonged period alongside, I suggested to McGrath that it would be a suitable opportunity to repaint the hull and draught marks. Stages were rigged, a makeshift pontoon constructed, and those not driving winches or working in the holds wielded rollers and paint brushes. The weather remained mostly fine during Wednesday afternoon, although towards evening the monsoon thunderclouds returned. Overnight, we were treated to a ferocious electrical storm, with near continuous flashes of lightning and massive thunderclaps accompanied by torrential rain. Or so I was told. After 36 hours without sleep and several rums, I slept like the dead, waking late on Christmas morning.

During the morning, word was sent to the launch commanders to be ready to sail at first light on Boxing Day. In the meantime, all the crews were given permission to celebrate Christmas, which we were now doing in the best traditions of the navy, eating and drinking as if there was no tomorrow. For some, that was likely to prove a fatally accurate prediction.

My own officers were doing their utmost to preserve the reputation of the merchant navy as a service full of disreputable drunks. Some of the engineers already looked as if they would have difficulty standing. Fraser was clinging to a bottle of Laphroaig, one of the dwindling number Poh had supplied him in Singapore. Cramp had wrapped a red bandanna around his head, which, together with his gold earring and heavily tattooed forearms, made him look even more like the piratical gypsy he was. The chief steward was eyeing the rapidly growing pile of empty bottles with an avaricious grin, as if in anticipation of the kickback he expected from the providore. Only Lakshman and I were relatively sober, so at least there were two clear heads in the event of an emergency.

Thus far, however, the Japanese had respected the birth of Christ and the air raid warning siren had been thankfully silent.

Amidst the babble of conversation and laughter, a commanding voice strove to be heard.

'A poem, gentlemen, a Christmas poem.' Flush faced, Lamont rose to his feet clutching a glass of whisky in one hand and banging the table with the other. The hubbub died away.

'It was Christmas Day in the workhouse.' A raucous cheer drowned him out.

'It was Christmas Day in the workhouse,' persisted Lamont. He thumped his fist again to command silence and began to recite.

'It was Christmas Day in the workhouse,
The happiest day of the year.
Our hearts were full of gladness
And our bellies full of beer.
Up jumped a brave young sailor,

His face as bold as brass.
We've got no room for Christmas pud,
You can stick that up yer arse.'

The rest was drowned out by cheering as the cook appeared bearing a tray on which sat an enormous boiled fruit duff. He placed it in the centre of the table. One of the naval officers sloshed rum over it and struck a match. Blue flames engulfed the pudding and spilt onto the table where they were hastily patted out.

McGrath rose, flourishing a carving knife and hacked the duff into generous portions which were topped off by a thick, yellow liquid poured from a large jug. Whether or not it was real custard I never discovered. Before I had a chance to taste it, Da Silva arrived at my side and whispered that Colonel Spencer and Commander Barker were awaiting my presence in my cabin.

I found them already sampling my whisky and puffing on Spencer's cheroots, the smoke of which assaulted my nostrils.

'I see you've helped yourselves. Why don't you come down and join us?'

'Sorry, Bill,' said Spencer, grinning. 'Didn't think you'd mind, seeing it's Christmas.' The noise of the party echoed up the staircase from the deck below. 'Sounds like they're all having a good time. We might pop down after, if there's anything left. Would you mind closing the door, old boy?'

I pulled it to and sat at the chair behind my desk. 'Why do I have the feeling you haven't come here just to wish me the compliments of the season.'

Spencer winked at Barker. 'He knows me too well.' He reached down to the briefcase at his feet, pulled out a map and laid it on the desk. 'May I?'

He unfolded a large map of Malaya.

'Commander Barker and I have just come from a briefing with Major Thorne and the Thorne Force commanders.' He jabbed a finger onto the map. 'We're at Port Swettenham, here, as you know. Have you got a soft pencil?'

I reached into the drawer, and handed him a 4B.

'As of yesterday, the Japs were here, around Taiping on the west coast, and here at Kuantan on the east. He drew thick circles around the towns and joined them with a diagonal line running south-east across the map.

My mouth gaped in surprise.

'That's right,' he continued. 'They've already gained control of over half the peninsula. It's not all bad news, though. As we fall back our lines of communication get shorter, the length of the front we have to defend gets shorter and we still have the Australian Eighth Division in reserve.'

Spencer paused to take a large gulp of scotch and a drag of his cheroot. I took the opportunity to study the map. In a direct line, the Japanese were just over one hundred miles from where we sat. Despite all the reassurances from the governor and army high command, they had made remarkably swift progress.

'I know what you're thinking,' said Spencer. 'If the Japs have already got that far, what's it going take to stop them. Correct?'

I nodded.

'Time. We need to buy some time while we consolidate defensive positions further south.' He tapped the map with the pencil. 'Here's Taiping. See this road?' He traced the pencil along it. 'It heads south and then east towards Kuala Kangsar and the bridge over the Perak River.' He drew another circle. 'If we can blow that bridge, it'll make it much harder for the Japanese to outflank us as we pull back behind the river. That's where Thorne Force comes in. They're going to blow it up on Saturday night.'

'Christ! That doesn't leave them much time.'

'That's up to Commander Barker and his launches. They sail at zero nine hundred tomorrow towing the motor boats. They carry the force to the mouth of the Trong River where they transfer to the boats. From there they have to find their way upstream to Trong. Hopefully it's deep enough all the way. After that it's shanks's nag.'

'How many men?'

'Two platoons of twenty-five, one in each launch. It'll be a tight squeeze with all their weapons and explosives. They're already here by the way. Holed up at the Mariners' Club, probably enjoying their Christmas dinner as we speak.'

I turned to Barker. 'It's one hundred nautical miles from here to the Trong River. You've got to get past the shoals at the mouth of the Perak, the Dinding Islands, and then find the right river mouth. They all look the same on that stretch of coast, especially in the dark.'

Barker nodded. 'We need to be off the river mouth by midnight tomorrow. That will give the boats five hours to get upriver to the landing site. The troops need to be ashore by daylight if they're to have any chance of getting to the bridge by nightfall.'

'Tricky piece of navigation.' I regretted saying it as soon as I opened my mouth, and even more when I saw the knowing smiles light up their eyes.

'Oh, no you don't. This is nothing to do with me. It's a military operation.'

'Ah, now there you're wrong Bill.' Spencer's grin was as wide and foreboding as a Cheshire Cat's. 'None of the naval officers know this coast as well as you. You're a commissioned lieutenant and Commander Barker is your superior officer. He could order you to go, but I'd take it as a personal favour if you'd volunteer.'

I yanked open the drawer, grabbed the tin of Senior Service and wrenched off the lid. My nostrils twitched at the familiar smell of strong Virginia tobacco. I pulled one out, tapped the end with my thumbnail and jammed it between my lips.

'I thought you'd given up,' said Spencer.

'Just pass me your lighter … and pour me one of those.' I pointed at the scotch bottle.

I took a deep drag, feeling the calming effect of the nicotine, reached for the glass and drained it. 'One of these days I'm going to wring your bloody neck.'

'That's a little unfair, Bill,' said Spencer. His tone almost sounded as if I'd hurt his feelings. 'It was you suggested we take on that U-boat in Palau in thirty-seven. And I didn't tell you to ram that one last year. Anyway, it's not as if you've got to do any fighting. Your job's just to pilot the launches there and back.'

I shook my head in resignation. 'Why do I have the feeling I've been outmanoeuvred yet again.' I took another deep drag of the cigarette, feeling a little light headed. 'Is there anything else you ought to tell me?'

'That's the spirit,' said Barker. 'Knew we could count on you.' He reached into his pocket and pulled out a thick envelope. 'Present for you.'

I opened it to find a pair of shoulder straps with a reserve lieutenant's interwoven, wavy gold stripes and a Royal Navy cap badge.

'You'll need to wear those. If you're captured looking like a civilian, you'll be shot out of hand, as a spy.'

'What happens to the ship while I'm away?'

'Nothing, she'll still be here when you get back.' His grin widened, revealing long teeth that suddenly resembled fangs. 'If not, your chief mate's got a master's certificate. I'm sure he's quite capable of taking her back to Singapore … or wherever we require her next.'

'Right then, that's all settled,' said Spencer. He reached for the bottle and topped up our glasses. 'Let's drink to good fortune for Thorne

Force, and then go and see what the gannets have left for our Christmas dinner.'

We chinked our glasses and drained them. The nicotine and the alcohol were doing their best to lighten my mood, but not enough to dispel the tingling that had returned to my fingertips.

CHAPTER TWENTY-THREE

Forenoon, Friday 26 December 1941

I f there were sore heads among the soldiers and sailors crammed into the launches, none were prepared to admit it. Not even me. Promptly at 9am, their twin Thornycroft diesels coughed into life, the mooring lines were cast off and we slipped away from the ship's side. In the leading launch, with the engines purring smoothly at 250 revolutions per minute, we eased through the roadstead with a motor boat towed close astern at the end of a short line. Entering the Klang Strait, I ordered starboard helm and told the coxswain to keep to the middle of the channel. At the transom, a seaman veered the tow line to its maximum length. Further astern, the second launch followed in our wake.

I turned to the young lieutenant in command of the launch. 'I'm sorry, can you remind me of your name again?'

'Perkins, sir.'

'Do you have to call me, sir? We're the same rank.'

Perkins glanced nervously at the collection of gold braid on the shoulders of Colonel Spencer, Commander Barker and the army's Captain Nettles who, together with the coxswain and me, were crowded into the launch's open bridge.

'Probably, sir. Especially seeing as you're a captain really.'

I ignored Barker's strangled cough. Perkins was probably just being polite, in deference to my grey hair and wrinkles.

'Well Mr Perkins, I think you can start working up to cruising speed, or whatever it is that keeps the towlines intact.' I pointed ahead to where the coast of Pulo Klang curved away to the west. 'When that point's abaft the beam, bring her round to three one eight degrees. You'll see Pulo Besar come into view to starboard and Pulo Angsa to port. Keep to the Angsa side. Keep going until you're well past and then come round to three zero five degrees. That'll take you clear into the Malacca Strait. Got all that?'

'Yes, sir.'

'I won't be far away.' I patted the gyro compass repeater in its gimbal bolted to the bridge wing. Unlike the binnacles on *Oriental Venture* with their magnetic compasses, the launch's gyro compass was constantly aligned to geographic north, and provided true bearings that did not have to be adjusted for variation and deviation. It was an expensive luxury most tramp steamer owners avoided.

Perkins rang Full Ahead on the engine telegraphs, the purring increased to a deep-throated roar, the deck throbbed and the launch surged ahead. The tachometer needles wound up to 800 rpm but, with the extra weight of 30 bodies and equipment, plus a towed motor boat, I estimated the speed at about 8 knots; enough to arrive at the Trong River by midnight, if nothing went wrong. The wake streamed astern like a giant jagged arrowhead. It was also crooked; the towed boat yawing back and forth across it. No wonder tow lines parted in rougher weather. It was not the coxswain's fault. He was working hard to maintain course, occasionally glancing up from the steering compass to check the horizon for anything to use as a mark to steer by.

'Do these launches always behave like this?' I asked Perkins.

'Yes, they have two over-sized rudders, but the keel ends thirteen feet before the stern. So they do tend to skate about a bit. They can turn on a sixpence, though.'

I ran my eye over the rest of the launch. It was not just the bridge that was crowded. The whole craft was packed with men and equipment. In addition to its crew of 12, whose sleeping and eating quarters were crammed into the hull, 25 Australian soldiers lounged about the open decks or had squeezed below. Their weapons and packs filled every available space from the crew's mess in the bow to the tiny officer's wardroom aft. As if that was not already enough, there was a sub-lieutenant, who hardly looked old enough to shave, and the two seamen who would crew the motor boat.

Mounted on the long, slender foredeck was a 3-pound naval gun. Abaft it was the squat enclosed chartroom with a secondary steering position. The armour-plated rectangle of the elevated bridge rose behind, with the main steering position and engine controls. A semi-circular blister on each side housed swivel mounted Lewis guns. Behind the bridge rose the signal mast, beside which two lookouts scanned the sky. Further aft was the raised coach house of the officer's wardroom with a 20-mm Oerlikon mounted on the roof. Empty cradles edged the narrow strip of deck either side. Their depth charges had been left ashore to reduce weight. Seamen manned each of the guns. There was little place else to stand with the boat so crowded.

It was a bright sunny morning and, with the steady, reassuring bass of the engines, the sparkling water flashing by, the cool breeze of our passage and the eager looks on the faces of the young naval officers, there was an infectious sense of excitement.

'AIRCRAFT, GREEN TEN, ELEVATION FORTY-FIVE DEGREES.' The lookout's yell momentarily drowned out the engine noise.

All eyes swivelled towards a swarm of black dots that rapidly transformed into a formation of twin-engined bombers. The Oerlikon and Lewis guns rotated to starboard, their barrels elevating to track the aircraft. Some of the soldiers raised their machine guns, while several more wrestled to find space to train a Bren gun.

'HOLD YOUR FIRE,' shouted Spencer. 'They're not interested in us, and they're out of range anyway. The port's going to cop it, though.'

The bombers flew steadily on towards Port Swettenham. Bursts of grey smoke filled the air as the anti-aircraft batteries opened fire.

We had a ringside seat as the bombers took turns peeling away from the formation to dive bomb and machine gun the port. We were too far away to make out damage to individual ships and installations, but the plumes of black smoke told their own story. It was not a one-sided contest. The anti-aircraft barrage was heavy, causing the bombers to jink in their approaches. At least two took hits. One of them smashed into the ground behind the town, while the other turned away to the north, trailing smoke.

I studied the plumes through my binoculars. Did *Oriental Venture* lie at the foot of one them? Packed with drums of diesel and other inflammables, she was a convenient target close to palm oil and fuel tanks. Was she already ablaze, while those not killed by explosion or fire raced to salvage their few possessions before watching her die?

I felt a nudge at my elbow. Barker had moved to my side and was gazing astern.

'It hurts, doesn't it. The thought of losing your ship,' he said.

I nodded. It was the simple truth. Except she wasn't just a ship, she was my life.

'I wouldn't worry. Chances are they missed her.' He waved an encompassing arm. 'Most of the men, both here and on the other launch lost their ships when *Repulse* and *Prince of Wales* went down. It's a common hazard for sailors in wartime. Why do you think they look so keen? This is a chance for them to hit back. The operation might seem like a gnat goading a bull but, for them, it's the best way of avenging what ... and who ... we lost.' He turned and shouted down the hatch into the chartroom. 'Pass the word to the cook. Have him brew up tea for everyone. It's going to be a bloody long day.'

The tea was strong and thickly sweet with condensed milk. There were insufficient mugs to go around, but the Australian soldiers solved the deficiency with their mess tins. With the novelty of departure and the excitement of the air-raid worn off, the soldiers settled down to endure the boredom, stretching out on the decks with their packs for headrests. The off-duty sailors went below to their mess, while Barker and Spencer ducked down to the chartroom leaving Perkins and me with the helmsman and lookouts.

For the remainder of the morning, the little flotilla ploughed steadily on. The sky remained empty and we sighted nothing other than the occasional fishing boat going about its normal business. The Japanese and British Empires might be locked in mortal combat for possession of Malaya, but its fishermen still had families to feed.

By noon, the Selangor River was abeam to starboard, the low, green clad hill at its mouth the only landmark for miles of featureless coast. At intervals I called down bearings for the launch's sublieutenant to plot a fix on the chart, confirming what I could see for myself, that we were making good progress. Shortly after the change of watch, the cook handed round plates of tinned stew warmed over the galley range. It was gristly and colourless, but better than an empty belly.

Relieved on watch by his sub-lieutenant, Perkins offered me a guided tour of his command. It took only a matter of minutes to walk her 72-foot length and her cramped interior made *Oriental Venture* seem palatial. There was a tiny toilet cubicle right forward, using it would be an interesting experience in heavy weather. Aft of it was the crew's mess with sailors and soldiers sprawled on each bunk. A shoe box sized alcove housed the galley with a single washbasin, a small coal fired range and just enough space to prepare the most basic of meals. A bulkhead separated the mess from the engine room where the twin Thornycroft diesels hammered away. Beyond another bulkhead was the tiny petty officer's mess with the radio cubicle opposite. A seaman sat at the tiny desk; headphones clamped over his ears. Finally, under the coach roof, was the officer's wardroom where Perkins and his sub-lieutenant enjoyed the luxury of curtained, padded bunks, a mess table, a spirit locker and their own tiny, but private washroom. Compared to the rest of the launch it was relatively spacious, but was still smaller than my own cabin aboard *Oriental Venture*. Perkins leaned forward and shouted over the thundering of the engines, offering me the use of his bunk should I feel the need to rest.

'You cheeky bastard, I'm not that old,' I replied, speaking too softly for him to hear over the noise. I grinned at his enquiring look and jabbed a thumb upwards.

Spencer was waiting for us when we returned to the bridge.

'Slight change of plan, old boy.' The smug smile on his face suggested he was doing a favour in telling me. 'Just received a wireless signal from HQ. Need you to put us into the mouth of the Bernam River. We have a rendezvous to pick up a local who can guide the boats up the Trong as far as the kampong. There's a landing place beside an old godown. From there, it's only two miles to the road along a track through the forest.'

I ducked below to study the chart. The coastline curving away to the north was flat and low-lying with few features to navigate by. There was deep water all the way to the mouth of the Bernam where a mud bank extended three miles from the shore. With the launches drawing only five and a half feet, there was sufficient depth to cross it and enter the river mouth. The biggest challenge, however, as in most Malayan estuaries, was the thickly planted fishing stakes. Getting in between them was tricky, but at least they marked where the water shoaled.

Back on the bridge, I ordered the coxswain to steer 330 degrees. The bridge was too small to pace, so I wedged myself into a corner.

As the afternoon wore on, the wind freshened. Spray bucketed against the bridge windows which only partially deflected it, to the increasing discomfort of its occupants. The motor boat towing behind jerked fiercely on the tow rope as it yawed across the wake. I was about to suggest the crew bend on another length of line, when there was a savage jerk and the tow parted. Perkins yelled to a seaman to haul in what was left and ordered the launch into a tight turn back towards the boat. Approaching it, he rang the engine to stop and ordered the coxswain to place us alongside.

With the engine ticking over at a soft rumble, we drifted towards the boat with seamen standing by with fenders and boathooks.

The lookout's frantic scream was drowned in the roar of an aero engine. A Japanese fighter streaked overhead, so low its belly seemed to brush the signal mast.

'FULL AHEAD.'

Perkins jammed the engine telegraph levers to the emergency position. The sudden surge of power caught a seaman off guard. Still clutching a fender, he stumbled against the hand rail, lost his balance and tumbled into the water. Perkins shook his head and craned his neck to look for the fighter. It had zoomed up to gain height, turned and was hurtling back towards us from astern.

The crash of the 3-pounder was loud above the engines' roar. The first shell bust behind the fighter. The second was closer, rocking its wings, but it bored on regardless. Adding to the noise, the Oerlikon and Lewis guns opened fire sending streams of tracer straight into its path.

HARD A STARBOARD,' yelled Perkins.

Pin pricks of light rippled from the fighter's engine cowling.

He was right. The launch turned on a sixpence. Bullets splashed into the empty patch of water where we had been.

I clung to the side of the bridge as the launch heeled steeply out of the turn, heading in the opposite direction.

Astern, the fighter had also turned and was lining up for another pass. Again, the Oerlikon and Lewis guns sprayed shells and bullets into its path until it seemed impossible for them to miss.

'HARD A PORT.'

The fighter's guns flashed. This time the pilot guessed correctly, banking steeply to keep his guns on target. Bullets zipped past my ears and zinged and whined off the bridge's armour plating.

Roaring overhead, its belly almost scraping the mast, the fighter climbed away and made a wide sweep to the east before turning in again.

'Bastard's going for the motor boat,' shouted Perkins.

We watched helplessly as the plane dived towards the boat, made a single pass spraying it with gunfire and zoomed skywards out of range of our guns. It circled for a few moments, as if deciding whether to press home its attack, before levelling out and streaking away north-east.

'Probably saving ammunition for more inviting targets,' said Barker, emerging from the chartroom. 'It's a Nakajima Hayabusa, looks very similar to the Mitsubishis their navy flies.'

By the time we pulled alongside the boat, it was already half full of water and settling by the stern. Perkins slowly scanned the surrounding sea through binoculars, but there was no sign of the sailor who had fallen overboard.

'Sink it and let's be on our way,' said Barker, curtly. 'There's no time for a search. Thank God he left the other launch alone.'

Perkins nodded to the Oerlikon gunner. He depressed the barrel and fired. Several shells punched fist sized holes into the boat's hull.

With the motor boat sinking behind us, we resumed course for the Bernam River. The other launch following closely in our wake.

'You realise this fucks up everything,' said Barker, banging his fist against the bridge rail. 'We can't land both platoons with only one motor boat.'

Spencer had remained silent during the fighter attack. Now he turned to me for confirmation.

'Afraid not, Colonel. High tide tomorrow is at five o'clock in the morning. There'll be nine feet of water over the bar, enough to land you at Pasir Hitam on the southern side of the estuary. There's even a jetty there, mostly used by junks. But there are five miles of jungle and two rivers to cross between there and the road to Trong.'

'How come you know so much about this damned coastline?' asked Barker.

I tapped the side of my nose. 'It's what you're paying me the big bucks for.' I winked at Perkins, who was watching with a sly grin. 'I read the pilot book and studied the charts before we left. A good memory helps.'

'Hmpph. We'll see what the local man has to say. He might know a way to get both platoons up river. He's meeting us in a boat. Perhaps we can press that into service. When do we get to the Bernam?'

'Another two hours. How do we find your man?'

'He'll be waiting at the river mouth, from sixteen hundred onwards.'

'Piece of cake. It's only three miles wide. And how do we know the Japanese won't be there?'

'Your job's just to get us there ... Lieutenant Rowden,' growled Barker, placing a distinct emphasis on the lieutenant. 'Just leave the thinking to the colonel and me.'

'As you like.'

'Sir.'

'What?'

'As you like ... sir.'

I turned away, feeling my face flush with anger.

'Would you mind if I had a word with Lieutenant Rowden, Commander Barker?' Spencer steered me aft out of earshot, before Barker had chance to reply.

'For God's sake, Bill. What do you think you're playing at? Making Barker look a fool, in front of his own men.'

'He was right, you won't get one of these launches up the Trong River. I just agreed with him.'

'You good as told him he couldn't read a chart or the pilot book. How would you like it if Lakshman or Lamont said something similar about you?'

'I'd boot them up the backside. Look, I never asked to come on this madcap scheme, you dragooned me into it.'

'Well, you want to be careful Barker doesn't do the same to you. Don't underestimate him. He won the DSC at Narvik last year and pulled dozens of men to safety from the *Repulse*, including her captain. He could make your life very difficult.'

'Yeah, and so could bloody Tojo. And right now, my money's on him.' I had heard enough. Turning my back on Spencer, I stepped back up to the bridge and jammed myself into the corner opposite the scowling Barker. Away to starboard, the coast was an indistinct smudge along the horizon. The Bernam River entered the Malacca Strait only 10 miles south of the Perak, the river behind which, if Spencer was correct, the British Army planned to stand and fight. Thorne Force's task was to slow the Japanese advance but, reduced to 25 men, how effective could it be? And would we land them in time, or had the Japanese already swept all resistance aside and hurdled the river? If so, picking our way farther up the coast in pitch darkness might prove pointless, and fatal.

CHAPTER TWENTY-FOUR

Evening, Friday 26 December 1941

R ain threatened as we slowly threaded our way through the maze of fish traps at the mouth of the Bernam River.

I pointed to the lighthouse, distinct against the dark-green trees of the jungle clad northern bank. 'Bring that onto a bearing of zero-four-zero degrees and you're in the centre of the channel. But you wouldn't think so with all these bloody fish traps. It'd be a nightmare trying to pick your way through them in the darkness.'

It was shortly after 4.30pm and the tide was just starting to ebb. The other launch, together with its tow, was waiting outside the line of fish traps, while we nosed our way into the river to look for the boat containing the local guide. Close inshore, the north-east wind dropped to a gentle breeze, cool with the scent of rain and rank with rotting vegetation. Mist shrouded the river banks and heavy grey clouds were piling up to the east. With the engine idling quietly, the occasional splash of a jumping fish and the hoots and screams of long-tailed macaques carried loud across the still water, adding an eerie sense of mystery that might have explained the slight tingling in my fingertips.

Cooking smells wafted up through the chartroom. The cook was making the most of the calm conditions to serve supper. A seaman thrust a bowl into my hand. A spoon was half-submerged in a congealed mess of canned stew. I picked at it mechanically, watching the bend beyond the lighthouse where the river turned sharply out of sight.

'If we're going to wait here, we may as well drop anchor.' Barker appeared at my elbow clutching a steaming mug of tea.

'I'd advise against it, Commander.' I caught the flash of annoyance in his eyes. 'There's enough depth, but the current will pick up as the ebb strengthens and the bottom is just deep, soft mud, nothing for the anchor to grip.'

A seaman offered me a mug. I sipped the strong, sweet tea to wash away the taste of the greasy stew. I had a strong urge for a cigarette, suddenly grateful for Barker's instruction that there was to be no smoking on the bridge.

'We also might need to leave in a hurry,' I continued. 'We don't want to be messing about retrieving the pick if a plane spots us.'

'I think you're worrying about nothing,' said Barker, his jaw set into a determined line. 'There's no reason the Japs should spot us here. That fighter was patrolling the Strait, looking for ships making for Singapore.' He moved away to join Perkins, who was scanning the river banks through binoculars. 'Any sign of a boat? Anything?'

'Nothing, sir.' Perkins glanced at his watch. 'The rendezvous was from sixteen hundred onwards. It's nearly seventeen hundred now, sir. How long should we wait?'

'Until I decide otherwise, Lieutenant,' said Barker. 'In the meantime, keep your eyes peeled and the lookouts on their toes.'

Spencer's capped head appeared in the hatchway. He scrambled up to the bridge closely followed by Captain Nettles in his slouch hat.

'Any sign of the local man?' asked Spencer.

'A little patience, Colonel. I'm sure he's on his way,' said Barker.

Captain Nettles removed his slouch hat and rubbed a hand through the dense thatch of dark hair covering his skull. He was lean and long faced, with a day's bristles sprouting on his square jaw. 'Not to put too fine a hone on the blade, Commander. The cockatoos'll be roosting soon. Probably time to make like a wallaby, and hop it.'

'That's all very well … Captain. But without a guide, how do you propose finding your way up river to the landing site?' Barker's nostrils curled with annoyance.

'If you can find the entrance to the right billabong, I'm sure we can manage from there. Keep between the banks. Blind Freddy could manage that.'

There was a chortled snort from one of the lookouts.

'Silence!' snapped Barker. 'We'll wait another half hour. It's less than sixty miles to the Trong. We'll still have you there with plenty of time before daylight.'

Spencer nodded his assent. Nettles thrust his way aft, squeezed his backside into an empty space on the coach house roof and pulled out a tobacco pouch. Deftly rolling a cigarette with one hand, he struck a match on his boot heel with the other and settled back to enjoy a smoke. Despite his bravado, it was not as simple as staying between the river banks. The deep water in muddy Malayan rivers generally followed closely along the concave side of the bends. With the moon setting before 2am and the promise of rain, it was going to be a very dark night. Not ideal for picking our way among islands and rocks to find the Trong River, let alone feeling the way up it.

Unable to anchor, Perkins held the launch mid-channel using short bursts of the engine to maintain steerage. A light patter of rain dimpled the river's surface. I could have called for a waterproof jacket, but a rain wet shirt was preferable to a sweat drenched one under a sticky oilskin.

After another burst of slow ahead, Perkins rang the engines to idle. The engine note died to a low rumble and the launch eased forward against the current. As the noise faded, the sounds of the jungle re-emerged, birds squabbling as they roosted for the night and macaques proclaiming their territory. There was also something else, the rattling throb of a badly maintained engine straining at maximum rpm.

The sound could only be coming from upriver. I trained my binoculars on the apex of the bend. Moments later, a native fishing boat surged around it and straightened course; its long, sharp ironwood prow pointing directly at us.

'Fenders over the side. Prepare to embark a passenger,' said Barker, a relieved smile written across his face.

I trained the binoculars. My fingertips tingled as I rotated the focus ring, and the familiar shape of an elegantly curved hull topped by a wooden deckhouse resolved into clarity. The helmsman's face was an indistinct smudge behind a small window. There was no sign of anyone else, but the boat surged on, clearly expecting to close with us. The river bend was about a mile away. The boat had covered almost half that distance and was coming on rapidly.

'Is there a recognition signal?' I wiped the drizzle off the lenses with my handkerchief and focussed again.

'I think it's pretty clear who we are.' Barker's reply was brusque. 'No one else knew we were coming, so that must be him.'

'D'ya mind if I take a butcher's, mate?' Nettles flicked the butt of his cigarette into the water and accepted my binoculars. He studied the approaching boat and handed them back to me. 'Looks harmless enough, but why isn't he slowing down?'

'He knows we're in a hurry, keen to get underway,' said Barker.

The fishing boat forged on. A shaft of sunlight beamed through a cloud break, bathing the surface of the river and spotlighting the boat. The brightly painted decoration either side of the prow gleamed. A flash of light reflected off something glass or metal. Caught in a slight eddy, the launch swung broadside to the current, presenting her vulnerable side to the looming prow. With only several hundred yards separating us, the boat had neither slowed nor deviated.

I nudged Perkins. 'Something's not right.'

'I think we should move, sir.' Perkins pale face added to the urgency in his voice.

Barker stared at the rapidly approaching boat with the transfixed eyes of a rabbit in a car's headlamps.

'Sir?'

'For fuck's sake,' yelled Nettles. He grabbed a Tommy gun and fired across the boat's bow.

Perkins rammed the engine telegraphs forward.

The gunfire broke the spell. Barker's yell of 'Full Ahead' was swallowed by the roar of engines thundering back to life. The launch surged forward as the racing propellers gripped the water.

The fishing boat was close enough now to clearly see the helmsman. His hands spun the wheel and the prow swung in towards us.

'Bastards are trying to ram,' shouted Nettles. He raised the Tommy gun and sent a stream of lead into the deckhouse.

Machine gun fire erupted from the boat. Bullets zinged off the launch's armour plate and smashed splinters from the wooden hull and decks. Men dived for cover. One, too late, fell clutching his stomach.

The fishing boat continued to turn, the prow swinging round like the horn of an angry bull trying to gore a tormentor. It slashed past the stern with inches to spare.

Recovering from their momentary surprise, the launches' gunners blazed back. Japanese soldiers spilt out of the deckhouse and jumped up from the fish hold to add their fire to the battle. Perkins yelled helm orders, zig-zagging the launch away from the fishing boat before turning to run seawards. The boat gave chase, but its machine gunners were no match for the hammering Oerlikon. 20-mm shells pulverised it to matchwood, from which flames erupted.

Leaving the smoking, sinking wreck, Perkins conned the launch through the fish traps. I kept an eye on the bearing of the receding lighthouse and called course corrections to keep him within the channel. With the light fading, we regained deep water. Perkins slowed the engines and called for a damage report. His young sub-lieutenant reported one soldier dead, his guts ripped apart by a Japanese machine gun, and one with a flesh wound through the thigh. A number of holes had been punched in the wooden hull, above the waterline fortunately, which the crew were patching with sheets of plywood. A Morse lamp flashed out of the dusk, and a few minutes later the second launch slid gently alongside.

'Council of war,' declared Spencer, beckoning us to follow him down into the chartroom. The soldiers and sailors lounging there made themselves scarce and we crowded around the tiny chartable, joined by the lieutenant in command of the second platoon.

'Well, that puts a spanner in the works,' said Spencer. 'The Japs must have rumbled the local guide and seized his boat. They were probably watching the river mouth for our arrival. Without him, we still have the problem of getting up the Trong River.'

'You hard hearted bastard! What do you think they did to him to make him spit out whatever he knew? And for God's sake! If they know what we're doing here, it's pointless to continue.'

'Take it easy, Bill. It's not the end of the world. He didn't know our exact destination, nor what we're going to do when we get there. Look, I know it's tough, but that's war. Whether or not we go on is a military decision. As navigator, are you quite certain there's no way we can land both platoons at Trong?'

I shook my head. 'Like I said. We can probably get the launches alongside at Pasir Hitam. Both platoons will get ashore, but they'll have to cut through miles of jungle and cross several rivers to get to the road.'

'Right then! Captain Nettles, you're the senior Thorne Force commander. Change of plan?'

Nettles had rolled himself another cigarette and was leaning against a bulkhead as calmly as if propping up the bar in his favourite watering hole. He pushed himself upright, edged between Spencer and Barker to the chart table, and spread out a map of northern Malaya.

'First Platoon was to blow the bridge at Kuala Kangsar tomorrow night, while Second Platoon caused a diversion on the coast road. Even if we get ashore at Pasir Hitam and make it to the road, it's twenty-five miles to the bridge. If the Japs are already on the alert we'd never get there and back again.' He took a drag of his cigarette, nipped it out and jammed the butt behind his ear. 'You can only piss with the cock you've got, so I say we take one platoon to Trong and hit the coast road here.' He traced a finger down the road south of the village. 'The jungle's thick on either side and there's a sharp bend which slows the traffic where we can set up an ambush. With luck we can hit a convoy, block the road and haul the flock out in the confusion.'

'That still leaves the problem of guiding the motor boat up river to the landing.' After his earlier hesitation, Barker had recovered his composure.

I didn't need the curl of Spencer's lips to know what was coming and bowed to the inevitable. 'Like Captain Nettles said. How hard can it be? Just keep between the banks. I'll get you and your men there, Captain.'

'Right, that's settled then.' Barker's smile contained more than a hint of triumph. 'How long will you need ashore, Nettles?'

The captain bent over the map stepping off distances with his fingers. 'It's seven miles to the bend in the road, three hours if we don't run into any nosey patrols. If you get us ashore by daybreak, we can be in position by nine. We'll break off no later than fourteen hundred. That'll give us five hours at the road and have us back at the landing well before sunset.'

It was fully dark when we got underway again. With the casualties transferred to the second launch in exchange for its towed boat and two men from Second Platoon, Barker ordered it to return to Port Swettenham. There was half-hearted grumbling from the soldiers who would miss the raid, which turned to cheers when Nettles reminded them of the beer they could consume before their comrades returned. Using the last plotted position west of the Bernam as our departure point, I scribbled dead reckoning calculations on the chart and set course north-west towards Pulo Rumbia, the largest of the islands off the mouth of the Perak River.

Flickers of lightning rolled along the eastern horizon, accompanied by the low rumble of distant thunder. Or was it the guns of two armies colliding in the darkness? Huddled into an oilskin with rain dripping down my neck, I gazed into the blackness ahead. Pulo Rumbia was over 600 feet high, easily visible in normal conditions. In the darkness, with rain obscuring visibility, I was relying on the keen eyes of the lookouts to avoid running into it.

The rain quickly cleared the decks of all but the watchkeepers and those of the soldiers whose stomachs had not adjusted to the rolling and pitching. For those crammed like sardines into the tiny accommodation spaces, sleep would be hard to come by. For Perkins, his sub-lieutenant and me, the night promised only to be long and wet, with the tricky task of finding the mouth of the Trong to keep us awake. The chartroom hatch slid back, releasing a shaft of dim light through which emerged the tall, stern figure of Commander Barker. The brief glimpse of his lined, drawn face, before the hatch closed to restore the darkness, betrayed the strain of commanding his small flotilla. If the Japanese had reached the Bernam River in force, then we were already well behind enemy lines. The local guide might not have been able to tell the Japanese exactly what our mission was, but the fact of our needing him to pilot us up a nearby estuary would put them on the alert. Come daylight, there was bound to be an aerial search. It was easy to hide a small boat in a jungle covered creek, but a 72-foot Harbour Defence Motor Launch would be much easier to spot.

Barker moved to the rear of the bridge and waited until his eyes adjusted to the darkness.

'Thick night. I hope you know where you're going, Pilot.'

He spoke loudly enough to be heard over the roar of the engines, and I sensed the question was more for the sake of conversation than reassurance.

'I'm aiming smack on the nose for Pulo Rumbia. There's deep water all around it to within about one hundred yards. If we don't hit it, it'll be a reliable fix from which to skirt the Dindings and run north to the Trong. Then we feel our way in on the flood as far as safely possible, before transferring the soldiers into the boat.'

'And if we hit it?'

'You can shoot me.'

'I like your confidence.' His hand gripped my shoulder. 'Tell me, how did you know something was not right with that fishing boat?'

I could have told him about the tingling in my fingertips, but I doubted he would believe me. 'I just had a feeling, I guess. I expected to see someone on deck, waving even. There was a brief flash, like sunlight glinting off metal.'

'Well, thank God you did. The hull is double layered mahogany, reinforced with ribbing. It's tough, but not enough to withstand a direct hit by a solid beam of ironwood with ten tons of fishing boat behind it.' He lapsed into silence and we all stared ahead into the darkness, our faces ghostly in the faint light thrown by the steering compass.

I had spent many long, sleepless nights on the bridge of *Oriental Venture*, but at least there I had the benefit of sheltering in the wheelhouse from the worst of the elements. There had also been Da Silva's coffee—the urge for one was strong now—and the temporary stimulation of cigarettes. I took several deep breaths to clear my head and stamped my feet to remind them to keep the blood circulating. The launch was bouncing along from crest to crest on the short chop raised by the breeze. The rain had stopped, but occasional sheets of lightning flickered along the eastern horizon.

Ahead, the sea and sky merged into a wall of total darkness. Stars glimmered above the … No! It wasn't a cloud bank.

'Slow ahead.' My command made Perkins jump, but he reached for the telegraphs reflexively.

Steep sided cliffs emerged from the darkness with the white crests of waves breaking at their feet. Perkins altered course to starboard and followed the coastline around until the island was clear astern. I took a final bearing as it slipped back into the night, and called out a new heading.

'That deserves a reward.' Barker sounded relieved. He slid back the chartroom hatch. 'Someone ask the cook to rustle up a brew.'

Half an hour later, with a mug of steaming tea in my hand, I ordered the launch onto a northerly heading.

'We'll be off the Trong in four hours,' I told Perkins. 'We've got the ebb setting us north-west at the moment. The tide will turn around midnight, but I've allowed for that.' I paused to permit a grin to spread across my face, knowing he could not see it in the darkness. 'Tell you what. I'll head down to that nice soft bunk of yours and get my head down for a few hours. A stiff tot of your Pusser's Rum wouldn't go astray either. You can call me when you get there. Okay?'

There was a sharp intake of breath followed by a stifled chortle.

'Nice try, Rowden.' Barker's voice floated out of the night. 'Pity the navy doesn't have a sense of humour.'

The tea was no substitute for Da Silva's coffee, but there was plenty to keep me awake. The rain returned and the strengthening wind whipped up short, white capped seas. I leaned against the rail to take some of the weight off my aching feet. Dawn was normally something to look forward to. The next one promised only the start of another long day.

CHAPTER TWENTY-FIVE

Saturday 27 December 1941

The eastern sky was paling as I helmed the motor boat away. A flickering Morse lamp wished us good luck, and the launch turned and disappeared into the western darkness. Colonel Spencer and Captain Nettles were crowded beside me at the tiny steering position in the half-decked boat. The rest of the soldiers occupied whatever space they could find. The luckiest of them had claimed the tiny forward cabin.

Beneath our feet, the Lister diesel chugged and coughed away, its racket surely loud enough to warn anyone of our arrival.

The rain had cleared and a few pale stars winked between breaks in the cloud. I blinked my gritty, sleep deprived eyes and checked the steering compass. Heading north-east would take us directly into the river mouth from where we had to feel our way four miles upstream to Trong landing.

Mangroves lined the banks of the estuary. I could sense their encroaching presence in the darkness, the rank smell of rotting vegetation and slimy mud filling the calm morning air. With the last of the flood under our keel, we passed easily over the outer sandbanks, the increase in engine note and the steep build-up of the wake the only evidence of the shallower patches.

Ahead, the low, dark line of the river banks slowly hardened against the lightening sky, the gap between them revealing the entrance to the river. I swung the boat into the channel, which soon narrowed to little more than 100 yards. The first couple of miles were fairly straight and it was, as Captain Nettles had said, no more difficult than keeping between the banks.

A right-angle bend marked the eastward turn of the river and I slowed the engine to a quieter throb, hoping the noise would not carry far beyond the mangroves. For the next couple of miles, the channel meandered back and forth in wide loops. I posted a seaman on the bow to watch for snags and mudbanks, and followed the outside of the curves looking for the deepest water. The wake sucked noisily against the river banks, disturbing wading birds and mud crabs. There was a large, white splash as something slipped off the mud into deeper water.

'Was that what I thought it was?' asked Spencer.

Nettles whistled in admiration. 'Bloody big saltie. Remind me not to go for a swim.'

The first rays of dawn wakened flocks of birds roosting in the trees, setting up a raucous squawking and chattering to which the macaques added their howls.

Spencer clasped his hands over his ears. 'Christ, that racket's enough to wake the dead.'

There was a hail from the bow and the lookout raised an arm in warning. I cut the engine to idle and followed the direction of his pointed finger. A submerged tree trunk slid past the side with inches to spare.

'That was close. I don't fancy walking from here. Not with that crocodile hanging about,' said Nettles.

I nodded and slipped the engine back into gear. The boat nosed forward; its progress slowed by the beginnings of the ebb tide. Narrowed now to only 30 yards, the river made a sharp turn to the north and then east. Native huts appeared in small clearings on the eastern bank.

'The landing place is just around the next bend,' I said, trying to keep the relief out of my voice.

'Good work, Bill,' said Spencer, patting me on the shoulder. 'Right-ho, Captain Nettles. Rouse your men. It's time we earned our keep.'

Muffled shouts and oaths, as men kicked dozing comrades awake, were followed by clicks and snaps as packs and weapons were checked.

I cut the engine to idle and the boat drifted around the final bend. Several small fishing boats were pulled up on the bank, and a low rickety jetty poked into the water beside a rusty roofed, galvanised iron sided godown. With a kick astern on the propeller, I placed the boat alongside the jetty and stopped the engine.

The sudden silence was broken only by the gurgle of the ebbing tide and the squabble of native crows. The acrid smell of a charcoal fire drifted through the trees, otherwise the tiny settlement appeared deserted.

'Fall in ashore,' ordered Nettles.

The Australians scrambled ashore and quickly formed up into sections.

Nettles pointed to the leading section and jerked his thumb in the direction of the track heading east into the jungle. 'Scout ahead.'

Hitching packs onto their shoulders and with Tommy guns held across their chests, the men sloped off along the track, their rubber soled, canvas boots making no sound on the hard packed earth. After a short interval, Nettles led off the rest of the platoon, one party of which carried a Bren gun.

Spencer stuck out a hand. He had swapped his cap for a slouch hat and a Tommy gun hung from a strap around his neck. 'We should be back by nightfall.' He shrugged his shoulders. 'The launch will be at the rendezvous in twenty-four hours. After that it's returning to Swettenham ... with or without us. If we're not back in time, don't leave it too late ... and give my love to Helena.'

I grasped his hand. 'We'll be here. Just come back in one piece.'

He released my grip, stepped ashore and marched smartly off down the track, disappearing around a bend into the jungle.

I beckoned to the two seamen who comprised the boat's crew. 'We can't stay here, we're too visible if any Japanese patrol decides to take a butcher's. There was a small creek just before the last bend, we'll hole up there for the day.'

With the engine cranked back to life, I swung the boat around and headed back the way we had come, as far as the creek mouth half a mile downstream. I slowly nosed the boat in between the banks while the bowman took soundings with a boat hook. The creek proved just deep enough to float us and we passed lines around the mangroves. The jungle canopy closed overhead, making us difficult to spot from the air. There were no huts visible and the only thing likely to see us would be boats passing up or down the river.

The concealment of the jungle was a two-edged sword. We were an inviting target for mosquitoes and sand flies. The former mostly disappeared as the sun rose higher, and the damp heat enveloped the boat like a sauna bath. The latter remained an ongoing irritation, darting onto any area of exposed skin and inflicting a sharp nip that rapidly turned into an itch, which the army issued anti-insect cream did little to dispel.

Despite the insects, my eyelids were soon drooping in the soporific heat. I pulled rank and ordered the seamen to remain on watch, while I stretched out on the narrow bunk in the boat's tiny cabin.

I awoke to the crash of gunfire and the rattle of bullets against the cabin roof. Grabbing a spare Tommy gun, I scrambled through the hatch to the steering cubby. The seamen were huddled together under its short roof. After the thunderclap, a torrential downpour blotted out visibility, the heavy drops splattering into the river making its surface hiss and smoke.

'Back wiv us then, sir,' said one of the seamen. 'Out like a light you was.'

I glanced at my wristwatch. I had slept for two hours. 'Any trouble.' I rubbed my aching hip, sore from lying on the bunk's hard surface.

'None, sir. Couple'a fishermen went downstream, but no one paid any attention.'

'Okay then. Why don't you two get your heads down for a bit.' I stepped to the transom, unbuttoned my fly and added my stream to the rain drops. The seamen grinned as I took shelter back in the cubby.

The one who had spoken nudged his companion. 'You 'ead below, mate. Fair's fair. I'll keep the lieutenant company for a spell.'

The other man mumbled his thanks and disappeared into the cabin.

I'd had little chance to study either man in the darkness. The remaining one wore the single fouled anchor of a leading seamen on the shoulder of his grubby white singlet. His shorts were equally soiled and his cap, pushed well back on his head, looked as if it had been sat on. His weather-beaten face and crooked nose suggested he had seen his share of bar fights and brawls, but his eyes sparkled clear and the blue pupils were piercing.

'What's your name, sailor?' I asked.

'Baxter, sir.'

'Well, Baxter. My apologies, I should have thought of this myself earlier. Did anyone think to stow any provisions aboard this scow. I'm starving and my mouth's as dry as a Welsh Sunday.'

Baxter's lips curled into a smug grin. 'Good job some of us did.' He reached into the cabin, retrieved a haversack and passed it to me. 'Selection of cans in there. Pot luck I'm afraid, the labels have worn off.' He pulled a clasp knife out of his pocket. 'Grab one, and I'll knock the top off for you.'

The can contained sliced peaches. I drained half the contents into my mouth, enjoying the sweet refreshing syrup, and passed Baxter the rest. He nodded his thanks and handed me a canteen of water.

'How about a gasper, sir? Don't think anyone's going to notice.' He pulled out a pack of NAAFI supplied Players.

The craving was strong. I reached out a hand, and snatched it back. 'I'm trying to give up, but don't mind me.'

'Is it true you're a captain in the merchant service?' Baxter lit a cigarette and I enviously watched him inhale a deep drag.

I nodded.

''Ow come you got roped into this little lot then?'

'It's a long story, Baxter. Probably dates back to half way through nineteen thirty-seven, when I got mixed up with that gung-ho Australian colonel you saw stride off into the jungle this morning. Maybe once this is all over, I'll tell you about it.'

The rain was easing, but the growing noise of an aero-engine interrupted our conversation. I stole a quick scan of the patch of sky visible between the overhanging trees, but saw nothing.

'Looking for us?' asked Baxter.

'I doubt it. Probably just a reconnaissance flight. We're safe enough here. It's the launch I'm worried about. Harder to conceal one of those.'

'That boatload of Japs that came for us at the Bernam River? Does that mean they're already south of the Perak? That we're behind the front line?'

'Might just have been a patrol that managed to sneak past our positions.' From the knitted eyebrows and the compressed lips, I could see Baxter was not buying my optimism. I didn't believe it myself. 'Anyway, you don't look like a man afraid of a stoush.'

'Bit different this, sir, than taking the leathernecks down a peg or two in Wan Chai. Bit different too, to being fished out of the China Sea with the *Prince of Wales* sinking under me. Still, I did see the *Bismarck* and lived to tell the tale, so p'r'aps I ain't used all me lives yet.'

The engine noise faded into the distance, leaving just the plop of water dripping off the trees into the creek.

'Your mate in there,' I jerked a thumb in the direction of the cabin. 'Off the *Prince of Wales* too?'

'Stoker Watson. Yes, sir. Joined after the *Bismarck*. Missed all the fun bits.'

'Well, you know what they say, Baxter. If you can't take a joke ...'

'Don't join the navy. Yes sir, I knows that one.'

With the rain clearing, the clouds drifted away and the sun beat down upon the tidal flats. By 11am, the receding water revealed the myriad of life sheltering among the roots of the mangroves. Fish skipped in the remaining puddles. Fiddler crabs emerged from their burrows, picking through the mud for shellfish and insects. The boat's keel bumped once or twice and settled onto the mud, heeling over slightly to rest its bilge against the near bank. We opened several more cans for a noon meal of bully beef and peaches, washed down with tepid water. Taking it in turns to doze in the sweltering cabin, we endured the early afternoon heat. The tide slowly crept back in, heralded by the waving claws of the fiddler crabs before they retreated to their burrows in the face of the rising water. When the keel floated free, I roused Baxter and Watson.

By 4pm, we were back alongside the flimsy jetty, bows out ready for a quick getaway. With the flood tide still over an hour to run, the rising water gurgled around the jetty piles. There was more life in the kampong. Malays drifted in and out of the shadowy interior of the godown. Children splashed in the shallows close to the river bank. Fishermen squatted beside their boats, splicing ropes and mending nets. Occasionally, someone would wander over to take a look at the motor boat and its sweating, pale faced inhabitants. Their smiles and head shakes suggesting amusement at the strange ways of Europeans.

Life appeared normal, which I hoped meant that no Japanese soldiers were about to descend upon us. As the hands of my watch ticked round to 5pm, however, with no sign of the platoon's return, the tingling in my fingertips added to the feeling of unease. I reached for one of the spare Tommy guns. It was a popular weapon amongst gangsters, even in the Far East, but I had never used one. Most of my shooting had been at close range with the big Webley. I had left it in my cabin aboard *Oriental Venture*. I was regretting that now.

'Can either of you show me how to fire one of these things?'

Baxter reached out a hand for the gun. He held it by the pistol grip, barrel pointed at the deck. 'You've got a safety switch here,' he flicked it back and forth with his thumb. 'This one's the firing mode lever, single or automatic, and on top's the cocking handle.' He used his other hand to slide it back. 'Two clicks and she's cocked. The magazines clip in here and release with this thumb switch. Got all that, sir?'

I took the gun back, slotted a box magazine in place and stuffed several more into my pockets. 'I'm going for a scout around. I won't be far away. If you need me in a hurry, fire a single shot.'

As I stepped onto the jetty, there was the faint rattle of distant gunfire. 'Get the engine started. I think we'll be leaving in a hurry.' I turned and trotted away from the jetty, following the track into the jungle.

After several dozen paces, I entered a different world. The jetty disappeared around a shallow bend. The tree canopy cast the track into deep shade, through which small shafts of light sparkled. Apart from my footfalls, the only sounds were the calls of invisible birds and the distant screeching of macaques. I stopped to let my eyes adjust to the gloom and stared into the jungle on either side. It was not as thick as I first imagined. The undergrowth provided concealment but was not so dense as to prevent movement. For all I knew, a small army could be hiding just off the track. I walked on, stepping warily, keeping to the side of the path, ready to dive for cover.

I jumped at the sound of another burst of gunfire, followed by the sharp crump of a bursting grenade. Dropping to one knee, I raised the Tommy gun and wedged the stock into my shoulder. I wrenched back the cocking handle and my thumb fumbled for the safety switch.

'Christ what have we got here. A fucking choco soldier?' A slouch hatted figure emerged from the bushes about ten yards ahead and ambled down the track towards me as if out for a stroll in the woods. 'Everything all right back at the landing place, cobber?'

'Yes. I heard firing. Thought I'd have a look around.'

The soldier pointed to the Tommy gun and grinned. My knuckles were turning white around the fore and pistol grips. 'I hope ya know how to use that thing, mate? Jap patrol picked us up a mile back. Captain Nettles has set up a rearguard ambush. The rest of the platoon will be along any mo.'

After another burst of firing, closer this time, soldiers appeared around a bend in the track and trotted towards us. They slowed as they passed; a sergeant brought up the rear.

'Back to the boat,' he panted. 'Japs not far behind.'

A volley of shots, concealed in the jungle, were followed by shouted commands in a language that certainly wasn't English. The sergeant waved at us to get moving, jogging along behind casting frequent glances over his shoulder.

As we emerged from the jungle track, the soldiers set up their Bren gun behind a hastily scrabbled earth mound beside the jetty.

More firing erupted, continuous bursts punctuated by the crash of grenades. The sergeant stood defiant, gazing towards the track.

'Here they come,' he shouted. 'Covering fire!'

The last few men of the rearguard burst out of the jungle and sprinted for the boat. I was thankful to see Nettles and Spencer among them. The Bren gunner opened fire and hosed a stream of lead into the trees behind them. Chattering Tommy guns joined in. I handed mine to a soldier who fired off the magazine and clipped in another.

What were they firing at? The track and the jungle still seemed empty?

Spurts of dust sprang up around the feet of the runners, and I caught a glimpse of uniformed figures crouching along the fringe of the treeline.

With targets to aim at, the Bren gunner swept his stream of bullets back and forth into the jungle's edge, slashing leaves and sending splinters of wood flying. The Japanese fire slackened and the runners jinked their way the remaining yards to the jetty. They had almost reached it when a soldier slumped forward as if his feet had caught a trip wire. Hardly pausing in his stride, Nettles reached down, grabbed the man by the webbing of his pack and dragged him on, leaving a trail of blood in the dust.

Most of the men were on board, only the Bren gun team and several others sprawled on their bellies beside the jetty. Had the Japanese had enough? The shrill pierce of a whistle was immediately followed by blood curdling yells. Over a dozen men, led by an officer brandishing a sword, dashed from the cover of the jungle and charged towards the jetty.

It was suicidal, the Bren gun cut most of them down before they managed 50 yards. The rest crawled back to the safety of the trees.

'LET'S MOVE.' Nettles' bellow blasted my ear. 'Before they regroup.'

The last of the men ashore hoisted their weapons and threw themselves into the boat, tumbling into the aft well deck. Baxter and Watson threw off the lines, I jammed the engine into gear and rammed the throttle forward. The boat leapt away from the jetty. Firing erupted from the shore, bullets splattered the water behind us and smashed splinters from the transom. I swung the wheel hard over and we rounded the first bend, leaving the jetty and the Japanese gunfire fading into the jungle behind us.

CHAPTER TWENTY-SIX

Tuesday 30 December 1941

'**I** could sleep for a week.' Spencer lay sprawled on the couch in my day cabin smoking a cheroot. His crisp uniform was in stark contrast to the sweat and mud-stained battledress he had worn for the last few days. I was also glad to return to familiar surroundings, with the four gold bars back on the shoulder straps of a fresh set of khakis.

'What have you been doing for the last twelve hours?' I sipped at a cup of hot, strong coffee, another pleasure I had sorely missed.

'I had to write a report and attend a briefing at Divisional HQ in Kuala Lumpur.'

'Did you get anything of value from the major-general's staff car?'

The car was among a convoy of vehicles Captain Nettles and his platoon had ambushed at Trong. All were forced off the road by machine gun fire and grenades, killing the occupants, including the Japanese major-general. His briefcase, stuffed with plans and documents, had been pulled from the burning wreck.

'We're still waiting for the full translations. But from what I can make out, the Japanese are expecting us to make a stand behind the Perak River. The ground there is good for defence. So they're attempting to outflank it, pushing down the coast as fast as they can.'

'So that's why they were already at the Bernam River when we got there?'

Spencer nodded and took a drag of his cheroot. 'If we can't hold them at the Perak, the idea is to retreat to Slim River and fight to defend Kuala Lumpur for as long as possible, while the rest of the army withdraws to Johore. In any case, you're not needed here anymore. You'll receive orders to return to Singapore shortly.

'And you?'

'Back to Kuala Lumpur to join General Heath's staff.'

I drank another mouthful of coffee. The commando raid might have been a shot in the arm for the defenders of Singapore but, being shot at and charged by soldiers wielding wickedly long bayonets, had made the war very personal. I was, nevertheless, awed by their courage; running into that deadly hail of machine gun fire. British soldiers had done the same time and again in the previous war in the dreadful battles of the Somme and Ypres. It seemed sheer madness, knowing death was inevitable. It was also madness to put to sea in thin-skinned merchant ships, knowing that a single bomb or torpedo could result in a variety of deaths, all of them horrific. But we still did it.

'You've gone very quiet.' Spencer sat up and stubbed his cheroot into the ashtray. 'Penny for your thoughts.'

'I was just wondering if it's too late to become a conscientious objector.'

'I'll make your apologies to General Tojo, shall I? Ask him to count you out for the rest of the war.' He reached for his cap and briefcase. 'Thanks for the coffee, but I have to get back to KL. I just dropped by to pick up my kit and let you know the news about returning to Singapore. Barker will send you official orders. His report spoke well of you.'

The hairs on the back of my neck bristled. 'Am I supposed to feel grateful for that? You know I don't give a toss for the opinion of a man just because he's superior in rank. He as near admitted he couldn't navigate, and you saw how he reacted when the fishing boat tried to ram us. He froze. If it hadn't been for the quick reactions of Nettles and Perkins, we'd have been matchwood. Did he mention that?'

The silence spoke volumes. I opened my mouth to continue, but Spencer raised a hand. 'Don't be too hard on him, Bill. He's had a tough time. He didn't just survive the loss of *Repulse*, his ship before that was nearly shot out of the water at Narvik.' He levered himself up off the couch. 'Look, I really must get a move on.' He stuck out a hand. 'Goodbye, Bill. Have a safe trip back to Singapore.'

His grip was firm and his mouth curled into a smile, but the normal glint in his eye was missing.

'So long, Arnold. I'll save a place for you at Raffles.'

He released my hand and headed for the door. Pausing in the opening, he turned. 'In case I don't get back before she leaves, give my regards to Helena. She did a good job in Bangkok, better than I deserved. I'm glad she shot that bastard Maslennikov. Tell her ... oh never mind, just make certain she gets out. Promise me that.'

'If it comes to that, I'll take her myself if I have too.'

'When,' he whispered, nodding slowly. 'When.' He raised a hand in salute and was gone.

His mention of Helena caused an unexpected tightness in my chest. I had hardly given her a thought over the previous few days. Now, with the possibility of seeing her again, I cursed myself for not having written a telegram for Spencer to forward from Kuala Lumpur. I could walk up to the Harbour Master's office and telephone her. I got as far as reaching for my cap, when there was a rap on the door and McGrath poked his head around it.

'Message just been delivered for you, Skipper.'

I beckoned him in, took the buff-coloured envelope and ripped it open. It was a typewritten order signed by Barker, instructing me to unload Thorne Force's remaining stores and equipment, and return to Singapore to await further orders. It had the usual naval bullshit about time being of the essence and proceeding with all due dispatch, as if a missed tide by one requisitioned tramp steamer was all that stood between the Japanese and the end of the British Empire. I handed the note to McGrath.

He scanned the contents. 'I'll get onto it right away. The sooner we get out of here the better. The bombers have been over once or twice a day. It feels like we're a sitting duck.'

'Go and get Lakshman started on it, then come back.' I pointed at the coffee pot. 'I'll save a cup for you.'

He returned a few minutes later and relaxed onto the couch, gratefully accepting the offered cup. 'Thanks, I needed that.' He swallowed a large mouthful. 'By the look on his face, Colonel Spencer seemed pleased with the results of the raid.'

'He bagged a major-general and stole his briefcase. Apparently, it contains all of Japan's plans for the domination of the Far East.'

McGrath's eyes widened. 'Really?'

'No. But whatever it does contain probably won't tell our brass hats much more than they already know. That the Japs are on their way to Singapore and there's not much we can do to stop them. If you want my opinion, the whole show was the over excited desire of men eager to play at Boy Scouts.' My voice had grown increasingly bitter. I paused, and continued in what I hoped was a more congenial tone. 'Captain Nettles and his Australian's did well though. I wouldn't give much for Japanese chances against them in anything less than a fair fight.'

Having returned aboard late the previous afternoon, ashen faced and shaking from hunger and lack of sleep, there had not been time to brief McGrath. I had taken a cool shower to keep me awake long enough to swallow a bully beef sandwich and a large rum, and turned in. McGrath was looking at me expectantly, obviously keen to hear more. I started at the beginning.

'Talk about Jason and the bloody Argonauts,' he said, when I finished. 'Sounds almost as exciting as hunting wild pigs with a pea-shooter. Can't say the same here. It's been as dull as a long Sunday sermon ... apart from when the Japs use us for target practise.' He took another mouthful of coffee. 'Actually, that's not quite true. Bullen's men have got the hang of the Oerlikons. I reckon they could shoot a gnat off the balls of a flea at a hundred paces. They've been credited with a share in bringing down a bomber. It crashed in the fields behind the town. Cramp's gone ashore to see if he can scavenge a piece of the wreck as a souvenir.'

I shook my head. 'He'll probably end up drunk on toddy, before looking for horizontal refreshment in whatever passes for the local cathouse. If he's not back when we sail, he can hike it to Singapore. And don't ask me for sympathy when he reports to you for a short arm inspection.'

McGrath returned my grin. Cramp had never quite shaken free of his cockney laced, Gypsy origins. He was a law unto himself. Serving time in Wandsworth gaol for tier ranging had just made him more careful. The wreck of the Japanese plane was probably under guard but, if the soldiers looked away at the wrong moment, they might find the whole thing mysteriously vanished.

'Have you had any more news of your father?' In my self-absorbed mooning over Helena, I had been too preoccupied to ask before leaving Singapore. After that, there had been no opportunity.

'Nothing.' His drooped shoulders betrayed concern. 'But hey, no news is good news. Isn't that what they say.'

'Send them a telegram from Singapore. At least tell them you're okay. And you never know, we might be ordered to Sydney next.'

McGrath put down his cup. 'Thanks for the coffee, Skipper. I'll go and see how Lakshman's getting on.'

While the crew sweated through the hot, humid afternoon swinging cargo nets of army stores and equipment onto the quay-side, I worked my way through the pile of bumf accumulated while I had been away. Rain clouds building up over the eastern hills, suggested a late thunderstorm, but the afternoon remained fine with a light sea breeze providing relief from the heat. Towards 4pm, Da Silva appeared with another pot of coffee. I poured myself a cup and carried it onto the bridge wing, taking a break from the paperwork. I found Bullen gazing at the sky, a hand shading his eyes.

'All quiet, Bullen?'

He turned at my approach. 'Too quiet, sir. We've usually 'ad at least one raid by now.'

'Aren't there lookouts for that?'

'Sometimes the siren cuts it a bit fine. Thought I'd take a gander meself.' He dropped his hand and gestured towards the quay where a squad of soldiers, their shirts stained with sweat, were hoisting boxes into the back of a truck. 'Is it true we're 'eading back to Singapore?'

I nodded. 'As soon as we've finished discharging. The navy doesn't need us anymore. For the time being anyway.'

Leaving Bullen searching the sky, I leant over the rail to look down on the main deck. The metal was painfully hot and I kept my skin clear. The last slings of cargo were swinging out of the holds. Lamont was bustling about issuing orders to replace the tween deck covers and hatch boards.

'How long?' I shouted down to him.

He glanced up and down the deck, assessing progress. 'One hour, Skipper.'

I checked my watch and waved an acknowledgement. 'Departure stations at five-thirty. Let McGrath know.'

There was an answering hail of, 'Aye aye.' I strode into the wheelhouse and asked the bridge seaman to fetch Lakshman.

By the time he arrived, I had scribbled a note to the Harbour Master, informing him of our departure. It hardly seemed necessary. The port had taken a pasting from the daily bombing raids. A number of the godowns had been reduced to piles of rubble and most of the ships had already left. I told Lakshman to deliver the note, begging or borrowing transport from whoever was in charge ashore.

While he was away, I nipped below to have a word with Fraser. He grumbled at the short notice and bustled below to set the stokers to work raising steam pressure.

Waiting for the clock to tick round, I watched the seamen busy on deck, lowering derricks and securing hatch covers. The rain clouds were holding off and bands of high-level cirrus stretched across the sky. Picking up the binoculars, I checked the signal mast for the state of the tide. Low water had been at 2pm. The ball at the northern yardarm confirmed the tide was flooding, the current flowing south along the line of the wharves. Without a tug and with the sea breeze pushing us alongside, lifting off the wharf would be tricky. If I had dropped an anchor while coming alongside, I could have used it now to haul the bow off. I smiled. Lakshman would have another evolution to record in his journal, provided I didn't make a hash of it.

He was gone for half an hour. When he returned, I set him to testing the telegraph and steering. A few minutes before 5.30pm, the piercing blast of McGrath's whistle blew the crew to their departure stations.

On the bridge, I made a final assessment of the conditions. The sea breeze had eased, and the tide was swirling past the wharf piles.

I beckoned Lakshman. 'Nip down aft and tell Lamont to single up to the backspring. He's to stand where he can see the bridge wing and wait for my signals. As Lakshman turned to go, I reached for the speaking trumpet and hailed McGrath on the forecastle. 'Single up to one breast rope.' He raised an arm in acknowledgement.

I rang the engine telegraph to Stand By and walked onto the bridge wing. Mooring lines were being slackened and let go, the seamen hauling them in as fast as they could. With only the two lines remaining, Lakshman sprinted back up to the wheelhouse just in time for my next order.

'Hard a port.'

On the forecastle, McGrath was waiting for the signal. 'Slacken away,' I yelled through the speaking trumpet.

The breast line went slack. For moment nothing happened, then an eddy caught the bow and the pressure of the current, assisted by the flow past the rudder, pushed the ship away from the wharf. Now, I had to get her moving ahead before the stern swung too close.

The air-raid siren drowned my first orders.

'Midships the wheel. Dead slow ahead.' I had to repeat the yell to be heard over the wailing. A clatter of boots sounded on the ladders as gunners raced up to the Monkey Island.

'Let go all,' I shouted, waving my arms for emphasis. The mooring lines went slack. Soldiers ashore yanked the eyes off the bollards, dropped them into the water and sprinted for cover. The rising throb of massed aero-engines assaulted my ears.

'SLOW AHEAD!'

The stern was still swinging towards the wharf as the current pushed the bow out.

STARBOARD TEN!'

The aft mooring gang strained to haul in the backspring. I said a quick prayer that it wouldn't foul the propeller.

Sharp cracks of anti-aircraft guns added to the noise. Louder bangs erupted from the forecastle as our 12-pounder joined in.

'MIDSHIPS ... STEADY'

The swing stopped. We were angled away from the wharf, only just stemming the tide.

'FULL AHEAD.'

The deck plates throbbed as the propeller sent a swirl of water astern. A thick cloud of black smoke burst from the funnel as the engineers flung open the fire dampers. Overhead, the sky filled with shell bursts, through which a vee-shaped formation of aircraft flew steadily on.

I cocked my head at the persistent wail, clear above the engine noise and gunfire.

'STARBOARD TEN.' The bow started to swing as I lined the ship up for the centre of the roadstead.

The wailing reached an ear-splitting crescendo.

'STEADY.'

Massive explosions erupted along the line of the waterfront. Bombs smashed into godowns, tossed vehicles into the air, tore up railway lines and started numerous fires. Several plunged into the water to starboard. Shock waves pounded through the hull. The deck heaved and I stumbled against the dodger, painfully banging my head. Huge geysers of cordite stinking water burst high into the air, collapsing onto the ship, drenching me and everyone else not under cover.

'PORT TEN.'

As we rounded the tip of Pulo Lumut, the ear-splitting cracks of our 12-pounder ceased, but the anti-aircraft guns ashore continued to harass the bomber formation as it turned away to the east. I had a final glance at Port Swettenham. Large columns of smoke marked where fires raged among the palm oil and diesel tanks. Flames leapt from a roofless godown that was probably filled with bales of compressed rubber.

'Midships.' I allowed the bow to swing until it lined up with the centre of the south channel. 'Steady as she goes.' Trailing water, I squelched into the wheelhouse.

Lakshman's brown face was abnormally pale. 'Are you alright, Captain?'

I glanced down. My shirt front was spattered red. I felt the lump on my forehead and my fingers came away covered in blood.

'I hit my head against the rail.' I reached into my pocket for my handkerchief and pressed it over the cut. 'Anyone else hurt?'

'I don't think so, sir. Mr McGrath has not yet reported.'

The burly figure of Chief Engineer Fraser appeared in the wheel-house doorway. His faced was flushed scarlet and he was breathless from the climb from the engine room floor plates.

'Everything okay down below, Angus?'

'D'ye think I'd come all this way to tell ya if it was.' His bushy eyebrows seemed to have a life of their own. 'The auld girl was ne'er meant to wi'stand bombs and she's over twenty years old. If they'd been any closer, we'd be seeing daylight through the hull. As it is, there's at least half-a-dozen rivets sprung leaks in the engine room. I've got men caulking them. God knows how many there are else-where. Ye'd better get yer man Cramp sounding the holds. And I'll need to reduce revs while I check the shaft bearings. If it's bent ... well there's nae much I can do.'

It was a long speech by Fraser's standards. In the convoys, ships had been bombed or torpedoed around us, but none had exploded as close. Fraser's agitated state showed just how near we had been to disaster.

'What speed can you give us, Angus?'

'Enough revs for seven knots, while we check the bearings. Let me know if the bilges start filling and I'll get the pumps running.'

McGrath's arrival coincided with Fraser's return below. He asked me to remove the wadded handkerchief to look at my head.

'It's just a scratch, Skipper.' He grinned. 'You'll have a nasty lump, but a bit of sticking plaster will stop the bleeding.'

'Thank heavens for small mercies. Cramp's already had enough practice stitching me up. What's the situation below?'

'Just a few sprung rivets. Bit of water trickling in, nothing serious. Cramp's plugging the holes.'

'Good work.' I pointed ahead, where a line of buoys marked the channel leading into the Malacca Strait. 'It's your watch Mister Mate. Keep between the cans. I'm going below to change my shirt and clean up. Sing out if you need me.'

I left him to it.

CHAPTER TWENTY-SEVEN

Evening, Tuesday 6 January 1942

With its doors and shutters closed due to the blackout, the Great World was hot and airless. The outside entertainment areas and street stalls were also closed, only the dance hall and the restaurant were admitting customers. Both were packed. People still needed to dance and eat, if only to temporarily forget the steadily advancing Japanese.

We were doing the same, taking our minds off the war while waiting at anchor for orders. The shaft bearings had passed Fraser's inspection, and the naval dockyard had caulked our leaky rivets and repaired the buckled plating. As soon as they finished, we had been sent out to anchor. There was no room at the docks, which were crowded with ships disgorging reinforcements and military equipment. A whole squadron of Hurricane fighter aircraft had even been delivered in crates.

I was also trying, unsuccessfully, to take my mind of Helena. It didn't matter how much rum I drank; I could still see the scorn on her face. The newspapers reported the temporary recall of Duff and Diana Cooper, but had not mentioned Helena accompanying them. I telephoned Raffles shortly after our return, but the reception desk refused to say whether she was there. I wrote her a note but, if she was still there, she declined to reply. The devil on one shoulder wanted to say good riddance. The angel on the other was clamouring to see her. There was also an observer watching both, claiming to be disinterested, wondering if the love-sick pain in my chest had ever proved fatal, and regretting it had never read sufficient Barbara Cartland romances to find out.

'Tell me again how this taxi dancer system works,' said Lamont. After an hour drinking Tiger Beer, why was he having such difficulty working up the courage to ask a girl to dance?

'Yer goes to the table over there.' Cramp pointed with his finger. 'Yer buys a book of four tickets for an Oxford scholar. Then yer goes to the taxi rank and chooses a girl. At the end of the dance, yer tears off one of the tickets and gives it to 'er. The ticket, that is.' He chuckled at his own joke.

Perhaps Lamont was spoiled for choice. Selection distress my old drinking buddy Captain Grim Jim Coffin called it, when trying to make his mind up in Manila's Santa Ana Cabaret.

'And if you want ... more than that?'

'It'll cost fifteen dollars to take one away from the taxi rank. That'll buy the right to negotiate,' said Cramp.

'And I s'pose they're all virtuous young ladies who'd quail at being asked for a quote. Do they charge by the hour or the inch?'

'This is Singapore, not Inverness,' I said, laughing. 'But if you're not quick,' I nodded in the direction of some sailors weaving their way among the tables, 'the best ones will be taken.'

Lamont reached for his Tiger beer and drained it. 'Och aye, tight purse never won fair lady.' He rummaged in his pocket for a dollar. 'If I'm no back in half an hour ...'

'If we're not here, we'll be in the restaurant eating supper,' I said.

Lamont waved a hand in reply and rolled his way towards the taxi table.

I felt a presence hovering at my elbow and turned to find the waiter pointing expectantly at our beer bottles.

'Half empty, sir. You want more?'

'Half full.' I reached into my pocket and dug out some notes. 'Bring us a bottle of rum and two glasses.'

By the time he returned with the bottle, the band had struck up a brisk version of *Let's Face the Music and Dance*. Lamont had chosen well, and was twirling around the floor with a lithe young Chinese woman whose lustrous eyes gleamed from an exquisitely painted doll-like face. Watching their quick, confident footsteps was a painful reminder of my clumsy efforts with Helena on the boat deck.

I reached for the rum bottle, poured a large shot and downed it.

'Like that, eh?' said Cramp.

'I'm not sure I need advice on women from you. Your track record's no better than mine.'

'What you need is the laurel leaf cure,' said Cramp, refilling my glass.

'Another one of your gypsy potions?'

'More of a spell really. The women use it, but I suppose it would work equally well for a man.'

'Go on then, make me laugh.'

'I'm serious. You sit cross legged in front of a Jeremiah with a basket of laurel leaves between your chips and peas. You gaze into the fire, grab an 'andful of leaves and sprinkle them over the coals. As they burn you chant, laurel leaves that burn in fire ... draw unto me my 'eart's desire.'

'Where the fuck are we going to find a basket of laurel leaves?'

'That's more like it.' He clapped me on the back. 'Women are like buses. There'll be another one along in a minute.'

Before I could reply, I felt a hand on my shoulder and Poh's immaculately dressed figure slipped into Lamont's vacant seat. He unbuttoned his cream linen jacket, pulled off his Panama hat and mopped his brow with a bright red handkerchief.

'I thought I find you here. What you drinking?'

I pointed at the rum bottle, but he shook his head, beckoned the waiter and ordered a gin sling.

'Any news?' I hoped his finding me meant orders that would take my mind off Helena.

'Sorry, Captain, not for you, but I do have other news.' The waiter delivered his drink and he took a sip. 'Cheers. First of all, Mr Khoo. He pull strings and book passage for wife and good self on British India ship sailing to Calcutta. They leave tonight.'

It took a moment to hoist it in. If Mr Khoo was leaving at such short notice that he didn't have time to wish me or the ship farewell, the situation was more serious than the authorities were admitting.

'Is Miss Markova travelling with them?'

'No. She still at Raffles.'

It hardly made sense. If she hadn't left with the Coopers or Mr Khoo, why was she staying on?

I shook my head. 'I don't understand?'

'Mr Khoo begged her to go with them.' Poh shrugged his shoulders. 'She say prefer to stay. Put her name down as volunteer at British Military Hospital.'

I managed a smile at the thought of Helena dressed in a Voluntary Aid Detachment uniform. She would be good for morale, too good perhaps. Men might be tempted to hide their recoveries, in order to stay where they could catch daily sight of her.

The music died away and the band shuffled off stage to take a well-earned break. Lamont rolled back to the table, red-faced and sweating but smiling contentedly. He greeted Poh, dragged up an empty chair and plonked onto it with a deep sigh.

'Yon taxi-lasses are rare good dancers. Hav'na had so much exercise since the Edinburgh Palais.'

'You got your dollar's worth then?' I asked.

'Aye, and worked up a right appetite. Did you say we were goin' to tak' supper in the restaurant?'

Poh held up a hand. 'Please, I would be delighted to be your host. Pepper crab, Singapore noodles, fish-head curry. Whatever you want.' He stood and beckoned us to follow him.

Without rationing, and alcohol cheap and plentiful, it was as good a meal as any I had enjoyed in Singapore. Most of the tables were occupied by Europeans, eating and drinking with gusto, as if anxious to take full advantage of the little time left of their lotus eating existence.

Cramp and Lamont did full justice to the banquet ordered by Poh, but I had little appetite. In typical Chinese fashion, as soon as the table was cleared of empty dishes, Poh waved his hand for the waiter and summoned the bill.

'Can I drop you back at Collyer Quay?'

Lamont and Cramp exchanged glances, like naughty schoolboys.

'Sure, the night's still young. Would you no fancy a wee bit more entertainment?' asked Lamont.

Poh was no saint. He and I had spent many a happy hour in the better establishments of Malay Street, but that was in more peaceful times. The brothels were busy with servicemen eager to make the most of their leave passes, and Cramp and Lamont were rapidly reaching the state where valour would override discretion.

'It's okay. We'll take a taxi. I'll see them back to the ship,' I said.

A relieved smile crossed Poh's face. 'In that case, I bid you good night.' He shook our hands and bustled away.

The taxi driver nodded when I gave him the address, and swung the taxi onto River Valley Road heading towards the city. Just before the Elgin Bridge he turned left and headed east past Saint Andrews Cathedral and the rear of Raffles Hotel. Even with the street lamps extinguished, North Bridge Road was bustling. Slivers of light spilt between the curtains of the shop houses and cheap hotels. The driver pulled over just past Middle Road. I paid him and we walked around the corner into Malay Street.

Mama-san welcomed me with less than the discretion she normally displayed. It was several years since I had last passed through her doorway, and she greeted me like a long-lost friend, which in a sense I was. I had performed favours for her in the past, helping her transfer—smuggle would be more accurate—gold and other valuable items to her relatives in China. In return, she allowed me free drinks and the occasional run of the house. Producing a bottle of rum, she ushered us into easy chairs and called her girls to join us. Although Mama-san was Chinese, most of the clientele and the working girls were Japanese. Those Japanese men that had not been interned were lying low. The women, however, had nowhere else to go.

It was still relatively early, none of us was noticeably drunk and we were far from the least attractive clients they could expect that evening. Lamont and Cramp were soon getting better acquainted with the girls perched on their knees. In less salubrious brothels—if that was not an oxymoron—the women often wore the minimum necessary to preserve basic decency. Mama-san boasted higher standards. Her young ladies were fully dressed in ornate cheongsams, albeit slit to the thigh, while for Japanese clients they often dressed as geishas.

After Lamont and Cramp had been led away to the delights awaiting them in the boudoirs, Mama-san eyed me with a mildly disapproving gaze.

'What the matter? You no like the girls? All clean, doctor come every week.'

'Sure I like, but not this time, sorry. Very tired. Working too hard.'

It was the lamest excuse that had ever passed my lips. Even with an apologetic smile, Mama-san didn't buy it.

'You sick, maybe? Need see doctor?'

'No. No, I'm not sick. Really. I'm just a bit ...' I shrugged my shoulders as if that would help explain.

Mama-san's frown cracked into a broad grin.

'You no sick here.' She grabbed her crotch, laughing. 'You sick here.' She placed a hand over her heart, laughed again and reached for my arm. 'You come with me. Free cure. Anything you want. I do Singapore grip.'

She waited patiently while I talked my way out of accepting her offer. Finally, she burst into giggles.

'It was joke, okay. What this lady name?'

I told her.

'And she love you?'

'I don't know.'

'*Ai yah!* Men never understand women.' She tapped her forehead.

'Before you go I give special medicine. Guarantee make woman love you.' She clapped her hands and one of the girls appeared. After a lengthy exchange in Cantonese, accompanied by sideways glances and more giggles, the girl disappeared through the doorway into the street.

'Okay, so you wait,' said Mama-san. 'You want tea, eat something?'

She allowed me to decline and our conversation was interrupted by the arrival of a couple of army officers. By the time Mama-san had fussed over them and they were escorted away, Cramp and Lamont had returned.

As we left, Mama-san pressed a small package into my hand. 'Put in her tea, this much.' She pinched her thumb and forefingers together. 'If no work, you come back, free jiggy-jiggy.' Her laughter followed me down Malay Street.

'What was that about?' asked Cramp.

'The Chinese version of the laurel leaf cure.' I hailed a taxi.

Helena had chosen to remain in Singapore. Whether or not I would ever get the chance to try the love potion, I had promised to see her safely away. Now I just needed to find a way to fulfil it.

CHAPTER TWENTY-EIGHT

Wednesday 7 to Thursday 29 January 1942

T he navy intervened before I had chance to try my luck telephoning Raffles again. Orders arrived the following morning to return to the naval dockyard. We were no sooner alongside, when an immaculately white uniformed Captain Mulock mounted the gangway.

I grabbed my cap, and took the stairs down from the bridge two at a time to meet him. The navy had strict protocols for the reception of senior officers. I remembered reading Captain Marryat, where boatswain's pipes, sideboys with pipeclayed gloves, and officers doffing hats were mentioned. I almost bumped into Mulock as he stepped through the accommodation door. He raised two fingers to the peak of his cap in response to my salute, then grinned.

'Morning, Captain Rowden. Sorry to come aboard without permission, but I'm too long in the tooth to be bothered by all the ceremony, especially as this is really a civilian ship. Do you mind if we head straight up to your quarters?'

I led the way. Five minutes later, we were sipping coffee fortified with a nip of Tanduay rum.

After congratulating me on my part in the Thorne Force commando raid, he got straight to the point.

'We're a navy without any ships,' he said. 'Yes, we've a few destroyers and a couple of light cruisers, but they're busy escorting convoys into Singapore. What we don't have are any of the small ships, the minesweepers, picket boats, gun-boats and the like. We've pressed as many civilian vessels into service as we can find, including yours, and now we've got another job for you.'

An hour and another pot of coffee later, he departed promising to send down written orders.

His feet had hardly touched the quayside when a party of boilermakers clambered aboard, and headed for the forecastle.

I summoned McGrath and briefed him on our new role.

'A minesweeper! A bloody minesweeper. How the hell are we going to do that,' he said, blue eyes flashing.

'We're going to be fitted with paravane gear. We'll stream otters either side of the bow. They'll snag any moored mines and bring them to the surface. Bullen and his DEMS gunners can blaze away and explode them with the Lewis guns.'

'What about magnetic mines. Won't we set those off anyway?'

'According to Mulock, the Japs don't have magnetic mines. Whatever they have or not, our job's to sweep the Durian Strait to make sure they haven't laid any there.'

'Now I've heard everything, Skipper.' McGrath shook his head. 'I think I'll put in for a transfer to the army. It can't be any more dangerous than looking for mines like an Irishman, sticking your fingers in your ears while stamping about with your feet.'

'If the name fits,' I laughed.

The following morning, a dockyard crane swung an A-frame aboard. Boilermakers attached it to the bow with bolted eye plates and chains. It was followed by two winches for streaming the otters. By the time they finished, the bow was a Heath Robinson contraption of steel girders, chains, winches and wires, with the A-Frame jutting forward towards the waterline like a battering ram.

A day later, a party of naval ratings trooped aboard while a crane lifted the otters onto the deck. They were tapered, cylindrical paravanes with bodies like a miniature torpedo, headed by a stubby wing. Once deployed, they would fly underwater parallel to the bow dragging the sweep wire between them. The petty officer in charge handed me instructions from Captain Mulock to take the ship out into the roads, so the ratings could demonstrate how to rig and deploy the otters.

A further twenty-four hours later, *Oriental Venture*, auxiliary-minesweeper, put to sea with orders to patrol the Durian Strait. Included among those orders was a list of naval radio frequencies and a code book. In addition to minesweeping, we were also part of Mulock's Extended Defences, responsible for reporting any warship or aircraft, friendly or otherwise, we sighted. Reporting was about the only useful thing we could do. As Petty Officer Bullen laconically observed, when he learnt of our orders, we were the exact opposite of a battlecruiser. Anything we couldn't outfight we couldn't outrun, and anything we couldn't outrun we couldn't outfight. It was not exactly consoling to know that we might, at least, die usefully. I handed the radio frequency list and the code book to Gilmore, and told him to practise his coding.

The Durian Strait ran for thirty miles south from the western approaches to Singapore, winding its way between the coast of Sumatra and the archipelago to the east. It was not the normal route from the Sunda Strait to Singapore, but it was the farthest away from Japanese planes operating from Indochina and Thailand. If the Japanese mined it, they would cut the city's lifeline. Our task was to keep it open.

To compensate for the fact that none of us had the first idea about minesweeping, the navy provided a handbook. It was full of complicated instructions. Boiled down, they amounted to steaming up and down the Strait with the otters deployed, hoping the sweeps would intercept any mines before they hit the ship. McGrath's description of Irish minesweeping was frighteningly apt.

Fortunately, the first week-long patrol was largely uneventful, at least by the standards of a war we had already been fighting for over two years. The crew quickly became adept at launching and retrieving the otters, while those on the bridge became intimately familiar with the islands and landmarks as we navigated within the Strait's confines.

Steaming between lushly forested islands, with the sea a sparkling turquoise and the breeze ruffling my hair, it was almost possible to imagine we were on a leisure cruise, instead of hunting a deadly, invisible enemy. At other times, with visibility blotted out by a thunderstorm and swift currents setting us towards the hazards for which the Strait was famous, it felt as dangerous as trying to weather an iron-bound lee shore in an unhandy sailing ship.

Whatever the weather however, the lookouts quickly learnt the value of keeping their eyes peeled. Japanese mines were not the only threat; those laid by our own navy in the Singapore Strait were just as dangerous. It only took the parting of a rusted shackle or a cracked link of chain for a mine to bob to the surface and drift into the shipping lane.

The first heart stopping cry of 'mine', summoned every available eye to anxiously search in the pointed direction. The DEMS gunners took turns taking pot shots with the Lewis guns. It was good target practise, and provided the crew with an opportunity to gamble on the most accurate. The finally resulting explosion was a satisfying boost for morale. More worrying, was an underwater explosion two days later for which there was no apparent cause. Perhaps a large, inquisitive fish brushed against the Hertz horn of a mine. The shock wave forced dead and dying fish to the surface, including beautiful, bright-red snapper, which the crew snared in makeshift nets.

Midway through the week, the lookouts spotted a lone Japanese aircraft. Interrupting its reconnaissance, it dropped low to investigate. Surprised by the accurate barrage from our Oerlikons and Lewis guns, the pilot attempted only one pass. His bullets zinged harmlessly off the decks and fittings, before he climbed away to look for more promising targets.

Unable to sweep in the darkness, the nights were spent patrolling the wider, regularly swept sections of the Strait, sometimes as far north as the western approaches to Singapore. As usual, I spent the hours from dusk to dawn on the bridge; catnapping whenever the conditions were quiet enough to allow it. Even when they did, sleep was hard to come by. Every time I closed my eyes, I could see Helena's reproach filled face. As we neared the end of our first patrol, I was anxious to discover whether she was still in Singapore, or if Poh had successfully persuaded her to leave. But even as I hoped she was on her way to safety, part of me longed to hear she had stayed.

We arrived back at dawn, to see fires burning among the docks and the godowns lining the Singapore River. Columns of black smoke rose over the city, obscuring the morning sun. The acrid stench of burning oil and rubber filled our nostrils. We were ordered to anchor while the dockside fires were brought under control, and then signalled alongside to top up our coal bunkers, stores and ammunition.

Poh made a brief visit, delivering the crew's mail and the news that the Japanese were still advancing. They had seized Kuala Lumpur on 11 January and resumed bombing Singapore; the planes targeting Keppel Harbour and the Naval Base. Helena was still volunteering at the military hospital and Poh waited while I wrote her a note. After apologising for my behaviour at Raffles, I begged her to leave for India or Australia. It was not what I wanted to say, not at all. The thought that I might never see her again, except perhaps on a cinema screen, felt like a dagger in the heart, but at least I would know she was alive.

I handed over the note, and Poh swore to do all he could to persuade her to leave. It would be none too soon. His departure was closely followed by the arrival of a young naval lieutenant. He handed me orders for a repeat patrol, another sweep of the Durian

Strait, this time lasting almost a fortnight.

Any relief I felt to be away from the bombing, was tinged by fear for Helena's safety if she remained in the threatened city. While we quickly settled back into the routine of daily sweeps and night-time patrols, a sense of gloom hung over *Oriental Venture*. For most of us, Singapore and Hong Kong had come to feel like home. For the Chinese crew, the latter was their home. All had family and friends there, and the stories of Japanese savagery as it fell did not bode well for Singapore.

The days passed frustratingly slowly. Even the Japanese reconnaissance flights took on a sense of the mundane, as if the pilots were simply going through the motions. They were searching for inbound convoys. A lone tramp steamer was simply an opportunity for gunnery practise, few bothered to waste a bomb. When they did, zigzagging under full helm, even at ten knots, was usually sufficient to keep the explosions far enough away to do little more than rattle the crockery in the galley.

Midway through the second week, a coded message ordered us to head south-east to Linga Island to investigate the report of a downed Hurricane. It proved correct. We sighted the aircraft's remains on a beach, but there was no sign of the pilot. After blowing the whistle and firing shots to attract attention, I was about to launch a boat when Gilmore handed me a signal ordering our immediate return to Singapore. It was Lamont's afternoon watch. I handed him the signal and told him to plot our return courses.

We were treated to a gorgeous sunset. The crimson ball, setting behind Sumatra, inflamed the clouds and sent tongues of fire flickering along the wave tops. As the first stars appeared, McGrath took evening sights. Distant headlands and islands were still visible, but I wanted as accurate a position as possible before setting course for the southern entrance to the Durian Strait.

The first quarter moon had long set by 3am, as we felt our way past the Rukau Islands. It was a clear night, ablaze with stars, and the island's low peaks were black sentinels silhouetted against the dark horizon. Once clear of North Brother, I altered course to the north-west. Three miles away the peaks of Great and Little Durian loomed reassuringly in the darkness. Having patrolled up and down the channel for the previous fortnight, the landmarks were almost as familiar as the callouses and scars on my hands. In any case, the night remained perfectly fine and dawn was not far off as we transited the two-mile wide gap between Middleburg and Melville Reefs.

The welcome smell of coffee drifted up from the pantry, and several minutes later Da Silva appeared with his tray. McGrath and I were on the bridge wing, scanning the slowly brightening horizon. I was already looking forward to a couple of hours of shut eye in my day cabin, when the lookout hailed.

'Two points off the starboard bow. Looks like something in the water.'

The something turned out to be wreckage: baulks of splintered timber, an upturned lifeboat, articles of clothing, empty lifejackets … and dead bodies.

I slowed the ship and ordered the rescue boat readied. After following the pathetic trail of flotsam for half an hour, we sighted the lifeboat. It was crammed with men. They had rigged a sail, but the morning was calm and the oars rose and fell in a ragged stroke as they pulled in the direction of Singapore.

I jerked the whistle lanyard. The deep blast pierced the morning and survivors clambered onto the lifeboat's thwarts to wave. I hove to two cables away and the boat came smartly alongside, upturned faces smiling with pleasure and relief. Painted on the transom, *Tai Ting* was the name of the ship to which it belonged. Most of her crew scrambled up the rescue nets unaided. The injured were gently hoisted aboard lashed into a bosun's chair.

Tai Ting's senior surviving officer, Chief Mate Ramsden, joined me on the bridge. He watched ruefully while Bullen's gunners shattered and sank the lifeboat, before telling me the short, tragic story of the ship's sinking.

They had struck a mine the previous evening, the explosion blowing the forecastle off and rupturing the forward holds. *Tai Ting* had gone down in minutes taking her captain with her. Most of the crew jumped overboard, but Ramsden and the other mates had managed to launch a lifeboat before the ship slipped under. In the moonlit calm, they dragged to safety as many swimmers as they found.

His voice shook as he gratefully accepted a mug of strong, rum-laced coffee. 'We were told the channel was swept free of mines. That was the last thing we were expecting.'

'A stray, broke adrift maybe. We spotted one on our last patrol. I'm sorry.' It was little comfort to a man who had just lost his ship and everything he possessed. 'Where were you headed?'

'Tanjung Priok and then Sydney. I guess you picked up our distress call? I didn't think the radio operator managed to send it before the engine room flooded and we lost power.'

I shook my head. 'No, we were on our way back to Singapore when we spotted some wreckage. It was just luck we found you.'

The disappointment on Ramsden's face spoke volumes. By rights, *Tai Ting* should have been halfway to Java on its way to safety. Instead, it was at the bottom of the Durian Strait and those that had survived were heading back to Singapore.

Ramsden excused himself and went below to check on his men. I turned my attention to the northern horizon, where full daylight revealed hazy columns of smoke rising above the direction of Singapore.

Three hours later we dropped anchor in the inner roads. The gangway had hardly been rigged, before a navy launch swung alongside, and the tall, unwelcome figure of Lieutenant-Commander Barker climbed wearily up the steps.

CHAPTER TWENTY-NINE

Thursday 29 January 1942

W
e sailed early the same afternoon. Ramsden and the crew of the *Tai Ting* were sent ashore soon after our arrival. The launch that carried them returning with a party of naval ratings, and six requisitioned sampans that now bobbed and tugged on their tow line.

Lieutenant-Commander Barker was once again pacing my bridge. He looked as if he had not slept for several nights. His uniform hung on his bony frame like grey, crumpled sackcloth. Bloodshot eyes glared from deeply sunken sockets surrounded by dark rings. His hands trembled as he took fierce drags at a cigarette. He downed several mugs of Da Silva's strongest coffee, holding them in both hands to avoid slopping the contents. Knowing the reason, I left him to pace alone and focussed my attention on getting underway as smartly as possible.

Trusting Lamont to navigate us out of the roads and into the Main Strait, I beckoned McGrath to follow me into the chartroom. The chart of the Malacca Strait was spread on the table, held down by brass paperweights.

I jabbed my finger over the entrance to the Batu Pahat River, 60 miles north-west of Singapore. 'That's where we're headed. There are several thousand soldiers cut off on the coast, behind the front line. Barker's spent the last two nights rescuing them. The Japanese don't know they're there, but they're bound to find out eventually.'

'No wonder he looks as if he's about to drop dead from exhaustion,' said McGrath.

'I don't think any of us look much better. And it's going to be another long, sleepless night.'

'I wondered what the sampans were for.' McGrath ran a hand through his ginger hair. 'We'll be anchored off, with scrambling nets both sides while the sampans ferry the troops from the beach.'

I nodded and pointed to the anchorage Barker had already plotted on the chart. 'There's enough water depth there to get within about a mile of the river mouth. They've been using motor launches for the last two nights, but they don't have enough space for all the men still left ashore. We're their last chance.'

Hearing Lamont's helm orders, I poked my head into the wheel-house. The outer shoal beacon was abeam and he had shaped course to safely round Saint Johns Island. I stepped back to the chart.

'Once we're round Tanjong Bolus, we'll head over to the Sumatran side of the Malacca Strait. The Japanese are attacking anything they see moving. We'll have to take our chances until sunset. Then we'll run in towards the coast in the darkness. We'll have until two o'clock at the latest to get as many men aboard as possible. If we're not well away by dawn ... we may as well paint a bullseye on the funnel.'

'I'll get onto it then.'

McGrath headed below and I returned to the wheelhouse. Japan-ese planes had bombed Singapore just before 11am, their regular calling time according to Barker. The smoke from the fires was drift-ing south, carrying soot and the stench of burning oil. Thunder-clouds ringing the horizon held the promise of rainstorms. The rain would be welcome relief to the men battling the fires and it, together with the smoke, might help conceal us from enemy aircraft.

Once past Saint Johns Island, Lamont altered course north-west through the inner passage towards Sultan Shoal. The channel through the minefields was narrow, smoke haze obscured the bea-cons and I breathed a sigh of relief when we cleared the shoal and headed west into the wider waters of the Malacca Strait.

Wider, but not safer. The lookouts anxiously scanned the horizon and the gun crews were at action stations, the muzzles of their Oer-likons and Lewis guns trained skywards. Bullen stalked the bridge wing, hands clasped behind his back, like a lean, grizzled heron. He was one of the oldest men aboard, his deeply creased face evidence of long years of service in all weathers, but his jaw was set with grim determination. Like Da Silva, he seemed to have lost the need for sleep. He snapped a salute as I joined him. I had given up telling him not to bother. In any case, Barker was watching us.

'We're going to rescue some pongoes, sir?' He saw my raised eye-brow. 'No secrets on the lower decks, sir. The leading seaman in charge of the sampans told me.'

'We have to get there first, Bullen. The Japs are doing their best to sink anything that moves in the Strait.'

He stiffened as Barker moved towards us.

'Keep your men on their toes, Bullen. There's still over a thousand soldiers on the beach at the river mouth. The enemy are so close they can hear their vehicles on the road.'

Barker's face was grey with fatigue and his left eye twitched continuously. The strain of another sleepless night might be enough to break him. I glanced at the sky. The smoke was thinning, but the clouds were steadily piling up. Rain was already trailing from the bases of the heaviest cumulonimbus.

I laid a hand on Barker's arm. 'Why don't you get your head down for a couple of hours, Commander. There's nothing more you can do now, and we might get lucky. The Japs will find it hard to spot anything through those thunderclouds.'

Barker jerked his arm away as if burnt by my touch. He seemed about to argue, then his head drooped in surrender.

'I'll use your day cabin, if that's alright, Captain. Call me if ...' He shuffled unsteadily away towards the door.

It was the first time he had addressed me as, 'Captain'. I put the slip down to tiredness. 'See that rain squall?' I called to the helmsman, pointing to the nearest one.

He nodded.

'Steer into it.'

If we could dodge from the shelter of one downpour to another, until the light faded, we might just make it to Batu Pahat unobserved. For the sake of those soldiers whose lives depended on it, I said a short prayer to Saint Woolos. He was the patron saint of pirates and smugglers. If anyone could help Barker sneak ashore in the dead of night, and smuggle away a thousand men from under the noses of the Japanese, he could.

By sunset, Saint Woolos was still keeping his end of the bargain. Several times we heard the drone of aircraft but, whether they were patrolling the Strait in search of a target or on their way to bomb Singapore, we were spared their attention under the thick cloud cover.

As soon as it was sufficiently dark to render us invisible from the air, I altered course to close the coast. With 20 miles to run, we would be off the river mouth before 10pm. At 8pm the watch changed, but the only difference on the bridge was the fresh helmsman and lookouts. McGrath was below organising for the soldier's reception; Lamont was navigating; Lakshman was standing by to run errands and I was studying the darkness ahead, hoping the calculations for set and drift were correct. A sandbank extended into the Strait north of the river mouth. The Japanese would be delighted to find us stuck on it at daybreak.

Shortly after the change of watch, I sent Da Silva to wake Barker with a pot of strong coffee. A few minutes later, he strode into the wheelhouse. His face was nothing more than a pale blur in the darkness, but the firm tread and the brusque voice announcing his arrival suggested the nap and the coffee had restored his vigour, if not his charm.

'Where are we, Rowden?' he snapped.

'Ten miles to go, we'll be dropping anchor just after nine.'

'Confident you know where you are?'

'As near as possible, seeing as we're feeling our way blind.' I was surprised how much easier it had become to bite my tongue. 'I'll have a man on the lead shortly, as we run over the sandbanks.'

I took the grunt from the darkness to indicate approval, and resumed scanning the horizon. The rain showers had eased since sunset, and the waxing moon was peeping through breaks in the overcast. With luck, the whaleback profile of Mount Formosa would guide us the last few miles to the anchorage. The shoreline was also not totally devoid of light. Pinpricks of fires marked the fishermen's villages clustered around the entrances to the creeks. I called down to the boatswain to start casting the lead, and listened to the regularly chanted soundings as we nosed closer to the coast.

In the quiet darkness it was hard to believe that two armies were locked in battle for the southern tip of Malaya. The Japanese had already pushed well down towards Johore, driving the British Army before it. Either the guns were silent, or we were too far away to hear them. I felt movement at my elbow and Lamont whispered in his Scottish burr.

'I can make out the summit of Mount Formosa. Four points to starboard. We've about three miles to go.'

I raised the night glasses. The bulk of the hill was silhouetted in the moonlight, right where it was supposed to be.

'Good work, Second,' I whispered. 'But I don't know why we're whispering. If the clouds clear completely, there'll be enough moonlight for anyone ashore to see us.'

I reported our position to Barker, and sent Lakshman below to alert McGrath. 'Tell him to standby to cast off the sampans, and warn Cramp to walk the anchor out. No unnecessary noise.' Voices were one thing, but there was no point announcing our arrival with several tons of anchor and steel chain splashing into the water.

I called to Lamont to ring the engine to half ahead and listened to the boatswain calling the soundings. The water depth shoaled as we crossed the outlying sandbar, deepened in the gutter and shoaled again as we eased towards the shoreline.

'Stop engines.'

The vibration died away as the ship slowed to a stop. Barker raised a torch and sent a series of quick flashes into the darkness. There was no response. My pulse quickened. Had the Japanese taken the beaches? Were we about to be riddled with gunfire? They could hardly miss and we would be a flaming wreck before I could get the ship underway again.

A light stabbed out of the darkness.

'That's them. Right, let's get going.' Barker bolted down the stairs to the main deck. Moments later, diesel engines coughed into life and the small flotilla of sampans slipped their tow lines and chugged towards the beach.

The clank of the chain, as Cramp walked the anchor out, sounded unnaturally loud in the darkness. Finally anchored, with ten feet of water under the keel, there was little to do but wait. Boarding nets were rigged and all the guns manned; their barrels trained on the shore. Barker had accepted the recognition signal without question. If it was a trap, we were a sitting duck.

The cloud cover continued to thin and the gibbous moon broke through, ringed by a silvery halo. The land breeze swung the ship until she pointed towards the shore. It reduced her profile, but a sharp-eyed lookout might just be able to pick out her dark silhouette. The breeze carried the rank odour of seaweed and jungle, overlaid with acrid tinges of smoke but, apart from the sough of the wind and the slap of water against the hull, the night was still. Or was it? I turned my head to confirm my suspicion. The growing throb of a diesel engine was approaching from the direction of the beach. I rubbed my fingertips together. If it was a trap, we were about to find out.

A sampan chugged out of the darkness and bumped alongside. Others followed close behind, crammed to the gunwales, with only inches of freeboard. As soon as they touched, a horde of darkened shapes swarmed up the side netting, their ghostly faces skull-like in the moonlight. Boots clattered on the ladder and a young army officer climbed onto the bridge. His stained and ragged uniform looked ghoulish in the pale light of the binnacle. He stank of rancid sweat and mud. There was a bandage around his head, his face was deep lined with fatigue, but his eyes still glinted.

'Captain Rowden?' He stiffened to attention. 'Lieutenant Childers, First Leicesters. Commander Barker's compliments, sir. That's the first three hundred men. There are about six hundred still ashore, many of them wounded.'

'Any trouble finding us?' I asked.

'You're bang on the compass bearing Commander Barker gave me. The moonlight helps.'

Da Silva appeared with a mug of coffee.

Childers reached for it and gulped the contents. 'The Japs are nosing around the eastern base of the hill, we can hear their lorries on the road. They haven't spotted us yet, though.'

'If you can see us in the moonlight, so can they. If they chance to look.'

'Right-oh, then. I'd better get back pronto and bring off the next batch.'

He handed the empty mug to Da Silva, turned on his heel and climbed back down to the main deck.

I watched over the side until the sampans were swallowed by the darkness, and turned to find McGrath had joined me.

'We've embarked three hundred men,' he said. 'On their last legs some of 'em. I've put them in the tween decks. They're out of the way there and they can smoke.'

'There are twice as many still to come, wounded among them. And the Japs are closing in.' I glanced around. Bullen, lean and ramrod straight was watching the shore through night glasses, his white shorts and shirt pale in the moonlight. Beside him, barrel chested Lamont sucked on the stem of his unlit pipe.

'Join us in the chartroom, you two.'

Under the light of the red lamp, I pointed to our anchored position on the chart. 'We're here, if the second mate can be believed.' I picked up the dividers and stepped off the distance to Mount Formosa. The summit was five miles away to the north-east. Its lower slopes extended towards the shore for about a mile and a half. 'According to that army lieutenant, Childers, the Japs have been spotted on the far side of the hill. What's the maximum range of our guns, Bullen?'

'About eleven thousand yards for both the 4-inch and the 12-pounder, sir,' he replied, without hesitation. 'About four and a half thousand for the Oerlikons, not very effective at that distance but they might keep some heads down.'

'When Childers returns with the next load, get him up here to mark on the chart where the Japs are likely to approach from. You never know, we might be able to offer some support.'

Highlighted by the red glow, Bullen's grin was devilish. 'Shooting blind on distance and bearing. My ballistics are a bit rusty, but I'm sure there are range tables for the guns somewhere. Nothing for the Oerlikons though, they're not usually used as artillery.' He paused and the corners of his mouth drooped. 'The muzzle flashes will give our position away.'

I nodded. 'Last resort. We'll only open fire if the Japanese tumble to what's happening and head for the beaches. I suggest you and Mr Lamont work out some signalling arrangements with Childers, telling you when to shoot and where.'

Bullen's grin returned. 'Aye, aye, sir. I'll go and find those range tables.'

'Go with him, Ian,' I said to Lamont. 'Talk to the gun crews. Make sure everyone's on the ball. Send Lakshman up. He can take over here.'

'Are you sure that's wise?' asked McGrath, as soon as they were both out of earshot. 'We'll be an easy target if the Japs spot us. And with all those men aboard—'

The distant crackle of gunfire cut McGrath off in mid-sentence. I dashed onto the bridge wing and whipped up my night glasses.

'Anyone see anything?'

'Nothing, Skipper.' Lakshman materialised out of the darkness.

There was another faint rattle of gunfire.

'Sounds like someone's made contact. Some way off, though.' I swept the glasses along the dark smudge where the coastline merged with the sea. Clouds rolled across the moon. Despite being only a mile away, the beach was invisible.

'Hear that?' The rising throb of diesel engines announced the sampans returning with the next load.

McGrath darted down the stairs to the main deck. I peered down at the rippled, inky water splashing softly against the ship's side. Sampans emerged from the darkness and bumped alongside. The scrambling nets sagged under the weight of dozens of dark shapes swarming aboard, materialising into men as soon as their feet reached the deck. They were followed by the wounded, hauled up on makeshift slings, trailing a pale wrack of loose bandages, or strapped into makeshift stretchers. Those capable of walking were harried down the access hatches into the tween decks. The rest were carried into the accommodation where McGrath and the chief steward were doing their best to make them comfortable.

Lamont's Scottish burr carried onto the bridge wing, accompanied by Childers' clipped, military tones. I stepped into the chartroom to see them hunched over the chart, Childers with a pencil gripped in his fist.

'Near as we can tell, the Japs are here, following a track towards the beach.' He marked a position on the lower slopes of Mount Formosa and drew an arrow towards the coast. 'No more than a platoon. They're wary, but they probably think they've made contact with a few stragglers. We've pulled back the perimeter, but they might push on to see what's what. A platoon we can deal with. Question is, what support they've got, if any? Answer ... no fucking idea.'

He pulled a map out of his pocket, unfolded it and spread it on the chart table. 'If you mark your position on that, then the best I can do is signal an approximate bearing and range. In extremis only, though. Once you open fire, the game's over. The Japs will realise what we're up to. And you'll be a sitting duck if they've got artillery.'

'Just what my chief mate, said,' I replied.

'Blistering sporrans, your map's about as much use as a balsa wood fid.' Lamont threw down the dividers. 'It only covers the land, and the margin's not wide enough.' He reached for a note book, ripped out a leaf and rummaged through the chart table drawer. 'Thank Christ for Sellotape.'

Taping the blank paper to the edge of the map, he swiftly plotted the ship's position and drew several alignment markers.

He slid the map back to Childers and tossed him the roll of tape. 'Take this with you, and stick the sheet back on if it comes unstuck. Follow the arrows.'

Childers' grin seemed to lift years from his haggard face. 'Thank God for the navy.'

'Navy be buggered,' said Lamont, returning his grin. 'You're in the company of real seamen. And we're not bad with the pop-guns either. Just flash the word and we'll shoot the lice off the balls o' them Japs.' He thudded a fist into Childers' shoulder for emphasis.

'Only if we ask for it. Which hopefully we won't. Unless the solids really hit the fan.' Childers folded the map, careful not to dislodge its appendage, pocketed the tape and straightened up. 'Right, I need to get back to the beach. There's men still waiting.' He glanced at the bulkhead clock. 'You need to be away by zero two hundred.'

'Any later than that and we'll be tiger bait at dawn,' I said.

He nodded; his mouth twisted into a grimace. 'Commander Barker said to tell you that if the sampans aren't here by then, you're to head back to Singapore. We've got the majority of the men off. The rest of us will have to take our chances.' He rubbed his bandaged head. 'Keep your eyes peeled for our signals. We'll let you know as soon as the last boat leaves. And if ... well if it comes to that it probably won't matter what you aim at.'

The other sampans had departed by the time Childers scrambled down into the remaining one. He glanced up at the bridge, waved a hand in salute and barked the order to cast off. The sampan chugged away into the darkness.

It was 1am. Most of us had been on our feet for over thirty-six hours. I could feel the familiar prickling on the back of my eyelids and was about to call for Da Silva, when the nose-tingling scent of coffee wafted up from the pantry. There was a tin of Senior Service in my day cabin. Fuck it! This was no time for a martyr's hair-shirt. Men's lives depended on our judgement. I slipped into the cabin, snatched a cigarette from the tin and lit up, dragging the welcome smoke deep into my lungs. The nicotine rush, assisted by several gulps of coffee, cleared the fog from my brain. After several more hasty drags, I stubbed the butt into the ashtray and bustled back to the bridge, announcing my presence with a brusque, 'Anything happening?'

'Nothing, Skipper.' Lakshman's reply floated in from the bridge wing.

I checked my watch. The green luminous dial revealed less than ten minutes had elapsed. I stepped outside to join Lakshman, raising my night glasses to scan the darkness. Nothing. I twisted my head from side to side, searching for any sound above the lap of water and the soft hiss of venting steam. Fraser was maintaining boiler pressure ready for instant manoeuvring.

The watch-hands slowly ticked off the minutes. Ten minutes became twenty, then thirty. Half an hour before we needed to be underway. I rubbed my fingertips to ease their tingling.

A prolonged rattle of gunfire broke the stillness. It was almost a relief to feel the surge of adrenalin banish the tiredness.

'TWO POINTS, STARBOARD BOW,' yelled Lamont, from the Monkey Island.

A cluster of faint, flickering red lights danced in the distance, like fireflies against a black curtain.

'What do you think they are? Muzzle flashes? Tracer?' I shouted. 'And how far away?'

'Could be broonies dancin' in the moonlight, hard to tell. The navy claims the flare of a match can be seen from over a mile. Can't be that far from the beach, though.'

'Watch the bearing and keep the guns trained.' It sounded ridiculous. We were a scruffy freighter, equipped with antiquated cannon manned by hastily trained seamen and soldiers, not a warship.

Bursts of firing continued; the rattle of machine guns, interspersed with the crack of rifle fire. Was it just a handful of Japanese soldiers that had bumped into the shrinking perimeter, or had they finally realised what was happening and attacked in force?

The firing increased in intensity. Through the night glasses it was possible to distinguish faint lines of tracer criss-crossing the darkness. The noise rose to a continuous roar. Bright flashes of explosions added to the crescendo, before the firing died away and an eerie silence settled over the water.

I glanced at my watch. The hands had just ticked past 1.45am. There was no sign of any returning boats. I cupped my hands and bellowed to Cramp on the forecastle. 'Haul the anchor short.' I waited for the answering hail before reaching for the engine room voice pipe to tell Fraser to standby the steam valves.

Turning away from the voice pipe, I saw Lakshman watching me. In the pale light of the binnacle, his normally cheerful face was a mask of strain and anguish.

'What a choice, eh Third? If we go, we leave three hundred men to the mercy of the Japanese, but we might get back to Singapore and save over six hundred. If we wait, we'll be caught by the bombers at daybreak.'

It hardly seemed any choice at all. We would be lucky to reach Singapore in one piece in either event. Commander Barker and his men had risked everything to save the soldiers from under the noses of the Japanese. Could I really abandon him just because the clock ticked past 2am? I didn't have a direct order, just the word of fatigue-drunk army lieutenant who might keel over at any moment.

I paced the bridge wing, watching the hands of my watch crawl towards the hour. The moon disappeared behind a bank of cloud and the night turned pitch black. The hands ticked past the hour and crawled on. The hiss of venting steam became a drawn-out sigh of anguish, as if the ship herself was on edge with waiting.

A light stabbed out of the night, the Morse slow and deliberate.

Lakshman called out the words, confirming my own reading.

'FIVE BOATS ON WAY REARGUARD FOLLOWS SHORTLY TARGET ZERO NINE FIVE DEGREES RANGE TWO THOUSAND YARDS STAND BY DO NOT ACKNOWLEDGE.'

'Did you get that Second?' I called up to Lamont.

'Aye, Skipper. But is that true or compass bearing? Do the pongoes even know the difference?'

'Your call. Maybe Barker sent the message.'

Lamont hailed the guns forward and aft. 'Target range two thousand, compass bearing zero eight six.' He lowered his voice. 'Christ, I hope I'm not second guessing the commander.'

'How do they know …?' Why the hell had I not thought of it before? The guns were only fitted with relative bearing indicators.

'Lifeboat compasses, Skipper. Not sure how accurate they are on the ship, but it's better than nothing.'

Ignoring the desire to kick myself, I swung my night glasses onto the target bearing. The darkness was impenetrable. Were there enemy soldiers advancing into the gun's trajectory? Or was Barker as blind as we were, hoping to lay a diversion while the last of his rearguard sprinted for the final sampan. Having run into opposition, perhaps the Japanese were advancing more cautiously. Or was Barker's rearguard already cut off without knowing it?

The horizon exploded with bursts of light and red streams of tracer.

'That can't be far behind the beach. Check the bearing,' I called up to Lamont.

'About right. I hope they judged the distance correctly.'

Bursts of firing continued, but there was no signal to open fire or any indication the rearguard was about to quit the beach. I clenched and unclenched my fists, fighting to stay calm.

'Sampans coming alongside!' McGrath's yell from the boat deck broke the tension.

I darted to the bridge wing and peered over the side. Dozens of men were scrambling up the netting. As soon as each sampan emptied it was cast adrift. Lieutenant Childers pulled himself up the ladder from the boat deck, the bandage around his head dark with fresh blood.

'Japs are less than half a mile from the beach.' He gasped from fatigue and the effort of the climb, sucking in lungfuls of air. 'There's more of them now, probably a company. The rearguard's holding them, but they'll make a break for it any moment. When they signal, just shoot at the gunfire. Our boys know to duck and run like hell. Hopefully the Japs'll cop it when they follow them.'

'You got that, Second?' I called to Lamont.

'Aye, aye. We're ready.'

More bursts of gunfire lit up the eastern sky, the crack and rattle of the shots sounding very close in the darkness.

Morse flashed from the beach. One word. Repeated. 'SHOOT.'

'SHOOT!' My yell would have reached a skysail yardarm in a full gale. It was instantly followed by the simultaneous crack of the 4-inch and 12-pounder guns.

The flash of the shell-bursts momentarily lit up the beach. Through the night glasses, I glimpsed the final sampan with men scrambling aboard. The delayed crump of the explosions buffeted my ears. The shots had fallen beyond the red flashes of machine gun fire. Lamont yelled an elevation correction and the second shells exploded amongst the flashes. There was a ragged cheer from the gun crews and they set to with rapid fire. Explosion after explosion ripped the darkness apart, revealing the curve of the beach and the dark silhouettes of the jungle trees behind.

A chattering roar added to the din as the Oerlikons joined in. Two streams of tracer hosed into the sky, the glowing red shells cascading into the jungle. To my untrained eye it was impossible to tell if they were landing anywhere near the target. Shouts from the Monkey Island suggested someone was trying to observe the fall of shot.

The wink of the Morse lamp stabbed out of the night. I shouted each word, calling them up to Lamont. 'LAST BOAT LEFT BEACH REDUCE RANGE TO ONE EIGHT ZERO ZERO YARDS.'

Hearing his answering hail, I raised the night glasses to search for the final sampan. It was already well clear of the beach, pursued by trails of machine gun fire from the Japanese troops spilling onto it.

'Those machine guns can kill at two thousand yards.' Childers was at my elbow. 'They'll fire at the muzzle flashes.'

I leaned over the dodger, cupped my hands and roared at the forecastle. 'Get the anchor up.'

Furious clanging of the forecastle bell confirmed the anchor was aweigh. I rang the engine full astern. Vibration surged through the deck plates as the huge cylinders beat to life. The threshing propeller dragged the ship stern first away from the beach.

'How's your head?' I called to the helmsman.

'Nor-east, sir.'

'Try and keep the stern heading south-west.'

The smaller target we made the better, we could turn once out of range.

The staccato of bullets ricocheting off the steel decks sounded like giant hail. The Japanese machine guns had found the range.

'Focus on those machine guns,' I yelled to Lamont, before grabbing the signal lamp.

I flashed a short message to the sampan, telling it to follow us, waited for an acknowledgement, and trained my night glasses on the shoreline. Shells exploded among the trees lining the beach. Twin streams of Oerlikon tracer cascaded among them. The Japanese machine gun fire slackened, then stopped.

'Stop engines,' I shouted. 'Get that last sampan alongside.'

Five minutes later, with Barker and the rearguard aboard, the sampan was cast adrift. I ordered full ahead and the helm hard over. 'Steer sou-sou-east.'

The helmsman nodded, his face a blank mask of oriental inscrutability. Was he relieved we were finally heading back to Singapore, with almost a thousand rescued soldiers cramming the tween decks? Or was he just looking forward to a few hours in his bunk before dawn brought fresh dangers?

Soft footfalls on the deck announced the arrival of Commander Barker. Childers managed to snap an approximation of a salute. Despite his filthy, dishevelled appearance the moonlight caught a defiant glint in Barker's haggard eyes. I raised my palm to the peak of my cap and received a regulation salute in reply.

'Bloody poor show. Your gunners couldn't hit a stone frigate at point blank range. I should have the whole shower locked in the brig.' Barker glared at me; his lips compressed into a tight line. I opened my mouth to protest.

'On the other hand.' His mouth relaxed into a grin. 'Four-inch bricks was the last thing the Japs expected. And the 12-pounder and the Oerlikons spraying everywhere. They must have thought we had a destroyer out here at least. Kept their heads down just long enough.' He shoved out a hand. 'Good work, Captain Rowden, thank you. There's over a thousand men will live to fight another day because of you and your crew. Thank them for me, will you.'

He reached for my hand and shook it firmly.

'Don't thank me yet, Commander. They'll come looking for us at dawn, and they know where we're headed.'

I turned away and stalked onto the darkness of the bridge wing. The moon disappeared again behind a thick bank of cloud. I sniffed the air for the approach of rain. If we were lucky, early morning thunderstorms might conceal us from the bombers long enough to ... I put the thought aside. If anyone deserved any credit for the evacuation it was Barker and his tiny navy. He had pulled off a miniature version of Dunkirk. I just hoped our part in the final act was not doomed to end tragically. But even if it didn't, what was left for Singapore? The Japanese were almost at Johore. The island was about to be besieged, with us and everyone else, civilians and service personnel alike, trusting to its remaining defences. That included Helena, unless she had finally decided to leave. I balled my fists and gently pounded them on the teak hand rail to ease my frustration. The better part of me hoped she had seen sense and gone, but a nagging voice insisted otherwise, that she was too stubborn to run away from the danger. I listened to that voice and rejoiced. I wanted to see her. I wanted her, and the Japanese, the British and my promise to Colonel Spencer could all go to hell.

CHAPTER THIRTY

Afternoon, Monday 2 February 1942

A s I had hoped, banks of thunderstorms shielded us from searching aeroplanes as we steamed towards Singapore with our rescued soldiers. With Fraser coaxing as many revolutions as possible out of the engine, all available eyes anxiously searched the sky. We heard the drone of engines but, by mid-morning on 30 January, we reached the safety of Singapore harbour without being spotted. The soldiers were ferried ashore and the wounded taken to hospital, leaving us to swing around our anchor again while we awaited orders.

The army retreated onto the island the following day, leaving Johore and all of mainland Malaya in Japanese hands. Singapore was besieged, but the news reports still confidently predicted that, with its back firmly against the wall, the British bulldog would teach the Japanese a lesson they would not forget. *The Straits Times* rang the praises of the rearguard from the Argyll and Sutherland Highlanders. They were the last over the causeway, quick marching to the sound of the regimental pipers playing *Heilan' Laddie*. Perhaps the Japanese were too busy shielding their ears from the caterwauling to stop them blowing a hole in the causeway.

Things did not look quite so rosy from the anchorage. Smoke towered from fires started by the shelling of the naval base. Palls of smoke also drifted over the city, from the smouldering remains of fires among the docks and godowns started by the previous day's air raid. We could expect another today, but for the moment the harbour was quiet. In any case, the bombers usually ignored ships anchored in the roads, only occasionally flying low enough to strafe once they dropped their bomb load. Thus far, we had been lucky.

Despite *The Straits Times'* confidence, plans for the evacuation of Singapore were already in motion. Liners were arriving to provide passage for the European women, children and male civilians desperate to get away.

Helena was not among them. Poh had ruefully confirmed she was still at Raffles and volunteering at the Military Hospital. I was determined to see her. Even if she refused to accept my apology, I had to convince her to leave before it was too late. I sent her another note, but there had been no reply and I impatiently awaited the arrival of the launch. It nosed alongside shortly after two bells in the afternoon watch. Leaving McGrath in charge, I climbed down the gangway and ordered the coxswain to take me to the Master Attendant's pier.

The imposing facade of the Fullerton Building loomed over Collyer Quay. As a symbol of British Rule, its permanence looked increasingly questionable. The Singapore River, normally crowded with sampans, was thinly populated. An intermittent stream of craft wound their way downstream, passed under Anderson Bridge and chugged seaward. Rats deserting the proverbial sinking ship, or the sensible ones getting out while there was still time?

I hailed a taxi and rode the half mile to Raffles. Saint Andrews Cathedral was untouched, but its white painted spires looked vulnerably fragile next to the bomb cratered Padang. A battery of Anti-Aircraft guns sprouted on the seaward side, their gun barrels bristling skywards.

Raffles looked as serene and permanent as ever and the uniformed Sikh at the entrance held open the door to admit me. I crossed to the reception desk and asked if Helena was available to see visitors. Was she in the hotel or at the Military Hospital? She had not replied to any of my notes, and I had no way of knowing. I was resigned to waiting for as long as necessary but, after telephoning her room, the receptionist returned with the encouraging news that I was to remain in the lobby and Miss Markova would join me shortly. I took a seat beside a large potted palm and reached for the newspaper lying on the table, hoping to distract the butterflies in my stomach.

The front page still advertised the availability of Australian groceries at the Cold Store, and extolled the beauty benefits of Palmolive soap. *Our Wife* was showing at the *Cathay*, the reviewer describing it as the most exciting love triangle that ever made a man run around in circles. There was also a reminder that martial law had been declared, and the usual reports of crushing defeats suffered by the Nazis and the Japanese. Despite the paper's steely optimism, its readers must have worked out for themselves that the Japanese army was on the doorstep.

I was reading a letter to the editor objecting to the requisition of bicycles, penned by someone calling himself, "A Voice in the Desert" when a waft of familiar perfume caught my nostrils. I glanced over the paper to see Helena frowning down at me. She had dressed casually in loose fitting, grey silk pants and a matching blouse. Her face was discretely made up and her auburn hair brushed and bobbed. Her jaw was clamped with determination, but I noticed the look of inquiry in her eyes.

'Are you going to ask me to sit down, or should I stand here all afternoon?'

I jumped to my feet and offered my hand. She raised a neatly plucked eyebrow, reached for the hand and shook it.

'Please sit down, Helena. Can I order you some tea?'

'You English and your bloody tea. Surely you haven't come here just to offer me tea.'

'Did you receive my messages?'

'Yes. I ignored them all. I wanted to see if you'd have the courage to come in person, rather than sending pathetic notes.'

'What if I'd never come?'

'What if you hadn't? I'm a big girl, I don't need you traipsing after me.'

I sat silent for a moment. I hadn't expected a reception as frosty as this. 'You're not making things very easy, Helena.'

'What did you expect?'

'I've been asking myself that same question. Look, are sure you wouldn't like some tea?'

'What I'd like …' One corner of her mouth creased upwards. 'Oh, for God's sake. Order your damned tea if that's what you think it will take.'

I waved for the waiter. It was approaching 4pm, the time at which, according to the old song, everything stopped for tea. Men were poised to slaughter each other not 15 miles away, but the trolley laden with scones and cucumber sandwiches was doing the rounds. Helena watched with amusement—it was a relief to finally see her smile again—while the waiter placed a selection on our plates.

'It was worth coming down just to see you fussing about like a dowager with tea and scones. Would it be too much to ask for a vodka, Rodnik preferably?'

I raised my arm, and snatched it down again at Helena's laugh.

'For God's sake, Rowden. I'm teasing you.'

'Well, that's better than snapping at me.'

Her smile hardened and her eyes narrowed. Icy fingers reached for my heart.

'What is it you want of me?'

The question threw me aback. What did I want? A friend? I'd take that if there was nothing better on offer. A lover? A wife? A mother for children I never expected to have?

'Surely it's not that hard a question. You've always struck me as a man of action, not a thinker.'

'I want to fulfil my promise to Spencer, and see you safely out of Singapore.'

'He's got nothing to do with it. Anyway, that still sounds like you want to get rid of me?' She broke off a morsel of scone and popped it between her lips.

I freed the sheets and threw caution to the winds. 'If I had my way, I'd toss you over my shoulder, carry you back to the ship and lock you in my cabin.'

'It's better than being dragged off by the hair, I suppose.'

'You'd be as safe there as anywhere.'

'But not safe from you. Look, don't you think you should at least apologise first, before playing Blackbeard?'

'I will, I am, but don't you think you overreacted just a little.'

Helena opened her mouth to argue, but I forged on.

'Okay, I'll admit Diana caught me off guard when she told me you and Duff had been lovers. She seemed to enjoy it ... and twisting the knife by pointing out how hard Beckwith was working to earn your favour.'

Helena tossed her head. 'Whatever Diana said, there was no need for you to speak to me the way you did.'

'I'm sorry. I let my feelings get the better of me.'

'Jealousy! That's what it always is when a man starts to think he has proprietary rights over a woman. As soon as he's made love to her a few times, he wants to lock her away so he can enjoy her in private, like some prized possession. It never occurs to him that a woman might enjoy sex with a man, without feeling the need to chain herself to him. And when he does realise it, he drags her off the pedestal he's placed her on and throws her into the gutter. Well, let me tell you, I'm neither virgin nor whore and I'm not a mother either for that matter. You can disapprove all you want, but I'll flirt with whom I please, spend time with whom I please and love whom I please. For a time, that happened to be you, so count your blessings but don't expect me to honour and obey, or listen for wedding bells and the patter of tiny feet.'

She spoke softly, but with such passion that the light in her emerald eyes seemed to dance like flames. I had never imagined any of those things with any woman. The most I ever dreamt of was retiring to a quiet tropical island and living off my ill-gotten gains with a woman to keep me company, love was a bonus. More than that I probably didn't deserve. In any case, Helena had spoken in the past tense. I looked again into her eyes that seemed as unfathomable as the ocean.

'So, Captain Rowden. You haven't answered my question. What do you want from me?'

I took a deep silent breath. 'Nothing.'

A soft snort flared her nostrils. 'Nothing! A moment ago, you were threatening to throw me over your shoulder and drag me kicking and screaming onto your ship.' Her long, scarlet fingernails tapped threateningly on the table top, and I felt like a rodent about to be ripped to shreds by an eagle.

'Listen Helena, I've said I'm sorry. I truly am, and I came here to apologise, but you aren't making it easy.' She shook her head, but I stood on. 'We're neither of us saints, I've forgotten the names of most of the women I've ever had sex with. But if I never saw you again, I'd still count myself the luckiest man alive, just for having seen you smile and the look of pleasure in your eyes.'

I glanced down at my hands, suddenly conscious that I was twisting my interlocked fingers. The tips were tingling, hopefully not in warning. Helena followed my gaze and a corner of her mouth lifted.

'Stop fiddling with your hands. Do want a cigarette?'

She flipped open her enamelled cigarette case and I eagerly reached for a Sobranie Cocktail, ignoring the bright pink wrapper. Out of habit, I was still carrying my lighter and lit us both. The nicotine hit from the rich Balkan tobacco was instantly calming. I took another deep drag and held the smoke in my lungs, before slowly exhaling.

'That really is not a good look, you smoking pink cigarettes.' Helena's face brightened with amusement. 'If I'm driving you to take up smoking again, at least smoke something that makes you look less like a lounge lizard in a Turkish brothel.'

'Speaking from experience?' I waved for the waiter and asked him to bring me a tin of Senior Service.

'Yes … seeing as neither of us are saints. Although actually it was in Paris. Anaïs persuaded me to go to one with her and Henry Miller. What an eye opener that was.'

'Never heard of either of them.'

'Anaïs Nin wrote short stories, some of them filthy. Henry Miller was her lover.' Helena delicately inhaled a lungful of smoke and let it trickle from her nostrils. 'Anyway, you're not changing the subject that easily. I thought you were about to get down on your knees and beg forgiveness.'

'It was you that changed the subject—'

The air raid siren cut me off and the hubbub of conversation died. For a moment, people sat frozen by the wailing. The head waiter finally broke the spell, calling for everyone to make their way to shelter.

Helena grabbed her purse and we followed the guests out of the side entrance and across Basah Road. On the playing fields behind the Raffles Institution, a hastily constructed brick walled rectangle greeted us. Beneath a concrete slab roof, its open steel doors revealed a dark, cavernous interior, already jammed with bodies and more pressing in.

Helena shook her head. 'If I'm going to die, I'd rather do it in the daylight, than in that Black Hole of Calcutta. She reached for my hand and we ducked away from the line of guests.

'This way.' I pulled her across the playing fields in the direction of the bridge carrying Beach Road over the Stamford Canal. The water was filthy and the canal bank muddy and littered with refuse but, if the bombing came too close, we could crawl under the safety of the arch. I dropped to the grass and patted the ground beside me. Helena sat down and we pressed our backs against the parapet. The wail of the sirens was drowned by the roar of approaching bombers.

A formation emerged among the scattered clouds, flying high approaching from the east. The crack of anti-aircraft guns buffeted our ears and shell-bursts flecked the sky in the path of the bombers. They flew steadily on, following the line of the coast, and released their loads over the docks. The whistle of falling bombs rose to a crescendo and we huddled against the masonry. The earth shook, our bodies rocked and our senses were numbed by explosion after explosion. Most were far enough away to pose little danger, but some strays fell much closer. A heart-stopping screech filled my ears. I pushed Helena back against the parapet and sheltered her with my body. The ground erupted, a shock wave blew the breath from my lungs, the world fell silent, falling earth and rocks rained down on me … and everything went black.

When I came too, Helena was wearing a light slip and brassiere and her pants were blood spattered. I tried to sit up, afraid she was hurt, but she pushed me back.

'Rest a moment.' Her voice barely penetrated the fog in my head.

I raised a hand to my pounding skull and found it wrapped in silk.

'You've taken a knock to the head. I don't think it's serious, but you were bleeding like a stuck pig. I've bound the cut with my blouse.'

The bombing had ceased and the drone of engines was fading. I tried to sit up again, feeling strength return.

'Do you think you can stand?'

I nodded and Helena helped me to my feet.

'Put your arm around my shoulders.'

My legs were wobbly, but improved with each step. By the time we reached the cool welcome of Raffles I could have walked unaided, but kept my arm around Helena. I was not going to let her go now. We joined the stream of guests returning from the bomb shelter. Hotel staff with anxious faces greeted us. Helena asked for the doctor to call up to her room and led me towards the elevator.

With the door to her suite closed behind us, she reached out her arms. My head hurt, my ears rang, my hair was matted with blood and the room whirled slowly around. None of it mattered. I pulled her to me, like a drowning man clinging to his saviour. I was not about to die but, even if I had been, I knew for certain that with Helena again in my arms I would never be happier.

CHAPTER THIRTY-ONE

Morning, Friday 6 February 1942

Helena refused to let me return to the ship until the doctor cleared me of concussion. The treatment she administered was highly effective, and would probably have raised approving nods from the medical profession, even if it was not something they commonly prescribed. The headache had faded by the time she released me from her room, a shaved patch of skull and a couple of stitches reminders of the rock that had tried to knock more sense into me. Back aboard, Cramp admired the doctor's needlework, while chuckling at yet another addition to the scars marring my increasingly battered appearance.

Despite my entreaties for her to move aboard the ship, Helena decided to remain at Raffles. The daily bombings were mostly aimed at the docks and military installations, the hotel barely suffering a shattered window. There was heavy shelling of the northern coast, but the Japanese had made no attempt to cross the Johore Strait, and *The Straits Times* remained confident that Fortress Singapore could beat off any attack. Reinforcements were arriving from India and more were expected from Australia. A convoy had berthed the previous day, disgorging troops that marched straight from the docks to the northern fortifications. Perhaps the predictions were correct and the Japanese had, finally, cut off more than they could splice.

The upbeat statements from Government House and Army HQ were reflected in the mood in the city. The morning was hot, but fine and sunny as I stepped ashore at Collyer Quay and weaved my way through the bustling traffic to cross the road. Between the grand edifices of the shipping and trading houses, the entrance to Change Alley beckoned. It was said you could have your pocket picked at one end and your wallet sold back to you before you reached the other. I pushed my way amongst the voluble throng ignoring the offers to change money, sell me a cheap Japanese watch, or a short time with someone's sister. At the far end, I patted my pocket to reassure myself the wallet was still there and stepped back into the sunlight of Raffles Place. Many of the buildings had suffered bomb damage but Malacca Street, on the far side, seemed mostly untouched.

Poh's office was half way down, a brass plate announcing that Poh & Co. were to be found on the first floor. I mounted the stairs, chuckling over Poh's well-worn joke whenever he was asked a question involving the expenditure of money: 'I'll have to consult my partner, Mr Co.'

His clerk, a smartly dressed Indian with circular, steel rimmed spectacles and slicked back hair, ushered me into the inner sanctum. As always, Poh was immaculately dressed in a freshly pressed linen suit. With the louvre shutters closed against the glare, and the overhead fan turning briskly, the dark, wood-panelled office felt much cooler than the street. Beaming, Poh rose to greet me, directed me to a chair and reached for the thermos jug.

'Iced water, Captain, or something stronger?'

'Water. And a coffee, if you can manage one.'

'Of course.' He rang a brass hand-bell on his desk.

While we waited, I sipped the iced-water and scanned the office. The desk and furniture were of dark rosewood or mahogany. The bookshelves were lined with leather bound ledgers and books of government regulations. It could have been the office of an accountant or civil servant, there was no indication that Poh controlled a commercial empire with tentacles extending into the farthest corners of the Far East.

'Ten cents for your thoughts, Captain.'

'It used to be a penny when I was young.'

'Ah, the benefits of inflation.' He paused while an elderly Malay served coffee. It smelled delicious, the beans dark-roasted to perfection and fine ground, just the way I liked it. 'I am glad we have this opportunity for little chat.'

'Yes, I'm wondering how much longer we're going to be swinging round the pick. We're supposed to still be working for the navy, but you seem to know more than they do.'

Poh steepled his fingers, his eyes grave. 'Not much longer. Japanese will attack on Sunday.'

'Is that official intelligence?'

'No. It is mine. Every day Malay and Chinese people flee across the Johore Strait. Plantation workers, coolies, fishermen. They see for themselves.'

'And you think the Japanese will win?'

'Fighting last two months already, and army not stop them once. In China we have a saying, "fish rots from the head." The generals already believe Japanese unbeatable.'

'But what about the reinforcements?' The columns of soldiers marching north from the docks had looked impressive.

Poh shook his head. 'The Japanese are thirty thousand. British side nearly three times more, but not fight so well. Once on the island, only one objective. Not the naval base, not the docks, just the water reservoirs at Bukit Timah. No water, no more fight.'

'Have you made plans to leave?'

'No, I shall stay. There will be much to do before the Japanese are beaten.'

'Surely you don't think the people will fight on? Why should they?'

He beckoned me closer, as if afraid someone might overhear.

'I tell you a secret. Many Chinese already raise money to help the Kuomintang fight the Japanese. We also send money and buy weapons for Communist resistance in Malaya.'

The Kuomintang, Chiang Kai-shek's governing party and Mao's communists were sworn enemies, but the Chinese in Malaya were backing both horses.

'I thought the Communist Party was banned in Malaya,' I said.

'Yes, but British government secretly agree to support them. You will see, many will fight the Japanese. It is their country, and they know the jungle better than you.'

'That's dangerous work. If the Japanese find out what you're doing, they'll kill you.'

'If so, they will look for rich man in expensive suit, silk shirt.' Poh chuckled and adjusted his tie, held in place by a diamond studded pin. 'But in blue smock, bare feet, straw hat. Just one more coolie.'

'How do you know so much about all this?'

The smile broadened into laughter.

'In every government office, every Tuan home, what you see? Indian clerk, Chinese cook, Malay amah. They speak English. They hear everything. How keep secrets?' He laughed again and reached for his coffee. 'It will be same when Japanese come. We will learn their language.'

'How much time do you think we have? My orders are to be ready to sail at short notice.'

Poh sat back in his chair and eyed me thoughtfully. 'One, maybe two weeks at most. Some ships already waiting, like yours. More coming.'

'So, we'll be part of the escape route, the insurance policy?'

'Yes. The navy already making plans for evacuation convoy. You must prepare for voyage to Fremantle, with maybe five hundred passengers, including women and children.'

I ran through a mental check list. 'We'll need coal, water, extra food and bedding, timber to construct bunk beds in the tween decks.'

'Let me know, Captain. I will do my best.' Poh reached into a drawer and retrieved a bulky Manila envelope. He slid it across the polished desk top. 'In the meantime, here is a cash advance, banker's drafts for additional funds and further instructions. The management of our ships has been transferred to Sydney. Captain Fairclough already there, making all arrangements.'

Fairclough had been Anglo-Oriental's Hong Kong manager. Stiff and stuffy as he was, I was glad he had escaped the city's fall.

'Once you reach Australia, the navy will hand *Oriental Venture* back to Ministry of War Transport,' Poh continued.

That, at least, was good news. I did not fancy sailing under naval orders a moment longer than necessary. Apart from making the ship even more of a target, I would be glad to get away from men who dreamt up hare brained commando raids from 70-foot launches. I shivered, despite the heat. Irrespective of what happened to the ship, I was still commissioned for the duration of hostilities. Spencer had already dragged me into too many of his schemes. As a naval reserve officer, I had even less chance of avoiding them.

'You have fever, Captain?' asked Poh, noticing the brief spasm.

I grinned. 'Someone walked over my grave.'

'Ah yes. Maybe a spirit. One of your ancestors keeping watch for you.'

'Looks like I'll need all the protection I can get. It's a helluva long way to Fremantle, even if we make it as far as the Sunda Strait. There'll be Japanese aircraft, warships and submarines all looking to add to their tally.'

'Quite correct.' Poh's smile faded and his round face slumped. 'You will be running the … what you say in English?'

'The gauntlet.'

'That is a glove, yes? I have never understood slapping with gloves for punishment.'

'The gloves were armour plated, worn by knights.'

'Ah, so. In China, use bamboo rods.' Poh's face brightened. 'But maybe not so bad. There is a Chinese proverb, the successful man make his own luck. You make own luck, Captain, always I think so.' He held up a hand and rubbed his thumb over the fingertips. 'Many times you tell me tingling fingers warn of danger. For you that is lucky, but my fingers tingle only for gold.' His smile broadened into a soft laugh. 'Sometimes gold is as good as a warning, but it not buy luck.'

I held up my hands and inspected the fingertips. They were not tingling, but that was hardly reassuring. 'Are you sure you want to stay? At least let me take your family.'

His smile hardened. 'That is not possible. The authorities only issue permits to Europeans.'

'Forget the permit. Send them with me, they can hardly deny them entry once we get there.'

Poh was silent for a minute, then shook his head. 'Our home is here. I have much *guanxi* ... you know what that means?'

I nodded. It was the network of connections and relationships that bound Chinese communities together. A man as rich and powerful as Poh could call in many favours.

'Please do not worry about me. I have plenty family in Malaya and the islands. My grandmother was an Iban from Borneo, remember. If we have to run, plenty places to hide.'

Poh had shown me his grandfather's grave near a small riverside township deep in the North Borneo jungle. The body was buried there, but the shrunken skull hung from the rafters of his great-uncle's long house.

'If it is not my fate to survive'—the corners of Poh's mouth turned up into an impish grin—'then you burn spirit-money at my grave, or maybe I come back as hungry ghost to haunt you.'

'Maybe it'll be me haunting you,' I said, returning the grin.

'I think not, you have still many steps to tread. Anyway, impossible you frighten me, you already *gwailou*.'

It was a pleasure to hear us both laugh. The term was an insulting name for a white man; in Cantonese it meant "ghost-man."

'And the *gwaipo*,' I said, using the equivalent for a white woman.

'Miss Markova has all the papers needed for exit. I am arranging ticket on the *Devonshire*.'

Helena had finally agreed that leaving was the only sensible course of action. But if the city was going to fall anyway, would she be any safer in a passenger liner departing on Sunday, than on

Oriental Venture a day or two later. It was a purely selfish thought. I checked my watch. It was Helena's day off from hospital volunteering. There would be time to call at the hotel before returning to the ship.

'Okay, I'll see her at Raffles now and tell her to pack. Unless you have anything more for me.'

Poh held up a hand. 'Miss Markova not at Raffles. She visiting the Military Hospital. I send car for her this morning. She go see your friend, Colonel Spencer.'

'Is he injured?' I had heard nothing from him since leaving Port Swettenham. I felt a twinge of guilt that Helena knew more of his whereabouts than I did.

'Not wounded, only malaria. You go there now?'

I nodded. Poh pushed back his chair and walked around the desk. I rose to meet him.

'It has been a pleasure as always, Captain.' He grabbed my hand and shook it. 'I hope to see you again before you depart.' He patted the envelope. 'You will find all you need to know in there. In the meantime, send me stores' list.'

I slipped the envelope into my attaché case and headed for the stairs. Back in the glare of Malacca Street, I took a moment to gaze at the brass plate fixed to the wall of the narrow, three story, building. It seemed to represent the solidity of the commercial heart of Singapore. Fluctuations in freight rates and commodity prices, of whatever magnitude, never seemed to fluster Poh. As he had told me many times, a rising or a falling market, both presented opportunities. Would that still be the case when the Japanese were masters of the island? One thing I was sure of, if anyone could take advantage of whatever pickings there were, it would be Poh; if he survived.

I walked back to Raffles Place and hailed a taxi. The driver was an aged Chinese with a crooked smile revealing a few remaining stumps of broken, dirty teeth. He wove the car among the carts and pedestrians, and swung into the line of traffic heading south-west down New Bridge Road. Chinatown had taken another beating in the previous day's air raid. Survivors, with bandaged heads and limbs, clustered around an outdoor dispensary. Wisps of smoke rose from the smouldering ruins of tenements and shop houses, and carts hauled away rubble. Impatiently blowing his horn to clear a path, the driver sped on to the junction with Outram Road. The traffic was still thick as we passed the General Hospital and the Tiong Bahru apartment blocks known locally as the "den of beauties". They were home to the mistresses of many of the island's wealthy business-men. As we headed out of the city, past the sewage farm and the cemetery, the traffic thinned. At Alexandra Road, the driver swung left with a squeal of tyres and raced the final mile, before turning into the tree lined drive leading to the white columned entrance to the military hospital.

The stiffly uniformed, sour faced nurse at the reception desk frowned when I asked where I could find Colonel Spencer. Civilian visitors were obviously discouraged, but I persisted, telling her it was military business. She sniffed pointedly, consulted a list pinned to a clip-board and directed me to the male convalescent wards.

The corridors smelled of carbolic and floor polish and the male wards were packed with European casualties of the fighting. Indian and Malay servicemen were confined to segregated wards in other parts of the hospital. A nurse directed me to the officers' ward and I pushed open the swing door. A double row of beds greeted me. Spencer's was easy to spot, Helena was poised at the foot of it with a wheelchair. Mine were not the only eyes drinking in the long, slen-der legs below the hem of her summer dress, or the auburn tresses tumbling from beneath her sun-hat. Spencer was already perched in the chair, in pyjamas and dressing gown. The smile Helena flashed as I approached fuelled an explosion of the love-hungry silkworms in my stomach.

'You're just in time to wheel Arnold into the garden for some fresh air. How's your head? And what are you doing here, anyway? Check-ing up on me?'

I raised my hat to reveal the stitches through which hair was re-sprouting. 'Poh told me I'd find you both here. Let me take that.' I grabbed the handles and wheeled the chair through the French win-dows onto the lawn. Small knots of walking wounded lounged in bath chairs beneath the trees. I found a vacant patch of shade and pulled up a couple of chairs.

'Poh said you've got malaria. Why didn't you send word? I'd have brought grapes and flowers.'

Spencer's unshaven face was pale and beaded with sweat, but his chapped lips cracked into a weary smile. 'Nice to see you too. Yes, it's a recurrence of the malaria I picked up in New Guinea. Damned nuis-ance that it's come back now.' His smile broadened. 'But judging by the way you two are looking at each other, you didn't come here just to visit me.'

'If you must know, I came to try and persuade Helena to leave on the *Devonshire* on Sunday. Looking at the state of you, I should probably give you the same advice. You don't look as if you could fight off a Girl Guide in a pillow fight.'

'What's the matter with you two.' Helena's eyes flashed sparks. 'Arnold's been banging on to the same tune.'

'He's right. The Japanese will be here any day. You need to leave now. It might be your last chance.

'And what about you … both of you?' Her eyes flicked between us.

'*Oriental Venture* will be part of a convoy evacuating the last European civilians,' I said. 'My orders are to head to Fremantle.'

'And when will that be?' asked Helena.

I glanced at Spencer.

'If I was a betting man, which I'm not'—he rasped his fingers against the gingery stubble on his chin—'I'd say by the end of next week at the latest. The air force is on its last legs and what's left of the navy will soon be withdrawn to Batavia. Without command of the sea and the air we can't hang on here. Once the Japs are over the causeway, Percival will have little choice but to send up the white flag, unless he wants to see the whole city reduced to rubble and have the blood of countless civilians on his hands.'

He slumped back in the chair, his feverish eyes burning.

'And what will happen to the army?' I asked.

'It's not going anywhere, other than into prison camps. There'll be quite a haul for Yamashita to brag about. Anyway, there's nowhere near enough shipping.'

'But you're not thinking of staying,' said Helena.

Spencer's smile was tinged with sadness. 'I'm ordered back to Australia. Seeing she's headed there, *Oriental Venture* will do nicely. But it sticks in my craw to run away, like a flea jumping off a dying dog.'

I turned to Helena. 'So, will you go on the *Devonshire?*'

'If Arnold's going with you, I might as well come too. Australia sounds like as good a destination as any.'

My heart leapt and I ventured a celebratory smile. 'You know, I really did think a while ago there …'

'Don't spoil things, or I'll throw myself at the feet of that Colonel Beckwith. I'm sure he knows what to do with a lady in distress.'

Spencer raised a knowing eyebrow. 'Lover's tiff, eh? Well, you know what Shakespeare says … or was it Burns?'

'It was Lysander, in *A Midnight Summer's Dream*,' said Helena. 'The course of true love … and all that romantic clap trap.'

'Honestly, Helena.' Spencer raised a dramatically weary hand to his brow. 'How can someone as lovely as you dismiss romance like that. You have no idea of the effect you have on mortal men.'

'It must be the delirium talking. So I'll forgive you.' Her eyes flashed at me, the smile in them further melting my innards. 'And don't you start talking like a theatrical ham, or I'll be tempted to find an asp and stick it to my less than heaving bosom.'

My eyes strayed towards the snug fitting bodice of her dress. I grinned guiltily, and reached into my pocket for the tin of Senior Service.

'For God's sake, don't let matron catch you smoking,' said Spencer, reaching for one. 'Anyway, I thought you'd given up.'

'I have, I'm just keeping you company.'

I waited for Helena to extract a pink Sobranie from her bag, rasped the flint on my lighter and lit the three of us. A cloud of blue smoke drifted up through the branches of the shade tree. Several heads turned to watch with envy in their eyes.

The moment was too good to last. A starched, white apparition stalked from the direction of the ward, waving her arms furiously. When satisfied we were sufficiently chastened, she instructed me to wheel Spencer back inside and leave him to the tender mercies of people who, she maintained, would take better care of his health.

After seeing him safely back into bed, I promised I would break him out as soon as it could be arranged.

As we walked back down the carbolic-reeking corridors to the exit, Helena reached for my arm. 'Don't take any notice of what I said back there. If you want to sigh like a furnace and sing a woeful ballad to my eyebrows, I won't object.'

I checked my watch. It was approaching noon. There was plenty of afternoon left and the Japanese were not expected until Monday. I hailed a waiting taxi, held the door for Helena and jumped in beside her.

'Raffles Hotel.'

The pressure of her hand on my thigh was firming reassurance that we would both be sighing like furnaces before much longer.

CHAPTER THIRTY-TWO

Forenoon, Monday 9 February 1942

As Poh predicted, the Japanese crossed the Johore Strait on Sunday evening, the brunt of the attack falling upon the Australian's defending the north-west coast. The following morning McGrath and I were in the radio shack listening to news of the fighting broadcast by the Malaya Broadcasting Corporation. It did not sound good. The Australians were fighting hard, the bulldog had roared, but it had not thrown the Japanese back into the Strait.

I jerked my thumb in the direction of my cabin. 'That smells like coffee, fancy a cup?'

Da Silva had left a pot and two cups on the desk. McGrath filled them both and spooned sugar into his.

'Did you send Poh a list of our requirements for the voyage to Fremantle?' I asked.

McGrath nodded. 'Think we'll get any of it?'

'I'm sure it's chaos ashore, and all the ships will be keen to stock up before they leave. But if anyone can find a little extra for us, Poh can.'

'Fresh water's going to be our biggest challenge. Even if the port's water mains survive the bombing, we've only so much tankage.'

'It'll be rationed for cooking and drinking only. We'll all be washing in salt water or not at all. That'll please the women.'

With the possibility of 500 hundred passengers, most of them likely to be female, all of our facilities were going to be stretched to the limit. Cramp and the crew were installing additional bunks in the passenger cabins. Mothers with children would have first call on them, and the officers would double up to make additional space. The single women and the men would have to sleep in the tween decks, in rough tiers of bunks, or on the deck if necessary. It would be hot, humid and uncomfortable down below, even with the ventilator goosenecks trimmed to catch whatever breeze there was.

Toilet and washing facilities were a bigger problem. Those in the passenger and officers' accommodation would mostly be reserved for the women. For the men, a row of wooden framed canvas screened heads and showers was being erected on the main deck aft. The engineers were completing the plumbing—sheet steel troughs and lengths of pipe with spaced holes drilled in them, all connected to the salt water fire main.

We were doing all we could to make the evacuees as comfortable as possible, but it was precious little. The voyage to Fremantle would take ten days. Ten long, hot, cramped days and sleepless nights with minimal food and water. And that was assuming the Japanese left us alone.

I drained the last of my coffee and poured us both a fresh cup. 'Have you thought any more about what you want to do when we get to Fremantle?'

I had suggested to McGrath that he sign off and take some leave to visit his parents. They were on the other side of the continent, but it was only a week by passenger steamer and a few hours on the train. He would have no difficulty finding another berth in Sydney as soon as his leave ended.

'I'll send them a telegram when we arrive. Hopefully, I'll be able to telephone as well. I'll decide then, if that's okay with you, Skipper?'

'It's fine with me. But don't feel you have to stay. I'll be sorry to see you go, but it's nearly five years since you were last home.'

McGrath said nothing, but I knew what he was thinking. His father was ailing, he wanted to see him and his mother again, but he was caught between the pull of home and loyalty to the ship. I waited for him to speak.

'It's not that I don't want to go home, Skipper,' he said. 'It's just that … well, you offered me a job, threw me a lifeline really, when no one else would, and bumped me up to mate when I least expected it. It doesn't feel right to walk out now, especially when there's a war on. There's thousands of others can't go home because they're fighting the Nazis or the Japanese, so why should I be special.'

I reached over to the drinks' rack for the bottle of Tanduay and slopped a shot into our cups. This was going to be a difficult conversation and I needed to lubricate my tongue.

'Listen to me, James McGrath. I'm not going to insult your intelligence by singing your praises. You've been a good officer and a damn good chief mate. I'll miss you when you go, the ship will miss you, but we'll manage. That's the life of a seafarer. Nothing lasts forever, the voyage always comes to an end. And when it does, most seamen, myself included, hang about the docks for a few weeks until the money runs out and then sign on again. Why, because there's nothing to hold us to the shore. No home, no family, no little corner of the world we can call our own. We're rootless, drifting, floating our way through life, and what we leave behind will be as permanent as a ship's wake. There are others though, the lucky ones, who look forward to the end of a voyage, not as an opportunity for an extended bender, but to tend their roots. Maybe there's a mother or a sister, a wife, children, a country cottage waiting for them. And they can forget, if only for a while, the crank ships, the lousy food and the sleepless nights in screeching gales. You've got a family, James. You've got parents and brothers, there's a farmer's daughter maybe, and a corner of Australia waiting to welcome you home. Don't miss that opportunity, it might not come again for a long time, if at all.'

It was a pretty speech, and I almost convinced myself, but it was rubbish. The smirk on McGrath's face told me he hadn't bought it either.

'Fair dinkum, Skipper, you'll have me crying into my rum next. I went to sea to get away from becoming a cow cocky, and there's no girl pining for me back home. Yeah, my dad's getting long in the tooth, but he's got my mother and my brothers. There'll be grandchildren one day. I'll telephone him from Freo, I promise.' He reached for the rum laced coffee and drained it. 'Thanks for the coffee. Now I'd better get back on deck and see how the crowd's getting on.'

I let him go. There was plenty to do to get the ship ready for the evacuation and, with all that the Japanese were likely to throw at us before we got there, Fremantle was a long way off.

I finished the last of the coffee and climbed up to the bridge. It was a beautiful morning at the anchorage. The sun sparkled on the water, fluffy piles of cumulus drifted across the deep, blue sky and a gentle breeze lowered the air temperature. It was not such a beautiful morning over Singapore. Clouds of smoke to the north marked where the fighting was at its most intense; the distant boom of gunfire was distinct on the breeze. There were also pale columns of smoke rising from the embers of fires started by the bombing. There would be more air raids today. The RAF still had a handful of fighters left and the occasional bomber was brought down, but the raids were pressed home relentlessly.

The blast of a steam whistle caught my attention, and a launch pulled alongside the gangway. A crewman clambered up. A few moments later he arrived on the bridge and handed me an envelope.

'Message from Mr Poh. I wait in boat for reply.'

I ripped open the envelope. Inside was a short note from Poh with orders to place the ship alongside the coal berth the following morning. After that we were to move to the main wharf to embark passengers. We were scheduled to depart for Fremantle before sunset on Wednesday evening.

There were also two letters from Colonel Spencer. The first told me we would be carrying a party of wounded and their nurses from the Military Hospital. They were also due to embark on Wednesday. Even better, he and Helena would accompany them.

The second letter contained the unwelcome news that Captain Lakshman had been officially posted missing. His company of Mahrattas had been cut off in the fighting at Slim River in January. Some of the survivors had fought their way through the jungle to regain the British lines. Captain Lakshman had not been among them. I was about to call Lakshman, when my eye caught the name Mohan Singh amongst the remainder of Spencer's news. He had been captured in northern Malaya, not long after his appearance at Raffles on the night I dined with Helena. According to Spencer, he had approached his captors with an offer to form a new army from among Indian prisoners of war, to help the Japanese liberate India. It had been accepted, and Singh was recruiting volunteers from the prison camps to join what he called his Free India Army.

I could imagine the outrage among the colonials when the news became public. The Indians would be condemned as traitors to the Empire and there would be calls for them to be shot or hanged, or worse. But were they traitors, or were they loyal Indians fed up with two hundred years of domination by foreigners? If the Japanese could help them achieve that sooner rather than later, then why not fight for a free India.

There was no point trying to tart up a pig with lipstick. I called Lakshman to my day cabin and handed him Spencer's letter. The confused emotions were written on his face. His brother had known Mohan Singh. If he, too, had been captured, would he answer Singh's call to fight against the British? Or had he fallen at Slim River, to rot away in an unmarked jungle grave?

'I'm sorry, Vijay. You could write to your parents, but it's probably too late to mail anything from here, and by the time we reach Fremantle they'll have received a telegram.'

Lakshman's face drooped. 'They will be heartbroken.'

'It's more than likely he was taken prisoner.' It wasn't, but there was no point facing the worst until it happened. 'Word will come through eventually. The military situation's chaos at the moment.'

'If he is dead, that will be terrible.' Lakshman's voice trembled. 'My mother will never get over it. But at least he will have died with honour. But if he joins Mohan Singh … and the Japanese …'

'If it hastens independence?'

'Of course India will be independent. It is only a matter of time, Captain.' His shoulders stiffened. 'My father has supported Congress his whole life. But not helping Britain with men and money is one thing, fighting for the Japanese is quite another. That is … dishonourable. The Mahrattas are one of the oldest regiments in the Indian Army. They fought with Colonel Wellesley, your Duke of Wellington, at Seringapatam. They fought the Ottomans at Kut and Sharqat. They …' His voice tailed off. 'Sorry, Captain. You are not needing a history lesson.'

I had never heard of any of those places. They had not ranked a mention in the Industrial School's list of the Empire's achievements, which included Afghanistan, Balaclava, Isandlwana, Ypres and the Somme. To which glorious line of defeats, Dunkirk and Singapore could now be added. If Captain Lakshman was dead, he had died in vain. If he survived to join Mohan Singh, I, for one, would not blame him.

'You know what Henry Ford said about history, Third?'

'That it is bunk?'

'More or less. He probably meant that what's more important is what's happening to us now. Which is, that we've got to get this ship to Fremantle. Maybe there'll be better news when we get there.'

'Yes, sir.'

'And if it's any consolation, we go alongside tomorrow and depart the day after. Colonel Spencer and Miss Markova are coming with us. We'll also be taking as many wounded soldiers, nurses and evacuees as the authorities can cram into us. It's going to get very crowded, so you'll have to double up with the second mate, hot bunking if necessary.

Lakshman's head wobbled and his smile returned. 'I will be sending for a charpoy. No offence to Mr Lamont, of course.'

'I'm sure there'll be none taken. Now, write to your parents anyway. I'm sure they're worried about both of you. When you're finished give it to the launch skipper. Maybe one of the evacuation ships is headed to India and Poh will find a way to post it.'

He had barely left, before Cramp appeared in the doorway bearing an enamel basin and a pair of surgical scissors.

'What can I do for you … nurse?'

He returned my grin. 'Time to have those hitches removed from yer loaf.' He inspected the cut and whistled softly. 'You've healed well, but whoever put this lot in won't win no prizes for needlework.'

'He probably didn't train at the same teaching establishment as you.'

'Wandsworth jail? Nothing like sewing mail bags in the clink, to learn how to stitch twelve to the inch. Now hold still in case I scalp you.'

CHAPTER THIRTY-THREE

Wednesday 11 February 1942

I n the darkness of the small hours, Singapore was a vision from hell.

The previous evening's air raid had left fires raging among the godowns lining the docks and the Singapore River. Flames licked the underbellies of the low cumulus, painting them blood red. Sparks whirled about in the rush of air sucked in by the inferno. Artillery shells exploded indiscriminately around the city like ghastly fireworks. Towards dawn, the desperately battling fire fighters brought the blazes under control, but daylight seemed only to lift the curtain on the final act of a Greek tragedy. Not that I had ever read one. An old shipmate and writer, Bill McFee, had tried to interest me with tales of Medea and Orestes as we sailed around the eastern Mediterranean. Perhaps I should have paid more attention, especially as, on the bridge of *Oriental Venture* alongside in Keppel Harbour, I was now dangerously part of the action.

In the early morning light, the wharf was a picture of devastation. Piles of rubble marked where godowns had been shattered by the bombing. Most of the few still standing were damaged, some severely. Corrugated roofs balanced at precarious angles on what was left of their supports. Daylight shone through jagged rents in the remaining walls. Japanese shells continued to howl in, the irregular crump of their explosions scattering across the island. The air was full of smuts and reeking smoke from the fires still smouldering around the docks and the river. Thick black columns rose to the north, where the naval base and its oil tanks were ablaze. The Australians, bearing the brunt of the fighting, were still resisting strongly. But once they gained a foothold, the Japanese pressed on and were already probing south towards the outer suburbs. The last of the RAF's Hurricanes had been brushed aside by repeated Japanese attacks, and the city was defenceless. The lookouts anxiously scanned the sky for the arrival of the next air raid. Whatever hopes there had been for the survival of fortress Singapore were dying before our eyes.

We had come alongside the previous day, first under the coal loader to top up the bunkers and then to the Main Wharf to join a rag-tag flotilla of steamers and coasters that would form the final evacuation convoy. True to his word, Poh had arranged for several truckloads of food to be delivered. It was mostly canned or preserved, perhaps the chandlers were holding back fresh meat and vegetables in the hope of selling them to the Japanese. The quantities were also far from adequate to feed the expected numbers. It would be short rations, only made palatable by the sauce of hunger, until we reached Fremantle.

Now we waited, with our holds open, ready to load whatever the authorities deemed necessary to save. Soldiers from the Pioneer Corps hung around in knots amongst the piles of rubble. The Chinese dockers had fled once the Japanese landed and the Pioneers had been sent to replace them. There were other soldiers too, deserters possibly, slinking around the remains of the godowns. McGrath posted extra gangway watchmen. One of them was keeping an eye on a hose snaking its way aboard from a fresh water hydrant on the quayside. Miraculously, considering the bombing, parts of the port's water main still functioned. McGrath was filling every available space, including ballast and deep tanks. Dosed with chlorine and boiled, the water would taste foul but at least it would keep people alive.

I reached into my pocket for the tin of Senior Service. In the face of the impending onslaught, the marginal reduction in risk to my health did not seem worth the price of denying myself the pleasure of tobacco. I repeated the half-serious vow to quit if I reached Fremantle alive, lit up and took a deeply unsatisfying drag. If we reached Fremantle? We still had to escape from Singapore. Despite all of our efforts, the simple truth was there was nothing we could do to protect against sustained bombing or strafing. Having gained air superiority, the Japanese were raiding day and night, sometimes multiple times a day. Each of the ships alongside added its meagre gunnery to the anti-aircraft barrage. Several of them had already been hit, their crews battling to extinguish fires and carry out makeshift repairs. None had been sunk, but it was only a matter of time. When would it be our turn?

A series of explosions to the north of the city was an equally unsatisfying reminder that Helena was still at the Military Hospital. Poh had sent word to expect her during the afternoon, together with the party of nurses and wounded servicemen. I said a quiet prayer to Saint Woolos to keep the bombs and shells away from the hospital long enough for them to safely leave.

By mid-morning, the eerie calm had given gave way to frantic, confused activity that suggested government control was on the verge of collapse. Groups of leaderless soldiers edged their way among the piles of rubble, looking for anything worth looting or for access to an unwary ship. Convoys of trucks arrived, squeezing into every vacant space, their backs crammed with packing cases, tea chests, furniture and military hardware. Civilian cars threaded their way among the trucks and the rubble, blowing their horns to clear a passage while searching for the ship to which their occupants had been allocated.

In the absence of definite orders, I ordered the gangway watchmen to let no one aboard without a permit.

At noon, some semblance of order was restored with the arrival of an army major and a company of soldiers. The looters melted away as the major and his officers set to work to sort out the jumble of vehicles and civilians on the quayside. It was very hot and humid with the sun beating down on the exposed concrete. Those with the foresight to bring water, soon found their bottles emptied. Those without suffered. Tempers were short, and frayed further when the major turned away lorries containing bulky personal items. Pianos, mahogany furniture, intricately inlaid cabinets, ornately carved beds and other long prized possessions were abandoned on the quayside, with the major turning a deaf ear to appeals, tears and screamed threats.

As the awful truth sank in, that they were fleeing Singapore in little more than the clothes they stood up in, some of the women wailed in despair. There were children too, whose crying reached up to my Olympian perch on the bridge wing. I grabbed the cap from my day cabin and bounded down the stairs. I found McGrath supervising work on the main deck and beckoned him to follow me.

Down on the quayside, the hubbub of women and children was drowned by the throb of engines and the grinding of gears as trucks carrying military equipment were waved forward, while those turned away backed and filled to retreat past the growing line of vehicles.

'Is there anything we can do to help?'

The major's red face streamed with sweat, beads of which dripped from the whiskers of his bushy moustache.

'And you are?' Despite his frazzled appearance, the military bark conveyed authority.

'Captain Rowden, *Oriental Venture*.' I jerked a thumb toward the ship. 'This is my chief mate, Mr McGrath.'

'Bad business. Bad business,' he grumbled. 'They were told to bring only one suitcase each and most of them are not supposed to be here until later this afternoon.

'The chaos of war, Major.' I hoped my grin was sufficiently disarming. 'Is there anything we can do for these women and their children. At least on board we can provide them with shade and somewhere to sit down.'

'They're not all yours, Captain. They've each got chits assigning them to different ships. My job is to get all the essential items loaded, not play travel agent.'

'If you can lend me some of your men, I'll get my chief steward to sort out the civilians. I'll take any on board who want to go to Australia. The rest we'll try and point in the right direction. If you can clear enough of a road, they can use their cars.'

The major was clearly not used to taking orders from a merchant seaman, even from one wearing the four gold bars of a captain. For a moment, it looked like he was going to tell me to mind my own business.

'Hrrmmph. Very well then, Captain. Good luck. Looks like you'll need it with this lot.'

He tipped his fingers to the peak of his cap. A few moments later, half a dozen squaddies detached themselves and reported to me.

The chief steward took to the task like a frustrated purser whose talents had been wasted in a tramp ship. With the soldiers maintaining order, he worked his way among the throng of civilians that pressed around him as if seeking salvation. Unsurprisingly, many chose the sanctuary of *Oriental Venture*—viewed from the quayside her size, and the naval guns at bow and stern, looked invitingly secure—irrespective of their finally intended destination. As Grim Jim Coffin had often reminded me, when an alligator was about to take a bite out of your backside, any escape route was a good one. Those who still preferred their originally allocated ships were directed along the wharf in what we hoped was the right direction.

Meanwhile, the major took charge of the Pioneer Corps stevedores and, with the crew driving the ship's winches, field guns, Bren Gun Carriers, trucks and other military hardware soon started to disappear into our holds. When they were full, attention turned to the decks until every space was crammed with anything worth saving.

Waiting for the afternoon thunderstorm to arrive, it was fiercely hot on the quayside. Runnels of sweat trickled down my chest and soaked my shirt. Many of the Pioneers were working shirtless, and would have badly sunburnt backs by the end of the day. Looking forward to the shade and the relative cool of my day cabin, I climbed back up the gangway and mounted the stairs to the boat deck.

With the remainder of the crew, McGrath had rigged as many canvas awnings as we possessed. With the addition of some bunting, the ship might have looked is if we were a pleasure steamer about to sail on a Thames River cruise to Southend. Women clustered in whatever shade they could find, sitting on the hatch covers or on the deck. Children played around their mothers, clambering over winches and ventilators and smearing themselves with grease. The men mostly leaned against the side rail, smoking and watching order slowly re-emerge out of the chaos ashore. If ever there was a lesson in the adaptability of the human spirit in the face of adversity, those people displayed it. Faced with the breakdown of everything they had taken for granted, boarding the ship offered a sense of refuge and stability out of all proportion to its capabilities.

For most, if not for all. As I approached the steps to the bridge, a formidable looking woman blocked my path.

'Might I have a word with you, Captain?'

It was an order not a question and I had to check myself from snapping to attention.

'I know you and your crew are doing their best,' she continued, pinning me to the spot with steely determination. 'But these conditions really are not suitable. We have mothers on board with young children.'

'I'm sorry, Mrs...?'

'Childs, Patricia Childs. My husband is Colonel Childs, commanding officer of the Observer Corps.'

I could almost see the colonel's rank patches on the shoulders of her starched, cotton print dress.

'How can I help you Mrs Childs?' I glanced around, hoping to spot McGrath and summon him for support.

'There is no food suitable for children,' she barked, as if addressing the most junior subaltern in her husband's command. 'The sleeping arrangements are far too cramped and there are ... *cock-roaches*. The laundry facilities are inadequate and the *ablutions...*' She raised a hand to her forehead, as if the mere thought of them had brought on a migraine. 'We'll never be able to manage in such intolerable conditions all the way to Fremantle.'

I could have added that fresh water would be rationed for drinking and cooking only, that we had sufficient food to guarantee only one half-decent meal per day and that it was more than likely we would never reach Fremantle. I smiled at the thought of Mrs Childs confronting the unfortunate commander of the Japanese ship that would rescue her, after it had sunk us.

'And it's no laughing matter, Captain. Really!'

'I'm sorry Mrs Childs—'

The piercing wail of the air raid siren cut off the rest of my apology. The crack of gunfire as the anti-aircraft batteries opened up sent everyone, including Mrs Childs, scurrying for the illusory safety of the accommodation. I darted up the stairs to the bridge in time to see Bullen pull on a tin hat and thrust his arm skywards.

'There! Looks like upwards of thirty of the bastards.' With an ear shattering yell, he called out the bearing and elevation to the gun crews.

Flying straight and level, apparently undeterred by the increasing barrage of gun fire, the bombers flew steadily towards the docks. The noise grew deafening, as the roar of aero engines was joined by the near continuous thunder of the guns and the crack of exploding shells. Bursts of grey smoke thickly cluttered the sky amongst the bomber formation. They looked harmless, until a bomber peeled away and screamed towards the ground trailing flames.

'OPEN FIRE!' Bullen bellowed.

As our guns added their contribution to the barrage, those on all the other ships along the Main Wharf also joined in. Another Japanese plane broke formation and limped northwards trailing a plume of smoke. The rest bored on, filling the sky above the docks like a flock of vultures.

Clusters of deceptively small, black dots detached from the bellies of the bombers.

I watched, mesmerised, as they plummeted earthwards, slowly at first then faster and faster. I gripped the handrail, fighting the urge to duck, as the screeching rose to a crescendo.

Deafening explosions rocked the ship. Gouts of earth and broken masonry sprouted skywards. I gasped for air, realising I had been holding my breath.

'They're aiming for the dockyard.' Bullen's leathery face was twisted into a savage grin. Was it relief?

The rolling thunder of explosions continued for what seemed an eternity, then died away as the last bomber dropped its load and turned to the west. The guns fell silent. Less than a mile away, a great pall of dust and black smoke hung over the ruins of Keppel Dockyard. I could feel the heat from the fires on my face.

'Not our turn, this time.' Bullen slipped the strap from under his chin and removed his helmet. 'Pity the poor bastards who were underneath that lot.'

'They'll be back.' I reached into my pocket for a cigarette. My fingers were trembling. Most of the bombs had fallen on the dockyard and West Wharf, but those less well aimed had scattered wider. Several had fallen dangerously close. Fragments of masonry and smoking metal littered the deck. I took a deep, calming drag and shook my head, amazed I was without a scratch.

'Let's 'ope we've put some sea miles behind us by then, sir,' said Bullen.

I nodded and checked my watch. We were supposed to sail before sunset, in order to find our way through the minefield before dark. It was already approaching 4pm. Our complement of civilian evacuees was aboard, but we still had to embark the nurses and their patients, Helena and Spencer among them.

As soon as the all clear sounded, I steeled myself for resumption of hostilities with Mrs Childs. I climbed down to the boat deck to await her arrival, but it was McGrath who found me first. The good news was that the ship had escaped scot free. The bad news was that the bombing had finally cut off the water supply.

'Get me an exact tonnage,' I said, making some mental calculations. 'And let Angus know that his evaporator's going to have to work overtime.' The steam raised in the boilers was fed by fresh water distilled by the engine room evaporator. It had some excess capacity, but nowhere near enough to satisfy the demands of hundreds of extra people. Every little bit would help eke out what was in our tanks, but it would be strict rationing until we reached Fremantle.

There was still no sign of Mrs Childs by the time I finished my cigarette. Perhaps the imminent threat of being blasted into bits had persuaded her that conditions aboard were better than the alternative. I was about to go in search of her, when an army truck threaded its way among the rubble and the abandoned vehicles on the quayside. There was a big red cross painted on its side. My spirits rose when it pulled up alongside the gangway and Helena climbed down from the passenger side. Apart from the driver however, Colonel Spencer was the only other occupant. His face was drawn with fatigue and his faded uniform hung loosely on his malaria wasted frame.

He jerked a thumb towards the rear of the truck. 'Medical supplies. Can you get them aboard?'

I beckoned one of the seamen and told him to fetch the boatswain. 'And the wounded?' I asked.

'Tomorrow. The roads from the hospital are blocked by rubble. We had the devil of a time finding a way here.'

Leaving the boatswain to see to the unloading of the truck, I led them up to my office. Helena was dressed in a nurse's uniform. The white apron was bloodstained, there were dark sweat patches under the armpits of her pale blue tunic and hair straggled from beneath the brim of her cap. She flopped onto the couch and rummaged through her shoulder bag.

'Blast, I've run out of cigarettes.' She reached eagerly for the offered tin of Senior Service. 'Do you think that darling man Da Silva can rustle up some coffee. Preferably strong, I'm shattered.'

The darling man had already anticipated her request. He bustled in with a large pot balanced on a tray. His sole eye shone with pleasure as he poured Helena a cup. The smile she returned would have lit up a room in any circumstances.

'The convoy sails this evening,' I said. 'My orders are to proceed with it. The accommodation's crammed with women and children. The men are in the tween decks. The army's stuffed our holds with whatever's worth saving. I've no orders to wait.'

'There are several hundred wounded … and a party of nurses.' Spencer's face turned grave. 'You know what'll happen if you leave them to the Japanese.'

I nodded. It was widely rumoured that, when they captured a hospital in the grounds of Hong Kong's Saint Stephen's College, the Japanese had bayoneted the wounded in their beds and gang raped the nurses. Still, I hesitated. I had the lives of my crew and several hundred anxious passengers to consider. The convoy was promised a cruiser for protection, all of the ships were armed and there was safety in numbers. Sailing alone in the convoy's wake, we would be easy pickings.

'It's a helluva choice, I know,' said Spencer. 'I don't envy you. But remember what flag you're flying. What would the navy do?'

'Court martial me for refusing to obey orders?'

'Did they court martial Nelson for breaking the line at Cape Saint Vincent, or for turning a blind eye at Copenhagen?'

It was a laughable comparison, except that I had experienced first-hand the madcap courage of Commander Barker and his men. They had taken the fight to the Japanese in a flotilla of small craft, and evacuated thousands of men to safety under their very noses.

I glanced down at my hands. They were trembling and my fingertips were tingling. I rubbed them together. When I looked up, Helena was watching me.

'You can't leave those women behind,' she said. 'Whether we leave tonight or tomorrow, what are our chances of actually making Fremantle?'

'Slim, in either case,' Spencer replied, his brows furrowed with misgiving. 'The Japanese have complete control of the air, and intelligence reports a naval fleet headed towards Sumatra to cover an invasion.'

'Then I vote we wait,' said Helena, shrugging her shoulders. 'I couldn't live with myself if I thought we'd abandoned dozens of nurses to be raped and mutilated.' She stubbed the butt of her cigarette into the ashtray. 'I'm bushed. Is there anywhere I can lie down and shut my eyes for a bit?'

I pointed towards my sleeping quarters. 'In there. I'll use my day cabin.'

She mumbled her thanks, dragged herself wearily off the couch and disappeared, pulling the door behind her.

I reached across to the drinks' rack and pulled out the rum and two glasses.

'Looks like we wait.'

CHAPTER THIRTY-FOUR

Thursday 12 February 1942

D awn was late, and the sun had to fight its way through the
thick layer of smoke blanketing the island.

A second air raid the previous evening, had again targeted
the docks and the godowns around the Singapore River. Numerous
fires were started and hardly a godown remained standing. Several
ships had been hit, and a party of late arriving civilians had been
caught in the open. The survivors had been helped or carried aboard
the waiting ships. Some were stunned into silence with shock,
others wailed and screamed with grief for loved ones whose remains
were scattered amongst the rubble. We remained unscathed, but
how much longer before our luck finally ran out?

Despite the bombing, the cook managed to turn out sufficient
quantities of curry and fried rice to feed dinner to the evacuees.
Amongst the vegetables swimming in the pungent sauce, were
chunks of what looked like bully beef. I had eaten worse, but the
evacuees included a number Singapore's great and good. Bully beef
curry would hardly be a staple of their kitchens. Perhaps it was relief at still being alive or just plain hunger, in any case there were no
complaints and, despite Mrs Child's misgivings, the children went to
bed with satisfied tummies. Most of the mothers had brought sufficient extra food for their own children to be able to share with those
with less foresight. So the evacuees settled down for an uneasy first
night in their unfamiliar surroundings.

It took until midnight before most of the fires were brought under
control. I watched from the bridge, alternating between pacing the
deck and dozing in the pilot chair. Finally, I retired to the couch in my
day cabin, until McGrath woke me at the start of the morning watch.

The bombing also delayed the convoy's sailing. Worried about
finding the entrance to the mine field at night, the captains waited

until first light. The ships slipped their moorings one by one and steamed slowly seawards down the North Channel. Many of the evacuees gathered on deck to wave them goodbye. Some, recognising friends on the departing ships, shouted greetings and promises to meet in the Savoy or the Ritz, or wherever their favourite peacetime watering hole had been.

Full daylight revealed we were not the only ship waiting to leave. A few still remained alongside what remained of the docks, or were anchored in the roads. Most were coastal steamers that had, like ourselves, been requisitioned by the navy.

The smell of coffee wafting up from Da Silva's pantry reminded me that breakfast was overdue.

He appeared in my sea cabin bearing a tray on which sat portions of bully beef, tinned cheese and several hard biscuits. There was also an object concealed under a cloth. I whipped it off to reveal a large pot from which the unmistakable aroma of dark roast, Java coffee emerged. I was probably the only person aboard enjoying such a luxury. I smiled, wondering what Mrs Childs would make of it.

A gentle tap on the door was followed by a manicured hand whisking the privacy curtain aside. Helena stepped into the cabin.

'I thought I could smell coffee. Have you a spare cup?'

I offered her mine and pulled another out of the cabinet.

'Did you sleep well?' I asked.

'Like a log, except during all that banging and crashing about before midnight. Very inconsiderate, some people.'

'I'll pass on your concerns to General Tojo.'

Helena reached for the coffee and swallowed a large mouthful. She was still dressed in her sweat stained uniform but had left off the cap and her blood-spattered apron. Her auburn hair tumbled onto her shoulders. The dark circles under her eyes had resisted her efforts with the makeup brush. She smiled.

'I must look an absolute fright, and ... I smell. I hope you don't mind.'

I caught the whiff of body odour behind the liberally applied perfume. 'We all smell. We're short of fresh water. It's seawater for washing, until we reach Fremantle.'

Helena raised a manicured eyebrow.

'Salt water soap,' I continued. 'Works on clothes too. You can rinse off in the rain.'

'Sounds dreadfully primeval.'

'Have you eaten?'

'Yes. Da Silva brought me up a boiled egg and toast with some ... tea.' She wrinkled her nose. 'I knew you'd have coffee.'

I slid the pot towards her. 'Help yourself.' I drained my cup and pushed my chair back. 'And make yourself at home. I need to find McGrath and Colonel Spencer to check we're ready to leave as soon as the wounded arrive.'

I left her sipping my coffee and nibbling a wedge of tinned cheese.

I found Spencer on the main deck, leaning against the rail beside the gangway, smoking and watching the quayside. He still looked tired, his face drawn and pale, but his uniform was pressed and his back straight. He gestured towards a ragged squad of Australian soldiers in distinctive slouch hats, skulking among the ruins of the godowns. Most were armed. Many carried bottles of liquor from which they took frequent swigs.

'Discipline's breaking down,' he said. 'The provosts should be rounding those men up and sending them back to their units. Where the hell's their officer?'

The loud rumble of exploding artillery shells was an unwelcome reminder that the Japanese were pushing ever closer.

'You know the worst thing?' asked Spencer.

I shook my head.

'There's over eighty thousand men trapped on the island, including the Australian Eighth Division. Good soldiers most of them. Soldiers we could badly use elsewhere.'

'Are you saying defeat's inevitable?'

Spencer's tired face crumpled. He nodded. 'Two or three days at the most.'

'Then we leave today. Is there any way you can find out when the party from the military hospital is going to get here?'

We were interrupted by the arrival of McGrath and Lakshman.

'Sorry to interrupt, Skipper,' said McGrath. 'We're almost ready to leave. The hatch covers are on and battened down. The crew are securing the derricks. The chief engineer needs an hour's notice to build full steam pressure. I'm just sending Lakshman ashore to read the draft.'

I nodded, as Lakshman climb down the gangway.

He arrived at the bottom just as a dishevelled squad of Australian soldiers burst from behind the nearest pile of rubble and confronted him. Their burly, hawk-faced sergeant forced the muzzle of his rifle into Lakshman's chest.

'Step aside ... wog.' The sergeant's sharp, nasal tones were overlaid with drink.

Lakshman's refusal was emphatic, and brave.

The sergeant spun the rifle in his hands and clubbed the butt into the side of Lakshman's head. He crumpled like a rag doll. Kicking the unconscious body aside, the sergeant charged up the gangway with his men pressing behind. They checked as they spilt onto the deck and saw me. The sergeant raised his rifle. 'Step aside mate, were not staying in this shit hole to become patsies for the fucking Japs.'

A shoulder barged me aside. McGrath jumped at the sergeant, grabbed the rifle barrel and twisted it out of his hands. Recovering from his momentary surprise, he leapt at McGrath howling with rage and lashing out with kicks and punches. Regaining my balance, I was about to intervene when Spencer grabbed my arm.

'Leave it with the colonials, Bill.'

Momentarily, it seemed good advice. I had seen McGrath fight before, but never with such fury. After fending off the sergeant's first assault, he grabbed hold of him and dragged him onto the foredeck, where there was more room to swing punches. They were evenly matched. McGrath was lean but muscular; his body hardened and his boxing skills honed by his four years as an apprentice in square riggers. The sergeant was an inch or two shorter, but what he gave away in height he made up for in weight and power. Each punch he threw was marked by a savage grunt and a string of obscenities.

After trading furious volleys of blows—blood trickled from the sergeant's beak like nose and McGrath had a swollen and cut lip—there was a pause as they eyed each other warily. Their chests heaved as they fought for breath.

The Australian soldiers were clustered together with their backs to the bulwark and their rifles at the alert. They watched the fight with sullen, menacing eyes. Opposite them, leaving a clear space for the combatants, some of the crew had gathered. Among them, Lamont, Bullen and the boatswain carried Bergmann machine pistols. Spencer's advice suddenly seemed less sensible. Things could very easily turn uglier.

I glanced around. Cramp was at the top of the gangway carrying the unconscious Lakshman. Men and women watched from the boat deck above. A mother covered the eyes of her young daughter and snatched her away from the rail. If there was going to be shooting...

A savage cheer went up from the Australians. Using his superior weight, the sergeant wrestled McGrath to the deck. Before he could fight free, he took several pile driving punches to the face. His head lolled and the whites of his eyes rolled back. The sergeant reached down to his boot and a fighting knife flashed in his hand. Before I had time to react, the knife slashed towards McGrath's throat.

BANG!

A bullet whistled past my ear. Blood spatters erupted from the sergeant's chest. Bolts clicked ominously as rifles snapped to the horizontal. Blood pooled on the deck.

With the Colt smoking in his fist, Spencer stepped over the dead sergeant.

'That man was a deserter.' His voice was surprisingly steady, considering the number of Lee Enfield 303s pointed directly at his chest. He stepped forward until his shirt front was almost pressed against the muzzle of the nearest one. 'Is there anyone else wants to desert?' He glared at the soldiers, looking each of them in the eye. Some looked away, others returned the challenge. No one moved.

'I'll take that as no. Who's the next senior man?'

A wiry soldier pushed to the front. His sweating face was pale despite the heat. 'Corporal Biggs ... sir.'

'Where are your stripes, Biggs?'

The fresh outlines on his sleeves showed where the chevrons had been unpicked.

'Er ... I took them off ... sir. In case—'

'Well get them sewn on again,' snapped Spencer. 'Now, take charge. Fall these men in and take them down onto the quayside. Find a couple of serviceable trucks and commandeer them. We're going to rescue some nurses and their patients.'

Biggs called the soldiers to attention and ordered them into single file to follow him down the gangway. There was some grumbling but, amazingly, they obeyed the command.

I whistled my appreciation. 'That was brave.'

'Bollocks! They just need to be led.' Spencer nudged the dead sergeant's body with the toe of his boot. 'He was a nasty piece of work. You could tell from the corporal's face they were scared of him. But they'll forget all about him once their minds are better occupied.' He slipped the Colt back into its holster. 'I meant what I said. I'm going to the military hospital to look for those nurses. The Japs might already be close. Killing a few's just what those men need to pull them together.' He turned towards the gangway, paused and called over his shoulder. 'Whatever happens, just make sure you get away before sunset. If we're not back, it means ...' He left the rest unsaid, raised a hand and stalked off down the gangway. Two trucks waited on the quayside with their engines revving. He climbed aboard the leading one and they ground their way among the piles of rubble towards the dock gate.

I beckoned Lamont. 'Tell the boatswain to arm the gangway watchmen with those Bergmanns. And no one's to go ashore without my permission. We don't want a repeat of that.'

'Aye, sir. That we don't.'

As Lamont headed for the gangway, there was a groan followed by a muttered obscenity. I reached out a hand and helped my battered chief mate back to his feet. His shirt front was spattered with blood and he gingerly felt his nose.

'I think it's broken. Jeez, his fists felt like mule kicks.' He glanced at the body slumped on the deck. 'Last thing I remember, he was using me as a punching bag. What happened?'

'He pulled a knife,' I replied. 'Colonel Spencer shot him before he butchered you.'

'Christ! And Lakshman?'

'Cramp carried him aboard. Probably took him to the sick bay. You need a visit there too. Apart from that broken nose, you're going to have two black eyes. I hope you weren't thinking of going courting tonight.'

McGrath's chuckle was strangled by a groan. 'Don't make me laugh it hurts.'

He followed me inside to the tiny sickbay with its single bunk and medicine cabinet. Lakshman was already sitting on the bunk nursing an egg sized lump on the side of his head. His mouth twisted into a grin when he saw McGrath's bruised and bleeding face.

'I am assuming the other fellow is looking much worse, sir,' he said.

'He's dead,' I replied. 'Colonel Spencer shot him … for desertion. He's taken command of the rest of them to go and find the nurses and the wounded we're supposed to embark. I suggest you patch each other up. It's going to be a long day, and an even longer night. Oh, and do something about that body on the foredeck. Dump it ashore, as far away from the ship as possible.'

I left them to it and returned to the bridge. If anything, the smoke had thickened. Combining with the thunderclouds building up over the island, it had turned the sky into a threatening, leaden dome. Ash and smuts of soot drifted down onto the deck. It looked apocalyptic, but there was a possible silver lining. The Japanese bombers might stay away.

I light a cigarette and strode onto the bridge wing. Soldiers—more deserters probably—were still slinking about among the rubble, rifling through the abandoned possessions looking for items of value. If morale was so low and discipline so slack that men were able to just walk away from the fighting, how much longer before resistance ceased altogether? The rumble and crack of duelling artillery suddenly seemed louder than before, and close-sounding gunshots were more frequent. Would Colonel Spencer return with the wounded and the nurses, or would Japanese troops come bursting through the remains of the dock gates? Spencer had told me to sail before sunset, regardless. But did we even have that long? Footsteps on the ladder signalled an arrival from the boat deck. Mrs Child's voice was almost a relief.

'Captain, is it true we're still waiting for the party from the military hospital?'

'Yes, Mrs Childs. But I've instructions to—'

'Quite right. I can't bear to think of those girls falling into the hands of … savages.' She spat the last word, as if trying to clear something foul from her mouth. 'Mind you, those Australian soldiers were hardly much better. I saw what that sergeant did to your officers. Thank goodness the colonel had the good sense to shoot him. Good riddance, I say.'

'The colonel's Australian too.' I managed to suppress a grin as her fiercely narrowed eyes widened in surprise. 'And he's taken command of them and gone to the hospital to find the nurses.'

'Well bully for him,' said Mrs Childs, regaining her composure. 'Now, we need to find a doctor. Some of the children have diarrhoea. I'm afraid of dehydration. In this heat …' She fanned herself with her hand for emphasis. 'And if it spreads…'

'I'll check the passenger list—'

'No point, I've already asked. There's no doctor on board. You must send into the city to find one.'

I was not used to taking orders on the bridge of my own ship. Before I had time to argue, Helena appeared from my day cabin. She had donned her apron and nurse's cap.

'Can I help at all, Mrs …?'

'Childs. My husband is Colonel Childs, commander of the … well never mind that now. Can you look after the children … nurse?'

'Markova. Elena Markova. Or Helen, if you prefer.'

'Markova? That doesn't sound very English?' Mrs Childs' eyebrows knitted with suspicion.

'That's because ...' Helena shook her head. 'Look it doesn't matter where I'm from. I've been with the VAD at the military hospital. Why don't you go below, Mrs Childs, and gather the children. I'll collect some things and follow.'

'Do you know what you're doing?' I asked, as soon as Mrs Childs was out of earshot.

'I might not have trained at Saint Thomas's Hospital,' said Helena, her eyes flashing. 'But the Red Cross taught me enough to make up a salt and sugar solution. I'll bet there's bismosol syrup in your medicine locker. And that your crew have a few bottles of Po Chai Pills stashed away. They work wonders for hangovers, as well as upset tummies.'

I grinned at her. I had used them on many occasions, both as prevention and cure.

'I'll also need the cook to boil some water.'

'Okay, but just for the children mind.'

She nodded, straightened her cap and tucked in the few loose strands of hair. 'Lead on, Captain. We can't keep the patients waiting.'

The sick children, together with their anxious mothers, were gathered in the saloon. For a hastily trained volunteer nursing aid, Helena swept to work with all the aplomb of a latter-day Florence Nightingale. Even Mrs Childs was all smiles.

'You missed your vocation,' I whispered to Helena, before heading towards the door.

'Bugger off,' she mouthed back.

Stepping out onto the deck, I smelled the approaching rain. It was almost noon, but the afternoon thunderstorm was early. The rumble of thunder merged with the guns as the first drops fell, quickly followed by a shattering downpour that instantly flooded the scuppers.

I retreated to my cabin, to find Da Silva laying out a plate of curry and rice. It looked suspiciously like the re-heated remains of the previous evening's dinner. I reached for the rum bottle, poured a large measure and drank it neat. To save water, I told myself.

By the time I had forced myself to eat enough to stop my stomach complaining, the downpour had ceased. I took my coffee up to the bridge and smoked a cigarette. Lightning flashes lit up the clouds and the pall of smoke hanging over the island.

How much longer could I safely wait for Colonel Spencer? The buoys marking the entrance to the minefield were unlit. It was approaching the new moon and, with the smoke from the fires, the night would be pitch black. Would I be able to find the channel in the darkness? I rubbed my hands together to ease the tingling in my fingertips.

The smell of pungent tobacco warned me that Lamont was approaching with his pipe.

'Any sign o' yon colonel and his nurses, Skipper?'

'No.' I pointed towards the eerie desolation ashore. Tendrils of smoke curled about the skeletal remains of the godowns like wraiths. 'See for yourself. It's as quiet as the grave. Even the deserters seem to have disappeared.'

Lamont shook his head and checked his watch. 'Sunset's in three hours. It's going to be black as the Earl o' Hell's waistcoat—'

'I don't need you to tell me that, Second. Why don't you ...' I choked off the rest. It wasn't his fault. 'Get on the blower to the chief. Tell him we're still waiting, but to raise steam pressure and be ready to move as soon as I ring standby.'

'Aye, Skipper.' Lamont scurried away trailing his own cloud of smoke. Twenty minutes later the watch changed and McGrath was pacing the wheelhouse, looking as anxious as I felt. There was a growing knot in my stomach, to which none of the possible choices offered any hope of relief. I turned them over and over in my mind, hoping that some new solution might emerge, like the final pieces of a jigsaw suddenly falling into place. If I left too soon, I might be condemning several hundred men and women to death, or worse. If I left too late, I might blunder into the minefield.

There were lookouts and gunners on the Monkey Island. McGrath and the helmsman were standing by in the wheelhouse. I was surrounded by people, but totally alone with the pressure of the decision. I could also feel the despondency hanging over the ship, as realisation dawned on the evacuees that the longer we waited the less chance there was for everyone.

Pacing the deck and chain-smoking Senior Service, my heartbeat measured the seconds as they ticked by. The sun was invisible behind the clouds and smoke, and with an hour to sunset the light was already fading. I shivered, despite the heat and humidity. The ebbing daylight felt more like midwinter England than tropical Singapore. I started as gunfire flared, worryingly close, the rolling thunder of the explosions interspersed by the chatter of machine guns.

'Ring stand by below and call the crew to stations.'

The jangle of the telegraph was followed by shrill blasts on McGrath's whistle.

I gripped the rail. Once the lines were cast off there would be no turning back. Lamont watched me expectantly from the forecastle. I reached for the speaking trumpet.

The low, insistent growl of engines pierced the crack of artillery. A truck nosed into sight around a large pile of rubble, followed by another and another. Moments later, a line of them snaked alongside the ship. Spencer jumped down from the leading one and waved.

'Thanks for waiting,' he yelled.

I waved back in acknowledgement. Did he have any idea how close he had come to being left behind?

CHAPTER THIRTY-FIVE

Evening, Thursday 12 February, 1942

As we slipped our moorings, the last rays of the setting sun finally pierced the underside of the smoke and clouds, painting them blood red. I ordered the engine to half ahead and conned the ship down the North Channel, past the bombed remains of the graving docks and the coastal steamer wharf at Tanjong Pagar.

With the addition of the wounded and the nurses from the military hospital, we had over 1,000 souls embarked. The non-walking wounded had all been helped below into the tween decks, where the nurses made them as comfortable as they could. Many had only a thin blanket to cushion the steel deck. Those that could walk lined the rail as the devastation of the Singapore waterfront slipped astern. Among them were the Australian soldiers. I had been inclined to leave them behind. Desertion was for the army to worry about, but attacking two of my officers made it personal. Spencer persuaded me to let them aboard.

'It's pointless leaving them to become POWs,' he said. 'We're going to need every available man to carry the fight back to the Japs. And the ringleader's dead. I'll take responsibility for them, I don't expect any further trouble.'

The wail of the air raid siren carried loud across the water, followed by the growing throb of aero engines. The cloud cover had broken, and it was only a matter of time before the bombers came. They were unlikely to bother us, but I pitied those left in the shattered city. Ignoring the bomb blasts, I lined the ship up with the signal station on Mount Faber right stern, and focussed on the spot where I expected to sight the buoy marking the entrance to the minefield.

'It ought to be fine on the starboard bow,' said Lamont, peering through binoculars.

The buoy was one and a half miles from Tanjong Pagar point, less than 20 minutes at half speed. If we missed it, we would blunder right into the minefield, the only warning the explosion that ripped the bows off. In the gathering darkness, the minutes ticked round on my wrist watch.

'I have it.' Lamont's call was a relief. 'A point to starboard, Skipper. Current's pushing us to the north. Suggest you come round half a point.'

I raised my binoculars to confirm the sighting, called the course change to the helmsman and rang the telegraph to full ahead.

Once abeam of the buoy, the swept channel ran southerly past the Outer Shoal towards Saint Johns. The island rose to almost 200 feet and was flanked by the jagged rock of Peak Island. On a moonlit night they were easy to spot. Without a moon, we just had to keep our eyes peeled and trust to dead reckoning to keep us in the channel. I had made the passage many times and knew the vagaries of the tidal streams. Lamont was a newcomer, but he learnt fast.

By 7.30pm we had safely rounded Saint Johns and were steaming south-east through the Main Strait towards Round Island and the entrance to the Phillip Channel. Behind us, an orange glow on the horizon marked the funeral pyre that was Singapore. Apart from that, the evening was disquietingly peaceful. A cooling breeze bathed the decks. The bow rose and fell, shouldering aside the gentle swell with a murmuring rush. The minefield ended half way down the strait, and at the change of watch I sent Lamont below to get some rest. In front of us were two and a half hours of open water steaming, before entering the narrows of the Durian Strait.

Eight bells brought McGrath to the bridge, as well as Lakshman.

'Have you eaten, Skipper?' McGrath asked.

I had turned Da Silva away earlier when he arrived on the bridge with a tray. Entering the minefield, food had been the last thing on my mind. Now, I realised my stomach was grumbling.

'No, what was for dinner?'

'Some sort of stew. Bully beef again. I expect there's some left. I can get Da Silva to rustle it up.'

'Please. But first, how did you go with the head count?'

'Including the crew, one thousand and fifty-seven. Do you want a breakdown?'

'Not at the moment. Just get the chief steward to make several copies. So, if anything does happen, hopefully there'll be a surviving record of who was on the ship.'

'Aye, Skipper.' In the pale glow of the binnacle lamp, his battered face, with both eyes blackened, looked deathly and the normally irrepressible grin was absent.'

'Are you okay, James?'

'Yes, sir. It's just … we've mothers and young children aboard. Wounded soldiers, some with limbs missing, some blinded, some still raging with fever. And those nurses. They look all in. They've given everything to take care of those men, and now there are sick children to look after.' He shook his head. 'I can't bear to think what will happen to them all if … well, you know.'

I reached for his shoulder and squeezed it firmly. 'We can only do our best, James. Captain Nettles, who lead that madcap commando raid, had a saying for this situation, "You can only piss with the cock you've got".'

The glimmer of a smile returned to his face. 'Wise man. My dad used to say the same, not to my mother of course.'

I grinned. 'Let's get safely through the night and we'll see what tomorrow brings. Now, beat the drums for Da Silva. And ask Colonel Spencer and Helena if they can spare me a moment.'

Da Silva arrived first. He dumped the tray on the chart table with a disgruntled bang and left without pouring the coffee.

'What's eating him?' asked Spencer, passing Da Silva in the chartroom doorway.

'Annoyed that I didn't eat my dinner the first time it was offered.' I shovelled a spoonful of stew into my mouth. It was barely lukewarm. 'Would have probably tasted better too.' I grabbed the bowl, and Spencer followed me back into the wheelhouse. 'See anything?' I called to Lakshman on the bridge wing.

'Nothing, sir. But the sky's clearing,' he called back.

'That doesn't augur well for the morning,' I said to Spencer, in between mouthfuls. 'We'll be clear of the Durian Strait by dawn, back in open water. It'll give us more room to manoeuvre, but there won't be anywhere to hide if the bombers coming looking.'

'If?'

'When. We'll go to action stations at dawn. Bullen and the DEMS gunners are pretty handy, they've had plenty of practice. But there's only so much they can do. What about your Australians?' I spooned the last of the stew into my mouth.

'*My* Australians?'

'You said you were responsible for them. They're the only other trained men aboard. Look, it's mostly about morale. It might not

279

make any difference, but the more lead we throw into the sky and the more noise we make the better. We've got Oerlikons and Lewis guns, the soldiers have their rifles. It might not deter the planes, but it'll make the civilians feel good that we're having a go. Britannia rules the waves, Britons never will be slaves and all that guff.'

I could sense Spencer smiling beside me. 'I think I saw a few Bren guns in one of the trucks you've got on deck. And there's always your toy Bergmanns. If the pilots get cocky and come too close, they might be in for a surprise.' He chuckled in the darkness. 'You know something, Bill Rowden, you're wasted as a tramp ship captain.'

'So you've told me. But I'm not sure that's a compliment, coming from you.'

'Bit below the belt, old boy. And just when I thought we were getting to be friends.'

It was my turn to chuckle. 'Perhaps, but it's another nice mess you've gotten me into.'

'Aw Ollie, I couldn't help it.'

'Are you two reduced to Laurel and Hardy routines now?' There was a waft of familiar perfume as Helena's lithe shape materialised out of the darkness.

'Well, you have to laugh, don't you,' said Spencer. 'It wouldn't be funny, if it wasn't so serious.'

'Very droll. You should be on the stage … there's one leaving in five minutes. Boom boom!'

'I was just leaving anyway. I've got to see a man about some weapons.'

'Put that on the tray for me, please Arnold.' I handed him the empty bowl and he disappeared into the chartroom.

'Sorry I took so long,' said Helena, running her fingers through her hair. 'I was in the bath. Da Silva filled it with hot seawater. Nearly as good as the real thing. I even managed to wash my smalls and uniform. They're a bit scratchy with salt, but at least I feel clean again.' Her hand reached for mine. 'Now, what did you want to talk to me about?'

'I wanted to—'

'I can see Round Island, Captain.' Lakshman's call was loud in the darkness. 'Two points to starboard.'

I released Helena's hand and raised my night glasses. The hump of the island was a dark smudge silhouetted against the horizon.

'Thank you, Third. Come round to sou'-sou'-west-a-half west when it's abeam. How far from there to Melville Reef?'

280

'Sixteen miles, sir.'

'Keep your eyes peeled and let me know when we've five miles to go.'

'Aye, aye, sir.'

It was all part of the performance. Check and re-check. Lakshman knew the courses to steer and the distances to each alter course as well as I did. If not, he would feel the rough edge of my tongue, and I was not leaving the bridge. His indistinct form scampered up to the Monkey Island to take a bearing. I turned back to Helena.

'Sorry. I wanted to ask how the wounded were faring, and the children.'

'You ought to be asking Matron Bulstrode.'

'I'd rather hear from you.'

'Most of the children are feeling better. Drinking regularly and keeping solids down. Some of the mothers just needed reassurance. Mrs Childs' got them well in hand.'

'And the men?'

'Matron's worried about a number of them. Fever, wounds turning infected, that sort of thing. We've precious little in the way of drugs to treat them. It's mostly cold compresses and sympathy. There's some won't make it to Fremantle, but the girls are doing their best.'

'Is there anything more we can do? The ship I mean.'

'Well, those spaces in the holds, the tween decks I think you call them. There hardly the best place to look after wounded men. Not much light or fresh air. And it's hard climbing up and down those ladders with buckets and bed pans.'

'It's the safest place if we're attacked by aircraft. But I'll get some of the hatch boards lifted off in the morning. And the crew can help with the fetching and carrying.' I mentally kicked myself for not having thought of it sooner. 'Anything else?'

'How are you with amputations? In case of gangrene.'

'The medical guide's probably got some instructions. Failing that, a sharp saw, a pint of rum and wad of leather to bite on.'

Helena snorted softly. 'I suggest you read up on those instructions.' She reached for my hand and pulled me farther out into the concealing darkness of the bridge wing. 'Is there anything else you want to talk about?'

I knew what she was asking, and I knew for a certainty that my usual attempts at deflection would be as unwelcome as they were unnecessary. I wanted to say them, just three little words to tell her exactly how I felt about her. They swirled around in my head, clamouring to be let out, but an iron band seemed to contract around my chest and my throat went dry. I opened my mouth, but no words would come.

Helena tightened her grip on my hand. 'Don't come over all strong and silent. If you want to say something, this might be your only chance.'

Still the words would not come, and I turned my head away ashamed by my own hesitancy.

'Don't turn away, Bill. It should be easier in the darkness. Just say it. Whatever is.'

I swallowed and took a deep breath, suddenly feeling a crushing weight lift from my shoulders. 'I love you, Helena, but I know it's impossible.'

She reached up and ruffled my hair. 'I know that, I just wanted to hear you say it. And it wasn't a trick question, I love you too. Probably from the time you buried me at sea off Formosa and certainly when you asked me to dance in the moonlight. I'd have let you take me right there on the deck, if that silly engineer hadn't blown soot all over it.'

'Lakshman would have seen us from the bridge.'

She pulled me close. 'Well, he can't see us now ... can he?'

'Probably not, but...'

Her deep throated laugh floated off into the peaceful darkness. 'I know, in case the crew find out you're human.' She nudged me in the ribs. 'I didn't come up here to seduce you. Don't get me wrong. I'm happy to ... if that's what you want, but I know you've got a lot on your plate. And, well it's not exactly the best time for me either.' She lifted her head and kissed me, pressing her open mouth against mine. When she let me go, her voice was husky. 'There, that's a taste of what you can look forward to once we're safely past Java Head.'

And what if we did not make Java Head? Helena raised a fingertip to my lips to stop me voicing the thought.

'Let's not think about that. In fact, let's not think about anything. I love you, Bill Rowden, but I know it's impossible too. I have to return to Hollywood. You've got a ship to command. There's a war on. And yes, I'll say it, we might all be dead tomorrow or the day after. If we get though them, then we'll have until Fremantle to work out what it all means. If we don't, then at least we have this.'

She kissed me again and I felt the tears wet on her cheek.

'I'm truly sorry for what I said at Raffles, I'd give anything to take it back,' I said.

'I really didn't think you were the jealous type.' Her fingers jabbed into my ribs. 'What time is it?'

I checked the luminous hands of my wristwatch. I had missed hearing Lakshman alter course at Round Island, and we were already well on our way to Melville Reef.

'Half nine.'

'Goodness!' Helena disentangled herself. 'I'm due on shift. Matron will have a fit if she knew what I was doing.' She pecked a final kiss onto my cheek. 'Keep us safe, Bill. Keep us all safe.'

Her footsteps tripped down the ladder to the boat deck, leaving her words ringing in my ears. Leaving me with tingling fingertips and not a clue as to what they meant. Desire? Foreboding? Fear?

A shooting star caught my eye, blazing a trail across the southern sky. As Lakshman had earlier predicted, the clouds had cleared. The sky was ablaze with luminous stars. Overhead, Orion aimed his perpetual bow while his dog, Sirius, dashed at his heels. Just above the northern horizon hung Polaris, the North Star. The Southern Cross had yet to rise but I looked forward to following its pointer all the way to Fremantle. It was easy to forget there was a war on under such a sky.

Soft footsteps padded across the deck towards me.

'Excuse me, Captain, sir. I believe I can see Mantaras Island, three points to port.'

I checked my watch again and raised the night glasses. In the starlight, the low island stood out clearly, exactly where it should be.

'Start a running fix, Third.'

The tide had been ebbing since leaving Singapore, and I had allowed for its northerly set. It would turn as we approached the two-mile wide entrance to the Durian Strait, between Melville and Middleburg Reefs, and the flood would carry us south at an additional two knots. The Strait ran between reefs and sandbanks to the west and a chain of islands to the east. Half way along, a sharp turn to clear False Durian Island was followed by another at North Brother. With a clear starlit sky, and the landmarks visible, there should be no difficulty finding our way.

Once clear of the Durian, there were 70 miles of open water before the approach to the Berhala Strait. With luck, I could doze for a couple of hours in the pilot chair. If the sky remained clear, McGrath's dawn star sights would confirm our position. Things were going better than I had any reason to expect but, on second thoughts, I put in a request to Saint Woolos for thick cloud cover in the morning.

Having taken several bearings, Lakshman announced he had a reliable fix. I checked the chart and took the opportunity to smoke a cigarette. Da Silva had forgiven me and the pot of coffee restored some energy. Just after 10pm, I brought the ship onto her new course and we steamed between the reefs. The unlit light towers and the water breaking around their bases were reassuring guides. So far, so good.

CHAPTER THIRTY-SIX

Friday 13 February 1942

Despite my prayers, Saint Woolos decided it would a beautiful tropical morning. The sea sparkled blue, a gentle breeze cooled the decks and the rising sun gilded the undersides of the fair-weather cumulus.

I had been expecting them since dawn, but hopes had risen as each minute ticked slowly by and the sky remained empty. It was approaching 10am when those hopes were finally dashed by the lookout's frantic yell and pointing arm. I blew a blast on the ship's whistle to warn everyone to take cover. All those enjoying the fresh air on deck dived for the illusory safety of the accommodation or scrambled down the ladders into the tween decks. The layers of steel shielding them might seem solid enough protection, but they were no match for a well-aimed bomb.

I counted six of them, dive bombers flying in loose formation, approaching from the north-east. For a minute or two it seemed they would ignore us. They held their course, as if intending to fly on towards Sumatra, faintly visible to the south, in search of a more worthwhile target. With a lazy waggle of its wings, one peeled away from the formation into a shallow dive.

'Coming down for look-see.' Bullen's sweating, leathery face was shielded beneath the rim of a steel helmet. 'Hold your fire lads.' His ear-splitting bellow was acknowledged by an arm wave from the gun crews. The Australian soldiers had set up makeshift gun positions using the deck cargo for cover. Bren gun muzzles bristled from them like porcupine quills, providing a welcome addition to our armament.

The snarl of the dive bomber's engine rose to a painful roar. It levelled out at mast head height and streaked overhead so close that the helmeted, goggled faces of the pilot and gunner peered down through the windshield. The crimson ball on the dark green fuselage looked like a threatening bloodshot eye. I resisted the temptation to raise two fingers.

'It's a Navy Val,' said Bullen, shading his eyes with a hand. 'Flown off a carrier somewhere.' He raised his fist and shook it. 'Bugger off and pick on someone your own size.'

'I don't think he heard you,' I said.

A mile away, the Val banked into a graceful turn and roared back towards us.

'OPEN FIRE,' yelled Bullen.

All of the gun muzzles had been silently tracking the Val. Hearing Bullen's yell, the gunners pressed their triggers. The sharp cracks of the 4-inch and 12-pounder were followed by the rapid whoof-whoof-whoof of the Oerlikons and the hammering of the Lewis and Bren guns.

The two larger shells burst harmlessly behind the Val, but it flew straight into the well-aimed torrent of Oerlikon and machine gun fire. The pilot was cocky, or raw. It cost him his life. Caught in a hail of lead, the plane disintegrated. Shards of metal and perspex burst away from the wings and fuselage. It staggered, dipped one wing and cartwheeled into the sea less than 200 yards away. When the waterspout subsided, there was nothing left.

A ragged cheer was instantly drowned by the scream of a power-diving Val.

All the gun barrels swivelled to near vertical, throwing a protective umbrella of fire over the ship.

The Val swooped down, rapidly growing in size until it filled the sky like a giant hawk. Its fixed undercarriage grasped for the ship like talons. The scream rose to a crescendo and the under-slung bomb dropped away from the fuselage. Almost scraping the mast, the Val pulled out of the dive and roared away unharmed. The whistling bomb fell straight toward the ship. I tensed myself for impact. At the last instant it plunged into the sea no more than 50 yards ahead. A fountain erupted and the ship shuddered and groaned with the shock wave. Cordite reeking seawater cascaded onto the deck, soaking me. Another screaming aero-engine announced the next attack.

'Hard a starboard,' I yelled.

The spokes blurred in the helmsman's hands. Every change of heading would make the pilot's job harder. But it would also make aiming the guns more difficult.

The Val hurtled down with its nose aimed directly at the bridge.

For an instant I though the pilot intended to crash onto the ship. The bomb separated. The Val screamed overhead, its wheels scraping the surface of the sea as it pulled up. The wind of the bomb's passing plucked at my hair forcing me to duck. A massive explosion rocked the ship and a column of fire erupted from the aft end of the boat deck.

'HARD A PORT.'

The ship had barely started to swing back the other way when the next bomber pounced. By now the gunners knew what to expect. As the Val pulled out of its dive, a hail of fire punched jagged holes in its belly. The bomb flew over the stern and exploded in the sea. The Val levelled off at wavetop height. Trailing smoke and with its engine coughing and spluttering, it flew away to the north-east.

'That's another one won't see the cherry blossom again,' shouted Bullen, a ferocious grin spread across his face.

'MIDSHIPS THE WHEEL.'

I glanced astern. Flames and smoke poured from a large, jagged hole in the boat deck engulfing the starboard lifeboats. Fire hoses snaked across the deck as the crew fought the blaze.

Having watched two of their number fall foul of it, the remaining Vals showed more respect for our gunnery. They attacked from higher up, coordinating their dives to split our fire. Over the throbbing howl of aero-engines and the crack and hammering of the guns, I yelled helm orders.

'HARD A PORT ... HARD A STARBOARD.'

The helmsman span the wheel. The ship jinked one way, then the other. On the boat deck, an Australian soldier aimed his rifle at the bombers. Shirtless and bareheaded he fired again and again, screaming obscenities with every shot.

Even divided, the fire was intense and the first Val pulled out of the dive too early. Its bomb plunged into the sea too far away to cause more than a shudder. The other pilot showed more determination. With bullets striking shards of metal from his wings, he held his dive until the last moment. As soon as the bomb dropped, I knew it was a killer. Falling straight and true it plummeted onto the tonnage hatch, just forward of the poop. The explosion blew shattered hatch boards, shackles and other lumps of metal into the air. The ship staggered under the blow. If the blast had damaged the propeller shaft in the hold below, we were a sitting duck. I held my breath, waiting for the frantic whistle of the engine room voice pipe or the silence when the engine stopped. Neither happened, and I mouthed another prayer to Saint Woolos as the ship forged on.

The guns fell silent as the Vals regrouped and circled overhead.

From aft, came the cries and screams of wounded and dying men. The 4-inch gun was ripped from its mount. The gun crew lay scattered across the top of the deckhouse. Nurses scrambled up the ladder to their aid. Smoke billowed from the gaping hole where the hatch cover had been. The stores and spare gear in the hold below had been set ablaze by the blast. McGrath was directing the fire fighters. There was nothing I could do to help.

Preoccupied with the dive bombers, I had paid little attention to our progress. Berhala Island was just abaft the port beam.

'Port ten. Come round to due east.'

I waited for the helmsman to repeat the order, and called to Lakshman.

'Plot me a course, Third, to take us safely into the Java Sea.'

'The Japanese fleet's probably out there somewhere, sir,' said Bullen, his eyes fixed on the circling Vals.

'What do you think they're doing up there?'

'Radioing our course and speed.'

'Exactly. If the fleet is out there, they're probably laughing at us. So, we'll let them think that's where we're heading, and when they bugger off we'll turn back towards the Banka Strait.'

It was a long shot, but the only one I had. Whichever way I went, they were bound to find us eventually. But if we could give them the slip until sunset. If we could get through the Banka Strait safely in the dark. If. If.

Overhead, the Vals circled like vultures. One peeled away and dived. Bullen yelled and the guns opened up again.

The Val jinked from side to side, dropped a wing and banked away, as if testing our defences like a boxer feinting a punch. It zoomed around us probing for an opening. Finally, it turned, lined itself up on the stern and roared in, the machine guns on its nose sparkling. The crew fighting the fire dropped their hoses and dived for cover. There was no shelter for those atop the deckhouse. A nurse flung herself over a wounded man. Another, kneeling beside her patient, was ripped aside like a rag doll. Bullets hosed along the decks towards the bridge. Bullen and I dropped flat. Jagged edged holes blossomed in the bulwark where we had been standing. The plane screamed overhead its rear gun blazing. Bullets rattled against the newly armoured bridge front.

I scrambled back to my feet in time to watch it re-join the others.

In loose formation they flew away to the north-east. The drone of their engines quickly faded but the ringing in my ears, deafened by the explosions and the gunfire, persisted. The whistle of the engine room voice pipe sounded far away and my voice faint.

'Angus, everything all right down there.'

'Aye Bill, but there's no need to shout. I can hear you quite clearly. There's no damage to the shaft or the bearings. The bomb exploded in the tonnage hatch. It's a shambles there, but the mate's got it under control. Any other damage up top?'

I dropped my voice several decibels. 'Two of the lifeboats destroyed. I'm still waiting for a report on the rest.'

McGrath appeared as I replaced the voice pipe cover. His khaki shorts and shirt were covered in soot and grime, and his eyes were red rimmed.

'Fires are out, Skipper. The bomb went through the boat deck before exploding in the engineers' washroom below. It and the junior engineer's cabin took the worst of it. They're both burnt out, but apart from some scorched paint the adjacent cabins are liveable. Lucky the bomb didn't sever the fire main.' He nodded towards the boat deck. 'Took out two of the boats, though.'

'Any casualties?'

'Burns to some of the men fighting the fire. There was no one in the washroom or the cabin.'

'And the other bomb?'

'Hit the 4-inch gun before penetrating the tonnage hatch and exploding. The fire destroyed everything, but that's mostly scrap ropes and wires. The gun's a write off.'

I could tell by his face there was worse to come. 'And the gun crew?'

'Two killed instantly. They must have been in its path. Both mangled beyond recognition. Another had his legs ripped off and bled to death. The others were luckier. Broken bones, concussion, burns from the fire. One of the nurses was killed too. Poor girl, riddled with bullets. She didn't suffer, thank God.'

'I saw what the other one did. Bloody brave to throw herself over a man like that. How is she?'

'Lucky to be alive. Not a scratch.' His soot smudged face creased into a grin. 'She made Lamont a happy man. He's thinking of proposing. He's got a broken collar bone and several cracked ribs, but they've strapped him up and put the arm in a sling. He can stand a watch, but he won't be holding a sextant for a while.'

'I'll have a word with him later, in case we need to read the bans. In the meantime, check the rest of the wounded and the passengers are okay. Warn them to stay below. We're not out of the reefs yet.'

With the fires out and the debris cleared away, the day resumed something resembling normality. I recorded the deaths in the log book. As I wrote the name of the dead nurse, I wondered what twist of fate dictated that the bullets that destroyed her had left another woman, lying only inches away, unscathed. And why was it easier to smile at the survival of the one than grieve for the loss of the other. Life was for the living, my father used to say. Perhaps that was easy when you were one of the survivors, but the mothers of the dead nurse and the three DEMS gunners would hardly feel the same. And how many more deaths were worth the price of our survival? So far, the balance sheet was about equal. We had shot down one plane and badly damaged another. That might be four Japanese airmen who would never see home again but, in exchange, we had also lost four souls. If that was the full price, we would be very lucky, but I doubted the grim reaper was satisfied yet.

I held the easterly course for an hour and then turned south towards the Banka Strait. At noon, Lakshman calculated we had 70 miles to run. Sunset was just before 7pm, so we would enter the Strait with the last of the light. If we made it that far.

Lamont appeared at the change of watch with a huge grin spread across his face. His left arm was strapped to his chest. I asked if he was up to standing a watch.

'Och aye, Skipper,' he responded. 'There's nothing wrong wi' my eyesight. And sure, it's only my left arm. I can still wipe my arse wi' my right hand.'

I fixed him with the steeliest glare I could muster.

'What's all this about wanting to get married?'

'Well, yon lassie pressed so hard against me that the shape of her body's imprinted on my …' He paused and tipped a wink at Lakshman listening to the conversation. 'Sure, it'd be the only decent thing to do.'

The laughter was a useful tonic, although there was nothing funny about four deaths. I sent Lakshman below and let Lamont stay. He shrugged off his narrow escape from the reaper, managed to fill and light his pipe with one hand and sent up enough smoke to attract a war band of Apaches.

Noon was followed by what passed for lunch. A hard biscuit, a slice of bully beef and a couple of tinned sardines might not have been anyone's idea of a decent meal, but that the cook had been able to rustle up enough to feed over a thousand was itself a minor miracle. Having just stared death in the face, it was also a miracle that anyone was hungry. I lit a cigarette and sipped coffee, impressed by the resilience and adaptability of the human spirit.

Despite the coffee, and a couple of hours dozing in the pilot chair during the graveyard watch, by mid-afternoon I was having difficulty keeping my eyes open. I lit a Senior Service and briskly paced the short length of the bridge wing to get my blood pumping. The cry I was dreading, banished all desire for sleep.

I grabbed the binoculars and followed the outstretched arm. It was a lone, single-engined float plane flying at about 10,000 feet.

'Reconnaissance I'd say, sir.' Bullen was again at my elbow. He seemed tireless. Perhaps he was old enough to have got past the need for sleep.

'Looking for us, or anything else fleeing Singapore.' He glanced around the horizon. 'He might miss us amongst all that.'

Scattered thunderclouds had built up during the afternoon. They promised rain and the possibility of cover. Frustratingly, none were close enough to conceal us. I glanced up at the funnel. The air above it shimmered with hot gas from the boiler fires, but it was clear.

'Keep your fingers crossed, Bullen.'

'Already crossed, sir. And my toes.'

The plane droned steadily overhead. If it saw us, it showed no sign. It flew straight on towards the west and disappeared.

For the next couple of hours, we had the sea and sky almost to ourselves. Shoals of flying fish launched themselves out of our bow wave and glided away, before dipping beneath the low swell. A pod of dolphins surfed and frolicked in the wake. The braver of the passengers ventured back on deck. They pointed excitedly at the dolphins, some even squealing with delight.

It was too good to last and the crossed fingers finally failed towards the end of the afternoon watch. This time, it was seven twin-engined bombers high in the sky to the north.

'Those are called Nells by the brass,' said Bullen. 'God knows how they think up these names.'

I shouted to Lamont to warn the engine room, reached for the whistle lanyard and blew a long blast. My stomach plummeted to my boots, but my fingertips felt nothing. Was that a good sign, or an indication they had delivered their final caution?

The bombers stayed high as they lined up to attack. Maybe they had been warned of the accuracy of our Oerlikons, and were keeping out of range. Bullen signalled to the 12-pounder to open fire.

Puffs of smoke from its exploding shells appeared in front of the bombers. The gun crew worked like demons to sustain the barrage, but only a lucky hit would bring one down.

I called Lamont out onto the bridge wing.

'You and Bullen watch those bombers. Yell out the moment you see one release its load.'

I gripped the teak handrail to stop my hands shaking and clamped my jaw shut. The bombers flew on in line astern, approaching from the port quarter. The throbbing roar of their engines and the crack, crack of the 12-pounder hammered painfully at my chest. Were they the last sounds I would hear?

'Bombs away,' screamed Lamont.

'Hard a port,' I yelled to the helmsman.

Slow and unhandy as she was, under full rudder the ship swung rapidly. I started to count. How long would the bombs take to fall? Could the ship swing out of their path in that time? A piercing whistle heralded the approach of the first stick. I held my breath. The helmsman's face was white with fear. His hands gripped the spokes like skeletal claws. The whistle rose to a shriek. The sea erupted off the starboard bow, the shock of the blast lurching the ship bodily sideways. The deck heaved and shuddered under my feet, thank God I remembered to bend my knees. Spray drenched the bridge.

'Midships, steady,' I shouted. Twenty-one seconds. Had they been enough or had the pilot's aim been poor?

'BOMBS AWAY.' This time it was Bullen.

'HARD A STARBOARD.'

The spokes blurred in the helmsman's hands. I counted … sixteen … seventeen … eighteen … the whistle was ear splitting.

The sea erupted to port. The blast lifted the ship and shook it until every frame and plate seemed to rattle. I was thrown against the rail and clung to it for support while tons of water cascaded over the bridge wing.

'MIDSHIPS.'

'Christ, that was close. Barely fifty yards away,' shouted Lamont.

I prayed the next plane was higher.

'BOMBS AWAY.'

'HARD A STARBOARD.'

Counting, I glanced astern at the wake. Either side of the dog legs, the disturbed water showed how sickeningly close the bombs had fallen. How long before their aim improved? Twenty ... twenty-one ... twenty-two ... I fought the panic crushing my chest.

The splashes were over 200 yards away. The sea exploded and boiled. The ship shook herself and forged on. Poor aiming again, or had the pilot expected me to turn the other way? It was a simple coin toss.

'MIDSHIPS.'

'BOMBS AWAY.'

'HARD A PORT.'

The fear on Lamont's face told me they would be close. I forgot to count, and grabbed the rail for support. The whistling rose to a terrifying crescendo.

There was a blinding flash. The ship staggered under the weight of a colossal hammer blow. Bullen and Lamont were flung to the deck. With my ears ringing from the blast, I thrust my head over the dodger, expecting to see a massive hole in the foredeck. The air was filled with flying spray and the reek of cordite. I blinked the salt out of my eyes. The ship's rail had been torn away as if by a giant can opener. The canvas cover of number two hatch was ripped to shreds and the hatch boards tossed aside like matchwood.

'MIDSHIPS.'

Had the bomb exploded in the tween deck? It would be carnage among the wounded sheltering there. Mercifully, there was no smoke or fire.

'BOMBS AWAY.' Lamont had regained his feet. 'OH CHRIST! ANOTHER, BOMBS AWAY.'

'HARD A STARBOARD.'

The ship still responded to the helm, and the thump of the engine throbbed reassuringly through the deck plating. *Keep going.* I banged my fist against the rail to urge her on.

After the last stick, the shriek of the bombs whistling down sounded less threatening. I was still counting at 25 seconds when both loads fell well wide. The shock waves rippled through the ship.

'MIDSHIPS THE WHEEL.'

'Missed, you bastards.' Lamont was almost dancing with glee.

It was a lucky escape. Maybe one pilot had flown to close to another, putting both their aims off. There was no time to celebrate. The seventh plane still had a full bomb load.

'Captain. Rain squall.' Lakshman's cry from the wheelhouse momentarily raised my hopes.

Our twists and turns had placed it in our path. The edge was only two cables away. It would take us well over a minute to reach it, but would the pilot know that?

'Quick, tell the engine room to make smoke.'

Lakshman leaped for the engine room voice pipe.

Moments later, thick billows of black smoke erupted from the funnel and streamed aft.

I looked up at the bombers. The last one was lining up for its run. It droned on towards us, ignoring the sporadic blasts of our 12-pounder shells.

'BOMBS AWAY,' Bullen yelled.

'DOUBLE RING FULL ASTERN. HARD A STARBOARD.'

Surprise flared in Lakshman's face, but he grabbed the telegraph, yanked it back and forth twice, and slammed it full astern.

There was an answering ring from below. For a moment nothing happened. Then the engine beat died away, stopped and restarted.

I didn't bother to count. If I was wrong it would hardly matter. The whistling of the bombs grew louder and louder. Water thrashed at the stern as the propeller fought against the ship's momentum. I watched the bombs falling, trying to estimate their trajectory. In the last few hundred feet I was certain. They sailed right over our heads and plunged harmlessly into the sea.

'Stop engine. Midships.'

My legs felt like jelly and my hands shook as I reached into my pocket for a cigarette. The tin had kept them dry and my lighter still worked.

I took a deep drag and felt the nicotine work its calming magic. A decent interval after the beat of the engine died away, I ordered it back to full ahead. The 12-pounder fell silent. The last bomber rejoined the formation and the Nells headed back the way they had come.

'Resume course, Third.' I checked my watch. It was almost 4pm. 'You'll have to stay and relieve the second. McGrath's going to be busy elsewhere dealing with the damage.'

The voice pipe whistle sounded. I had been expecting it.

Angus Fraser's voice was surprisingly heated. 'I'm assuming that double ring was absolutely necessary.'

It was a struggle to hold my temper. 'Spot of trouble up here, Angus. In case you hadn't heard.'

'Aye. But the engine's too old for that caper. And those last bombs missed by a long way.'

'Yes, thanks to you. The sudden rush of smoke made the pilot think we were speeding up, running for the cover of a rain squall. Going astern took just enough way off to make sure he'd miss.'

I slapped the cover back without waiting for a reply. The faces around me were grinning with relief, but it was too early to celebrate. How much damage had the bombs done?

'I'm going below. Blow the whistle if you need me.'

CHAPTER THIRTY-SEVEN

Evening, Friday 13 February 1942

A bomb had not exploded inside number two hold. Instead, the stick had plunged into the sea right beside the ship's hull. The force of the blast had bent and fractured the shell plating and blown the hatch covers off. In between the frames, the plates were buckled and bowed inward. Rivets had sprung and shot across the tween deck like bullets, killing or maiming anyone in their path. Water poured in through gaps and rents each time the ship heeled to port. McGrath, Cramp and the crew were furiously working to shore the buckled plating, and constructing patches of canvas and wood to plug the largest holes. McGrath saw me and handed his hammer to a seaman.

'We were very lucky, Skipper. She must have rolled at just the right moment. The worst of the damage is above the waterline.'

I hardly heard him. I stared at the jagged wounds in the ship's side. Suddenly, the war had become very, very personal. Japanese pilots had deliberately injured my ship. I could almost feel the pain of those ragged tears. I ran my hand over the buckled plating feeling the cuts and scars. She was over 20 years old, and had already survived one war. The Maccams on the River Wear had built her well, but not to withstand a bomb exploding alongside. She had taken severe punishment; her side was rent, but her heart was still beating and the propeller still turned.

'It's all right, Captain.' McGrath gripped my shoulder. 'We're not going to lose her. The bilge pumps are keeping up with the flooding and we'll be able to stop most of it.'

'Make it good, James. Use anything you have to. Get the chief engineer to lend a hand. Whatever you do has got to last until Fremantle.'

It was the height of the cyclone season on the north-west coast of

Australia. It would tragically ironic if we survived the bombing, only to be sunk by a storm. I shook my head, annoyed at my indulgent self-pity. The ship was safe, for the moment. There were more important things to think about.

Fortunately, others had thought of them first. Matron Bulstrode and the nurses were tending the freshly wounded. Those who couldn't walk had been lifted to the other side away from the worst of the water. The rest were being helped up the ladder to the main deck by the Australian soldiers under the watchful eye of Colonel Spencer. I picked my way towards him among the corpses of those cut down by flying rivets.

'Your men are doing a good job,' I said.

'They just needed to be led.' He nodded in the direction of Corporal Biggs, who was rigging a hoist to lift out the stretcher cases. 'Amazing how a man can blossom when he's given a bit of responsibility. They must all have been terrified of that sergeant.'

'He was no loss then.'

A grim smile creased Spencer's drawn face. 'It's against King's Regulations to shoot a man without a court martial. Army command might not take kindly.'

I returned the grin. 'I won't tell them if you don't.' I glanced around at the nurses. 'Have you seen Helena?'

'Last I saw of her, she was in the saloon helping to comfort the mothers and children. The blast blew some holes in the accommodation.'

I darted for the ladder, scrambled up to the main deck and ran aft to the saloon. Helena was seated on a chair surrounded by a circle of children. They listened quietly as she related the story of Br'er Rabbit and the Briar Patch.

Mrs Childs strode to my side. 'She's marvellous with the kids. Had them singing Waltzing Matilda during the bombing. I wish all the nurses were like her. Wet blankets some of them.'

I reached for her elbow and bent my head to her ear. 'I'll let you into a secret, Mrs Childs. She's not really a nurse, just a volunteer aid. Actually, she's a Hollywood actress.'

Realisation dawned on Mrs Child's face. 'That explains it. I thought I recognised her. What was she doing in Singapore?'

'Another time, if you don't mind, Mrs Childs.' What would she think if she knew who or what Helena really was? 'If you'll excuse me, I need to inspect the damage and get back to the bridge.'

The outboard passenger cabins had also suffered. The blast had ripped off the accommodation ladder and hurled it against the bulk-head. Several portholes had shattered and flying metal had punched holes through the thin steel. Some of the women had burst ear-drums. They were already resting with compresses bandaged to their heads. Other passengers had swept up the broken glass. The holes were small enough that wooden wedges would keep out wind and water.

Fraser's report was also reasonably reassuring. The explosion had blown holes in the shell plating of the cofferdam—the smuggler's hold as it was commonly called—between number two hold and the bunkers. Even flooded, it wouldn't threaten the ship's buoyancy, so Fraser left it sealed. The coal bunkers were a different matter. Being almost full of coal, it was impossible to see whether there were holes in the plating. The stokers could shovel the coal away from the ship's side to expose any leaks, but there was the danger of it sliding back and trapping them. Fraser suggested we wait until all the other holes were plugged. If the flooding didn't ease significantly, it would mean we had more to deal with, and we would attend to them then.

By the time I returned to the bridge, Monopin Hill on the northern tip of Banka Island was visible off the port bow. Its jungle clad peaks gleamed bright green in the rays of the setting sun. The western horizon was ablaze with reds and golds and the last of the soft light bathed the ship, smoothing her battered appearance and taking years off her age. We were making good progress and, as the sun sank behind Sumatra, we passed through the six-mile gap between Transit and Frederick Henry Rocks to enter the Banka Strait.

Nestled at the foot of Monopin Hill was the town of Muntok. The Dutch had built a fort to protect the town. The flagstaff was bare and, through the binoculars, the fort looked deserted. Muntok was worth protecting: tin was mined in the hinterland and the town boasted a smelter. There was brisk trade with Batavia and Singapore, and ships were usually anchored in the bay or moored alongside the jetty. The tin mines and smelter would soon be helping the Japanese war effort. Had the Dutch already fled?

With the last of the daylight, Lakshman took cross bearings to confirm our position. There was clear water ahead until the next alteration of course at the Nangka Islands but, with landmarks mostly invisible in the darkness, and strong, unpredictable tidal eddies that could sweep us onto their reefs, our dead reckoning needed to be spot on. I slipped into the chartroom to refresh my memory from the pilot book, scribbled some calculations on the margin of the chart and ordered a slight course correction.

When I returned to the bridge wing, the north-easterly had picked up driving a bank of heavy cloud before it. The rain started, and I ducked back into the wheelhouse to find Da Silva with a tray holding what passed for dinner. I had little appetite, but the meagre helping of fried rice—in the darkness, I didn't bother to check the other ingredients—was enough to fill my belly. Freshly brewed coffee washed it down. A cigarette would have capped the meal but, navigating blind, I dared not leave the bridge for a smoke.

The rain became heavier, falling in torrents that blotted out visibility, until we seemed to be steaming at the base of a perpetual waterfall. The temperature dropped dramatically, and I spared a thought for the lookouts blinded by the rain and shivering in soaked clothing. I knew exactly how they felt. I had kept lookout on the bow of a topsail schooner in the freezing rain of the North Sea. It was a sailor's lot to be wet and cold, but I still felt guilty sheltering in the comfort of the wheelhouse, while they suffered the elements.

After an hour, the rain eased and the faint shadow of the horizon re-materialised. There was nothing in sight; not a star penetrated the overcast and I periodically checked my watch as the minutes ticked slowly towards 11pm and the alteration of course.

With half an hour to go, there were still no reports from the lookouts. I raised my night glasses and slowly swung them around the horizon. Nothing, but the tingling in my fingertips was like having an extra lookout.

'Third, send someone down to call the bosun and get him casting the lead.'

We might not be able to see, but by sounding the water depth we were not totally blind. If we were on course, there should be twelve to thirteen fathoms of water depth. Close to the islands was a sandbank where the depth shoaled to eight fathoms, enough for the ship to safely pass over. A mile of deeper water on the far side, separated it from the outlying reefs. As soon as the soundings showed we were past the shallowest point on the sandbank, we could safely alter course to clear the islands and remain roughly in the centre of the strait. It was not fool proof, but it was the only tool I had.

A hail from the main deck told me the boatswain was beginning his cast. I rang the telegraph to half ahead.

'By the mark, THIRTEEN.'

It was a relief to hear we were still in the deeper part of the strait.

'And a half less, THIRTEEN.'

In the darkness the boatswain would be feeling for the different materials spliced into the line to mark the depths. Some leadsmen even ran them across their lips to make sure.

'By the deep, TWELVE.'

The boatswain's regular chants continued as the water shallowed. We were feeling our way over the sea bed like a blind man tapping across the road with a white cane.

'By the mark, TEN.'

The rain started again and all trace of the horizon vanished. As I had expected—hoped, rather—the seabed shoaled as we crossed the sandbank. Despite the tingling in my fingertips, I felt more comfortable we were on course.

'SHIP, RIGHT AHEAD.'

The yell from the Monkey Island sounded loud enough to raise the dead. My heart leapt into my mouth and I snatched up the night glasses.

A destroyer. Half a mile ahead. Heading north. Towards Mundo Bay perhaps?

'Pipe down,' I hissed. If her watchkeepers hadn't seen us, had the lookout's yell alerted them?

'By the deep, nine.' The boatswain's chant continued, albeit more softly, as if nothing had happened.

Its dark profile blurred by the rain, the destroyer was steaming slowly, probably groping its way through the strait the same way we were. It crossed our bow, leaving us abaft its beam. If the lookouts were straining to see what was ahead of them...? Better not find out.

'Starboard ten. Steer south-south-east. Full ahead.'

The telegraph rang and the beat of the engine increased as the engineer flung open the steam valve.

'And a half less, nine.'

Apart from the boatswain's call there was deathly silence on the bridge. I whispered a prayer to Saint Woolos. He had let me down earlier. Perhaps he would make amends now. As the destroyer swung astern, the rain fell more heavily. She was just a faint shadow in the darkness.

A blinding flash was followed by the bang of a gun.

Star Shell!

I punched my fist against the rail. We had come so close to escaping detection. And now? I waited for the shell bursts that would destroy us.

Instead, the heavens opened and torrential rain blotted out all visibility. Even the star shell was swallowed up by the murk, like the faintly sighted glow of a gas lamp in a London pea souper.

'By the deep, ELEVEN.'

Had the destroyer turned to pursue us? Or had her captain decided that a fleeting glimpse of a dark shape—nothing more than a fishing boat perhaps—disappearing into a rain squall was not worth investigating. It was pushing my luck to appeal to Saint Woolos again. Instead, I prayed the torrential rain would conceal us, long enough for the destroyer's captain to decide that a dry and comfortable night safely anchored in Mundo Bay was better than chasing shadows in the Banka Strait.

I called down to the boatswain to stow the lead and go below. The rain was still bucketing down, but the strait widened and deepened for the next ten miles and the tide was flowing with us.

As my heart rate slowed, I allowed myself a smile. Apart from the obvious fact that, in daylight, we would have been easy meat for the destroyer or any bombers that found us, it was a pity we were transiting the Banka Strait in darkness. The next thirty miles were the most attractive. Banka Island was covered in thick forest, ridges of steep sided hills edged the shore, and the peaceful bays with tree-fringed sandy beaches were most people's idea of what an island paradise should look like. I had sailed past it many times, sometimes dropping anchor in one of its more secluded bays to load shipments of smuggled tin. The Dutch had a monopoly, but the islanders, assisted by Chinese merchants, found ways to circumvent it. Poh always had buyers ready to take whatever quantities we managed to load, at prices that kept everyone, me included, satisfied.

They had been happy days, but they were almost certainly over.

An hour later, there was still no sign of pursuit and, at midnight, Lamont arrived to take over the watch. I had been on my feet for almost twenty-four hours and watched Lakshman disappear below to his bunk with more than a touch of envy. If he was lucky, he might snatch several hours' sleep. The rain had eased half an hour earlier and I was hopeful—desperate might have been too strong a word—that, as the horizon cleared, we would sight some landmarks to check our progress. Out on the bridge wing, with the breeze cool on my face and a mug of Da Silva's strongest coffee in my fist, I felt a little more alert. But with two days of stubble on my chin and a sweat soaked shirt, I was in need of a bath and a shave.

Shortly after the change of watch, McGrath also arrived on the bridge. From his weary voice and slumped shoulders, it was evident he was just about done in. He reported the state of the damage and the repairs. We were still taking on water, but the pumps were keeping on top of it and we were in no immediate danger.

'Good work, James,' I said, when he finished. 'Go and get your head down for a couple of hours. Lamont and I can manage up here.'

'You sure you don't need a spell, Skipper? Change of shirt?'

I managed a chuckle in the darkness. 'That bad, eh? No, I'll be fine. Might be able to doze off in the chair after we round Pangong Point. If the sky clears and we can see where we are.'

He had not long gone below, when the breeze picked up and the thinning cloud revealed a couple of the brighter stars. Lamont joined me out on the bridge wing.

'Looks like the weather's clearing,' I said. 'Can you see anything?'

'About time too. Aye.' He raised a shadowy arm and pointed. 'Four points, port bow. If I'm no' mistaken I can just make out the Parmassang Range. The peak in the middle's over sixteen hundred feet high. Looks like one o' the Paps of Jura.'

'That's a great help. I've never seen them.' I raised the night glasses and searched the eastern horizon.

'A wee bit to the left. Aye, you should be on it now.'

All I could see was darkness. 'You've got better eyes than me.'

'Must've been the carrots Mum forced me to eat. I'll try and get a bearing.'

'Can you manage with only one arm?'

'Nae problem, Skipper. I'll hold the pencil in ma teeth if I have to.'

The cloud cover continued to thin and the clearing sky revealed more of the peaks along the eastern shore. They stood out as darker blobs against the star lit sky. Lamont took cross bearings which I plotted on the chart to save him straining his injured shoulder. We had drifted a little across to the western side, which was fine as it gained us extra sea room to clear the outlying sandbanks on the Banka side.

At 2am, past the sandbanks and abeam of Pangong Point, I ordered the helmsman to steer south-east by east to keep clear of the aptly named Nemesis Bank, which stretched down the middle of the strait. Further east it merged into the shoals fringing the Stanton Channel, the final section before entering the Java Sea. By then there would be enough daylight to pick out the buoys marking the deep water.

It was safe enough to leave Lamont alone for a few minutes while I went below to change my sweat stained shirt.

Helena stirred when I pushed open the door to my cabin.

'Is that you, darling?'

I checked the blackout curtains and flicked on the light switch.

'Sorry to wake you. I need a shave and a change of shirt.'

Helena sat up in the bunk and rubbed her eyes. She had fallen asleep in her uniform.

'What time is it?'

'Half past two. Dawn's in three hours.' I slid open a drawer and pulled out a clean shirt. 'You stay in bed, I'll only be a minute.'

'If you wanted a hot seawater bath, I could join you and wash your back.' She reached for the buttons on her uniform.

It was desperately tempting. 'Sorry Helena, I really can only spare a minute. Lamont's on his own.' I saw the disappointment in her eyes. 'Listen, in twenty-four hours we'll be almost to the Sunda Strait. Tomorrow night, we can fill a hot tub and wallow in it for as long as you like.'

Helena lay back on the bed and pouted her lips. 'Well, you know what they say. The one you knock back is one you never get.'

I raised an eyebrow. 'I only know one person who ever said that.'

'Yes. Your precious friend Grim Jim Coffin. I think he thought it might convince me. And the answer is ... no it didn't. Although why I should tell you that...' She smiled wearily. There were crinkles around the edges of her eyes and dark smudges beneath them, but her pupils still sparkled like emeralds. 'Turn out the light when you leave. I'm not going anywhere so I'll hold you to that bath tomorrow.'

Back on the bridge, shaved and wearing a clean shirt, I felt a whole lot better. There was also a smile on my face I was glad the darkness concealed. That was the first time I had ever had a woman call me darling ... and mean it.

CHAPTER THIRTY-EIGHT

Forenoon, Saturday 14 February 1942

T he skies cleared during the remainder of the night, and morning twilight revealed the twin peaks of Gadong and Mount Saint Paul silhouetted against the eastern horizon. At their feet, still hidden in the shadows, lay the small port of Tobo Ali, guarded by yet another Dutch fort constructed to maintain their tin monopoly. Dapur Island, marking the end of the Stanton Channel, was fine on the port bow. Once passed it, we were clear of the Banka Strait with open water ahead for the twenty-hour run to Sunda.

My eyes were scratchy from lack of sleep, and the shave and change of shirt were a distant memory. Despite the brain numbing, heavy limbed tiredness, I still managed a smile at the thought of Helena sleeping in my cabin. Her offer to wash my back was something to hold onto as I wearily dragged my feet back and forth across the bridge wing.

Dawn revealed an empty sea under a vast blue dome of sky. The temperature rose rapidly. It was going to be a hot day, with the only relief a gentle north-easterly breeze ruffling the surface of the low swell. There was no sign of the ships from the convoy that had left Singapore ahead of us. Had they survived being bombed in the confines of the straits? Were they already approaching Batavia or forging on towards Fremantle? I had to hope so, if only to stop fearing the worst.

McGrath fixed our position as Dapur passed abeam and corrected our course for the Sunda Strait. He joined me out on the bridge wing.

'Do you want to get your head down for a spell, Skipper.' A few hours of sleep had restored his youthful vigour; his cheerful grin another reminder of how tired and prematurely old I felt.'

I shook my head. There would be time enough for sleep when we cleared Sunda. Or if not, we would all be sleeping with Davy Jones. I forced the thought aside.

'Has Cramp sounded round?'

'Yes. The pumps are still holding their own. And he's checked the hull patches and shoring. They're all holding well, too. Touch wood'—he rapped his forehead with a knuckle—'we'll make it to Fremantle without any trouble.'

'I hope so. I don't fancy having to explain to Mrs Childs why she'll have to swim part of the way.' It was a poor joke but only intended for those within earshot. I beckoned McGrath closer and dropped my voice. 'We're not out of the woods yet, so pass the word for everyone to keep below as far as possible. I know how uncomfortable it must be for the wounded in the tween decks.' I raised my voice so the lookouts could hear. 'But if we make it to sunset, we'll be in the clear. The navy have patrols in the Timor Sea. Hopefully they're expecting us.' That was probably wishful thinking, but it was the best I could come up with.

The aroma of freshly brewing coffee wafted up from the pantry and, moments later, Da Silva arrived on the bridge with a pot and two cups. McGrath took his into the wheelhouse where the boatswain was waiting to receive orders. I balanced mine on the handrail and lit a Senior Service. Astern, the arrow straight wake stretched back towards Dapur Island. To starboard, the low-lying coastline of Sumatra was an indistinct brown smudge running away to the south. Ahead and to port were the sparkling waters of the Java Sea. I took a deep drag at the cigarette and felt the nicotine brush away the cobwebs. Perhaps the situation was more hopeful than it had appeared in the darkness.

His footsteps heavy on the ladder, Spencer climbed up from the boat deck. A mug of coffee steamed in his hand and a cheroot was clamped between his teeth.

'I'll have to have a word with Da Silva about handing out my coffee.'

'And good morning to you too, Bill.' The cheroot waggled between his lips. He removed it and puffed a cloud of pungent smoke before continuing. 'It must have been a quiet night, I slept like a log. Where are we?'

'In the Java Sea.' I pointed astern. 'That's Dapur Island, and over there's Sumatra.'

'Can you show me?'

I lead him into the chartroom and stabbed a finger onto the chart. 'We're here.' I traced along the course line to the Sunda Strait. 'We'll be through there by tomorrow morning. With any luck.'

Spencer nodded. 'We have been bloody lucky so far, so you might be right.' He saw the scowl cross my face and grinned. 'I'm not down-playing your part in this. Your handling of the ship yesterday, dodging bombs falling left and right, was nothing short of miraculous. Even so, you'd have to admit there was some luck involved.'

'If you say so. I'm not sure how much further we can push it.'

'Well now, that's the question. What are the Japanese up to? Are they hunting us or have they bigger game?' He pointed to the Gaspar Strait, between Banka and Belitung Islands, separating the South China and Java seas.

'The last intelligence reports I read before we left Singapore, indicated that a fleet was assembling north of Belitung Island to cover the invasion of Sumatra. The landings are expected around the mouth of the Musi River. They'll be accompanied by air strikes on the airfields and whatever defences the Dutch have scraped together.'

'We spotted a destroyer in the Banka Strait in middle of the night.' Spencer raised an eyebrow.

'Managed to give it the slip in a rainstorm.'

'Probably scouting ahead of the invasion.' He traced the line of the Musi River as it twisted its way into the Sumatran hinterland. The river mouth was already 100 miles in our wake. 'Point is, their bombers should all be headed in that direction and their fighters flying cover either for them or the carriers, against Allied attack ... if we have anything left to attack with.'

It was a glimmer of hope. 'So, they might not come looking for us?'

'Let's just say that ships escaping Singapore might be lower on their list of priorities. And even if they do spot us, how much attention can they spare to deal with one tramp steamer?' Spencer drained the coffee cup and took another drag at his cheroot. 'By the way, I bumped into Mrs Childs on my way up here. She's on the war-path again. Claims Cramp's been making advances.' He tapped his nose with a forefinger. 'Forewarned is forearmed.'

After he had gone, I sent for Cramp. He cheerfully admitted the offence.

'That's right, Skipper. I asked her if she'd like to take a drink in my cabin after supper. Something to wash away the taste of bully beef fried rice. The only mistake I made was to do it where one of the other women over'eard me. She was the one was outraged. Mavis would've said yes otherwise.'

'Mavis?'

'Yair 'er names Mavis, and we was chattin' away like China plates in the snug of The Blind Beggar. Until the other bint turned up.'

'You do know her old man's a colonel.'

'Poor devil's going to see nothing but the inside of a wire cage for the next few years. Least I could do was make sure his cheese and kisses had some fun before … well who knows where we'll be this time t'morrer. Pushin' up sea anemones most like.'

It would have been hypocritical to argue with either his intentions or his sentiments. 'I'll tell her I've had you flogged and keel hauled. And if you talk to her again, make sure she's on her own.'

'Aye aye, Skipper. Nod's as good as a wink.' He flashed me a grin. 'Course it's the gold earring and the gypsy charm that does it. Works every time.'

'Don't push your luck, Brian.' I scowled for better effect. It was pointless, we knew each other too well. Instead, I changed the subject. 'How much more timber have we got?'

'I could knock you up some chairs and a chest of drawers, but not much else. We used most of it yesterday.'

'Well, go round the ship and scrounge every bit you can find. Doors, tables, even the tween deck hatch boards. Colonel Spencer thinks we might get through Sunda unmolested. Says the Japs have bigger things to worry about. I hope he's right. But best be prepared … just in case.'

By the time I finished with Cramp the watch had changed. The lookouts and helmsman were relieved and Lakshman replaced McGrath. Da Silva returned with a tray on which rested a bowl containing what looked like gruel, with bits of vegetable floating in it.

'Jook … rice porridge,' he explained. His sole eye glinted menacingly, almost daring me to complain.

It was filling and, along with two cups of coffee and a cigarette, went some way to restoring my energy. I was even invigorated enough to look forward to being bearded by Mrs Childs, but she must have had second thoughts or perhaps Cramp had stolen a moment to whisper into her ear. In any event, the morning progressed as peacefully as it had begun. Bullen took station on the opposite bridge wing, his tin hat slung around his neck. He and his gun crews had been on the alert since dawn. Despite his age, he seemed impervious to fatigue and his crisp white uniform would have done credit to the bridge of the Royal Yacht.

By the time the chronometer hands had ticked their way past

9am, I was starting to feel that Spencer's optimism might be justified. Banka Island had long since disappeared astern, and the coast of Sumatra, 20 miles away to the west, was only the faintest stain along the horizon. The Java Sea stretched out ahead and every beat of the propeller felt like another step towards safety.

Lakshman was preparing to take an early sun sight, and I was enjoying another cigarette when the lookout's shout and the frantic ringing of the ship's bell broke the spell.

I grabbed my binoculars. Three antiquated looking biplanes swam into focus, like ponderous ungainly moths. They were too high to see any markings.

Bullen was beside me in an instant. 'Could be ours, sir. They look a bit like Fairey Albacores. Could be from *Indomitable,* if she's still in the vicinity.'

A ragged cheer from the boat deck suggested others had reached the same conclusion. Despite my instructions, some of the soldiers and the male passengers lined the rail and waved excitedly at the biplanes as they droned towards us.

'Get down below!' I roared at them.

I didn't wait to see if they obeyed. Bullen's face had frozen into a frown. 'The pilots are in open cockpits. They look very much like the old Stringbags ... Fairey Swordfish, same as hit the *Bismarck* last year. Except ...'

There had to be an 'except.'

'... *Indomitable's* not flying Swordfish.' He scratched his head. 'Could be from *Hermes,* but last I 'eard she was in Ceylon.'

How Bullen kept abreast of the navy's dispositions was a mystery. Perhaps he had a direct line to the Sea Lords. Whatever it was, he was seldom wrong.

The biplanes flew in a loose V formation, steadily overhauling us from the north. They looked too flimsy to do much damage, but Swordfish had delivered *Bismarck* the killer blow, despite the weight of metal she could throw against them. If they were ours, and were just coming to check us over, we had nothing to fear.

If not.

'Christ! They're Yokosukas ... Jeans we call 'em,' shouted Bullen. 'I didn't know they was still flying. PREPARE TO OPEN FIRE'

Sure enough, through the binoculars, the evil eye of the rising sun burned on their fuselages. Spencer had been right ... and wrong. The front-line bombers were hitting targets way to the north. But the B team could still pack a punch. I checked their payloads. Three bombs hung nose to tail below each of their bellies. They looked like eggs, but eggs filled with high explosive. Still, there were only three Jeans with nine bombs between them. We had dodged many times that number the day before.

'Warn the engine room,' I shouted. If anyone was still on the open deck, they could take their chances.

Overhead, the Jeans took station line astern. The leader waggled his wings and dropped into a shallow dive. The other two followed.

'OPEN FIRE.' Bullen's yell was hardly necessary. The rapid whoof-whoof of the Oerlikons was punctuated by the sharp crack of the forecastle 12-pounder.

The Jeans swooped down; roaring in from the port quarter. The Lewis and Bren gunners opened fire, adding their weight of lead to the deadly stream pouring into the bombers' path. Shell casings cascaded onto the deck. The roar of engines rose to an ear-splitting crescendo. The leading pilot was starkly framed behind the windshield; demonic in flying helmet and goggles.

'HARD A PORT.'

The Jeans roared overhead. I grabbed hold of the rail, and the whole world exploded. Geysers erupted all around the ship. Hammer blows rocked and pounded her until the hull shuddered and groaned in agony. An explosion tore open the after deck. Splinters of metal and wooden hatch board cartwheeled into the air. A column of fire blazed skywards, followed by a belching mushroom of black smoke. Bullen lay bleeding at my feet, cut down by the final burst of the rear gunner as the last Jean zoomed away. For a moment I was stunned with shock; ears deafened by the noise and limbs frozen into helpless immobility.

The sight of the wake carving a circle onto the sea's surface restored my senses.

'Midships! Lakshman, get the ship back on course.'

The Jeans had re-grouped and were returning the way they had come. With the ship ablaze, and having suffered no losses, they could chalk up another success. I stumbled into the wheelhouse on legs that felt like jelly. Ashen faced, Lakshman repeated the order to the helmsman and watched as he brought the ship back onto its original heading.

Lamont emerged from the chartroom. 'I've plotted our position, Skipper. Do you want me to give the coordinates to the sparky?'

'Yes, but tell him to standby until he hears from me. Take over here. I'm going aft. And get someone to see to Bullen.'

It was a mess down there. Flames and smoke billowed from the hatch opening to number four hold. The bomb had smashed through the covers and exploded in the tween deck. The force of the blast had blown the hatch boards to pieces; the deck was covered in wooden chunks and splinters. McGrath was directing the fire fighting. Cramp and the boatswain gripped fire hoses; playing jets of foam into the base of the smoke. A seaman was spraying water down the ladder access hatch.

'It's carnage down there.' McGrath was soaking wet and his uniform stained with soot. 'The explosion must have killed almost everyone in the tween deck. There are bodies all over the place, nurses as well as soldiers. I'm cooling the ladder so we can get down.'

'What's burning?' The tween deck had been empty, apart from the wounded and those caring for them.

'The blast must have carried on down into the lower hold. As far as I can make out it's set fire to one of the lorries. Hopefully we can get it under control before it spreads.'

'Have we taken any other hits?'

'None. It's a bloody miracle. Bombs exploding all around us, but only one hit the ship.'

It wasn't the one I was worried about. Provided it could be extinguished, the fire was unlikely to sink us and the damage was probably confined to the hold and what was in it. My senses, however, told me there was potentially mortal damage elsewhere. It wasn't just my tingling fingers. The ship had slowed and her motion felt heavy and sluggish beneath my feet.

'Tell Cramp to check the rest of the holds. And get a report from Fraser. Those misses must have done more damage to the hull. We're taking on water, I can feel it.'

The access ladder was cool enough to climb down. The tween deck reeked of burning oil and rubber, but most of the smoke was venting through the hatch opening. I bent down to touch the steel deck. It was hot, but not burning; the water and foam sloshing about had thankfully cooled it. As McGrath had said, it was carnage. The more heavily wounded soldiers had been berthed in the tween deck, with the nurses working in shifts to tend them as best they could. In the enclosed space, the blast had been catastrophic. Bodies were blown apart. Shards of flesh and clothing were spattered against the hull frames and stringers. Dismembered limbs lay scattered about the deck. Other bodies looked unharmed; the life merely blown out of them by the shock wave.

The boatswain joined me, shaking his head at the devastation. Behind him, seamen dragged fire hoses down the ladder from the main deck. They gingerly opened the access trunk to the lower hold and shoved the nozzles down it. I stepped to the edge of the opening in the centre and looked down through the remaining shards of the hatch boards. The fire had subsided, although the smoke was chokingly thick.

I grabbed the boatswain's shoulder as he reached for the ladder. 'Take care down there. I'll send someone to look after the bodies.'

I didn't need to. By the time I reached the deck, and had gulped in several lungfuls of fresh air, Spencer had mustered the Australian soldiers. Wrapping wet rags around their faces, they dived down the access ladder. The remaining nurses were huddled by the rail waiting to assist. There was pain and grief etched into all their faces, but also grim determination. Not a single cheek was tear stained.

'Anyone alive down there?' asked Spencer, equally grim faced.

I shook my head. 'I doubt it. Poor bastards wouldn't have known what hit them. I guess the least we can do is give a decent burial to what's left of them.'

McGrath and Fraser were waiting for me when I returned to the bridge. Their news was grim. The explosions had buckled and fractured the hull plating in numerous places on both sides of the ship, including the engine room. There were also several cracked steam pipes. The engineers were working to repair the piping, and Cramp and the rest of the seamen were scrambling to stem the leaks.

'It's nay looking good, Bill.' Fraser's face was deep red. The sleeves of his boiler suit had been ripped off and there were livid burns on his arms from scalding steam. 'If we canna stop the leaks, the pumps'll no keep up. Even when we get full steam pressure back.'

'Use everything we've got,' I said to McGrath. 'Strip the accommodation, rip up the timber sheathing. I told Cramp to use the hatch boards if he had to. Just keep the ship afloat. We'll have to forget Fremantle. Lamont!'

'Aye, Skipper.'

'Plot a course for Tanjung Priok and give me an ETA.'

'Already done, sir. South by east. We'll be there at seven thirty tomorrow morning, if we can hold speed.'

'Aye. Well there's another thing,' said Fraser. 'The explosions near shook the engine off its foundations. I hav'na checked all the shaft bearings, but I expect one or two at least will be out of alignment.'

I nodded. 'Let me know when you've checked them all, Angus.

We'll reduce speed if we have to.' I glanced down at his scalded forearms. 'They look as if they need seeing to.'

'Later.' Fraser turned for the ladder to the boat deck. 'I've work to do.'

McGrath followed him. Lamont ordered the helmsman to bring the ship onto her new heading and pulled his pipe out of his pocket. Stuffing the bowl with tobacco, he called to Lakshman. 'Best get another sight, Third. We'll need a good fix at noon.'

Provided we were still afloat by then. The ship felt heavier with tons of water sloshing about her bilges and holds. Her roll was already more pronounced. My hands trembled as I lit a Senior Service. There were a thousand souls on board, but lifejackets and space in the two remaining lifeboats and the rafts for less than a quarter that number.

I took a deep drag of the cigarette hoping the nicotine would calm my nerves. Lamont seemed preternaturally calm. Billows of smoke emerged from his pipe as he puffed contentedly, and even Lakshman seemed to have regained his normal cheerfulness as he bustled onto the bridge wing with his sextant. I felt as if I was the only one with nothing to do. In fact, there was nothing for me to do ... except worry. McGrath and Fraser were battling to save the ship. My looking over their shoulders would be a hindrance rather than a help. Colonel Spencer and the nurses were looking after the wounded. Blood still stained the bridge wing planking. Bullen! What had become of him?

I yelled for Lakshman. Instead, Mrs Childs answered my hail.

'Can you come below, Captain. It's ... it's ... Miss Markova.'

CHAPTER THIRTY-NINE

Late morning, Saturday 14 February 1942

S pencer met me at the door to the sick-bay. I didn't need to ask how Helena was. His face told me everything.

'How long?'

He shook his head. 'I'm so sorry, Bill, it's a miracle she's survived this far. She must have taken almost the full force of the blast. We found her wedged under the timber sheathing at the side of the tween deck. There can hardly be an intact bone left in her body and she must be riddled with bomb fragments.'

'Conscious?'

'Just. One of the nurses pumped her full of morphine, but it's barely touching the pain.'

I pushed open the door. Helena lay on the bunk, her body cocooned in white sheets through which blood seeped. Her head was propped on a pillow. Her face was unmarked, the eyes were closed and she appeared to be asleep. For a moment, it felt as if I had stepped back in time to her rescue from the *Admiral Altfater* two years before the war started. We had faked her death and persuaded the Soviet captain to let us take the body. She lay in the sick bay until the neurotoxin Spencer administered wore off. She lay there again, but this time there would be no miraculous recovery.

A nurse sat in a chair beside her, holding a cloth with which she wiped beads of sweat from Helena's brow. She stood up when I entered.

'I'll be outside, Captain. Call if you need me.'

I sat in the nurse's chair and reached for Helena's hand. It was almost as white as the sheets and felt like ice.

I squeezed gently.

'Is that you, Bill?' Helena's eyes opened. Her pupils were like translucent saucers behind which the dying embers of her life appeared to flare for one final effort.

'Yes.' An iron band wrapped itself painfully around my chest and I struggled to draw breath. 'I'm … sorry.'

'What for?' she whispered. The corners of her mouth twitched slightly; she winced and shuddered as a spasm of pain racked her.

'I should have kept you safe.'

'Don't be,' there was a sharp intake of breath as she fought the pain, '… ridiculous. There's … nothing you could have done.'

'I should have made you leave Singapore while there was still time.'

'I wouldn't have gone … without you.' Her face clouded over and she screwed her eyes shut. 'Ohhhh! It hurts so much.' Her moan, muttered through clenched teeth, ripped through my chest like a dagger.

'Morphine! I'll fetch the nurse.' I tried to let go of her hand, but she clung on with surprising strength.

'No point. It'll be over soon.' She opened her eyes again. There was pain and sadness deeply etched around them, but they were mercifully free of fear. '*Here is my journey's end. Here is my butt, and very sea mark of my utmost sail.*'

Shakespeare? *Othello*, maybe? Had I not quoted from it myself … how long ago was it? But then, I had never imagined this.

I raised her hand and pressed it to my lips. 'Helena. How will I ever …?'

'You will … you will.' She released my hand and stroked my face. Her fingers traced the line of my chin and a tear rolled down her cheek. 'Is it getting dark? I can hardly see you.'

'It must be sunset.' I clamped my jaw shut to stop it trembling.

'Is the ship safe, then?'

'We'll be in Batavia tomorrow.' Would it matter if it was not true? Would anything matter ever again if Helena was not there when we made it?

'Tomorrow is … another country.' She reached for my hand again and pulled me close. Her voice was barely a whisper. 'You won't forget me, Bill Rowden?'

My chest heaved and I swallowed hard. 'I won't forget you. No one will ever forget you.'

'Promise me. Cross your heart …'

And hope to die? Gladly. 'I promise. Cross my heart.'

She sank back on the pillow and closed her eyes. Her short, shallow breathing slowed to a faint murmur. Perhaps the morphine was finally kicking in and allowing her the blessed release of sleep. The faint rustle of air between her lips was measured by the tick of the bulkhead clock as it counted every priceless second of her ebbing life. I felt for the pulse in her wrist, but it was too weak for my fingers to register.

Her eyes flickered open and a soft gurgle forced her lips into a grin. 'You'll have to bury me at sea again. I won't miss it this time.'

The chuckle died but the light continued to flicker in her eyes. I had read the burial service as we dropped a weighted canvas shroud into the sea off Formosa. The log declared it to contain the mortal remains of Lady Helen Ashworth. Helena had remained hidden in her cabin to avoid suspicion among the crew. I would have to write another log entry. This time the truth ... for all the good it would do. If we didn't make it to Batavia no one might ever know what became of any of us. Even if we did, what was one more death amongst the countless that had already been killed. Except it was not just one more death. It was Helena.

'Don't cry, Bill.'

I reached up to my cheek and felt the moisture on my fingertips.

'It doesn't hurt anymore.' Her grip tightened on my hand and there was a sudden feverish urgency in her voice. 'Do you remember what Russians do when we set out on a journey?'

'Yes.'

'You'll have to drink one for me. Moskovskaya, the special one with ... the green label. It was my father's ... favourite vodka.' Her voice faltered and her eyes lost their focus, the enlarged pupils searching the ceiling as if looking for something. 'It seems so dark. What time is it?'

The clock was still half an hour shy of noon. 'It's evening. Sunset.'

'It's late ... nearly time to go home. My mother is coming for me.' Her eyes fixed on something behind my head. 'Matushka ... mama ... is papa there, and Grigor?'

She lapsed into mumbled Russian, talking with people only she could see and hear. Her father had been shot by the Bolsheviks after the revolution. Her mother had taken her and her younger brother to Paris. Was she still living there under Nazi occupation? How could I contact her?

'Bobby, is that you?'

The sudden switch to English caught me by surprise and it took a moment to recall that Bobby—Lord Ashworth—had been her husband. He had died in Shanghai before the Japanese invasion of China.

'I won't be long, Bobby. You do want me to look my best.'

She reverted to Russian jumbled up with French and English, talking to the memories of people who flitted in and out of the remains of her consciousness. It suddenly felt as if the sick bay was full of the spirits she had summoned to ease her crossing of the bar. I opened my mouth to speak ... and closed it. Would any words of mine make any difference now she was surrounded by friends and family?

I held her hand and listened. In between the tortured rasps of breath, the words tumbled from her mouth. She talked on, as if in doing so she could fend off the arrival of the one presence she was trying to avoid. Useless, of course. Finally, the words slowed, her breathing grew more laboured and her unseeing eyes widened with alarm.

'No! You can't. Not yet.' Her voice rose. 'Rowden ... Rowden.'

I held her in my arms, feeling her grow heavy as the last runnels of life trickled away. She drew a final breath that rattled deep in her throat. One second she was there, and the next she was gone. I laid her corpse back on the bed and straightened the sheets. There was almost a look of reproach in her emerald eyes which, even in death, seemed to gently smoulder. I smoothed my fingers over the lids to close them and called the nurse.

Spencer was outside the sickbay.

He extended a hand towards my arm. I recoiled and pushed past him.

'Bill!'

He followed me as I bounded up the stairs.

'Bill, I'm sorry. Do you need to talk?'

Outside my cabin door I rounded on him.

'No! And certainly not with you. If it hadn't been for your fucking spy games ... she'd still be alive.'

'Bill, wait—'

I slammed the door in his face. I had no vodka but there was rum. There was always plenty of rum. I grabbed the bottle, wrenched out the cork and filled a glass. It barely touched the sides on the way down and I felt the warmth explode in my belly. I paused with the second glass at my lips.

What had Helena said? 'In Russia we don't say goodbye. It's, *dasvedanya* ... until we meet again.'

'*Dasvedanya*,' I whispered through clenched teeth. I drained the glass and hurled it against the bulkhead where it shattered into crystal shards.

I reached for the bottle. It was a quarter full.

'Das ... fucking ... vedanya,' I shouted. I drained the bottle. It smashed satisfyingly into the bulkhead, strewing more glass fragments across the linoleum. I reached into the cabinet for a fresh one.

The door burst open. The burly figure of the shipwright filled the entrance.

'What the fuck do you want Cramp?'

He held out a hand. 'That won't do no good.'

'You think?' I twisted the cork out.

'It won't bring 'er back.'

I waved the bottle in his face. 'I don't want to bring her back. I want to go with her.'

I held the bottle to my lips and upended it.

Cramp's ferocious slap caught my cheek knocking the bottle out of my grasp. It, too, shattered against the steel. Rum splattered the bulkhead and trickled to the deck.

I raised a fist and lunged at him. He blocked the blow and fended me off. The look in his eyes was ... what? Pity? Disgust? Contempt?

'Get out. Now! Before I kick you out.'

He shook his head and kept his fists raised. 'You don't wanna do this, Rowden. I get that you're angry, that you're hurting. But for Christ's sake, don't be so bloody selfish. You're not the only one hurting. There's women who've lost their 'usbands. Parents who've lost their children. Men who'll never see their families again. What makes you so fucking special?'

I raised my hand to my cheek and rubbed it. It stung and I could feel the swelling. 'You've got no idea how I feel. So why don't you piss off and mind your own business.'

'Because it is my business, damn you. The ship's slowly sinking and there's a thousand frightened souls wondering whether they'll live to see another sunrise. Fraser's battling to keep the screw turning and young McGrath's at his wits end trying to plug all the leaks. They can't do it alone, and last time I checked there was still four stripes on ya shoulders.'

There it was. The burden of command. The world might be unravelling around me, but I was still Master under God. Whether He—or possibly it—cared or not, didn't matter.

'There endeth the lesson.' I reached for my cap. The tarnished gold leaf around its brim was a metaphor for the transitory nature of authority. 'But hit me again without saying sir, and I'll personally keel haul you. Now fuck off and send Da Silva to clean up the mess. Oh, and one more thing. You owe me a bottle of rum.'

Eight bells rang for noon and the change of watch, as I stepped onto the bridge.

Lamont was plotting the position on the chart. He glanced up and nodded as I passed into the wheelhouse. The helmsman stared doggedly at the binnacle. Lakshman was keeping watch on the port wing, studying the horizon through binoculars. I stepped out on the other side.

It was a glorious afternoon.

Lambswool cumulus decorated a bright blue sky. A gentle breeze ruffled the crests of the sparkling, cobalt swell.

It was a dreadful afternoon.

The ship wallowed deep in the water, rolling slowly to almost ten degrees and hanging for several heart stopping seconds before rolling back the other way. A few moments' observation confirmed she was listing several degrees to port. The same few moments were enough to feel the change in vibration as the propeller shaft rotated in its misaligned bearings.

I called to Lakshman to find McGrath and bring me a report on the condition of the leaks.

While I waited, I paced the bridge wing, the mask of command forced across my face.

Behind it, I felt as if I was being crushed by a burden too heavy to carry. I wanted to go back to the sick bay and take Helena in my arms. I wanted to tell her that everything would be alright, that she was just sleeping and would wake when I kissed her, like a princess in a child's fairy tale. I wanted the impossible, and the knowledge clawed agonisingly at my heart like the razor-sharp talons of a vulture.

Focus on the possible. If McGrath could contain the leaks. If Fraser could keep the propeller turning. If the planes stayed away.

McGrath mounted the stairs from the boat deck. Staying afloat was the first priority. I listened silently while he detailed the damage, the progress with plugging the holes and his estimate of the flooding. If it got no worse—what was it seamen said when they were safe ashore in bars or the arms of a woman: "Don't worry, things could be worse. So I didn't worry … and things got worse"— we might float long enough to reach Batavia. But even if we did, a part of me was past caring. The bodies were piling up around me. The bodies of shipmates and of men and women I had liked and respected, and loved. David Griffith cut down by a shell splinter, Olwyn De Angelo murdered by Jeffreys, God rot his soul, and now … Helena.

Helena. Her name whirled through my brain, firing agonising sparks as it brushed each raw nerve.

I might make it to Batavia. Unlikely as it seemed, I might even make it through the war. But at that moment I wanted nothing more than Helena, and I would willingly have embraced Davy Jones if he could have returned me to her.

CHAPTER FORTY

14-15 February, 1942

At sunset, as a mark of respect, I stopped the ship and read the burial service. Most of the evacuees and the walking wounded lined the rail as the canvas shrouded remains of Helena, Bullen and the dozens of victims of the previous two days' attacks were consigned to the eternal peace of the deep. Some of the shrouds were little more than jute bags into which had been gathered the dismembered limbs and torsos of those torn apart by the blast.

After the ceremony, Mrs Childs pressed a sturdy wooden box into my hands.

'If you'll forgive me, Captain, we've distributed Miss Markova's clothes among the other women. Her jewellery and everything of value is in this box. I expect you'll be able to return it to her family.'

I mumbled my thanks and took it to my cabin. There were necklaces, rings, earrings and broaches all sparkling with diamonds, emeralds and sapphires. Among them nestled her cigarette case. The enamelled surface shimmered in the lamp light. I flicked it open. It was empty and the interior bore a hallmark in what looked like Cyrillic script. At the bottom of the box lay a slim bundle of papers bound in ribbon. They included letters and her travel documents. I slipped them back, intending to examine them later. Hopefully, they contained her mother's address in Paris.

Apart from Da Silva's, there were surprisingly few tears shed for the dead. They would probably come later. In the meantime, all the thoughts of the living were focussed on their own survival. We had seen through the day, the Japanese had left us alone, but we were sinking. Slowly, by drip, trickle and stream, the water level was rising. The pumps were battling hard, like the rearguard of a defeated army struggling to stem an orderly retreat from turning into a rout, but it was simple arithmetic. At best, it would take us thirteen hours to steam to Tanjung Priok. If the pumps maintained the fight we could float for a further hour or two after that, but no more. It was not just the flooding, though, it was where it was. The water sloshing back and forth in the holds was quite enough to make the ship sufficiently unstable to roll right over. We ballasted double bottoms and deep tanks to keep her upright, or as close thereto as possible. Even so, she had a pronounced port list. McGrath, Lamont and I pored over the stability curves and tank tables, pooling all we had ever learnt about free surface effect and angles of loll.

So, thirteen hours. Could Fraser keep the propeller turning?

Several shaft bearings were out of alignment and running hot. Playing fire hoses onto them might keep them at a safe temperature, but added to the bilge pumps' task. Fraser had reluctantly accepted the inevitable and agreed to maintain maximum engine revolutions for as long as possible. If the vibration got worse. If one or other of the bearings overheated and seized. More ifs to add to the accumulation that already threatened our survival. At least the peril from Japanese air attack had lessened with the coming of darkness. The grim news of the ship's condition quickly spread among the evacuees but, free of the imminent threat of being blown apart, a hopeful silence settled over the ship as those who could afford the luxury of sleep bedded down for the night.

Both McGrath and Fraser had worked themselves to a standstill. McGrath was reeling with exhaustion when he finally reported there was nothing more that could be done to minimise the flooding. I ordered him to get his head down for a few hours. Lamont and Lakshman had also been on their feet all day, but they were young enough to survive another night without sleep. I stopped looking in the mirror. I hardly recognised the haggard, greying haired, old man that peered back at me through half closed, bloodshot eyes. But as bad as I must have looked, I didn't feel in the least sleepy. Cigarettes and strong coffee had been my go-to on the long, cold nights of the Atlantic convoys. This time, they had nothing to do with my new found energy. Spencer pulled me aside after the burials and thrust a packet of Benzedrine tablets into my hand. There were rumours of convoy escort commanders and bomber pilots swallowing them like chocolate Smarties in order to stay awake. They were not issued to merchant ship crews. More was the pity.

With McGrath turned in, Cramp had taken charge of monitoring the leaks and sounding the tanks and bilges. He reported hourly during the evening watch. The water levels continued to rise slowly, but no faster than before. By midnight, with less than eight hours to go, the larger question looming was whether I could get the ship repaired in Tanjung Priok. There had been two floating docks there, either of which could accommodate *Oriental Venture*. After the Japanese declaration of war, the larger had been relocated to Tjilatjap on the south coast of Java. How many damaged ships were queued to use the remaining one? More importantly, how long before the Japanese turned their attention to Java itself? Weeks? Days?

'How's the bennies?'

I had not heard Spencer arrive on the bridge. His darkened shape leaned against the rail beside me.

'I'm wide awake. Feel better than I have in years.'

'It's only temporary. You'll crash once the effects wear off.'

'As long as they get me through the next twenty-four hours.' I was not just wide awake. There was also a feeling of euphoria. That too, would only be temporary, but it provided some relief. 'I'm sorry I slammed the door in your face earlier.'

Spencer's hand gripped my arm. 'Don't give it a thought, old boy. Anyway, I deserved it.'

'I should have made Helena leave Singapore while there was still time.'

'She would never have gone. Poh secured her a passage to India, but she volunteered as a nurse so she could stay on. To be close to you. Surely you knew that, Bill?'

'Yes, she told me.' The admission pierced the succour of the Benzedrine like a white-hot poker.

He gripped my arm again. 'I'm sorry, Bill. I know it doesn't help, but I'm truly sorry. If I could bring her back...'

A shooting star blazed across the constellation of Orion.

'I saw you, you know. The night you danced in the moonlight. What were you dancing to?'

The memory of it flooded back, and I had to clench my jaw until it stopped trembling. 'From, *Follow the Fleet. Let's Face the Music and Dance.*'

'I always knew you were a romantic at heart. You made a lovely couple.'

Had he been spying on us; a voyeur watching from the shadows? It didn't matter now. None of it mattered now. Helena had sung the lyrics. I could still hear them. *There may be troubles ahead.* How prophetic they had proven to be. We had faced the music alright, only the band was still playing.

'What will you do when we get to Batavia?' I asked.

'Hand those Australians over to the army and report to command.'

'Will you report them for desertion?'

'No. I'll probably read about it in the history books, but no. We'll need every man before this is over. What about you?'

'Get the ship repaired, and push on to Fremantle.'

'Who's that Saint I sometimes hear you mumbling prayers too?'

'Saint Woolos. Patron saint of smugglers and fishermen.'

'I think we're all going to need his help. Put in a good word for me next time.'

He had done nothing for Helena. Perhaps he had stopped listening to me. 'Not sure how he feels about soldiers. He was a warrior himself, until he found God.'

'Listen, Bill.' There was desperation in Spencer's voice. 'I never wanted any harm to come to Helena. Believe me, I'd give ... I'd give my right arm.' He grasped my hand. 'Whatever happens ... well, good luck, Captain. See you around.'

He let go of my hand and was gone before I had time to reply.

'Good luck to you to, Colonel,' I whispered. My fingertips weren't tingling, but I felt sure we would both need it.

I paced the bridge wing for the next hour, and at four bells Da Silva arrived with a pot of coffee. Of us all, he seemed to need the least sleep. The coffee was good, but my eyelids had started to feel prickly and I popped another Benzedrine tablet as a precaution. I would pay a price, but what the hell as long as we made it to Batavia.

Lamont gratefully accepted a cup and took it back out onto the bridge wing. He normally liked to chat, but must have sensed I was in no mood to talk.

Alone on the other bridge wing I allowed my thoughts to wander. It was a mistake. Images of Helena crowded my head. I tried to push them aside, only to find them replaced by Olwyn De Angelo. She had promised I would find the right woman one day. 'Let me know when you find her,' she said in my cabin, the afternoon we escaped from the U-boat off West Africa. 'You won't ever have to save me again.'

I had not saved her then, and I had not saved Helena now.

I raised my hands and gripped my pounding head, as if that would stop the recriminations whirling around inside it.

'Good morning, Skipper.'

McGrath. Thankfully, the darkness concealed the extent of my torment.

'Watch has been relieved. I've made a round of the holds. Not great news I'm afraid.'

I glanced at my watch. The luminous hands showed 4am. Two hours had flown by while I had been wrapped in misery.

'Tell me.'

'The deeper we sink in the water the more pressure on the lowest leaks. Cramp and the bosun are doing what they can. But it's a losing battle.'

It was inevitable. 'What about the engine room?'

'Water's above the floor plates, but the pumps and the boilers are still clear.'

I spared a thought for Fraser and his men, up to their ankles in water as they struggled to keep the boiler fires burning.

'How long?'

'Four hours at the most. Provided it stays calm.'

The deeper we sank, the less freeboard we had and the smaller angle it would take to roll the edge of the main deck under. If we rolled too far, the free surface effect of the water in the holds would hold us there, at an angle of loll. If we rolled any further we could turn right over.

'Best say our prayers, then.'

Saint Woolos having abandoned us, was anyone else listening?

'We'll make it, Skipper. Or we'll get close enough to swim the rest of the way.'

'Better get the boats swung out and the rafts ready. Anything that'll float.'

'I've turned out the crew. Might be an idea to turn on the deck lights so they can see better to work.'

It would also light us up like a Christmas tree, but it would be daylight in less than two hours anyway.

'Do it. And get everyone out of the tween decks and up on deck. Including the wounded. Lifejackets for those who can't swim.'

McGrath scurried away in the darkness. Moments later, the ship lit up in the yellow glow of the deck lamps. By their light I saw Lakshman had returned to the bridge to relieve Lamont.

'You go and help the chief mate, Third. Mr Lamont and I can manage here.'

Lamont joined me on the bridge wing. Hammers clashed on retaining pins and blocks squealed as the remaining two boats were swung out.

'Did you hear that, Second? If we're not in Tanjung Priok in four hours most of us will be swimming.'

'What's that about swimming?' Angus Fraser's head appeared above the stairs as he climbed up from the boat deck.

'I'm preparing to abandon ship. It'll be touch and go whether we'll get there before we sink.'

'Aye, I'm aware o' that. We're already up to our knees down below. The lads are giving it all they've got. Boiler pressures are already into the red. The shaft's rattling like a bag o' bolts. She'll not take it for much longer.' He shrugged his shoulders. 'But long enough, maybe.'

'Thanks Angus. Best get everyone not essential up on deck, just in case.'

'Who're ya kidding? There's no passengers down below. Just make sure we get sufficient warning.'

He was breathing heavily after his climb from the engine room floor plates and a dark pool of water circled his feet from his dripping boots. He tilted his head back and gazed at the blaze of stars.

'Aye it's a grand sight, right enough. Sometimes I envy you deckies. Night like this. Breathing fresh air instead of sweating your bollocks off.'

'And in winter at sixty north? Warm and dry in your engine room. No salt water boils on your neck and wrists.'

'Never said there weren't some advantages.' He raised a hand to rub his chin, then took me by the elbow.

'Listen, Bill. I'm right sorry about yon lass, Helena. Didnae have a chance to say so earlier. If there's anything I can do …?'

Other than bringing her back, was there anything anyone could do? A shoulder to cry on? Someone to put me to bed when I drank myself into oblivion?

'Thanks Angus. I appreciate it.'

'Aye, well I'll get back down to the paddling pool. I'll let you know if there's any change.'

The squelch of his sodden boots faded down the ladder. Lamont hovered at my elbow. I might not have wanted to talk, but he wanted to add his tuppence worth.

'We're all sorry, Skipper. If there's …'

'Okay, Second. Thanks, but let's get the ship to Tanjung Priok first. There'll be time enough for that later.'

There was enough light to see the surprise in his eyes, before the professional mask clamped down.

'Aye, Skipper. You're right. It'll be dawn soon. I'll get ready for stars.'

It hardly mattered now, we would sight the coast of Java soon enough, but the routines of navigation helped keep the demons at bay.

The coming of dawn made it painfully clear to everyone how close we were to foundering. With the ship listing several degrees, the edge of the main deck was almost awash. Most of the evacuees had clustered on the boat deck.

Surprisingly, there was no panic. Lifejackets had been issued to all the children and their mothers, and to those unable to swim. The boats were swung out and ready. McGrath and Lakshman had numbered off as many of the evacuees and wounded as they would hold. There were still hundreds without lifejackets or a place in the boats. They would have to find space on the rafts, or cling to whatever floated free as we sank. From the bridge wing I watched Mrs Childs make her away among the women. She seemed to be offering words of advice or encouragement. A man started the first line of *Waltzing Matilda*. A few ragged voices joined in. More took up the chorus until the whole boat deck was signing lustily. *It's a Long Way to Tipperary* was followed by *Keep the Home Fires Burning* and then by *There'll Always Be an England*.

Scottish though he was, Lamont joined in; removing the pipe from his mouth so he could belt out the lyrics in a Harry Lauder baritone.

Ahead, the coast of Java with its backdrop of low hills slowly firmed in the growing light. To the west, the Thousand Islands stretched along the horizon.

With all the extra weight of water, the engine finally lost the battle to maintain speed and we limped along at little more than six knots. Still, the ship swam, the islands crawled by and the coast drew slowly closer.

Eventually, we were inside the enfolding headlands of Batavia Bay with the breakwaters of the outer harbour clearly visible, like two arms welcoming us to safety. But the distance was closing too slowly. The sea lapped higher up the main deck and the singing died away. My knuckles turned white from gripping the hand rail and the whole ship seemed to be holding its breath.

Gradually, the breakwaters crept closer, each turn of the screw closing the gap by a few more precious yards. Through my feet I could feel the tortured vibration of the shaft forced to turn in its damaged bearings. The ship was clawing herself towards the shore, like a wounded animal seeking refuge.

A light flashed from the signal station on the breakwater. I reached for the Morse lamp, sent our name and asked permission to enter harbour.

After a short delay, the signal station asked our condition.

I replied.

Another delay.

The light flashed, permission denied. A collective groan rose from those who could read Morse.

'What the fuck do they expect us to do?' There was disbelief and anger in Lamont's face.

'They're afraid we'll sink in the channel and block the harbour,' I said, reaching a decision. 'Port ten, steer south-east.'

The ship swung onto its new heading and the eastern breakwater slid slowly astern. Ahead was the villa lined beach of the bathing resort of Zandvoort. No less than the British, the Dutch awarded their colonial possessions names that reminded them of home, in this case the seaside resort on the Dutch coast, west of Amsterdam.

I turned to Lamont. 'Warn the engine room to expect a bump, and send someone to the boat deck to tell everyone to sit down. Then take Cramp onto the forecastle and clear the anchors away.'

I turned my attention back to Zandvoort. Men in tropical white suits, and women in sun dresses and gaily decorated hats, were breakfasting in the gardens of the villas or standing among the trees. Just like the planters and merchants of Singapore, they were determined to enjoy their last days of colonial luxury before the Japanese arrived. Many heads turned to watch, no doubt wondering why we were drawing so close.

Abeam of the centre of the beach I ordered the helm to starboard. 'Steer south.'

The faces ashore gawped in astonishment. Hands pointed. Arms flapped.

I looked over the side, the bottom was invisible through the muddy water but I knew the beach shelved gently.

There was jolt as the bow touched, then a judder as the keel rode up the sand.

As the ship ground to a halt, I yelled to Lamont to drop both anchors.

I reached for the engine telegraph and, for the final time, rang *Finished with Engine*.

EPILOGUE

1 March 1942

The coast of Ceylon had been sliding by since dawn, its jungle clad peaks silhouetted against the rising sun. Colombo lay ahead. The unknown lay ahead.

The Dutch authorities had been none too pleased at my beaching *Oriental Venture* at Zandvoort. It spoiled the view for those whose heads were still stuck firmly enough in the sand to believe the Japanese could not invade Java. They were also surprised we had survived the voyage from Singapore. Only two other ships from all those that had sailed in the final convoys had escaped the deadly attention of the Japanese. Reports were filtering in of parties of desperate survivors holed up on the islands bordering the Durian and Banka Straits.

After taking my statement, together with depositions from the mates, as to the perilous state in which we arrived at Tanjung Priok, they grudgingly accepted that I had little choice but to ground the vessel for the safety of all on board. By then, they had already ferried all the wounded, together with the nurses and the evacuees, ashore and embarked them on the Dutch ship *Plancius,* bound for Bombay.

Colonel Spencer and the Australian soldiers had followed them and marched off to the nearest army base. The Allies were scraping together every able-bodied serviceman for the defence of Java. I wished him luck. He would need it. The bulk of the British Far Eastern army had gone into captivity in Singapore. There was almost nothing to stop the Japanese continuing south through the islands to Australia.

The rest of us had been placed in temporary barracks while it was decided what to do with us.

The boatswain solved that problem for the Chinese crew. He took me aside and asked that I pay them off in Batavia. I had emptied the contents of the safe before leaving the ship. Poh had provided more than enough cash and banker's draughts. I asked why, and whether he was not afraid the Japanese would seize them. He replied that it would be easy for them to blend in with the Chinese population of Java. As was often the case throughout the islands, they had clan connections stretching all the way back to Hong Kong and the mainland. Anglo Oriental had agents in Batavia. I arranged to call on them, and signed the crew off in the presence of the head clerk. Neither of us was sure of its legality, Ministry of War Transport regulations probably required their consent, but we could claim the confusion of war. He negotiated a banker's draught and paid all of us the balance of our wages. The boatswain shook my hand and lead the crew away without a backward glance. He and many of the others had sailed in the ship since it first arrived in Hong Kong. They had served it loyally. Now it was gone, their loyalty had gone with it. It was hardly surprising, they owed me nothing as soon as the articles ended.

I left a copy of my report with the agent, who promised to forward it to Mr Khoo at the earliest opportunity. I also left him the balance of the company's funds. The Chinese had ways of secreting and transferring money that were best not delved into.

Several days later, the welcome news arrived that we were all to be shipped out in Paddy Henderson's *Yoma*. Originally built for the Glasgow to Rangoon service, she had been converted to a troopship in January 1941. She was a popular ship, and her comfortable, well-appointed, first-class cabins were lined with teak panelling. We never saw any of them; they were reserved for senior servicemen. Instead, I shared a four berth second class cabin with my three mates. A similar cabin was allocated to Fraser and his engineers. They were cramped and Spartan, without a porthole, but we had the freedom of the upper decks and at night it was cooler to sleep under the stars.

The chief steward discovered that his counterpart on *Yoma* was an old friend. They had sailed together as boys, years' before. As a result, he and Cramp enjoyed a cabin to themselves somewhere on a lower deck. Da Silva and the cook were pressed into service, the cook in the galley and Da Silva to look after *Oriental Venture's* officers and engineers just as he had always done. The DEMS gunners were absorbed into *Yoma's* gun teams. The stokers and firemen were allocated berths in the troop quarters. I visited them daily to ensure they were treated well. I need not have worried. They were not the only Somalis on board. Most of the Empire's races were represented, survivors of multiple sinkings, being carried to wherever the Ministry of War Transport thought fit to send them.

A week with nothing to do but sleep or watch the brilliant waters of the Indian Ocean slip by, did wonders physically, but I still tried to avoid looking in the mirror. The haunted face of the man who stared at me while I shaved, brought back too many painful memories.

Lakshman was leaning against the rail beside me watching the coast slip by a mile or so away.

'An anna for your thoughts, Vijay?'

There were 16 annas to the rupee and about 15 rupees to the pound. If my mental arithmetic was correct, I was offering him ... about a penny.

'I was just wondering about my brother, sir. Whether there will be any news when we reach Colombo.'

According to Spencer, Captain Lakshman had last been seen leading his company into action at Slim River. The Mahrattas had fought hard but suffered very badly. Only a handful had answered the roll call after the battle. Lakshman was not among them.

'It was chaos at the end. He was probably among the stragglers that found their own way back to Singapore. He'll turn up in a prison camp eventually.'

'My mother will be worrying. Would it be possible to send a telegram from the Colombo Post Office?'

'Possibly, but we can do better than that. Bombay's the next port of call. You must have some leave due. I can speak to the authorities. Get permission for you to see your family for a few days. After that you'll probably find a berth in an Indian ship.'

His face lit up. 'That would be most kind, but ...' the smile faded '... that would mean leaving you, sir.'

'Yes, it would. But I don't have a ship, or a berth to offer you. Let's wait and see what news there is in Colombo and you can decide then.'

'Thank you, Captain. What about you, sir?'

What indeed? I was employed by Anglo Oriental at Mr Khoo's pleasure. Even in wartime, the casualty reports issued by Lloyd's Shipping Agents would quickly reach him. Even if he was prepared to overlook the loss of his ship, it was unlikely he had another to offer me. The best I was facing was fronting up to the Pool and taking my chances with whatever was available.

'I haven't given it much thought, Third.' It was simpler to lie. I had commanded *Oriental Venture* for over seven years. She had been my entire life. The thought of her beached and abandoned at Tanjung Priok was still painfully raw. If the Japanese could not repair and press her into service, they would cut her up for scrap. Whatever I sailed in in the future, nothing would erase the memories of her.

Yoma slowed as we passed the Galle Face. The lawns looked fresh, and the white walls and red tiled roof of the Galle Face Hotel gleamed in the morning sunlight. The narrow strip of land separating the ocean from Beira Lake drew astern. McGrath and Lamont joined us at the rail.

'Late breakfast?' I asked.

'Aye. Porridge and finnan haddie,' said Lamont. 'Well, porridge anyway, and a greasy fried egg of indeterminate age.' He yawned and stretched his good arm above his head. 'And nothing to do. I could get to like these passenger ships.'

'Make the most of it,' I said. 'There could be orders waiting for us when we dock. Might be some dirty old tramp rescued from a Calcutta breaker's yard. Or, if you're very lucky, you might get a few more nights of luxury before we get to Bombay.'

'Either way, I was looking forward to stretching my legs ashore this evening. Anyone care to join me?' asked Lamont.

'The last time I was here,' I said, finding a memory to smile at, 'I was walking up Church Street. A man thought I was lost and offered to sell me a map. When I turned it down, he offered me his sister. I wasn't lost, but I thought the map was the safer bet.'

'I'll go with you, Ian,' said Lakshman.

Lamont looked him up and down with an exaggerated stare. 'I think not, young Vijay. Your mama would no' approve of the wickedness of a Scotsman determined to sample the best of the fleshpots of Colombo. I've no' been here before, but I've a flair for these things.' He tapped the side of his nose.

'You can come with me, if you like,' said McGrath. 'Although I thought you'd feel right at home here.'

There was a strained silence, during which Lakshman struggled to keep his mouth shut.

Lamont broke the silence. 'Now then Jimmy. You canna judge a book by its cover. Young Vijay is a Hindi speaking Hindu. Most of the people here are Sinhalese speaking Buddhists. He'll no more be understood than you trying to purchase a short time in the Anderston Drag in Glasgow.

'There are some similarities between the languages,' chipped in Lakshman. 'I could probably get by.'

'Just as long as you can order me a beer.' The embarrassed flush faded from McGrath's face. 'No offence meant, Third.'

'None taken, sir.'

'Actually, we can drop all that,' continued McGrath. 'We're off articles.'

They continued to chatter while I turned my attention back to the slowly changing vista of old Colombo. We were passing the fort. The Union flag streamed from its flagpole. Beyond it, another Union flag topped the white painted Victorian pile of the King's House. Beyond that again, the breakwater jutted north, enclosing a large chunk of ocean. Dozens of ships were anchored inside it, including many smaller warships, although the bulk of what was left of the Royal Navy's Far East presence was at Trincomalee on the east coast.

Even with the warships, it all looked very familiar. With the Union flags flying proudly over the city, and white, red and blue ensigns fluttering from the sterns of most of the ships in the harbour, it was hard to imagine that, only days before, the Empire had suffered the greatest blow to its prestige since the Indian Mutiny. It looked normal, but it wasn't. The future was unknown territory; a different country, as Helena had said.

Nothing in that country would ever be the same again, not least of all for me.

I had lost my ship.

I had lost Helena.

I felt as if I had awakened into a new world in which everything looked the same but was utterly different. This time, I was afraid the feeling would last, that their loss had left an aching pit in my heart so deep that nothing would ever fill it.

AUTHOR'S NOTE

*O*riental Valiant is a work of fiction set against the backdrop of the historical events surrounding the fall of Singapore in 1942. All of the main characters are fictitious, but a number of the minor characters are based on real people. Duff and Lady Diana Cooper, Captain Mohan Singh, Rear Admiral Spooner, Colonel Ashmore and Captain Mulock, for example, all participated in the roles ascribed to them. For dramatic effect, other minor players have been substituted for those who actually took part in the operations to defend and evacuate Singapore. Most notably, Lieutenant-Commander Barker is entirely fictitious and in no way intended to cast any shadow over the heroic actions of Lieutenant-Commander Victor Clark, the inspiring commander of both the naval elements of the commando raids, and the evacuation of several thousand stranded soldiers from the beach at the Batu Pahat River, on which parts of the book are based.

As far as I know, there was never a joint British-Soviet intelligence operation in Bangkok to establish Japan's military intentions in the Far East, but I have no doubt the intelligence services of all the major powers were actively seeking them. It does seem likely, however, that the Soviets actively worked to forestall a possible Japanese attack on themselves by bringing the USA into the war.

The NKVD allegedly used a number of double agents and communist sympathisers inside the Roosevelt administration, said to include Harry Dexter White in the Treasury Department, to fashion a policy designed to provoke the Japanese into attacking the USA and to withhold intelligence that might have alerted the commanders in Pearl Harbour. Such has been suggested by: John Tolland in *Infamy,* the controversial and revisionist historian Harry Elmer Barnes in *Pearl Harbour After a Quarter of a Century* and, more recently, by John Koster in *Operation Snow.* So, while General Maslennikov's actions are entirely fictitious they may be plausible. The real Ivan Maslennikov was indeed an NKVD General, but he was not assassinated in dubious circumstances. He fought throughout the war, and afterwards remained in the NKVD and its successor the MVD until committing suicide in 1954, reportedly fearing repercussions for his association with the infamous Lavrentiy Beria.

For those navigators who read the book, I would ask they do not attempt to plot the progress of *Oriental Venture's* voyage from Bangkok to Singapore. Time and distance were necessarily flexible in order to accommodate the narrative.

Many of the principal events are based on historical actions of the campaign. The 3/17th Battalion of the Dogra Regiment did defend the beaches at Kota Bharu. They did so with such ferocity that the Japanese later commented that it was some of the hardest fighting of the entire campaign. An RAAF Hudson did spot the invasion fleet 24 hours before the landings, but its warning was largely unheeded. *Repulse* and *Prince of Wales* did sail on the afternoon of 8 December 1941, but their course would not have placed them within sight of *Oriental Venture*. Nevertheless, I like to think they would have returned the salute from a dipped Red Ensign. Royal Navy ships always exchanged salutes with British merchant ships when I was at sea.

The Thorne Force raid is loosely based on the Rose Force commando operations mounted by men drawn from battalions of the 8th Australian Division and planned by Major Rose of the Argyll and Sutherland Highlanders. Harbour Defence Motor Launches 1062 and 1063 were used much as described to transport the commandos and tow boats for river use. HMS *Medusa* is the sole surviving HDML (1387) in service today, and I am grateful to Captain Alan Watson OBE of The Medusa Trust for assistance with technical information pertaining to their design and operation.

To support Rose Force, the Straits Steamship's *Kudat* was requisitioned by the navy as a stores' ship based in Port Swettenham. Less fortunate than *Oriental Venture*, she was bombed and sunk.

The progress of the Japanese down the Malay peninsula is largely as sketched, however I am not an historian so please forgive any howlers. For those interested in learning more, *The Defence and Fall of Singapore* by Brian Farrell is an excellent history of the campaign. The extent to which a merchant navy captain would have been briefed on the strategic situation and then ordered to participate in a commando raid is open to fiction writers to speculate.

Due to a shortage of smaller naval craft, a number of civilian ships were pressed into service as patrol boats, minesweepers and for the final evacuation convoy. *Malay Waters* by H.M. Tomlinson, describes the adventures of the coastal steamers of the Straits Steamship Company while serving as auxiliary naval vessels. It was their *Jarak* which patrolled the Durian and Rhio Straits in the final days before the evacuation (although not as a minesweeper), rescued the crew of Jardine's *Tai Sang* after she was sunk by a mine and participated in the rescue of the soldiers from under the noses of the Japanese at Batu Pahat. She did not shell the beach but the idea is not entirely fanciful. I have read accounts which suggest that one of the merchant ships of the D-Day invasion fleet fired at the German defences.

Richard Pool's, *Course for Disaster* details the activities of the HDMLs in the Rose Force commando raids, and Geoffrey Brooke's, *Singapore's Dunkirk* is excellent source material for the fate of the ships that took part in the evacuation of the Europeans.

Some 40 ships sailed in the final evacuation between 12 and 14 February. Most were sunk by the Japanese. Two of the survivors were Blue Star's *Empire Star* which safely reached Fremantle and Heap Eng Moh's *Scott Harley* which made it to Tanjung Priok. *Oriental Venture's* final voyage is a synthesis of the sufferings of both. Captain Capon of *Empire Star* did indeed have an officer observe the fall of bombs, and managed to zig-zag between most of them. The final attack on the *Scott Harley* was conducted by biplanes that were, initially, misidentified and cheered as British. Tragically, however, hundreds died either in the sinkings or of mistreatment by their captors.

When I ventured to sea in 1970, many serving merchant navy captains had been younger officers in the Second World War. One with whom I sailed had served in the Arctic convoys, been sunk and pulled from the icy water seconds before freezing to death. Another told me he was visiting the waterfront of an Engish south-coast port in his merchant navy cadet's uniform, mistaken for a Royal Navy midshipman and Shanghaied aboard a minesweeper. By the time the mistake was discovered, he claimed to have been absorbed into the Royal Naval Reserve where he served for the remainder of the war.

He was not entirely pulling my leg. He had, in fact, been a cadet aboard *Strathallen* when she was torpedoed off the North African coast in December 1942 by *U562*. There were over 5,000 souls aboard of which all but 16 were rescued. My future captain abandoned ship in a lifeboat together with 88 nurses. He later said he regretted having no opportunity to do anything more than count them. Subsequently, he was commissioned into the naval reserve and sailed in minesweepers for the rest of the war. A charismatic captain and a superb ship-handler, but also capable of quoting the classics at two in the morning, he once told me his ideal job in retirement would be as a parking meter attendant in Winchester.

While I was studying for my Foreign Going First Mate's Certificate in London, in 1976, I ate my daily lunchtime sandwich in Tower Hill gardens, home to the Merchant Navy Memorial. The names of over 36,000 thousand seafarers who lost their lives during the First and Second World Wars are inscribed on its tablets. Their courage cannot be underestimated. I can hardly begin to imagine how, as civilians, they faced the constant strain and threat from bomb, torpedo and gun fire, while coping with the normal hazards of the ocean. What is often forgotten is that many of those seafarers were not British. Indians, Chinese, East and West Africans, West Indians, Arabs and others all sailed in British ships during the two wars. Sadly, their sacrifices were not always respected. It was not until May 1941, after almost two years of war, that a seafarers' wages were guaranteed if their ship was lost due to enemy action. Prior to that, their wages stopped from the day their ship was lost. Adrift in lifeboats for weeks or held captive as prisoners of war, they suffered the additional hardship of knowing their families were unprovided for.

The affair between Anaïs Nin and Henry Miller in Paris in the 1930s is well documented and they did visit a brothel together. Anaïs did not, however, start writing erotica until the 1940s. So, while it is possible for Helena to have accompanied her, it is unlikely she read any of her short stories.

I am grateful to Chief Engineer Tony White for his advice regarding ship's boilers and steam powered engines, as well as for various idiosyncratic turns of phrase that he will recognise. I am also grateful to Helen Hagemann, Leanne Searle, Kelly Boulter and Rose van Son for their comments, suggestions, corrections and encouragement.

As always, however, any remaining errors are entirely mine.

Having lost his ship, Captain Rowden faces an uncertain future but, hopefully, he will weigh anchor again before too long.

ABOUT THE AUTHOR

Richard Regan

Richard Regan joined the British Merchant Marine in 1970, at a time when the Red Ensign still flew at the stern of a quarter of the world's shipping. Seeing service in freighters, tankers and passenger ships, followed by thirty-five years working ashore for shipping companies and shipbuilders, Richard has visited almost every corner of the globe, and has  amassed a wealth of sights, settings, experiences and characters that are the inspiration for his writing.

'Oriental Vagabonds', his first novel, was set a generation prior his own career, but some of the ports and locations described had changed little when Richard first visited them. The ageing tramp ship at the centre of the story is also little different from one in which he twice circumnavigated the world. 'Oriental Vengeance', his second novel, is both prequel and sequel to 'Oriental Vagabonds'. His third novel, 'Oriental Valiant' takes up the story when Captain Rowden is ordered to take his ship back to the Far East at the end of 1941.

Richard now lives in Fremantle, Western Australia. When not writing he enjoys travelling, cruising, reading, photography and walking the family dog, Bosun.

www.ingramcontent.com/pod-product-compliance
Lightning Source LLC
Chambersburg PA
CBHW061928170626
46813CB00006B/2342